The Gift

STEPHANIE M. MATTHEWS

Copyright © 2017 by Stephanie M. Matthews

All rights reserved. No portion of this book may be reproduced, stored in a retrieval system, or transmitted in any form or by any means—electronic, mechanical, photocopy, recording, scanning, or other—except for brief quotations in critical reviews or articles, without the prior written permission of the author. If you would like to use material from the book (other than for review purposes), prior written permission must be obtained by contacting the author at stephaniemmatthewsinfo@gmail.com. Thank you for the support of the author's rights.

Author's Note: This novel is a work of fiction. Names, characters, places, and incidents are either products of the author's imagination or used fictitiously. All characters are fictional, and any similarity to people living or dead is purely coincidental.

paperback ISBN 978-0-9953132-0-0

To my mom and brother who didn't call in a "missing person" report when I disappeared for weeks at a time into my work hole. To my "Nicholas" whom I will always trust with my life.

But modesty and circumspection are required in pronouncing judgment . . . since there is always the risk of falling into the common fault of condemning what one does not understand. And, if it is necessary to err on one side or the other, I should prefer that the reader should approve of everything than that he should disapprove of much.

Quintilian, *De Institutione Oratoria,* X.1.26

PROLOGUE

The dining room was thick with the curling smoke from thinly rolled cigarettes and it smelled of new liquor, stale sweat, and mud. There was one electric light in the dining room, another in the adjoined kitchen, and a few candles on window sills extending the light's reach to expand the feeling of hospitality. The house was heated by a central fireplace where a fire was licking at the brick hearth and, while it wasn't much, everyone inside the house, including Lars Dreschler, was grateful just to have the wind off their back.

Dreschler peeked at the hand he'd been dealt, then carefully eyed the black, dented helmet collecting the bets of the other four men who were also assessing their hands. Across from him sat Johanne Schmidt, the eldest man at the table at thirty-five, and he tapped his cards twice on the table—his tell of a good deal. Dreschler tossed his bet into the helmet.

The youngest of their squad, Franz Fitschen, who'd lied about his age and was only fourteen, was flipping through a box of records nearby as the serenading bells of Rosita Serrano's voice crescendoed to an end. An unlit cigarette hung from the corner of his mouth and the straps of his helmet swayed across his smooth and dirtied cheeks as he held up his newest find, grinning, "Lili Marlene!"

The popular song was met with enough approval by the table for them to break their concentration and voice it, and the kid didn't wait for Rosita Serrano to finish before he flicked the gramophone's needle to one side and swapped one record for the other. Within seconds the warm sounds of an accordion crackled to life and Marlene Dietrich's husky voice sang to them through the cigarette smoke.

"I haven't heard this since basic training," Fitschen reminisced, closing his eyes to the song. Dreschler rolled his eyes. "She was one of the cooks and she gave me the dance." Fitschen sang back to Marlene Dietrich with love in his blue eyes as he joined the table. He slung his gun off his shoulder and hung it off the back of the wooden chair, stealing von Gottberg's matches, which had been lying unclaimed on the table beside his poor winnings.

"How long has it been since Dolfo and Fuhrman were supposed to be back?" Schmidt asked as he dealt another round. He was a short man and had to reach to sail the cards to the far end of the table.

"An hour, maybe more," von Gottberg said, casually scratching his scruffy face.

"If they're not back in ten, take Dreschler to find them." Schmidt said to Hausser who nodded.

Dreschler didn't appreciate being picked for the job. There wasn't any real danger in this village and his jacket still hadn't completely dried out. More important, he was comfortable. "They'll be back in nine," he said.

His company had been en route to join up with the regiment at Bastogne, touting their good luck charm, a Panzer III tank and its driver whom they found separated from his company. It was a welcomed diversion when orders came to reroute to this village and pick up more forced labor. Dolfo and Fuhrman had been chosen to be part of the recruitment team.

"The Hauptmann probably has him braiding the hair of all the pretty blondes," Fitschen said with a long, sad drag on his cigarette, and Dreschler wondered why Schmidt hadn't picked him to go back outside. "I should be babysitting them; I'll braid their hair so pretty…" Fitschen let his thoughts hang as he lost himself in his dream.

Von Gottberg snorted, "And then what, hündchen, question and answer period to help you learn what happens next?"

Dreschler laughed and decided to fold. Dolfo had first called the kid hündchen a couple days earlier, puppy, and Fitschen hated it. After abusing him with the name all afternoon they'd dropped it but, apparently, it wasn't ready to die just yet.

"My German naughty is better than anything these sprouts have ever had," Fitschen said stiffly.

That made the rest of the table break into laughter, and von Gottberg almost fell off his chair, a quick grab on the table's edge stopping him. Dreschler recovered his voice first. "Your naughty is stealing cake from under your mother's nose."

Before Fitschen could show his youthful offense, the front door slammed open. Dreschler jumped; von Gottberg and Schmidt were the fastest to grab their guns. "Frohe Weihnachten, boys!" Dolfo strolled in with a pleased grin on his face and Schmidt swore at him in welcome. Dreschler relaxed and sat back down. Dolfo's helmet was upturned in the crook of one arm and overflowing with pastries, while he grasped two dead chickens in his other hand, and a bottle of wine was barely secured under his armpit. "The Führer sends his Christmas greetings."

"Where'd you steal those from?" Fitschen asked, running his hand through his pale blond hair to get it out of his eyes. "A pretty girl gave them to you, didn't she?"

Everyone ignored the puppy and listened instead to the debrief Dolfo was giving Schmidt for why he'd shown up with supper instead of his partner. "The Hauptmann wanted Fuhrman to finish questioning one of the villagers. He'll be back when he's done. As for these"—Dolfo shook the dead birds in the air— "these will make a nice Christmas meal to complement all the canned vegetables and barley bread these people live off of. You know how to cook, right?" Dolfo aimed the question at von Gottberg.

Dolfo dropped the chickens on the kitchen counter, which still had a small stack of dirty plates left by the house's owners, who'd been taken to the town hall for holding along with two hundred other men and women. They'd be shipped out in two days to work in Germany's factories. Their honor of contribution to the war effort was driving the German war machine, and more of their weak blood in the fields and on production lines meant more Germans, like himself, could spend Christmas in a lovely Belgian's home rather than on the march or in a foxhole.

Dolfo grabbed the half-empty bottle of brandy from the table, took a long swig, then went into the kitchen to rummage through the cabinets and drawers. He laughed for joy when he found a giant can of coffee but then swore when he opened it to find it empty and hefted it with annoyance down the hall. Hausser laughed at his false hope and Dreschler decided to offer him some more brandy and a chair instead. Dolfo slid himself down with a happy sigh, the coffee apparently already forgotten, and half unbuttoned his shirt, breathing more freely.

"What about that sprout Fuhrman is talking to?" Fitschen asked, excited, "Is he a part of the Belgisch verzet, the Resistance? Are we going farming, digging up those sprouts?!"

Mirroring the opposite of Fitschen's enthusiasm, Schmidt turned to the young soldier. "There's no S.S. watching your back here, boy. If you live to see next Christmas, it won't be in a place like this—so forget about those stupid Belgians playing hero. My god, why did they have to send you as the replacement?"

"The man was telling ghost stories," Dolfo said to answer the first question, watching as von Gottberg tossed his bet of two cigarettes into Schmidt's helmet. "He was half-crazed with his story, but his German was the best of them all and Fuhrman has the best French. The villagers were all saying the same thing, telling us to leave them alone for our own safety. Pretty sure that's the first time anyone's tried to scare us with ghost stories. Though they were kind enough to suggest a few empty buildings and houses to wait in until the morning. Apparently 'death' comes out on Christmas Eve around here." That got a couple of snorts.

Schmidt dryly added, "and here we are."

"Why is the Hauptmann even listening to these stories?" Hausser asked as he flipped another card face-up only to promptly fold too.

"One man's superstition is truth for another," Schmidt replied, "and I'm grateful for the Hauptmann's caution, preferring us alive," he added, though the words were nearly lost to the neck of the bottle he lifted to his lips.

Hausser and Dolfo soon wandered to the living room to nap on the couch and chair, respectively.

They finished the hand and started to get hungry, so Dreschler finally kicked von Gottberg to the kitchen to work his magic with the chickens while he dealt the next hand.

They were about ten minutes into it when a clangor went up from the kitchen; von Gottberg came shouting and running back to the table, to grab his gun. Dreschler jumped up, ready and waiting for what would happen next, though Fitschen's cigarette smoke was drifting into his nose. Dreschler grabbed the cigarette from his mouth and tossed it naked on the table.

Von Gottberg cocked the gun, glued himself to the side of the wall, and poked his head around the corner back into the kitchen. His gun was quivering from his uneven breathing and his face had blanched of all color. Schmidt prodded him in a loud whisper, "What did you see?"

"Outside," the answer was laborious, "The window over the sink, I only saw one, maybe more . . . it . . . it was . . ."

Hausser was not impressed and he lowered his gun. "It? Not a he or she, but an it?"

"You're drunk, von Gottberg." Dolfo was equally unamused. "The schnaps has gone to your head."

Hausser kept the complaining going, "So help me, if you woke me from my nap for some bitch dog looking for scraps—"

"Shh!" Schmidt shot Hausser an angry glare and ordered everyone to blow out the kitchen candles. Easing himself past von Gottberg, Schmidt edged into the kitchen; Dreschler stepped out and followed behind. The barrels of their guns led the way, and the floorboards squeaked protest as they inched into the kitchen. Schmidt gingerly stepped over the fallen roasting pan and creeped up on the window with his gun aimed straight, his eye never leaving the sights. A white-washed cabinet blocked Dreschler's view of the window itself, but it was impossible for him to miss a faint iridescent green light reflecting off Schmidt's face.

"What the—" Dreschler was caught off guard by the loud crack of Schmidt's gun firing a single shot, shattering the window. The sound of five other guns cocking behind him picked up where the ringing from the shot echoed off.

Schmidt lowered his gun, turned from the window and brushed past Dreschler back into the dining room. His face was set hard, but the quivers from his mouth told a less sure story.

"Board up that window; it's cold out. Curtain the rest of them; light every candle you can to brighten this place up."

"Did you kill it?" Fitschen asked, flipping his hair out of his eyes again.

"Just do it. Now."

The order had barely left Schmidt's mouth when another gunshot echoed from outside. That one was quickly followed by a dozen more shots being rapidly fired, and it sounded like a firefight had broken out. Schmidt dumped out the forgotten bets from his helmet, and Dreschler raced for his, throwing the rest of his gear on, too.

The firefight grew louder as more guns joined the battle, but Schmidt held the men inside as he listened to it drawing closer. Dreschler began to get antsy. Peeking through the window curtain, he saw soldiers madly retreating from their base camp at the town hall.

"I only hear the Mauser," Hausser said, "Unless the Belgisch verzet got a cache of our guns, no one's shooting back."

"Then, why are we retreating?" Fitschen asked.

Dreschler, who had crouched beside the puppy, answered in a tone that made the kid hug his gun even closer. "They said the village was haunted."

Heavy boots stormed up the steps outside, with Fuhrman yelling his arrival and a command not to shoot, before he banged open the door. A gust of wintery air followed him in. Fully dressed and armed, his helmet's chin strap was fastened. His gray fatigues were as muddy and worn as the rest of theirs.

"We have to go. The Hauptmann said to regroup at the basilica."

"What's happening? What's going on out there?" Fitschen again.

Fuhrman, only a young man himself, bore an age on his face that was beyond his years. "I don't know. No one knows. The man I was interrogating, I can't explain it. He just . . ." Fuhrman trailed off as he ran out of words.

"You will explain. He just what?" Schmidt pressed him.

"I don't know, he just . . . everyone we rounded up, all the villagers, within a few minutes just . . . like the bodies in the field left unburied for too long, but, but they weren't dead," Fuhrman had the confidence of a sane man. A scared one, but a sane one. "I went and looked in the holding room myself. Kleist shot our man, I shot him. He didn't fall."

"Then you missed."

"The bullets landed in the wall behind him, there was an entrance wound! He—it—came after us. The whole lot of them, all the villagers. There was a, a green fire, jellyfish-like, I . . . I . . . don't even know, it squeezed them like a bellow. The Belgisch verzet planted gas canisters on these people to poison us. That's what the Hauptmann said."

The gunshots arrived outside their house, and Schmidt finally gave the order to move out. "Save your ammo and just get to the basilica. Green is not a Christmas color this year."

With Schmidt leading the way out, Dreschler took the rear, and their small group joined the stream of men from their company falling back, shooting behind them into the chemical-green haze growing on the streets' horizon.

Schmidt hollered at the dozens of men fleeing past to save their ammunition. Some listened, and others were too wide-eyed with fear to hear anything other than the sound of their own gun. Someone was shouting for the radioman; another was demanding to know where the driver for the Panzer was—the streets had become a mad retreat. The spires of the village's basilica could be seen from anywhere, and men ran to it like a lost ship to a lighthouse. Some went down one street only to come running back shooting their guns and yelling; others were shooting out windows as they ran past.

It quickly became clear to Dreschler which men had come from the town hall, as they wore their gas masks and sprinted past everyone else without looking back. Those coming up from the rear shouted that the Hauptmann changed their rendezvous to the North city gate, while others said that the basilica was still the place. The chaos was growing. Dreschler joined his voice with that of Schmidt and a few other seasoned souls angrily yelling for men to hold their fire.

He watched as two men tackled a third who was raving madly, tearing at his ribs with ten fingers glowing green. Another soldier began shooting at anything that moved, which meant his fellow soldiers. Five, then six men dropped to the ground, one of them screaming like a woman in labor, rolling around clutching his shoulder. A *pop*, then the wild man's body went limp, fell, and his gun was snatched up by another man.

Men cried out "GAS ATTACK!" as they scrambled for their gas masks. The newer soldiers stopped in the middle of the street to untangle the mask while others just ran faster. Dreschler grabbed one of the boys by the coat and dragged him along. "Figure it out as you run!" Word came along that the villagers had escaped, and Dreschler didn't care. No one did.

He found the radioman, crouching in the entryway of a building trying to raise a signal, his partner standing guard nearby. He kept repeating his call signs trying to pick up a response, but none was coming.

Dreschler, Fitschen, and von Gottberg arrived together before the small Gothic basilica to no more sense of order than there had been on the streets and no sign of the Hauptmann. Schmidt came running in, only a few seconds later, with two others and started calling the men to him and commanding everyone coming in who hadn't yet put their gas mask on to do so.

And then, in the midst of all the madness, the beautiful, simple musical notes of "Stille Nacht" began to drift out from the cracked doors of the basilica and penetrate the dark and chaotic Christmas Eve. Singers skilled enough to sing for the Führer himself sang, their voices reaching out like the soft touch from a loving mother. It was peaceful and it clashed with the war and fear being battled outside of those wooden doors. It was an odd thing, Dreschler thought, his thoughts slowing down. Not everyone was paying the song attention, but those who were seemed as bewildered as he; it was hard to tell through the alien-looking masks.

Schmidt was doing his best to calm the frightened boys and to rein in the veterans as their little formation grew and grew, his booming voice carrying. Those who had been close enough to see what chased them couldn't coherently describe what they had seen, and the stifling gas masks didn't help. One said that the graves of the Celts had been opened, another that the nightmares had left his head, or that the ghosts of the killed Belgisch verzet had returned to the fight.

"We can't wait much longer," Schmidt announced, unimpeded by a mask since he had traded it months ago for a bottle of smuggled Russian vodka. "Has anyone seen Fuhrman?"

The only answer Schmidt got was the shaking of heads. "Dreschler, von Gottberg, wait here to pick up any stragglers. I'm taking these men to the North gate to the Hauptmann." It was a statement of conviction. "Leave in five minutes, meet me there." Looking around at the group they had, there were maybe ninety men, a third of how many had come into this village. "Whatever the Hauptmann wants to do next, I'm sure he'll want more than this."

But Dreschler saw the men who were with them, and they were in no condition to do anything but put as much distance as possible between themselves and this place.

With one last threat to waste no more ammunition, Schmidt headed out with his group. The luminescent green shadows grew larger and larger on the building walls as though the light itself was the monster. The gunshots became less frequent, the shouting men not as loud, and a few more stragglers sprinted in, the radioman and a medic shouldering a limping man between them. The medic pointed his bloody fingers into the crowd and volunteered someone to help him stretcher the wounded man.

Von Gottberg took the moment to ask, "What did Schmidt see in the window?"

"What did you see?" Dreschler asked back.

Von Gottberg grunted. "A rotting head."

Dreschler nodded, his focus averted just then by telling the stragglers to get ready to head out. "He shot his reflection between the eyes. Dark magic or the devil, either way, bullets won't matter." He looked back to the basilica doors. Was it ignorance or idiocy that kept them singing? And how did they escape the roundup? "They won't survive the war acting like that," he murmured.

They were out of time. Dreschler gave the order and their little group of stragglers fled.

1

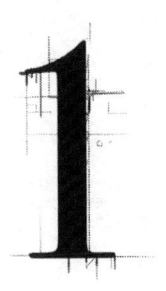

Thump, thump.

Thump, thump.

Thump, thump.

The subtle bumping of the train car lulled Fae Peeters awake from the nap she had slipped into. Her eyes sleepily opened to the sound of the train's rhythmic thumps, easing her into passively taking in the landscape rolling by.

The Google image searches she had done before she had set out hadn't lied—southern Belgium was beautiful. The land extended out from the tracks for miles until it rose into rolling mountains. Coniferous trees were the only real color in the snowcapped landscape as their naked deciduous counterparts melted seamlessly into the bright gray sky.

Having lived in Belgium for over a year now while studying for her Masters in architecture, Fae had found a piece of her heart in this little country. It wasn't saddled with the same expectations as England, Italy, or France and, because the country was often overlooked next to its flashy neighbors, its people were free of any expectations other than to deliver a beautiful country and amazing chocolate. So far she hadn't been disappointed in either.

A small town appeared on the horizon, and she lazily watched it as the train rolled by. As much a part of the landscape as the mountains, the town was neatly defined even though it sprawled across the land. She saw only one building outside its perimeter in the middle of a snowy field; a barn no doubt. Tall, slender houses with pointed roofs picketed the sky, and the always present church with its tall spires came and went, leaving Fae wondering how similar her destination would be to that place.

With a muffled groan, she stretched out in the upholstered seat, then settled into a proper sitting position. The car was about half full; two days before the Holidays, most people were already home with their families getting fat off too many sweets, drunk on too much warm wine, and exhausted skiing or hiking the hills.

Fae took stock of her fellow passengers. A bottle-blonde sat kitty-corner to her in the facing seat with her fashion magazine. Across the aisle, a middle-aged man was passed out next to his wife. Chatter from three elderly women who hadn't stopped gossiping since they sat down kept a soft buzz in the air. Then there was the man just up the aisle whose gaze she kept interrupting. As soon as she caught him he would look away, and then vice versa, making for an awkward game. But he smiled the last time she caught him, which she returned, before she'd drifted to sleep. He was handsome, and her grandmother had made no small show of expecting her to return home engaged to a good Belgian boy. She briefly flirted with the idea that maybe this man was her fairy tale.

Only, she knew he wasn't.

Fae reached under her seat and wiggled out her travel bag. Plopping it on the empty seat beside her, she took out one of the two letters carefully placed in the front pocket alongside her tickets and passport. The one she left was from her best friend, Analyse, back in Vancouver. She had sent a picture of herself in a pumpkin patch posing with a scarecrow. The scarecrow was dressed up to look like Fae, and the picture had the words "a poor substitute" scripted across the front.

The other envelope was a letter from her grandmother, and this was what had chased her out of her Brussels apartment to her grandparents' village.

For the most part, the letter was everything expected from a grandmother:

lighthearted complaints about preparations for the annual family Christmas feast, how she hoped Fae was having a good time at school, an update on her friends' knitting projects, et cetera, but it was the last part of the letter that Fae had read over half a dozen times and which she read again.

> *Fae, few people know that I was adopted as a young child. Having been found wandering the roads near the village I was soon to call home, inquiries discovered that my birth parents had been killed in an industrial accident; I was left with no relatives. While I was blessed to have been taken in by a wonderful family, not everyone would agree to call me blessed for being taken in by my village. Every old settlement has its secrets. When I was twelve years old and mature enough to see those secrets and mysteries for myself, I understood firsthand that I could never truly be one of the villagers; it would be impossible to share by adoption what they carried by birth. But even so, the life I lived in that village was a good one full of love and laughter and I was never bitter nor felt outcast.*
>
> *As time passed there were those of us who saw Adolf Hitler for what he was. Despite the difficulties in the decision, I begged my husband to move us away. It was difficult for him because the secret he shared with the other villagers would isolate him anywhere else, but he understood, and so we fled Belgium in wake of the German destruction across the East, bribing our way onto the first boat that was leaving across the Atlantic. The rest of the story once we landed in Halifax, you know. Leaving a childhood home is not easy, even less so in those days, but eventually your grandfather was able to live a normal life and celebrate Christmas, our favorite holiday, without incident.*
>
> *Fae, I want nothing more than for you to come to our village and learn what I did when I was twelve. It is the world's greatest secret and, as such, its greatest gift. Knowing that you will have it will be gift enough to for me, so please don't spend any of your small student budget on me this year. I have already arranged everything for your stay. You must follow my instructions perfectly or risk serious consequences . . .*

THE GIFT

The sway of the train slowed and the pressure of the brakes grinding steel on steel pushed Fae forward. This was going to be her stop. Glancing out the window she could see that, like the previous villages they had passed, this one sprawled across the land like spilled milk, the spires of the church rising above the troubles of life below. Unlike the other villages, however, this village was wrapped in a wall and that made the story of the German invasion her grandparents told even more fascinating. The thought brought her back to the letter.

It was cute, really, how her grandmother tried to be so serious as though she were still a little girl easily scared into obedience. What gift was so secretive and so intense that deviation from the treasure hunt led to serious consequences? She had taken bets from two of her Brussels friends as to what her present could be. A puppy and a stash of old family bonds were up against Fae's throwaway vote of the village being the keepers of the Kraken's bones. The guesses were lighthearted but the small knot, which appeared in Fae's gut whenever she thought too much about the gift, wasn't. The only reasonable answer was some sort of hidden relic from the Knights Templar, booby-trapped a la Indiana Jones, and that idea was just as silly as the Kraken's bones. That her usually levelheaded, sweet grandmother would tell her so much without telling her anything was out of character.

She put the letter back into her travel bag and stood up to collect her things: a black felt winter jacket, blue plaid scarf, faux leather and fur gloves, and her duffle bag.

The train ground to a halt and Fae dipped her head to see through the window and confirm the name on the station. Then she claimed her spot in the main aisle even though no one else got up. The handsome man looked up at her and smiled.

"Good luck," he told her in English with a thick French accent.

"Merci. Ciao." She smiled back hoping he might say more. He didn't.

Hauling her small load behind her, she trudged through the car and with a small push on the exit door, descended the three steep, steel steps to the platform. She shivered with the sudden change of temperature. As the train slowly rolled away, Fae saw she was completely alone.

"What a warm and welcoming place," she said, assessing her location. Extending outward from the station was a plain brick wall that quickly joined up with a stone wall that wrapped around the perimeter of the village. It wasn't adorned with decorative battlements or nicely dressed stones. It was just a plain, functional wall with equally bland turret towers. There was only one prominent piece of graffiti near the platform: a picture of a snow-covered gravestone with a dove sitting on top. It read, "You must die to leave alive. Joyeux Noël." She frowned at the art but dismissed it as nothing more than the dark thoughts of a disturbed teenager.

The only thing that welcomed her was a lonely Christmas tree, standing beside the glass door leading into the station. It was nicely decorated in gold, silver, and red but was also littered with advertisements masquerading as ornaments in the form of words such as, "joyeux" and "amour." She passed by the tree. She could respect people's attempts to force the Christmas season to bring love and joy, but Christmas wasn't a yearly reset button for humanity. People only gave during the season because they were told to and not because they genuinely wanted to; otherwise, they'd do it all year long. Good people did good things with love, joy, peace without looking for a reward or a seasonal validation.

Posted on the station door was a temporary sign written in all four major languages of Belgium—Dutch, French, German and English. At the bottom was the official crest of the village: *Visitors welcomed December 25th - December 23rd. The provincial and federal governments are not responsible for visitors during non-visitor hours.*

Again, Fae frowned. Today was December 23rd. Her grandmother said she'd arranged everything, did she know about this rule? She wondered if she could actually be kicked out of a village for a single night. What could possibly demand that non-residents leave for Christmas Eve?

She pressed through the station door with a shrug. She'd embrace the village holiday scene for what it was worth; she really did enjoy the holiday; and they would have to embrace, or endure her, just the same. On her last call with her grandmother, she'd said it might be possible to wave down someone in a car to drive her to the hotel but if not she would have to walk.

Apparently, the people who lived here were nice enough to chauffeur visitors around but kicked them out at the most giving time of year.

But as she was shifting her thoughts to figuring out how to get around and settle in, the words from the graffiti crept back into her mind, *You must die to leave alive.* Why would someone write that?

2

There were no taxis outside the station, and Fae wasn't comfortable with flagging down a stranger. The streets were pretty quiet anyway, and the hotel wasn't far even by foot. Pulling her phone out Fae saw that, just as her grandmother had predicted, the data coverage was too poor to be effective, so it was a good thing her grandmother had been smart enough to include a hand-drawn map. Repositioning the bag on her shoulder, she headed out.

The train station was fronted by a plaza, which was little more than a roundabout with a memorial to the Second World War standing in the middle of it. A block of concrete rose like an industrial stain on an otherwise quaint scene, on top of which stood a German war tank, the Panzer III. She knew that thanks to her grandfather. There were enough bronzed Karabiner 98k rifles, otherwise known as Mausers, and iconic Stahlhelm helmets haphazardly stacked beside it to arm and outfit a platoon of men, but her grandfather told her it was actually a company that had failed here. He said a miracle had forced the Germans to flee so quickly that they had left half their equipment behind. He always thanked God whenever he talked of that event.

Fae had no problem finding her hotel, as it stood above most other buildings with its true three stories. Once a house, the entire bottom floor had been renovated to provide a real hotel feel rather than show itself as a bed and breakfast. The décor was a fusion of modern and turn of the century, wallpaper and wingback chairs with Ikea-styled footstools and a Zen water fixture. It somehow all came together for a satisfying welcome at journey's end. Christmas carols escaped from hidden speakers to greet guests in the lobby, and it was tastefully decorated with modern glass balls and a glittery forest theme, accented with porcelain heirlooms that looked generations old. There wasn't an artificial Christmas tree to be seen. Even the miniature tree standing on the desk was real. Fae breathed deeply, relishing the smell.

There was no attendant at the desk and no other guests were relaxing in the lobby, but the service bell brought a woman in her late twenties out from the back room smiling warmly. She was thin and wore a skirt suit, her dark hair tidily pulled back in a claw clip.

"Bonjour, hallo," she said with a welcoming smile. "Joyeux Noël, how can I help you?" she continued on in French, a language Fae was fluent in thanks to her grandparents. Fae responded in kind.

"I have a reservation under Peeters."

The woman, Elise according to her golden nameplate, immediately began looking it up, though Fae couldn't imagine she had many reservations to sort through.

Elise looked up from the monitor, her face a blank slate. "I am sorry, there is a problem with your reservation. It says you want the room from the 23rd through the 26th but we are closed tomorrow night. The whole village closes down Christmas Eve. There is a train that passes by tomorrow. I can book a ticket for you."

"No, that can't be right," Fae said, resting her forearms on the counter. "This reservation was confirmed. I was told to ask for Eva Lemmens if there were any problems."

Elise's face softened. "She is the owner. Please excuse me for a moment while I confer with her." Elise disappeared into the rooms beyond and soon returned, accompanied by an elderly woman leaning on a cane. She was tall and thin like Elise, her white hair pulled back in a housewife's bun. If it wasn't for the cane, she looked healthy and strong for her age.

"This is Mats and Maria Peeters' granddaughter! So lovely!" The older woman was delighted as she came around the counter and grabbed Fae up in a deep hug as though she were her own family. Her cane slapped Fae in the back as she was pulled in. "Maria has written to me often of her family and no less of you. We were best friends since we were little girls." Eva released Fae from her embrace. "Elise told you there is a problem with your reservation. It was my fault for forgetting to tell her. There is no problem. You are more than welcome here for the duration of your stay."

"Thank you. I know my grandmother did a lot of planning for me to come."

"Of course she did, child," Eva said solemnly. "I invite you to share Christmas dinner with my family, naturally, though you probably have been claimed by your own relatives already. They are so excited to meet you, too! But if not, then my table is open."

"She is to stay then?" Elise asked Eva, her eyes betraying immediate alarm. "Misseur . . . it is not allowed—"

"It has been *arranged*," Eva interrupted. Elise said no more but kept her eyes on Fae, the distanced look of mistrust unmistakable.

"Here, dear." Eva went behind the counter and reached up to the pegged wall with a perfect grid of well-marked skeleton keys. "Room 3A. It is the best room we have. You will pay only regular room rate, of course."

Elise opened her mouth to protest but Eva held up her hand. "The granddaughter of my dear friend has come to visit and we will be the best hosts." To Fae she said, "There are no elevators here like the big city hotels you must be used to, but if you have need of anything, please, I will make it my personal cause. Are you hungry? I have a delicious meat pie in the fridge."

"No, thank you, I'm still good from breakfast." Fae smiled her thanks as she took the skeleton key from Eva. She could see why this dear old woman and her grandmother were friends. "Your village is very charming, and I look forward to exploring it more." And she meant it . . . the last part anyway. The letter had suggested enough things to check out to ensure that.

"You will learn much about your family history here. I promise." As an afterthought, Eva added, "I'm sure Maria has already told you, but you absolutely must see our church, the Basilique de Notre-Dame du Seigneur. Maria told me that you are interested in cathedrals and basilicas."

Fae smiled politely and tried her best not to come off as rude. "I don't want to give the wrong impression, I don't know if my grandmother mentioned, but I really don't care for the institution churches represent. It's their art and architecture that attracts me."

Fae watched as a little disappointment fell in Eva's eyes as she spoke, and a small twinge pecked at her for coming off cold when Eva had been so warm. "No one will be forcing you inside, dear," she replied with a smile, making it easier for Fae to shove aside the creep of guilt. "We don't have much for tourism, but we're proud of what we do have."

Fae returned the smile, thanking Eva again for her hospitality, and picked up her bags taking herself to the stairs. They were steep and in short angular flights, three flights per floor. The same renovations that had transformed the first floor hadn't yet reached the green carpet, threadbare from constant wear, and the old wooden stairs tended to creak. Small rectangular stained glass windows marked each floor. By the time Fae rounded the corner to the second floor, her heart was beating faster than she would have liked—the result of spending much more time in the books and on the drafting table than the gym, but the short-term physical sacrifices were worth it. She knew she was a talented designer and so did the firm where she had an internship. It was just too bad for them that being a landscape architect wasn't an exciting prospect.

Room 3A was directly on her right once she reached the top of the stairs. The door itself was made of carved wood, bearing years' worth of scratches and dents, and Fae wondered how many stories lay behind it. How many kids once ran up and down these stairs? What happened to them? Did German soldiers steal in here for a night before they turned tail and ran? Oh, if the wood could speak.

Jiggling the skeleton key in the lock, Fae let herself in and tossed her bags to the bed. She walked to the shuttered window and flapped aside the thin, white cotton drapes, dramatically throwing open the shutters just like she had seen any number of Disney princesses do, to behold the beautiful sight of . . . the roof of the neighboring house.

Fae's heart sank. The best room in the hotel and her view was another building's roof. Deflated, she shuttered the window and turned her attention to the rest of the room.

A second door led to a private bathroom, which was probably what made this the "elite" suite, though it still didn't give her too much to get excited about. The bathroom was compact, as most things in Europe were, but it was so small that she could almost use the toilet, wash her hair under the shower, and brush her teeth in the sink all at the same time. But still, it was a small luxury. It wasn't uncommon for similar lodgings to have a shared bathroom, or even the bathroom split into different rooms—the toilet in one, the sink in another.

Her room was clean though, and appropriately decorated for the Holidays with a small pine Christmas tree in the corner. Underneath its green boughs, lovingly arranged on the tree skirt, was a beautifully crafted Nativity scene. Kneeling, she took a closer look at it. Porcelain, hand painted. The humans had skin as white as snow and the animals had almond-shaped eyes. The three Wise Men were there with their heavily laden camels, as were two shepherds, one with a lamb wrapped around his neck and the other standing beside a cow peeking under his shoulder. Mary and Joseph had their eyes stoically cast downward to the straw-laced crib where a newborn Jesus stretched his arms above his head. His expression was as emotionless as his parents'.

"Not too excited about this whole 'Jesus, God with us' stuff, are you?" Fae said out loud. "I guess you guys were smart enough to know a myth when you heard one. But did you know you were living one?"

The Nativity scene would have to go. Despite her years in academia, she sometimes still found it difficult to look at religious icons as just art; they had the ability to spark an emotional response, to say it nicely. She'd ask the front desk for a simple exchange. It was a lovely enough ornamental set that it deserved to be appreciated by someone who could. Carefully gathering up all the pieces, Fae placed them near her jacket to take downstairs. She wouldn't make a special trip for it.

She took her time settling into her room and cleaning herself up before finding the remote for the old television hanging in the corner. Fae turned it on and dug out the letter again to plan the rest of her day. Her grandmother had practically written a tour guide, from arranged meetings with relatives, to naming old friends she should meet if time allowed, and even where to find the best baked goods. As she moved through the pages her eyes caught a paragraph she had already read multiple times. It was a paragraph that continued to mystify her even though it was borderline insulting, so she read it again hoping maybe another pass would help make sense of it.

My dearest Fae, to my last breath I will always tell you how I daily contest for your soul on my knees; every miracle begins with a prayer. The refusal of God's existence which you say grants you religious neutrality, and the judgment you pass on those who can't agree with your assertion, has led to a life I pray will not leave you in eternal regret. This is not new for you to hear from me. The offenses and hurts you suffered growing up can no longer define your worldview. You have a talent in your art that touches people, so it is for the souls you will inspire that has brought me to this point, this point of revealing to you, my dear, the most closely guarded secret. Your father does not even know everything that will be made known to you, and your grandfather took it with him to his grave, as must you, and yet even beyond it.

She loved her grandmother but sometimes she just couldn't let a sleeping dog lie, as her grandfather loved to say. The paragraph had gotten her mind turning again about the nature of her gift. It was both a secret taken to the grave and the pinnacle of a breaking point toward Fae's worldview, which apparently was dragging a few people down to Hell with her. And yet it was a Christmas gift, which meant it had to be a good thing. But it was a village secret that the world couldn't handle. She shook her head. It still made no sense.

A documentary about Frankie Valli was on TV and she watched it for a few minutes until they cut to a clip of him singing, "Can't Take My Eyes Off You" and had to turn it off. That had been her mother's favorite song. She'd play it when doing housework or anytime she needed to feel happy again, or when she was happy, and when Fae's father was home the three of them would dance to it together. But that was back when Fae still thought of them as having a functioning family, or, at least was still in denial about it.

It had been over seven years since her mother had been killed. Hearing the song was still too soon. Naturally, she had included the song in the list for her mother's funeral, and later the same day she had submitted the playlist, Pastor Blake had paid her and her father a visit.

"Fae, thank you for getting the playlist to Sam in time for tomorrow. Look, I don't know how to say this, but I'm sorry to say we won't be able to play the Frankie Valli song. You know church policy—"

"Excuse me?" Fae asked, indignant. "I'm sorry, what?"

"Blake," her father quickly interrupted, "you have to let us play the song."

"I'm sorry, Luc, but this isn't a personal decision. It's a mandate from God that our church is to be a holy place and secular music doesn't fit the bill. It's a place to lift Him high, not ourselves."

"You wrote that policy," Fae told him, "not God. It is your decision. How do you know what music is secular or not? Half that music on Sunday could be sung to anyone. God is love? This is a song about love."

"Physical love. Fae, I don't want to make this time any more difficult for you—"

"Then play the song. It's the only thing left to this family that means something." She glared at her father, didn't mean to. He seemed similarly inflexible, and this was a rare time they were on the same side. But she was just hurting so badly right now . . .

"Blake, it's innocent . . ."

Fae's fists tightened as she stared down now at the pile of Nativity figures. Pastor Blake didn't relent. Instead, he once again showed the true colors of his religion.

Fae smothered a yawn and despite her anger she suddenly felt crazy tired. It was still before noon and so she decided to slip in a short nap to help erase those memories she'd rather forget. She laid her head on the pillow and let the sleep wash over her.

She was in the back of a taxi. The driver had a messenger's hat on, but she couldn't see his face in the mirror. The landscape outside was charcoal gray, desolate and overgrown by twisted, harsh-looking weeds. Her grandparent's village suddenly came upon them, the hundred-foot-tall blackened walls crumbling in spots. The only entrance was through two spiked iron doors. As they passed through, gargoyles at the top of the doors turned their heads to watch them enter, tracking her with their beady stone eyes.

They arrived at her destination but it didn't feel right. She tapped the driver on the shoulder and told him as much. He didn't respond. She showed him the paper with the address and again asked the driver to take her there, and again he didn't respond. A third time she prodded the driver and she could feel him getting annoyed. He snapped his head around 180 degrees and met her with a full-toothed grin from a fleshless skull. Fae didn't scream, she just dove for the door handle only to find that she had been manacled in. A deep, rumbling cackle came out of the driver's skull. His messenger cap morphed into a lopsided World War II German helmet. A few stray wisps of dehydrated hair escaped from beneath it and he lifted an arm off the steering wheel and reached for her. His fleshless bony fingers were like little spears and she pressed herself back against the seat as far away from him as she could. It wasn't enough. The arm knew no limit and kept coming for her. *I've brought you to your gift,* the skeleton driver said, *it's been too long since the Peeters family has celebrated the Holidays here. It's nice to finally meet you in person. Let's go for a ride.* The head snapped forward and the car lurched forward. Fae wrestled with her fetters trying to reach the door handle, only to find that the handle was now gone and the window had been barred over. "You didn't bring me to my present! Where is it?" Fae demanded with rising panic. The driver said nothing but his bony hand kept stretching out for her. It just kept coming and coming while they kept driving. There was no way to get out . . .

Fae awoke with a jolt and bolted up, breathing hard. She never had nightmares, so what the heck was that? Gripping her head between her hands as though by physically grasping her brain she could better control it, she tried to slow her heart and forget everything she'd just seen. It had been so real; she could still feel the weight of the iron fetters dragging her down. She looked at her hands and found only her watch, the same one she always wore.

Looking up she found herself in the giant mirror. She was white and panicked; so much for freshening up. Why was she even here? Honestly though, what did her grandmother have stored away for her after seventy-odd years that was such a big deal? She could still leave on the train tomorrow and go back home to Brussels. Her good friend Yanna had left her with an invitation to join her family for Christmas. But that would be letting her grandmother down.

"What are you doing, Fae Peeters?" she asked her reflection.

Fae sighed a heavy breath and half-heartedly fingered through the knots in her hair. A little fresh air would clear her head, and the lingering haunted feeling was already starting to be crowded out by the resurging words from her grandmother's letter.

You must open your eyes to see that there is more than one world inhabiting Earth. When it comes to your soul there is no neutral ground, and by trying to live there you've become dangerously skeptical to this battle between life and death, which you are unable to see as a result. I pray that you will be able to, soon enough . . .

Fae was staring off into space and she began to feel so heavy. Her mind was stuck on repeat and she felt terrible looking at herself in the mirror. When had she gotten such bags under her eyes? This must be what the start of depression feels like. Either that, or madness.

You must die to leave alive.

Fae groaned. "Just everything shut up."

I'm in your head . . . That wasn't her voice! *I'm in your head . . .* She wasn't thinking those words, they weren't hers! The words repeated through her mind in a singsong taunt. *I'm in your head, I'm in your head, I'm in your head . . .*

She started to panic. First nightmares and now voices. She paced the room trying to talk herself back to reason. "I am smart and strong. I don't have mental issues. I am a normal, levelheaded human being. I am focused on my goals and I achieve them." *I'm in your head, I'm in your head . . .* "I am amazing at what I do, I am focused. I am grounded with a good life, good friends, good . . . things!" . . . *I'm in your head, I'm in your he—*

Gritting her teeth, Fae shot her eyes upward into the mirror to drill some sanity back into herself. But what she expected to see reflected there, wasn't. A humanoid horror, repulsively disgusting was staring back at her instead.

She yelled and tripped backward over the bed, falling onto the floor. She covered her head defensively and buried her face in the floor, trying to smother the sounds of her own panicked breathing. She was still dreaming, she was still dreaming, this was still the dream, that mirror wasn't real, it wasn't real . . . !

I'm in your head, and you're dead.

3

Newly waxed floors smelled like rotten eggs. It was a smell that lingered for only about a week, so when Fae realized she was wondering if she could smell the wax—rather than focusing on blocking out whatever had just happened—she knew that she had control of herself again. What she'd seen was just a residual image of the nightmare, that simple. With the trepidation of a child knowing something scary was going to jump out of the darkness, Fae rose and looked in the mirror. This time there were no surprises. It was just her own reflection.

Adrenaline still coursed through her body and she was scared that dwelling on what she had just seen and heard would conjure it back. She needed fresh air to clear her head and this time she meant it. And some strong coffee. Grabbing her purse and her jacket, Fae couldn't get out of the room fast enough.

In the lobby, Elise greeted her from behind the desk though Fae barely acknowledged her as she rushed by. The outside chill hit her like a plunge into a cold lake, refreshing and invigorating. Fae turned her face toward the sky and breathed deeply. She listened to a car driving by, a man across the street talking business on his phone, an engine revving in the distance. The wind stirred. A bird of prey called out. Fae listened to it all like rejuvenating music. Taking in all these sounds of normalcy, she breathed deeply again and the horrors were cleared away. She gathered herself and looked around. The train station and the roundabout were to the right, so she decided to explore to the left.

Since being in Belgium she had grown to admire the traditional Mosan Renaissance architectural style typical of the seventeenth and eighteenth centuries. Usually flat-fronted, uniformed buildings, they favored a combination of stone and brick for their flair. She had thought she'd seen a few examples on her way into the village. Architecture hunting was maybe just the thing she needed to reset her head.

Fae took her time wandering the village. She guessed that the core of the village would take only two or three hours walking to see it all, even at a leisurely pace with copious window-shopping. After finding the nearest store for the coffee stimulant she needed, she loitered at one of the two tables reading a copy of the local four-page newspaper. It highlighted the *bourgmestre's* Christmas greeting to the municipality, the success of recent school repairs, the results of a sledding tournament yesterday, and some local photography. There was nothing interesting to keep her reading past the bottom of her coffee cup so she headed back outside, deciding to start her self-guided tour with the village's outer wall.

Getting to the wall took a bit of determination. The village was a maze of misleading main roads, and vital connections were found on inconspicuous tangled side streets which were barely wide enough for a car. She decided to let the village take her to the wall as it wanted to which allowed her the opportunity to experience the village as it was meant to be known.

By every definition it was a quaint place well looked after by its residents with clean windows and maintained buildings. The streets were cobbled with black paving stones, and patches of pavement showed a slow invasion of the modern world. People drove small cars but biked even more and bike racks were found nearly every block. The downtown buildings squeezed together with roofs poking up like triangles of a red, brown, and black Toblerone bar. The farther the houses and buildings were from downtown, the more space to they had to breathe, with little lawns adorning them. Ivy grew more freely on the outskirts and the trees lining the streets were less uniform, the streetlamps less frequent. There were also more landmarks at the intersections; Fae didn't know what else to call the permanent displays on the street corners. One was an old well that still looked functional but was circled by little stone angels dancing around it on the ground. Another was a tall, boxy shrine with bird perches inside and a painted portrait of Jesus beside a man, woman and little girl on the back. A handwritten sign hung on the front that said, *les oiseaux seront de retour à l'été*, the birds will return in the summer. So it seemed to Fae that this was a village that had been left alone, not forgotten, and one that brought the modern world in as it chose.

When at last her journey landed her in front of the wall, she found a wide brick path lined by a hedge of trees running parallel to it, for as far as she could see in either direction. Beyond the trees was the wall itself, just barely overreaching the treetops. She decided to follow the wall, though twice she had to take detours where her path had been cut off by developments. She soon found the first of two gates which the village possessed. In this case, it was the South gate, which led out to the snow-covered fields beyond. From her grandmother's map, she knew that the North gate was the only other road exit.

By her judgment, the wall wasn't as old as she had first suspected. She found an opening in the ivy and brush and ducked down on the other side to rub her gloved fingers over the icy stone. Thin turret towers, no wider than a set of stairs, were set wherever there was a corner or a curve. Vines and moss grew unopposed and Fae began to realize that for all the effort in keeping their village postcard pretty, this wall was forgotten in the same way that a prison warden could be forgotten in the hope that he would somehow just disappear. For a village as insignificant as this one with no enviable resources or strategic land position, Fae could only imagine that the wall had to have been some politician's pet project. Still, why did it look so martial, as serious as the walls from the age of siege warfare, if it wasn't actually from that era? It had to be no more than five hundred years old, less more likely. Architects were artists at heart and they always wanted to add their own flair, and yet there was no flair in this wall, so it must've had purpose beyond a pet project. It had been built with expansion in mind, judging from all the free space the buildings closest to it had—which was interesting in its own right. It was a mystery that helped her forget and she began to feel like her normal self again.

Most of the government buildings were in the Mosan style: flat fronts of a nice reddish pink color and tall, thin windows set in a flawless grid across the front. She had gotten lost looking for a textile factory, which she did eventually locate. It was drab-looking in comparison to the downtown, having been built in the conservative Walloon mode of gray rock and a simple roof. It had always reminded her of Scotland. Including the farming industry, which she expected, she was starting to understand this village's place in the world.

She came upon the downtown naturally as it was quite literally the center of the village. There were no major rivers to build around, no hill, or even a valley; there was just the basilica. A relatively large plaza surrounded the basilica giving the building a wide berth for an impressive scenic framing. Restaurants, and shops, but mostly apartments, formed a circular perimeter around it.

The basilica's aggressive spires stabbed high into the air and leered over the otherwise modest skyline. It was small compared to its European brethren, well-crafted though, and still grand in its setting, looking too big for the village to hold. Church architecture was pivotal to understanding the progression of design, and she loved to draw inspiration from the boldness of the cathedrals. If those old Catholics got anything right, that was it.

Everything about the façade of the Basilique de Notre-Dame du Seigneur was textbook Gothic. Two bell towers extended up into spires at its center and another two progressively shorter towers descended toward either end. The main doorway, the portal, rose tall between the bell towers and there were two smaller portals, one on either side, which, by the rather permanent-looking nature of the bronze doors, were rarely, if ever, opened. Along the outside of the main portal was an ornamental molding which followed the curve of the arch, hiding the door beneath in shadow. This archivolt was made up of four decorative tubule columns of vertical low-relief sculptures which told a story from the ground up. The story was probably the ascent of Jesus to heaven, or the life of Jesus and the disciples, or some other common theme. Above the portal was a series of thick-framed stained glass windows, ideal for letting as much light as possible into this fortress. But the rest of the basilica confused Fae, for behind the dramatic Gothic façade was a Renaissance basilica with its fluid lines more like a love song living in harmony with its surroundings and less like a rock opera bristling for a fight.

Basilicas took generations to complete from start to finish. New design influences inevitably found their way into blueprints created generations before, but never had Fae seen anything so starkly distinct in one building. Had there been a giant fire that destroyed everything but the façade? But then why not better integrate the design in the rebuild? Now she really had to find out what the inside looked like. She had to find out the story of this curious, incredible building.

The cast iron guard door of the main portal was pushed back to reveal a heavy iron wood one behind, on which was hung a fresh evergreen wreath. Its bright green boughs and red and gold ribbons stood out like the only color in a black and white photo. As she walked beneath the archivolt and its story, she stopped to try to read it, her professional curiosity piqued. She wasn't much of an art historian but she was familiar with the language of sculpture.

Each tubule column of the archivolt was wide enough to hold one human figurine, tall and solemn. To her right was a typical scene of Jesus' ascension. The disciples were looking up as Jesus rose into heaven, surrounded by angels who populated nearly three-quarters of the scene. On her left side, the evil side by ancient tradition, was a different story.

Two people stood in the two center columns and on either side of them two demons. It was easy to identify the evil forces because snake tails coiled out from beneath their long cloaks. Blank, smooth stone marked the place where their faces should have been peeking out from beneath their droopy hoods, and one of them had stylized wings. As she followed their story upward, the demons reached out at the two people, pulling them into their cloaked grasp and putting their long, split tongues into their ears. In the next scene, the demons' heads had replaced the people's as their own and their now skeletal hands wore thick manacles, the chain held by the demons. In the frame above that, the demons' tongues twisted in, around, and through the people's skulls robbing them of sight, hearing, and speech. In the second frame from the top, Jesus appeared, and above that, before the artist ran out of space, the two people were restored as they had been, and the demons nowhere to be seen.

This had to be the most macabre piece she'd ever seen displayed on the exterior of a church. She had never seen anything like this before in church low-relief, never in any picture, scholarly article or even as an example in a lecture. Surely this was the Fall of Man, or some obscure tale of two saints? Christians of the past had an unsettling comfort with death but it was always hidden inside where bodies were buried in the floors and walls, and marble skeletons adorned the altars. Most dramatic was the interior of the Church of Bones in the Czech Republic. Its interior was designed entirely out of human bones and looked normal from the outside, but this basilica, to add to its curiosities, made the death visible for all to see.

Her attention drifted back down to the demonic people with manacled skeleton hands, captured by its disturbing imagery. An unsettling feeling began crawl up her spine and slowly reach its cold tendrils through her chest and out to her heart. She found herself trying to decode its message and symbolism, wanting to be objective and emotionally detached, but the similarity of these images with those from her nightmare and the gripping of fear made it impossible. A green fog began to seep out from the very pores of the demonized stone people. What was this, some sort of trick to entertain tourists? She should've been looking for the vent where the fog was coming from but she was as transfixed with the fog as she had been with the carved figures. The phosphorescent green was unearthly. This was no parlor trick—the fog came out too smoothly to have been mechanically released. As she watched, rooted to the ground, it fell to the earth and shifted toward her. Her heart began to race and it was getting hard to breathe. The green fog was reaching out for her, she had to get away, but she couldn't move! *I've never left your head . . . Sweet is surrender. Fighting hurts more than my love.*

"It speaks to you, doesn't it?"

Fae jumped as a man behind her snapped her out of the strange trance. The voice belonged to a priest, a middle-aged man with stylish eyeglasses and a balding pattern.

"It speaks to all of us," he continued when Fae didn't respond right away. "Dead we all were, transformed to look like our master, sin, before Jesus came and set us free."

"I had thought they were demons," Fae said with surety, pointing to the cloaked figures. The green fog was gone without a trace. She had been imagining it, that had to be it. The chill brought on by those hideous figures washed back down her spine like a receding tide until it disappeared.

"No. They are anthropomorphic representations of sin. The artists knew a thing or two that we have forgotten. Sin is as forceful as any person, as domineering and mean as a slaver. It gives you no choice in your actions, playing you like an instrument." The priest smiled warmly at Fae. "Were you going in? There's only two of us but my associate is on duty if you have any needs."

Fae instantly lost her taste to go inside. "No. I was just passing by and some movement caught my eye. Turned out to be a pigeon."

"Well then, I was heading out for a late lunch, would you care to join me? It appears we might have a lot to talk about."

"We have nothing to talk about." Fae said, a little more abruptly than she'd intended. "Sin is just what religious people call personal choices the Church doesn't like."

The priest didn't look surprised by her answer. "Do you believe evil exists?"

"Of course I do." She had no intention in debating a priest but that seemed to be what he wanted. "But evil and sin are different. One exists and the other doesn't."

"Are they so different? Or is one just a verb of the noun?"

"I am sorry, Father, but I'm not interested in your religious thought. I'm comfortable with what I believe and if you let me be, then I won't have any trouble with what you believe, OK? Please, enjoy your lunch."

Fae trotted down the stone steps.

"Fae Peeters," the priest shouted after her, "your grandmother told me of the gift she wants you to have."

THE GIFT

Fae stopped cold.

"How did you know I'm Fae Peeters?" she asked. Tricking her into talking to a priest would be something her father would do, not her grandmother.

"I have never met your grandmother, Miss Peeters, but she has a heart of gold that shines beyond her presence here. And I know who you are because you're the only visitor this village has right now. Word gets around. If your grandmother wasn't involved, I would have seriously asked if you wanted to be here tomorrow night."

"I'm not sure I do, but the mystery grows." She paused and considered what the priest seemed to be offering. "How do you know about my present? Does everyone in this town know about it except me?" The priest just smiled. "Look, I really have no idea what is going on here. I saw the sign at the train station, if I'm breaking any laws—"

"No, no. Not official ones anyway. All will be revealed in good time, Miss Peeters. I'm sorry that you don't want lunch. I was hoping we could be friends before the festivities begin."

The priest continued down the steps, then stopped and looked at her. "When the time comes you will remember this church of God. When you do, you will have the gift your grandmother wishes you to have."

"My grandmother wouldn't lure me inside your church like a sheep about to be fleeced." Fae forced a smile. "Sorry Father, I'll go inside to admire the workmanship but that's it."

The priest eyed her carefully and gave a short, "Hmm," then began to walk away into the sparsely crowded plaza.

"Just where do I find this present, anyway?" Fae called out after him.

The priest turned around and asked her seriously, "Did your grandparents ever tell you why the Nazis fled our village?"

"No." She didn't understand what his question had to do with hers. "They always said it a miracle."

He looked at her silently for a long drawn-out moment.

"Indeed. Well then, God bless you Fae Peeters and Joyeux Noël. Don't miss the festivities tomorrow—it's the most dramatic celebration of Christmas you'll ever see. You could say that its frighteningly accurate." He smiled slightly. "The doors to the church are always open Miss Peeters. Always."

And then the priest left, disappearing down one of the streets.

A dozen or so people milled about the plaza around her, some walking with purpose, others not so much. There must have been a waffle vendor nearby because a group of four giggling pre-teen girls walked by with fresh ones in hand. They didn't seem anxious about the mystery of tomorrow and appeared to be even less concerned with her presence, though they did eye her as they went by.

Fae shivered but she wasn't sure it was because of the cold. Her thoughts went back to the graffiti on the train station wall: you must die to leave alive. She was starting to worry that it meant something much darker than just the expression of a disturbed teenager.

4

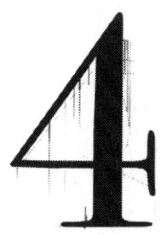

Pondering the oddness of this village and her grandmother's riddle, Fae walked away from the basilica. She found the waffle vendor the girls had advertised and made a meal out of the treat.

. . . it is for the souls you will inspire that has brought me to this point, this point of revealing to you, my dear, the most closely guarded secret . . .

And that was her grandmother's explanation, as though it would be enough to acquit her of any and all pains it would take to suffer through the mystery of the "world's greatest gift." What could she possibly mean by that? For a kid, it might mean getting a puppy or meeting a favorite celebrity. For an adult, it might mean enough money to pay off debts and a bit left for some beer. But Fae was certain it wasn't something quite so simple. She had to wonder if maybe her present was something that used to be more valuable than it currently was, something more akin to guarded Chinese wisdom rather than something to do with religion, though the latter was starting to sadly seem more likely. She knew her grandmother's heart was in the right place, but that kind of "gift" would be severely disappointing. Then again, maybe it was simply the opportunity to retrace her grandparents' childhood steps, and that idea was kind of sweet.

She took the rest of the afternoon to window-shop. The industry of mass production had either passed by this village or had been rejected, since nearly everything was handcrafted and made with such obvious passion that it was impossible not to feel cheated by the world of Ikea. There was one corporate store she recognized, which spoke of the younger generation, but everything else was a piece of art. Men's suits were tailored by hand, jackets were custom-made within twenty-four hours, custom shoes within forty-eight. Furniture and jewelry came from family businesses advertising themselves as yesterday's quality with today's designs and, based on their window displays, they left nothing wanting.

The sky had clouded over and snow was falling lightly though steadily. It caught in her hair and it collected in the trees and on the window sills. Thanks to winter's early darkness, many of the Christmas lights were turned on, creating a true wonderland. Old-fashioned black lampposts with large red bows stood sentry, elegant gold-colored angels swinging beneath in midflight, their horns raised to their lips in announcement. In the storefronts, white lights shone from beneath evergreen boughs and reflected off-colored balls, highlighting hand-painted toys. Angels hung from the top of window frames and St. Nicholas dashed across cotton snow with his furry reindeer frozen mid-stride. Every store featured a detailed, colorful window display. Some of the Christmas displays depicted familiar narratives—like that of St. Nicholas, and others provided a smorgasbord of Christmassy items which invited you to create your own story.

One of her favorites was the Ski and Outdoor Shop, which showcased a mannequin riding on a lightweight toboggan, outrunning the Abominable Snowman—a six-foot stuffed costume. The display case wasn't very wide so the Abominable was maybe half a foot from stepping on the back of the toboggan, but the marketing message was clear. It was there, in that display, that she noticed a stainless-steel camping cup filled with dark liquid and a chunk of bread laid out on an unzipped sleeping bag.

Communion.

Once noticed, she began noticing the same elements in other windows. Most of the businesses kept it simple, a simple glass and bread placed on a tray, but other shops were more clever and made their patrons search the Communion elements out like a game of I, Spy.

The flower shop had an entire wreath made out of the elements. Fae had to admit that it never looked more attractive to her than it did in that wreath. The wine and liquor store had set the elements on the extended tray of a realistic-looking wooden butler, waiting to serve at the fanciest parties. A shop for handmade paper and leather products had made a display of the Nativity and added St. Nicholas, a Christmas elf, and even Jack Frost to the traditional Nativity scene. All were kneeling in front of the manger. The gifts of the Wise Men weren't gold, frankincense, and myrrh but wine, bread, and napkins. They did call them *wise* men for a reason, after all. Despite herself, Fae let out a little laugh at the wit. If only there were a fourth wise man with a bottle of Tylenol.

The mystery behind the Communion displays, a symbol most often associated with Easter rather than Christmas, intrigued her. She entered the paper and leather store expecting an interesting insight into this newest oddity. Within seconds, all the snow that had fallen onto her head began melting and running down her scalp. It tickled.

An elderly man sat behind an even older-looking desk. Tall chestnut-stained bookcases went from floor to roof all the way around the small store, making the small space feel even more compact. In the middle of the floor stood a well-worn table made of the same dark wood, housing an assortment of wax monogramming equipment and inkpots. It smelled of leather and dye in here, and she loved it.

The old man was working on a project behind the counter with a bright desk lamp shining down on his work space. What hair he had left was snow white and, though he looked as frail as a cracked tea cup, the skill and precision with which his fingers punched holes in a purple piece of leather suggested that he wasn't ready to break just yet. When Fae walked in he looked up just a little bit, dipped his head in acknowledgment and returned to his work. But as Fae approached him directly, he took off his glasses and looked at her expectantly.

"I like your window display. It's clever."

He bobbed his head. "My daughter-in-law's idea," the old man said with a ragged voice that probably came from copious amounts of smoking.

"I'm just visiting, leaving tonight of course," she lied trying to clear the air about the subject before it became an issue, "and I keep noticing the Communion elements in everyone's windows. What's the reason behind it?"

Again, he bobbed his head before answering. "Do you know of our Gift?" She noticed his use of "our" and immediately knocked a few guesses about the gift off her list.

"I do. My grandmother is from here, she told me all about it," she lied.

This time he shook his head. "If you knew our Gift, you would not have asked the question." The old man didn't seem to care about her lie, he just returned to punching holes.

"No, OK, so I don't know . . . but look, I need to find out what the Gift is, it's why I've been sent here. If you could only tell me my next clue or—"

The old man cut her off by shaking his head again. Fae wanted to roll her eyes. "Not many visitors find us, not many care to, what with all the sights and wonders everywhere else in the world. How did you arrive here?"

"By train." After realizing how obvious an answer that was, Fae tried again. "I mean, my family is from here." That part was true.

"I know the name of every person who has lived here since I was born, and I know the face of every person who has left and never come back. Tell me whom I have the pleasure of addressing." He stood up to take a better look at her. She told him her grandparents' name and he cracked a small smile. He back sat down again, nodding his head.

"How is Mats doing? Still alive and punching, is he?"

"He died two and a half years ago. I'm sorry."

"Life comes and life goes." The old man went back to punching holes in the leather. Fae half-wondered if he had forgotten their conversation, when he spoke again. "We have always placed out Communion for as long as anyone remembers. It is one of our Christmas traditions. The bread and wine are signs of power, the flesh and the blood. The power over darkness, over death. Once not so long ago, a beautiful woman, both inside and out, was given the job of gatekeeper for our Gift. She loved to see people receive it, though not everyone wants to."

"So the priest told me," Fae said. "Where is this woman now? Or this story older than her life?"

"No, no she must be still alive," he said with another smile pulling at his mouth, "but she has left us. Everyone's lost trust in the outside world now that she's gone." He paused to cough. "The hours before Christmas Day are the most turbulent. Darkness fights hard to keep its rein. The power of love keeps darkness away from our doors until the light comes again."

Fae nodded, feigning understanding. He had given her something at least, but if he expected that that cryptic mumbo jumbo was going to satisfy her curiosity, then these people really *weren't* used to outsiders. "If you're trying to keep darkness away, shouldn't there be a blowout sale on flashlights?" She said dryly, too dryly. The old man didn't laugh. Maybe if she had smiled . . . ? He made a sound like a *grumph* and shook his head but, before he could dismiss her by returning to his work, Fae tried to keep the conversation alive.

"Can you tell me about the history of this village? I'm a student of architecture, and I would love to know more about how or, even better, why your walls were built, and learn more about the uniqueness of your basilica."

He coughed again, this time to clear phlegm from his throat. "I could tell you what I know, or you could learn all that you want at the library. It's not far from the war monument."

Fae asked for more specific directions and he offered to show her on a map, which she didn't have, nor did he offer any paper to draw one, which she thought was a bit cinchy since this was a leather and paper store. She did, however, have a small pad of paper she always carried for moments of inspiration, and he inked out a shaky map, then handed it back to her.

"Now, are you going to buy anything or do I have to charge you an interview fee?"

Fae couldn't tell if he was kidding or serious, but it was clear he was done talking. Before taking her leave, she took a small tour of his tiny shop, then thanked the man for his time. She walked back out into the falling snow feeling more thwarted than ever. She got the impression that she would get the same non-answers from anyone she approached, especially since she couldn't trust herself not to stick out like the insensitive tourist they were expecting her to be. Against the backdrop of more window-shopping, she accepted the fact that she was going to have to figure out the mysteries herself.

If her grandmother had arranged everything so well for her, why hadn't she thought of including a visit to a tourist information booth, such as the library, or even a Christmas survival pamphlet? She wanted to call her to discuss the nature of what "everything has been arranged" meant exactly, and to interrogate her about all the secrets and mysteries popping up, and all the other wonderful little details she had failed to properly discuss. The time difference killed that idea, though. Her grandmother's schedule was predictable; she would be out with her girls, sorting at the local food bank until early that evening when Fae would be well asleep.

The craziness in her head had thankfully quieted down, but it had all seemed and felt so real. Maybe she'd stumbled upon some sort of magnetic field or something like the Bermuda Triangle. She shook her head at the silliness of her theory, and yet . . . ? If the impossible could be entertained long enough, it could be proven possible.

Fae took out her smart phone to look up solar flares, lunar phases, even aurora borealis occurrences, and then she turned it in off in defeat when an error message reminded her that there was no data coverage. She would have to wait until she was back at the hotel.

5

Fae flicked up the collar on her coat to help fight the cold that had begun eating at the back of her neck. The sun had disappeared below the roofs and took its warmth with it. She tightened her blue plaid scarf and snuggled deeper into her coat. A native of the temperate and often rainy Vancouver, she wasn't used to the cold fronts that could stage successful coups d'état of Belgium's normally mild air. After leaving the leather and paper shop, Fae had gone directly to the library only to discover that it had closed at noon yesterday and wouldn't re-open until December 27th; a detail the old man had likely kept to himself if only to get rid of her faster. Such was life.

It was early evening and the streets and squares were mostly empty. The people she had been sharing them with having silently slipped away like someone trying to escape a party unnoticed. Fae realized she only had a little longer before everything shut down for the night, so she decided to pick up something warm to carry back with her to the hotel.

Following the Christmas lights and vintage streetlamps, she found a little coffee shop still open called Café Noir which struck her as familiar. Then she remembered it was the shop her grandmother had recommended for its coffee—so long as its standards of brewing hadn't changed in the last couple of decades. She pushed open the acid-etched glass door and a bell rang with a welcome. She walked down two steps and stamped her feet on the mat at the bottom to rid them of the snow.

The café was long with a curved ceiling like an underground subway. The plaster of the roof was uneven and edgy, earthen in tone as though the designer wanted it to look like the entire place had been hewn from living rock. Atmospheric lighting came from streetlamp cages that hung from both sides of the walls, contributing to the illusion that the tunnel-like coffee shop was just another side street going deeper into the village. The lamplight stuck in the craggy surface of the walls and created as many mini-shadows as it eliminated, and the effect was as mysterious as it was comforting. Most of the wall space was tastefully covered with posters and framed pictures from years gone by, along with the one no-name celebrity who had signed their image with a Sharpie, a page from The Travel Magazine highlighting their little town, and an old license plate or two. To her right, benches with small wood tables lined the wall. One couple still lingering there was drawn too deeply into each other to notice anyone else. The only other customer was an old man sitting secluded at the back, lost in his newspaper.

"Hallo, Vrolijk Kerstfeest!" The barista behind the glass counter welcomed her with a Merry Christmas in Dutch. His freckled face and shaggy hair would have been cute, if Fae had still been fifteen. She guessed he was sixteen or seventeen and probably the owner's son.

"Happy Holidays," Fae responded in English, paying more attention to pulling off her gloves than to the language she was speaking. Through her peripheral vision as she gave her reply, she could see his face becoming suddenly energized.

"You are American t'en! You speak English!"

"Canadian, actually. Je suis encore à apprendre le néerlandais, mais je suis à l'aise en francais," she said. I'm still picking up Dutch but I'm fluent in French.

"I do not want French, no, I will practice my English wit' you!" He looked thrilled, as if he just got a new video game, but Fae didn't mind. As an English speaker she had met many a wonderful person. It was lamentable, she thought, that most North Americans didn't know what to do if they met someone who *didn't* speak English.

"I 'eard t'at our visitor come from t'e nord. I believed you could speak Dutch," the barista apologized.

"Well, I am living in Brussels," she offered.

An appetizing selection of pastries and refrigerated sandwiches stared out at Fae from the spotless glass display case that wound its way back toward the wall. She admired their craftsmanship, so carefully made, so delicious-looking, and as if on cue, her stomach reminded her that it had been a couple of hours since she had last eaten. The barista must have seen the look on her face because he was quick to slide open one of the display-case doors. "What do you want? Somet'ing to eat?" Fae waved him down. Her stomach was empty but it was a warm drink that she really craved.

"Coffee, please. The temperature has really dropped out there."

"Coffee for your journey 'ome, good choice. Americana?"

"Whatever you're best at making."

The teenager laughed. "I'm good at everyt'ing!" He nodded at himself and smiled big. "I will make a very good surprise." He turned around to the back counter and began mixing ingredients into a small metal cup that looked almost gold in the atmospheric lighting. "You must be leaving on t'e 8:30 train, last one of t'e night." He said over his shoulder, "I will be fast or you will be late. Do you have no luggage?"

Fae looked quizzically at his turned back. "I'm not leaving tonight."

The teenager stopped what he was doing and looked at her, confused. "No outsider stays for Christmas Eve, not without . . . well . . . eh, it is not easy. Not since I remember."

Fae stifled a laugh. "An understatement. How hard is it to bring your girlfriend home to meet the parents?" Fae had pieced together that visitors were anomalies, but just how private an affair was Christmas in this place? "What if I am staying?"

"No." The old man who had been hiding behind the day's newspaper rose slowly, purposefully. He was thin, had a well-trimmed white beard that couldn't hide the sternness of his face, and wore a thick wool pullover on top of a cream-colored shirt, buttoned to the nape of his neck. A short-beaked cap covered his head and he leaned heavily on the tables to navigate around them.

His eyes never left her as he came closer, and she didn't know what to do. Was she supposed to rush to give him her arm to help him along his way, or let him keep his pride? Or, even better, ignore him? Though this man was too old to be a physical threat, the way his gaze pierced her as he leaned on each table in succession, like a crotchety old king coming to put her in her place, was making her uncomfortable.

Fae looked over to the barista for some guidance, but he was fixated on the old man with fearful reverence. Fae turned to her right where the lovers had been lost in each other, only to see that they were staring at her like an outlaw. She suddenly felt very isolated.

Fight or flight, she told herself, *you need to make friends for answers, not enemies.*

She shifted her eyes between the three sets of people. "Hey, I'm sorry if I offended you somehow, but Belgium is a free country; I can stay wherever I want for the Holidays," she apologized. Well, apologized on their behalf. Maybe if she could convince them that she had some sort of high ground . . .

The old man was still giving her a dark look as he leaned against the counter to stabilize himself. He began talking to the teenage boy in German, not hiding the fact that he was talking about her.

She barely knew any German, only enough to make out the odd word which was useless without context. She turned to the boy across the counter. The teenager replied to the old man first, who shook his head and pointed adamantly at her.

The boy looked apologetic for what he had to translate, but he didn't appear to have a choice.

"Misseur Drechsler says you cannot stay 'ere. He knew a visitor come . . . came, today. He says you are welcome to return Christmas Day in t'e morning. He is able to pay for your drink, but you must leave. If not tonight, t'en t'e final train tomorrow at two o'clock."

Fae frowned. What right did these people have for kicking her out of a public village?

Fae looked back at the lovers. They were still watching her, but keeping their distance. She steadied her voice.

"Tell Misseur Drechsler that I'm not leaving on any train until I get the present I was sent here by my grandmother to pick up—my *Christmas present.*"

The teenager looked begrudgingly at her; he clearly didn't want to be the messenger. He tried to silently plead with her, but the longer he waited the more agitated both the old man and she became until she couldn't wait any longer.

"What is it about Christmas Eve in this village that I can't be here for it? What don't you want people to know? Does the Pope come out in his pajamas to play the part of the Shelf-Elf? Do you still sacrifice little children to pagan gods? Do you have a pretender-savior you bring out of solitary confinement who walks among you and hands out chocolate to all his good little followers?"

"Please, please, madame," the teenager threw up his hands defensively as though her words were actual strikes in his face, "please don't speak such 'urtful words." He looked at her in defeat, then reluctantly translated to the old man.

With the message delivered, Misseur Dreschler shook his head with finality and bore into her with his icy blue stare. His eyelids were sun-bleached nearly white, and the skin beneath them sunk in saggy, concentric, half circles; the old king he might've been, but he had the tortured eyes of a prophet. She wanted to laugh in the face of those eyes, if only to rob them of their power, but they stole her laughter right out of her throat. Instead she began to feel something else.

Fear.

This time when the old prophet-king spoke he did so directly at her. He spoke his few words of German carefully so she wouldn't miss what he was saying.

The dull scraping sound of a chair behind her broke Fae's concentration. The lovers took their cue and quickly headed to the door, hastily fumbling with their jackets and gloves as they went. The cheerful tinkling of the bell announced their exit.

Fae glanced sideways at the teenager, demanding he translate. Again, the boy looked reluctant, but she didn't care and didn't relent.

"He says you must leave because of le cadeau, the Gift." As he said "the Gift" his voice wavered. "Any present you might have will wait for you under a tree at Christmas morning."

This was beginning to sound like the start of a cheap campfire story, yet she couldn't deny the transformation of the atmosphere around her as the phrase was spoken. She told herself it was the effect of the creepy prophet-king, the fleeing lovers, the residue of her nightmare and the hallucinations at the Notre-Dame du Seigneur, but she couldn't deny it. The golden light of the cozy shop, at first so warm and welcoming, had darkened to a sinister glow. Even the delicacies behind the counter had lost their allure, looking as tempting as poisoned apples. She almost thought she could hear the foreboding sound of a pipe organ concerto resounding through the curved walls.

The transformation was just another trick of her mind, Fae told herself, again. But the very real nervousness of the teenager and wild warning of the old man left her with a feeling she couldn't shake. Her grandmother had said everything had been arranged. Did it include this meeting? It wasn't her grandmother's style.

"You can't be serious." The skepticism Fae tried to convey sounded weak to her ears. The organ she was imagining played louder. "The Gift is like, what, a curse?" The question came out as a nervous laugh.

The old man answered her directly again and this time he spoke perfect but accented French. "Why are you here?"

"My family was born here," she responded back in French. "My grandmother sent me to see where she grew up and to get my Christmas present from her."

The old man stared at her. But instead of wanting to be sarcastic, Fae was compelled to satisfy him, give him what he wanted if only to leave her alone.

"What are their names, your family?"

"Mats and Maria Peeters. They're my grandparents." The old man's eyes squinted even deeper. "They moved in the wake of the Nazi uprising."

The barista inhaled sharply and his eyes grew wide. "*You're* Maria Peeters' granddaughter? Mon Dieu, I see the similarity from t'e picture!"

The old man glared at the boy just long enough to shut him up, as a nerve twitched at the edge of his wrinkly old eyes. Fae hoped it was recognition and not something more concerning.

The old man huffed out a gruff puff of air and turned to make his way back to his newspaper. He spoke to them over his shoulder in German.

"Misseur Drechsler says you can stay if you will not listen to reason. He knows Elise at t'e 'otel tried to dissuade you and probably ot'ers too. Also, he says t'at he hopes Maria told you everyt'ing or not'ing about your present. It does not come wrapped."

Lars Dreschler's capitulation didn't seem to calm the boy. He kept looking in the old man's direction as though waiting for another order. Dreschler had let her go after she'd named her grandparents. That had to mean something.

"Let me finish your coffee," the boy said awkwardly when it was apparent there would be no more direction coming from Dreschler. He turned back to the coffee station.

Fae wasn't sure she wanted the coffee anymore, but she let him ply his trade if only to give her a moment to figure out what had just happened.

"What is the Gift?" she whispered to the boy, hoping the old man couldn't hear her.

The teenager didn't give any indication that he heard her. He put the metal mixing cup up to the steamer. The machine's loud hiss filled the room for a moment, and when it was finished she asked again. In response, he merely he presented the coffee to her with a polite smile. He had created a maple leaf in the foam.

"For Maria Peeters' granddaughter t'e coffee is free."

"Thank you," Fae said, genuinely taken by the generosity and pleased that her grandmother had left such a pleasant impression behind. But it wasn't enough to distract her. "Why won't anyone answer my question?" She tried her best to sound curious rather than impatient. "What is the Gift?"

The barista nodded subtly showing that he had heard her the first few times. "Le cadeau . . ." He began to say then cast his eyes back to the old man. He lowered his voice and leaned in close. "Germans came into our village early in t'e morning December 24th,1940. T'ey marched in and collected our men, women, children to work in t'e factories and fields. On Christmas Eve came le cadeau. T'e next morning t'ere were no Germans in our streets. T'ey all fled and never returned."

He stood back up and started to wipe an already clean counter.

"I know the Germans fled, there's a monument to that right outside the train station. What made them run away?"

"You should leave tomorrow. But if you do not, take your sleep and, no matter what you see or 'ear, do not leave your bed until after t'e sun arrives Christmas Day, or you too may be like t'e Germans and never return."

"And if I don't go to sleep?"

"Then go to Basilique de Notre-Dame du Seigneur. You must ask permission; I don't know if you are allowed."

Lars Dreschler dropped his newspaper and looked their way disapprovingly. Fae knew then that the teenager wouldn't be answering any more of her questions. He had found some dishes to wash and he turned his back on her, busying himself with his task.

Fae took a sip of her drink. It was amazing, but the bittersweet taste didn't leave her tongue twitching for more as she knew it should have. The eerie atmosphere of the coffee shop hadn't dissipated and she felt like the walls themselves wanted to squeeze her out. She took one last look at the old man buried in his newspaper. Her stomach tightened.

She took out a bill from her purse and placed it on the scratched counter. Hastily doing up her coat, retying her scarf, and wiggling her fingers back into her faux fur gloves, Fae put the plastic lid on the coffee, thanked the boy, and hurried out into the cold wintery night back to her room.

Upon hearing the bell, Lars Drechsler set down the newspaper he had been reading. More unrest in the Middle East and more immigration issues at home, nothing new or unexpected.

A raspy cough arrested his chest before he called out to the boy behind the counter.

"Julien, follow that woman. If Maria Peeters wants her here, then so be it."

"Misseur?"

"Find out if anyone is talking too much. No one is to tell her about the Gift until, or more likely if, she makes it through the Eve. Cooking and shopping, those are the only conversations I want her having."

Julien looked alarmed. "I . . . I can't. I have to stay here. I have to watch the shop."

"No one else will be coming to buy your sandwiches tonight, boy. Don't lose track of that woman. Tell Elise to nail her door shut if she has to—no more questions!"

"The windows and mirrors, Misseur—"

"Should do the work for us and she'll leave. If that woman is meant to know the Gift, then it will be God's gift to her and not mine. Now, go!"

Julien hurried to carry out the orders. He ripped the white apron over his head but it got stuck in his hair. He managed to fling it off while simultaneously untying his work shoes, balancing on one leg though he almost toppled over. The boy managed to collect himself without breaking anything before running to the corner to get his winter wear. He threw it on as fast as he could.

"She turned right!" Lars yelled after him as he fled up the stairs.

With Julien gone, the café grew silent, which was just how Lars liked it. Watching the acrobatic show the teenager had just put on, Lars was amazed at how he or any of his war friends ever made it out of a foxhole much less a war. That had been the real Christmas miracle, he thought, because it needed to happen more than once.

Elise had come earlier that day on her lunch break to tell him about this woman who had arrived by order. He wanted no details about the woman. They weren't supposed to have mattered. Now, he wished he had asked.

The news of the woman's arrival was an annoyance but not worthy of the panic Elise had come to him with, but that changed when she told him about hearing Miss Peeters' screaming in her room. Elise's belief that the Gift was manifesting early was the only logical conclusion and that was unsettling. On the rare occasion an outsider stayed for Christmas Eve, the Gift usually manifested the day of. The last time it was early was when a member of the Belgian royal family vacationed here six years after the war had ended. He had seen the Gift everywhere, not just in a bedroom, as early as the 22nd—if Lars remembered correctly. The royal had left on his own accord before Christmas Eve and to preemptively cover any rumors about his departure, Lars had planted a hallucinogenic drug in his rented house; the drug laws were broader back then. The housekeepers reported the find to the village police, an official report was made, and thankfully the blackmail never had to be used.

But that was the incident which had led Lars to overturning Maria's Christmas Eve policy. Maria believed that if a person came for Christmas, then they were here by divine intent. Some still shared Maria's opinion, but Lars had seen the world; and those who had seen the world as he had, knew how it was changing. He had, and continued to insist that they were better off shutting the world out for a few days. Keeping themselves and the village unmolested was more important than accommodating one or two people who may or may not make it through the night. His company hadn't. And to this day, Fuhrman was listed as MIA. Lars had his suspicions, but some things were best left alone. That wasn't to say no one ever stayed the night. There had been three cases in the last sixty years and he had managed them well enough, but not without certain risk.

Lars had told Elise to prepare contingences for Miss Peeters, but that was before he knew whose young, pretty, offspring this woman was. That Elise hadn't told him that Miss Peeters was Maria's granddaughter bothered him—that information mattered. If Miss Peeters' compulsion to stay was greater than sound advice from the locals, then he would have to deal with her in another way.

Slowly leveraging himself up from the tabletop, Lars struggled to get his feet solid beneath him. The cartilage in his knees was virtually gone, and arthritis had ravaged the rest of his lower joints. Since the coffee shop was empty, he let his pain and weakness out, not caring about the depth of his groans.

He shuffled to the glass countertop, to an old black tank of a telephone.

Its receiver sat in a tarnished metal cradle and its yellowing keypad waited patiently to serve. He picked up the heavy receiver and held it firmly to his ear. With his knobby finger, he pressed each number with a soft *click*. The phone rang twice before it was answered.

"Elise, Lars Drechsler."

6

When Fae arrived back at the hotel she immediately asked about the Wi-Fi connection. Elise regretted to say that they had no public computers and the Internet was misbehaving in any case; she even showed Fae her screen of an unloaded web page to prove her point. Fae shook her head and rolled her eyes, then trudged up the three arduous flights of stairs, tired from her day and determined to learn something about this village, even if it was when the first gas station was opened.

The night was still early but all she cared about was crawling in bed, maybe turning on the TV, or picking through the journal articles and blueprints she had downloaded for their relevance to her thesis, before leaving Brussels. She was developing a system that could be used to determine a European society's devotion to religion based on the designs and location of non-ecclesiastic buildings. The final part was designing the plans for a number of buildings to reflect her findings and in her enthusiasm, she already had sketched a number of designs, of which she was pretty proud.

She decided against the TV and instead opened her laptop. She began reading an anthology of biographies on the architects and artists who had influenced and shaped the landscape of Europe. She had been reading for nearly twenty minutes when her screen froze and then went black. Her computer had never frozen before. She moved her finger around the touchpad and was pleased when a few seconds later the display returned. After a moment of working through the lag, all was good again except that she had lost her page. She found herself instead at the start of a chapter on the Spanish painter Francisco de Goya. Even though Goya wasn't part of her research, she kept reading out of fancy.

His was a typical biography for one of the great artists. He showed talent early on, benefitted from the patronage of the wealthy, got caught up in the political scene, then found himself in over his head but survived because his art demanded it. As Fae read she found herself dreaming of reading her own biography, and instead of Goya's name it was hers, and instead of Goya's works being trumpeted by his contemporaries, it was her designs which were redefining what a beautiful building was. It was a fun exercise, no different from an athlete imagining winning gold. The biography became less routine though with the introduction of his illness, at first a physical malady and then a mental one which some called a madness. The sounds in his head and the demons from his nightmares evolved his works into dark horrors. However, at the same time, his ability to speak for those who had little expression of their own—the mentally unwell—grew, and the works from that era became no less respected than his earlier portraits and altarpieces.

It all gave Fae pause. Was she going mad? It was something of a genius's trademark to be unstable, and being a bedmate with a darker side might actually help her career, especially with the resurging interest in Gothic culture. If she was already mentally . . . more open . . . learning how to tap into it would be smart rather than trying to fight or deny it and then being unprepared when it snapped. Who was it who once said that death was the only great adventure? A mind unleashed could go places others were too bound to go. *There are probably good reasons why mental illness is called an illness,* she thought, *and there are also probably some things better left unexplored.*

A voice spoke then, interrupting her thoughts, and like earlier, it wasn't her own and she could feel her eyes widen. *The darkness holds such beautiful secrets.* Hearing the extra-voice again alarmed her but for some reason, she wasn't scared. *The journey of exploring them will make you the person you envisage becoming. All you need is a guide; someone who understands you, someone you trust so deeply it would be impossible to become misled.*

Not being afraid didn't last long, as she became aware that it was happening again—the same dark mood from this morning. She no longer cared about the when and how of the mood occurring; the fear was back, crawling up her spine. Whatever this was that caused her to see and hear things wasn't something that could easily be solved with a Google search. Phases of the moon and magnetic fields were bad ideas and she couldn't believe she had even entertained them. *You must die to leave alive.* Was that really such a strange command? When living in this world was enough to wear you down to the bone, putting on a smile every day and chasing after success was as much an act of defiance as it was a show of the strength to live. Most people walking the streets were already half "dead." The graffiti artist must have been talking about dying to the stress and troubles of this life in order to truly start living, to truly experience life. Or maybe the artist believed that there was life after death, and that that was the real life.

Once you die and start to live, everything you wanted to know becomes embarrassingly clear. Let me stay and I will show you how to access that knowledge. It was still the voice. *Gold is valuable because of its rarity and you, Fae, are gold. I've been investing in you since birth. We are a team as close as twins in a womb.* It was her own mind, it had to be. She was talking to herself. Her own self was the only twin she could have had all these years, her own mind. It just . . . made sense. But it didn't because, literal or figurative death, she loved living the life she had now, had worked so hard for it, and wouldn't suggest death of any sort to herself. She had dreams and success to look forward to and she was enjoying it all without mad genius . . . it just, *didn't* make sense. So, maybe this mess really *was* just a new path of communication her mind was exploring?

No. It was madness to think that madness was somehow a desirous thing. A surge of determination rose up and she stormed to the mirror in front of her bed and pointed at herself.

"You, Fae Peeters," she commanded, leaning forward to stare deeply at her reflection, "are alive. Right now, you are alive. Not dying, not interested in death or dying. Your life is happy and full of potential. Your brain is normal; your mind is normal. My artist's quirk is eating plain toast on Saturday afternoon!" *But where is your guide in all this?* "I don't need any more than I have. You, Fae Peeters, are alive and focused. Now get ahold of yourself and stop this, it's Christmas for God's sake!"

She felt her resolution strengthen, but as she stared at herself in the mirror she couldn't help but notice how old she looked—deep bags under her eyes, dull flesh. She was either much more tired than she had suspected or the lighting in the room wasn't doing her any favors. She cast a look around for another light source but came up empty. She returned her eyes to the mirror, looking for an angle where the light didn't age her so much, but what awaited her in the mirror wasn't her reflection, but the head of a decaying corpse.

Seeing it for the second time was worse than the first because it wasn't supposed to be real—she'd already explained it away. Panicking, Fae grabbed the nearest thing and hurled it at the glass. Unfortunately, the nearest thing was her room key, which did little damage. She tried but she couldn't wrestle her eyes away from the corpse reflected instead where her own face should be. She reached for something else to throw, one of her gloves, then a pen, then the other glove, the corpse matching her every move. This couldn't be real, couldn't be REAL! The taunting from earlier that day echoed in her mind, *I'm in your head, I'm in your head.* Finally, her hand found a ceramic mug to hurl at the mirror, but an unexpected softness stopped her short.

Shhhhh. Shhhhhhh, now. It's not so scary when I'm here, is it? This voice in her head was her mind, right? It had to be. She had lost her mind and now it had come back. Her skin crawled when it spoke. She wasn't sure if it was creepy or alluring, but she needed this voice to be on her side so she chose the latter. A heaviness had settled in the room. With the coffee mug trembling in the air, she slowly set it down. *Let us take a look together. We can replace fear with knowledge.*

Fae nodded like a little girl hiding behind her mother's skirts. The corpse remained in the mirror gazing out at her but not seeing, its eyes clouded over. No muscle was left to the face so the thin, gray skin sunk deep into the pits of the skull. The skin itself was both dehydrated and spotted with rot revealing bone in spots where the flesh was no more. The nose was eaten away leaving only a stub showing the nasal cavities beneath. Those looked even larger by the curling of the lips which had dried and shriveled to a hellish grin. Only long, stringy patches were left of her hair, and she could easily count her vertebrae.

Her stomach weakened. From behind the corpse a thin cloud of luminescent green mist began to swirl in gentle rolls like a fog coming in off the ocean. Fae immediately thought of the relief carvings at the Notre-Dame du Seigneur and the tenuous calm the hushing voice had brought evaporated into fearful panic once again. She quickly checked behind her expecting to see green fog but saw only a normal room. Backing away from the mirror, she raised the mug again, eyes glued, hands shaking.

The green fog continued growing thicker in the mirror and the heaviness dropped to a crushing weight, threatening to squeeze every breath from her lungs.

She needed to get out of here. But the fear wouldn't let her move, and like a mouse caught in the crush of an eagle's talons, she couldn't escape, transfixed on the corpse staring at her.

The mist became so thick only the corpse's dulled white eyes and gleaming white teeth could be made out. Then, the same voice spoke out of the fog. It was deep and smooth and it resonated so heavily in her brain that she didn't know if it came from inside her or from without. It was a human voice, a beautiful one, and she instantly called it a friend.

Fae, the power of life and death is in your hands.

She tried to speak but was out of breath. "I . . . I am alive . . . there is no . . . choice."

Oh, but there is. Life and death. The voice repeated calmly, a patient correction from a caring teacher.

"I am alive."

Life and death! The voice reasserted. A pause, then the same smooth tone again. *Choose your hand to play.*

"Life then, I choose life!" The fear was escaping through tears blurring her vision, and her insides began to quake.

An amused chuckle resounded deep within her, and she knew then that she had said something wrong.

Do you, now. It wasn't a question. *Ring, ring.*

And then like a snap the green fog disappeared, taking with it the oppressive weight and the corpse, leaving Fae Peeters staring back at her blanched face and watery eyes.

The room phone rang, and Fae jumped with a yelp. *The phone, it's only the phone,* she told herself, trying to calm down. She didn't move right away. She couldn't. She had been dreaming, hallucinating, talking to her own consciousness. She was trying to rationalize, but she was still terrified. The phone kept ringing.

"Hello?"

"Miss Peeters, this is the front desk." There was a pause but Fae was barely keeping the receiver to her ear much less able to form a response so she let Elise continue. "Mrs. Lemmens thought you would be hungry and has put a hot plate for you in the kitchen. It awaits you at your convenience. It would be my pleasure to direct you to the kitchen, either by phone or in person at the front desk." Elise had barely finished her last word before Fae curtly thanked her and hung up. She inhaled deeply and then let out a long, slow exhale. It felt good so she did it again, and continued taking deep breaths until she stopped shaking. Soon her lungs moved in and out at a normal pace and her heart decided it wanted to stay in her chest.

The very thought of putting food in her mouth made her ill, but the idea of a warm, home-cooked meal was a welcome enough motivation to leave the room—though she would've gladly left for any excuse.

There was a knitted throw blanket resting on the corner chair and, before Fae left, she threw it over the mirror to cover the hellish portal; the apparition wouldn't happen a third time. She sat back on the bed and appraised her work and considered it acceptable, until she remembered that this wasn't the only mirror in her room. She couldn't move fast enough as she frantically rushed to grab one of the three pillows from the bed. Wrestling the cover off one of them, she dashed into the bathroom and draped it over the mirror there too, averting her eyes from looking into it as she did. She could almost feel the skeletal corpse waiting for her on the other side of the glass.

Before she left to go downstairs, Fae remembered to grab the unwanted Nativity set. With another deep breath, she collected it and composed herself, then fled the room.

At the bottom of the stairs Fae found Elise working behind the desk. She looked up as Fae came down the last of the steps.

"Your dinner is this way, if you'd follow me." She began to stand up then her eyes flicked down to the Nativity set and she raised an eyebrow. "Is there a problem with your furnishings?"

"I'm sorry. It's obviously valuable, but I'd prefer something else. Do you have a Christmas moose, or snowmen, or, I don't know . . . anything else? A menorah?" Fae carefully set all the pieces on the counter to hand them over to Elise's care.

Elise's other eyebrow raised.

"Any questions about room décor must be handled by Mrs. Lemmens directly as she has everything cataloged to each room. Unfortunately, she is no longer here. In the meantime, I'll return this to its place in your room until tomorrow when Mrs. Lemmens will personally take care of your problem."

"Don't bother." Fae told her. "You can leave it down here and Mrs. Lemmens can readjust her catalog minus three floors of travel."

"I have very strict instructions—"

"If I take it, I'm just going to put it in the closet, and it's nice enough art that it deserves to be seen. A decoration exchange makes sense. So just . . . do your job and . . ." She'd said too much, but she was too stressed to care about anyone else right now. Elise's face reddened, but to her credit she suffered the offense silently.

Elise paused before calmly replying, "If you'd allow me to advise you, that if you don't like baby Jesus, you'd be best to find another room for tomorrow night."

Fae would end up sleeping on the street if she chose to take her business elsewhere, but now she had been drawn into an argument she didn't want to have with this woman and that irritated her.

"I don't want to see that mess in my room again."

"We do our best to accommodate all requests, Miss Peeters. Is there anything else I can do for you?" The fact that Elise remained so calm was nearly as annoying as if she had gloated. But she didn't. She just waited for an answer.

"No," Fae said curtly, putting on her emptied coat in sharp motions to show just how agitated she was. She wasn't even going outside. "I'll take myself to the kitchen."

"Through the hall beside the stairs there, turn left, then the first doorway on the right."

Stop talking so perfectly, woman, this isn't a Hilton. Get mad at me for being such a stain on my family and for being such an irritating whiner! As she passed Elise, Fae heard herself ask, "How many Germans stayed in this house during the war? You can help me with that."

"Excuse me?"

"Germans. Nazis. Did any of them die here?"

"Perhaps. Maybe, I really don't know. May I ask why?"

Fae sighed to try to calm down. "My current line of research is correlating hauntings with specific styles of architecture," Fae lied. It was the only way. "I wanted to get some work done while here."

"I honestly can't help much in that area. I can tell you where the library is, though."

"It's closed."

Elise smiled. "Enjoy your dinner."

Elise waited just long enough for the pretentious girl to be out of earshot before she slipped into the back room where Mrs. Lemmens was bent over a ledger book. A desk lamp added extra light and the gold chain from her reading glasses drooped down her cheeks. A duet of cello and piano playing "Carol of the Bells" carried through the air.

Pulling up a chair beside the older woman, Elise waited patiently until she finished her work and set her pencil down.

"Is everything all right with our guest?"

"Just a minor cultural misunderstanding," Elise said. "It wasn't anything I couldn't clear up."

"Good. You do know why Miss Peeters is here?"

Elise took the question to be rhetorical. "Miss Peeters is asking about hauntings. I've heard screams coming from upstairs. It's begun already; the Gift is coming."

Eva nodded. "Then it has come earlier than usual. Miss Peeters must truly be destined to be here."

"I don't trust her. Outsiders don't belong here for the Eve. They can't make it through, so they can't understand."

"Maria Peeters made it through."

"She grew up here, that's different." Elise was tired of making the same argument over and over again. Rules were made for the majority, not the exception.

"And the immigrant families?" Eva pressed.

"There's a reason why Misseur stopped that."

"My dear Elise," Eva reached out and lovingly patted Elise's hands, "what is the purpose of a gift but to give it away?"

Elise didn't want to answer because she didn't want her complaint to go unresolved.

Eva tried another approach. "Does God ever let a tree fall without bringing a beaver to build a new dam from it? Even though God does not bring calamity, does anything ever happen where God cannot bring good out of it?"

"Someone should at least prepare her."

"And would she believe them any more than the world will believe her when she leaves here?"

Elise sighed because once again Eva was right. "The freak shows and ghost hunters would believe her and, unlike Area 51, we would actually give them what they came for and *that* is why she can't stay. What would happen to the Gift when the governments force us from our home in the backs of black SUVs, hooked up to heart and brain monitors? What if removing us from the city limits releases *him* to follow us and he's *loosened* into the world? We can control him, we have the Gift, but everyone else?"

"Careful, Elise, dear, undervaluing an enemy because of familiarity can make even an ant dangerous. My dear old friend, Maria, is very concerned for the future of her granddaughter. I don't know what that all entails but I do know Miss Peeters considers herself to be somewhat more enlightened to spiritual realities by simply believing that there are none. That is not so much her fault but our own. We've done this to ourselves after centuries of abuse. I know you never met Maria, but you must trust that she would not have sent Miss Peeters here if she didn't truly believe it would be a good thing. Once Miss Peeters does receive what she has come here for, you may find her a little less averse to my Nativity." Eva nodded toward the front desk. Then, she added, "Maria would never betray this village."

"I don't trust Fae," Elise reasserted.

"Misseur Drechsler has had his way with your generation, hasn't he?"

"He's kept our village safe all these years. Was he told about Miss Peeters?"

Eva set her reading glasses back onto the bridge of her nose, picked up her pencil, and began working on her books again.

"No," she said simply. "Maria did not wish him to know . . . though by now that wish is destroyed."

"Then everything hasn't been arranged, as you had said," Elise said without accusation.

Eva did not respond but kept working.

A boy choir's rendition of "Joy to the World" began to play and Elise left her boss alone.

7

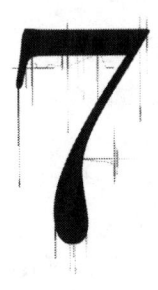

Despite little advance notice, everyone Elise had asked to come to her apartment arrived on time, except for Michele who'd come fifteen minutes late, citing traffic as his excuse. That was laughable in a place where there was almost never any traffic congestion except when Misseur Bourbon took his 1928 tractor from one field to the other through the middle of the village. It was a wonderful piece of living history, until you got stuck behind it.

With the arrival of Michele everyone settled into the living room. Denise and her twin Franc were here and Simone cradled her sleeping newborn over her shoulder. Maël sat to her own left and his group of friends filled the rest of the room: the newly arrived Michele, Marc, Alain, Tristan, Iakob, and Paulina. They had all known each other since birth, they represented the future of this village, and they would all grow old counting their Christmases behind these walls.

They, along with the rest of the village, knew the Gift not so much as a present but as a curse. It manifested once a year on Christmas Eve and then went away, and that was enough to completely define them. Most had accepted living with it, though over the generations some had been broken by it, and others had tried to fight it, smuggling in exorcists with their holy water and religious artifacts; they'd all been exorcised themselves before they could ply their trade. Elise had learned to cope, and so had everyone here. This group was dedicated to protect what they loved from those who would threaten it: They would contain the dark secret of their hometown's Gift, and tonight they would do it under Misseur's forged auspices.

This wasn't the first time that Elise had spoken on Misseur's behalf, but this was, however, the first time she spoke without his knowing. Nevertheless, she was confident. This was the perfect opportunity to show everyone that she was ready for his responsibilities. People knew she would take over his role; they had already begun treating her like his successor, which was highly validating as it was a role that needed trust. The position came with high respect, but it wasn't envied.

"A Christmas visitor has arrived," Elise began, a pad of paper and pen resting on her crossed knee, "and she needs to be dealt with."

"You and Misseur can deal with her in your crafty ways," Franc said, setting the tone. "You don't need us." It wasn't the first time he'd voiced that opinion. A ginger-haired man with a scruffy beard, he clearly didn't want to be here.

"In case you haven't heard," Elise responded calmly, "our visitor is Fae Peeters, Maria Peeters' granddaughter, sent by Maria herself." Of course they'd heard. Any other time of year, Fae's arrival would've incited excited gossip rather than protectionism. "As such, Misseur has decided to handle her with due appropriateness." Elise eyed Maël watching for a reaction. He was Fae's first cousin. Now that she knew what to look for, she could place the family resemblance. Like Franc, Maël appeared to be missing the cause for concern as he eyed his lap where he was thumbing a pick in his jeans. "Maria has been coordinating heavily with her old friend Mrs. Lemmens to make sure that Fae's comfortable stay allows her to get her gift as painlessly as possible."

Franc choked back a bitter laugh. Maël didn't react with even a nerve twitch. Elise suspected Maria had already contacted his family to help Fae, and the question was now whether Maël's loyalty was to a cousin or to his home. "I've asked around and, apparently, Maria has developed quite a network of helpers. I don't need to remind you what is at stake if this woman goes through the Eve with us. I've met her, heard her speak, and she is not our friend. I promise you, she'll be dead before the night is done."

"And she won't leave," Paulina assumed. "So what's the plan?"

Elise smiled a small, self-accomplished smile. "The pit of Ne—"

"Don't say his name!" yelled Paulina, practically jumping off her seat. Elise was sure Marc called her an idiot under his breath, too.

"It's his name," Elise said, trying not to roll her eyes too obviously, "not a summoning chant."

"Do Jews like the name of Hitler tossed around so easily?" Paulina asked with a glare.

"Fine. The pit of *him*. We throw her in and close the door, essentially burying her there for safekeeping, hidden from sight." She knew it wasn't going to be a popular plan, and she was ready for the immediate backlash of outright rejection, which erupted. She cut it off before the rancor grew into a movement. "It's the only way we can both let her stay and protect ourselves."

Denise, very much the opposite of her twin, Franc, frowned. "This is Misseur's plan?"

"He agrees with it." That wasn't exactly true.

"I don't know. The only thing Misseur is more against than visitors during the Eve is the pit."

"It's too dangerous, Elise," Iakob agreed, "you're talking about—"

"I know what I'm talking about. Nobody is without a weakness and *his* is the oldest: pride. We can tap into that and make this plan work. Fae will be caught safely in his pit and he won't concern himself with her until—"

"He represents everything that's wrong with this world; of course, he'll concern himself with her," Marc said, but Iakob talked over him and their two thoughts almost got lost in each other's. "We'll be gift-wrapping this woman for him and that's not going to protect her or us."

These people have no sense of opportunity, Elise thought. *If only they would calm down long enough for me to explain . . .*

"Come on, Elise. You can't play his game and expect to come away clean," Iakob was still talking.

"Thank you, Iakob, for that reminder." Elise held up her pen to bring order back. "Allow me to finish? Skipping to where we have her locked in the pit, she stays there for the night—"

Denise interrupted, "You lock her in there, Elise, and she's dead. I won't do it."

"How about," Maël spoke up for the first time, "you tell us how you expect to get the best of both worlds. You're asking us to send an unsuspecting outsider to sleep in the devil's bed and then snatch her out untouched and unharmed the next morning. Maybe you know something we missed." The others chuckled as though his comment was sarcastic, but Elise couldn't tell if it was or not. Instinct told her that he had been; desire wanted him to be genuine. "And then tell us why you're doing this without Misseur knowing because I won't believe he's OK with this."

Elise's insides scrunched up in annoyance at having been caught but she didn't let it show. "Thank you." She meant it. "One thing we can all agree on is that Fae cannot remain in her hotel room. That would solve nothing, nor can she attempt to get her gift. Misseur wants to stuff her into a windowless room at the Notre-Dame du Seigneur—drugged, then wake her up after she's missed everything and all is back to normal. But he'll still have to navigate around Maria's long reach and come up with a defensible explanation for the drugging."

Elise continued. "If she sees any part of the Gift, it'll be the beginning of the end for us because she won't understand. So, rather than doing what Misseur wants, we'll steal her into the pit instead." Seeing the doubt on Maël's face, Elise sped on to prevent his interruption. "Misseur's methods aren't adequate anymore, not with our generation. The pit is the only place that can create a plausible enough story Fae might believe. The gases there will make her forget everything before and even after she's brought back out."

"*If* he leaves her alone," Maël clarified.

"His arrogance will make him complacent toward her. We shouldn't be afraid of the pit or of him. We can *use* both. Why are we afraid to flex our muscle over him?"

"Because, one," Iakob said, "we aren't strong enough to fight him and, two, a caged animal is still dangerous. If even one thing goes wrong, one delay, one forgotten detail, one assumption, this woman's life is destroyed."

"Can you repent for something like that?"

"So dramatic, Franc," Elise said. "Like most everyone else outside our walls, Fae already *is* his creature, but by being here she lost her anonymity to him—if she had it at all. So, we risk making her life worse, yes, but that's an acceptable risk since he *already* knows she's here. It's just that instead of playing hide and seek in the Notre-Dame du Seigneur, we're doing it in the pit."

Denise added, "Maria and Misseur have gotten people throu—"

"Yes, I know," Elise interrupted, then continued on. "Every Eve, we're forced into being Ne—... I mean, *his*, disgusting show puppets. And because of that, our own people have tried to bring about our extinction and the Gift's with it; Danielle Sauvageon?" She asked the question to jog their memory. "In the eighteenth century, she wanted to kill all the children to eradicate the next generation, and she's the famous example. Lyon Layfette? He would've poisoned the whole water supply six years ago, if that one woman didn't stop him."

His case was the first time Misseur Dreschler had asked Elise to help him. After he was stopped, Layfette took a trip to Rochefort and she'd helped him book a room at a bed and breakfast owned by a retired psychiatrist. Lyon hadn't thought anything of it, but it made for the perfect start to a discrediting history, should he begin to talk.

"We survive the Gift and the risks it brings," Elise concluded, "Fae Peeters will too. Just, in the pit."

Simone shifted her baby and Franc offered to take him. "Fae's different, and you know it," she said. "We get through the Gift because those are the terms *he* has to adhere to—Fae isn't included in those terms. When Maria was here, there would never have been any conversations like this."

For the first time that night, Tristan spoke. He was a tall, skinny guy who had yet to grow into his body and probably never would. "Elise, have you ever been inside the pit? I know more stories than fact about that place, and I think the same goes for everyone, except Misseur. Do you know that what you want to do is even possible?" It was a genuine question and Elise took that to mean a step in the right direction. She hesitated. To convince them, she had to tell the truth. Her hesitation was almost answer enough.

THE GIFT

"I have been to the black door, yes." Her revelation silenced the protests, leaving only wide eyes and gaping jaws in its wake.

The black door. Shrouded in as much legend as the rest of the pit, it was the pit's entrance, buried away on an abandoned side street called la Rue in the most isolated part of the village. With la Rue's entrance sealed by two metal doors, only Misseur could walk that haunted street, and it was the only location in the whole village monitored by video. She had seen footage of that place that had robbed her of peaceful nights and could make the skin crawl of even the biggest cynic. Anyone who thought they were tougher than a few ghost stories and broke through la Rue's locks never made it far. Except her. She had just been smart enough to do it in the middle of the day.

"It was a few months after Lyon Layfette's incident. I had to know if the stories were true."

"And?"

"And what I saw was real enough to believe that the other stories are, too."

"How did you—"

"Just know that this plan is grounded in reality, OK? This doesn't leave the room."

There was an awkward silence for a few moments and this time she let them take as long as they wanted. Alain was the first to break the silence.

"Are you going to involve Misseur Dreschler in this?"

"Misseur has taken care of this village for decades and we all trust him to do what's best. Except in this case. He's doing what's safe, and outdated, probably because he doesn't want to cross Maria. I can make the hard decision. Putting Fae in the pit is the best solution to this problem, risks and all."

Iakob spoke again. "I don't like it, Elise. You're playing with someone, some*thing*, that is beyond all of us. This is a plan made off the *hope* that nothing goes wrong, and off the *hope* that he'll ignore her."

"You must understand," Elise said pleasantly, "I didn't ask you all here looking for permission. I'm asking for your help."

"To do what?" Maël asked.

"Someone needs to get her to the pit an hour or two before we—" Elise side-glanced at Paulina who was subtly shaking her head, discouraging Elise from vocalizing anymore. "They need to get her into the pit, and then someone to help lock her up, and then to dig her out Christmas morni—"

Franc interrupted. "Why don't you get her to the pit? This is your brilliant idea."

"Let's just say we didn't get off on the right foot. She wouldn't go anywhere with the irritating hotel receptionist. Alain, Marc, I'll need you to help get her into the pit. Maël, can you get her there?"

Alain began to protest at being volunteered but Maël spoke before he could voice his displeasure. "She's spending the day with my family. My grandparents have talked of nothing else since they heard she was coming and I won't rob them of their time with her. They won't get another chance."

"There's all Christmas Day and however long she stays afterward."

"If there's a morning for her to see."

Elise shot a warning look at Franc. She shouldn't have invited him.

"All I'm asking is that sometime early tomorrow evening you take her out to pick up a friend whose car broke down, or something, get creative, and bring her to the pit. When you return, you can tell your grandparents that she got tired and wanted to go back to the hotel to sleep."

Maël was hesitating. "I don't trust *him*."

"Look, we've been puppets in this hell-play all our lives. We know the script, so let's start directing it instead of being directed. What have we been saved into, if not to use the resources at hand to protect ourselves? If you get her to the pit by nine, that will be enough time to allow for a good buffer."

Elise surveyed the room and set her face. The group would still need convincing, but Maël hadn't refused. Where he went, the others tended to follow. Except for Franc, but that wasn't unexpected. They had all fantasized before of how to non-criminally stop the Gift, and her plan could be the first step down that road of taking control.

The contemplative silence in the room spoke of their interest. Given a little more time they'd support her. If only Fae Peeters knew how much of her soul she had shown in turning away Mrs. Lemmen's Nativity, she might have been spared this fate for Misseur's simple kidnapping and drug-induced sleep. But she would never know, and tomorrow night she would be buried alive for her sins.

8

The next morning, Christmas Eve, Fae came downstairs alert and refreshed after a surprisingly peaceful night. The lobby was cleaned and prepared for another day of business, though none would come, emphasized by an undisturbed stillness and an empty front desk. Fae had it in mind to wait for Elise; she was in no rush. She had returned to her room last night and found the Nativity back under the tree, set up exactly as it had been before. The only difference was that it had been joined by a stack of old newspapers and an empty box. If she wanted baby Jesus gone, she was supposed to wrap him up and stuff him away herself. She'd been angry last night, but after the good sleep she was ready to start the same conversation afresh, the box of wrapped Bible characters tucked underneath her arm. It was the principle of the thing now, nothing more.

The small fire in the lobby was burning strongly and the Christmas carols gently played on. A plate of fresh scones rested on an elegant side table between the large, overstuffed chairs that sat in front of the fire, offering themselves for the taking. Fae was happy to not let the offer go wasted.

Neatly tossing her coat, scarf, and gloves on the other chair, Fae put the box on the floor beside her and sat down, allowing herself to become lost in the flickers of the flames, their warmth and searing color a comfort. The beautiful thing about fire was that it was always the same no matter where, or when, you were. It was mystical, Fae thought, how something so wild and indiscriminately destructive, could be so comforting, lusted for, even, when tamed.

Fae was halfway through her scone when Elise appeared at the desk. She wore a black pantsuit, hair pulled back in a simple ponytail. The only thing she wore to indicate that Christmas was tomorrow were dangling silver snowflake earrings.

That woman definitely belonged in a Hilton or a Westin, Fae thought.

"Good morning," Elise greeted her politely, complete with a complimentary smile.

"Morning." Fae set down the remainder of her scone and picked up the box. She went to the counter and set it down on top.

"There has been a series of misunderstandings between us and, if you wouldn't mind, I'd like to talk to Mrs. Lemmens."

"I know Mrs. Lemmens would love to address your concerns; however, it is Christmas Eve and she is with her family."

"Isn't that convenient." Fae had expected something like that. "Are you the only other employee of this hotel?" Elise nodded affirmation. "Then with Mrs. Lemmens' absence, it would fall to you to act as Mrs. Lemmens, would it not?"

"Miss Peeters, this hotel is officially registered with the tourism industry for not only Belgium, but also this village. As stated on the official announcement clearly placed at all ports of entry, neither the federal nor provincial governments are responsible for visitors during non-visiting hours, which is the 24th of December. Today. Therefore, the responsibility of your stay falls under village jurisdiction which means that only Mrs. Lemmens is suitable for handling these issues. I'll make sure she attends to it first thing when she's back in the office. Is there anything else I could do for you, Miss Peeters?"

"You know what? There is nothing you can do for me. Just keep that box with your stupid Jesus away from me." Peaceful sleep or not, her mind was still way too close to the edge to just be an easy customer, and she was just as annoyed with Elise as she was with herself for how childish she was being.

"Please speak nicer of him. It's not just the porcelain you yell at."

"You care more about where the effigy of a half-mythical baby lays his head than where I do." Fae went back to the fireplace. "This isn't even worth a fight. If it has to stay in my room, throw it in the closet and forget to tell me."

She grabbed her coat and went outside, fumbling with the buttons. She hated stupid people. Like construction projects, they never ended and they were everywhere; in the return lines at Walmart, in the newspapers and, most certainly, behind pews and pulpits.

Today her grandmother's instructions were to wait outside the hotel where she was going to be picked up, today at 9:00 a.m. *I want you to meet my beloved, adopted sister and her husband, your great-aunt and uncle. She has never let me forget that she has yet to meet my granddaughter. Since you so enjoyed the stories of your grandfather, I think you will like their stories too.*

She settled herself on a wooden bench to wait. To her right was the station where the last train would leave at two this afternoon. The fact that she was still even thinking about that last train made her feel guilty. She'd connected with her grandmother just before she'd come downstairs. She'd apologized for the frosty welcomes but she still wouldn't give anything away about her present. Instead, she kept insisting that Fae attend the Christmas Eve concert tonight at the basilica. Fae could accept that. Today was a new day. It couldn't be as bad as yesterday. Besides, if she went back to Brussels now, she'd be giving these villagers what they wanted. She checked the time on her phone, 8:57. If her relatives were anything like what her grandmother said Belgians were like, they'd be too respectful to be late.

Despite what Elise probably thought, Fae loved the Christmas season just as much as any adult would admit. She loved seeing little kids get excited about flying reindeer and she loved the copious amounts of inexhaustible food, even the repetitious songs played and remixed so many times they edged on mild torture. She loved the rich colors and the Hallmark moments the gentle snow made in the streetlamps . . . though maybe not so much the wrapping paper people put over their broken and unhappy hearts. It was just that Christmas was kind of like biting into a chocolate chip cookie only to discover that it was full of raisins instead. She loved the cookie but took issue with the deceptive raisins, because Christians loved to use Christmas to lure people into their religion. They lulled them into a false sense of love and peace promised by a religion that actually brought little of either to the world. They got people to let down their guard by parading cuddly animals and a cute baby, then pounced on their checked-out brains and stimulated emotions.

At the very least, it'd be nice if Christians could acknowledge that Jesus wasn't even born on December 25th. It was a fact, not the premise for a religious outcry. Historical Christians had renamed the popular ancient Roman holiday of Saturnalia to suit their agenda, or was it that other holiday for, Sol-something . . . Sol Invictus, Fae thought fairly confidently, having heard something on campus about it recently. How Christians tried to convert the world to their cult of myth-believing, bigotry, and crusading was a stain on humanity. Of all their religious iconography, the Nativity reminded her the most of all the reasons why she tried to put as much distance between herself and Christians as possible: It advertised the start of something that was better having never begun.

Christians could keep the cross, for all she cared. It only looked worse for them worshipping a device of torture. They always showed Jesus dead on a cross as though they didn't even realize that they were telling people to worship a dead body rather than the living one they preached about. If they wanted to keep Jesus dead on a cross, then it was no less damning for their cause than having an iron maiden hang around their neck, or a slave ship as a symbol of racial equality emblazoned on the back of their car. She could accept that the historical figure of Jesus did likely exist but, being human, he was long dead.

Right on time, a small black Fiat from the 1990s rolled to a stop in front of her. A young man about her age was driving, but she couldn't get a good look at him because the windows were still dangerously frosted up. The passenger door swung open and an older woman got out with an expectant look. She wore a matching black and teal exercise outfit, and a black toque nearly covered up the stumpy ponytail resting at the nape of her neck. She looked prepped and ready to set out on some cross-country skiing.

"Fae Peeters?" Fae nodded as she stood up to greet the woman. "I'm your father's cousin, Veera Dupont." She spoke in English with only a minimal accent to give her away. "My son, Maël, is driving." Maël peered out at her through the open door and waved. Fae recognized him from the photos her grandmother had distributed en masse once she figured out email attachments. "Mere and Papa are waiting back at the house. Ready to go?" Veera climbed into the back seat, leaving the front for Fae and continued talking as Maël took off. "Maël will take you back to the house and I'll join you later in the day. The snow came late this year and we don't know how long it will last, so my ski group couldn't let a beautiful day like this go, Christmas Eve or not." She cocked a smile like a kid and it took ten years off her age. Patting Fae on the shoulder, she said, "We're all so excited that you came, Fae."

"You seriously have no idea how nice is it to hear that." Both Maël and her Aunt Veera smiled, making Fae believe that maybe they did know.

Stealing his eyes away from the empty street, Maël spoke, revealing his also nearly flawless English. "I recognize you from the photos Great-Aunt Maria sends. The last one she sent was of you in the mountains—*almost* as beautiful as our Alps. Where was the picture taken?"

Fae had to smile and, as it broke upon her face, so broke the morning's frustration with Elise. "Banff, in the Canadian Rockies. Grandmother was always talking about this one particular waterfall where she and Grandpa had come face to face with a grizzly bear when they were younger. After Grandpa died, she wanted to go back but couldn't make the long hike, so she made me promise to try to find it for her, and maybe the bear too." Fae laughed a bit and then said, "the problem was she didn't remember which trail led to the waterfall."

"And what of the bear?"

"I found a stuffed one in the gift shop."

Her cousin looked better in person than he did in his any of his pictures. His dark hair was gelled and his bright gray eyes were matched by a solid gray scarf that hung loosely from his black jacket; one similar to her own. There was a necklace hanging around his neck made up of a gold ring, a miniature key, and a shark tooth.

The three of them spoke easily as Maël drove. He and Veera told Fae about the village as they passed this or that noteworthy place. They drove out through the South gate and dropped off Veera to a group of people waiting for her along the side of the road, their skis pitched in the snowbanks. Driving back into the village, they came into an older neighborhood near the wall where thin houses had been built with a bit more room to breathe.

The house they stopped in front of was from the turn of the century and possessed about six feet of front yard to call its own. The sidewalk and driveway were neatly shoveled, and the house windows all had fake snow sprayed on them with the center wiped clean as though some eager boy had been trying to look in. Real candles were placed in all the windows but it was too early in the day for them to be lit, so they stood in quiet sentry waiting for their watch to begin. Carved into the front door and painted in gold was the word "forgiveness"; the calligraphy was beautiful but it seemed like an odd decorative choice. Fae asked Maël if chiseling words into front doors was popular here. He just shrugged and said, "sometimes." With his hand on the doorknob he looked at her and said, "My grandparents have talked of little else than your arrival since they were told you were coming, so excuse them if they maul you a little bit. I kept telling them not to overwhelm you but . . ."

Fae chuckled. "It's OK, Maël."

Maël opened the door without knocking, announcing their arrival with a shout and as Fae followed him in she was instantly enraptured in a tide of warmth and hominess only the house of grandparents could provide. It was like walking into a sunbeam from the shadows. The scent of gingerbread was so overwhelming she could practically taste it with every breath and automatically she became hungry. Real evergreen boughs and sprigs of holly were wrapped up the stair banister and shaped into a giant four-foot wreath hanging on the nearest wall. Ribbons and balls were tied onto every corner and on the entryway table there was a large bowl of oranges, each with a little bow glued to the top, and placed beside an Advent wreath burning brightly.

She looked around and saw little tin soldiers and nutcrackers, cross-stitched pictures of snowmen and crocheted dolls in winter outfits sitting on the stairs. There was an old toy train from the North Pole Express and more greenery placed upon anything that would hold it, children's homemade ornaments, and a hand-carved Nativity. There was so much to look at, Fae didn't have time to take it all in before she was richly welcomed by her great-aunt and uncle who came out from the sitting room on the left. She had heard them shouting and bubbling as soon as Maël opened the door and, though it had taken them a few seconds to emerge, she loved them instantly.

Great-Aunt Claire appeared first, balancing herself with graceful dignity by the edges of any object she passed. A respectable white silk blouse was tucked neatly into a Christmas-red knee-length skirt and she had stylishly draped a hand-crocheted Christmas scarf around her neck. Great-Uncle Emile came only a step behind her, his hands steadying his bride from behind as she walked, the stiffness wearing off with every step she took. He wore brown, pleated pants, the kind only the elderly seemed to be able to wear convincingly, a light blue, button-up shirt and a Rudolph the Red-Nosed Reindeer tie, which was blinking with embedded lights. They were practically yelling with delight that, "she's here, she's here!" the whole way, but it was their bright eyes and wide smiles that captured Fae, for they seemed to defy all the age that tried to weigh them down. They were beautiful, dignified people and any reservations Fae had about being here were thoroughly evaporated.

"Fae! Be-utiful granddaughtaire!" Aunt Claire exclaimed in English, pulling Fae down into a warm hug. Her accent was thick and awkward, and Fae knew that she was probably leaning on all the English vocabulary she possessed. She smelled of an old perfume, nice though, roses maybe.

"Welcome to our 'ome!" Uncle Emile exclaimed, trying as best he could to make the foreign words bounce off his tongue. He too pulled her into a deep hug and Fae was taken aback by how strong he was. "We are . . . in large t'anks t'at you come!" Uncle Emile pushed her out, took another look at her, then grabbed her back in for another hug and this time Aunt Claire added herself to the pile, kissing her face with grandmotherly lips.

That her great-aunt and uncle would greet her in English despite the difficulty of it was touching, and when she returned their smile she felt as though she had not truly smiled in years. Now she knew what it was like to fall in love with someone at first sight. "Thank you," Fae said dearly, "thank you so much." Then she continued in French, "If there is one thing my grandmother loves to talk about in her life here, it is you two. I am so honored to finally meet the legends."

Aunt Claire's eyes sparkled but Uncle Emile waved his hand dismissively. "Nonsense, your grandmother exaggerates us so." But his eyes sparkled too and Fae knew he was pleased to hear it. Fae took the moment to present an elegant box of chocolate truffles she had bought yesterday, which they graciously accepted before giving them to Maël to put in the kitchen.

Fae was ushered into the sitting room. There was a comfortable fire burning in the fireplace and a winterized painting of "Footprints in the Sand" hung above it. The furniture was about as old as their marriage but was still in surprisingly good condition, and a small, picturesque Christmas tree in the corner perfected the room. Two end tables were covered by a miniature village complete with working lampposts, and there were small magnets underneath the pond to make the little people skate in circles, and ski up and down a small mountain.

"A gift from your grandmother," Aunt Claire proudly declared, as Fae leaned in closer to look through the tiny windows of a house. A little boy and his dog peered back at her. "Every year for Christmas she sends me a new addition." She began pointing out, in reverse order, each addition by year, and she probably would have gone through the entire village set if Emile didn't interrupt and tell his wife to offer Fae a seat.

Whatever space wasn't taken up by the miniature village was filled with plates and bowls full of fruit and cookies, little waffles with powdered sugar, and neat slices of cake. "I am the baker of this house," Emile said patting, his well-fed belly, "and my bride is the chef. Together we always have a complete meal—meat, vegetables, and something sweet."

The three of them sat down and Maël soon joined them with warm drinks. Fae couldn't remember the last time she had such a great time with family.

THE GIFT

"Tell us about your life, Fae," Emile said, settling next to his wife, "Maria has kept us up to date, but stories are always better from the source." So, Fae obliged. She glossed over the part where her mother died in a car crash and the fallout from her father's epidemic absences. They knew enough of her life not to ask about either. Then Fae asked them the same questions in return. She learned, for a second time, about all the details of Maël's year in the military after university and then his acquisition of a government job in a nearby city. He looked bemused, hearing his life described in detail and he interrupted only to correct a detail or lessen an exaggeration. Such respect seemed like a long-lost art and it was enlightening to witness. Eventually, the focus shifted from catching up to telling stories.

At one point, Maël asked if Fae had really stolen all the neighborhood dogs and cats into her pet lost-and-found when she was younger. He grinned like a mischievous older brother bringing it up.

Fae groaned but, with a little bit of coaxing, she told them the story. The part that made all the difference, and had apparently never made it across the ocean was when, after building her pet lost & found in her front yard, her mother had suggested that it wouldn't be complete until there were some animals inside; she had been thinking of Fae's stuffed animals. "In my logical, six-year-old mind," Fae said in her own defense, "all the neighborhood dogs and cats were lost pets because they ate so much of the chicken I fed them. They were hungry!"

The shameful stories continued throughout the morning and Fae learned so much about the history of not only her family but also of the land. She even found out when the first gas station was opened.

Soon the lunch hour came and Fae accepted that she wasn't going to leave on the last train. To separate herself from these amazing people with an excuse would be a tragedy—not only to Claire and Emile, but also to her grandmother. A few unhospitable locals and a looming mystery weren't justification enough to break three elderly hearts. Besides, there was no guarantee that the voice in her head or the mirror-terror would return. So, she sat down to Claire's lunch of warm bean soup with fresh crusty bread. At first Claire was embarrassed about the simplicity of the meal but insisted

Maria said it was Fae's favorite, which it was. It was the best soup Fae had ever tasted and, after the first spoonful, she wouldn't let her aunt say another word about it.

Soon after lunch, Claire and Emile nodded off in the sitting room while she and Maël cleaned up the kitchen. He was a smart man, Fae decided, and the only thing she held against him was his religious belief, which was a pretty personal thing anyway.

"Many Christians say Jesus is the son of God," he told her as he put away a stack of bowls he had just finished drying, "but not everyone will tell you that Jesus is a fierce fighter and a passionate man."

"Really," she tried to sound interested. "So are you a Premier League, or Europa League kind of guy?"

"More of a basketball guy. And a good discussion kind of guy. I'm interested to know how they teach people about God in Canada. You don't really think about Canada and religion going together like you do in America or Italy."

She looked at him, trying to gauge his intention in bringing up the topic.

"So maybe you're not such a discussion kind of person." He shrugged and grabbed some cutlery. Fae decided to oblige him.

"Jesus is always shown as a delicate, weak sheep herder with doe eyes and perfect nails; that doesn't add up to being an impassioned fighter. If he was a fierce man, he might interest more people but, even then, his followers would ruin him. Christians are pretty much the worst people ever." She watched Maël's reaction and saw that he wasn't challenged or even offended. Maybe he really had just been trying to make conversation.

"Think about it this way," he said placing some silverware into the drawer, "he's supposed to be a king of kings, right?" Fae agreed. "Throughout history, how many standout rulers are remembered just because their herds were fed and their people felt appreciated?"

"Rulers are gauged by their successes in the economy, war, justice—that kind of stuff."

"Of course."

"Jesus doesn't have any of those points checked off except maybe in worldwide Bible sales, mass slaughters, and brainwashing."

"I think he scores higher than you think. What if you've been giving credit for his good efforts to other people this whole time?" Fae paused. It was a legitimate point. He continued, "Jesus, the king of kings, is called 'good' so how could he be known as good if all he does is watch sheep, moisturize, and sit back to watch a disastrous holy war?"

"My point exactly."

"So something has to change to correct the contradiction. I believe it's his resume that's wrong."

"If he's not a king at all that solves both sides of the question."

"What makes a king? People following him as a king, for one."

Fae didn't know how to respond to that, so she let his words hang. Coming from the mouth of a church person, the picture Maël painted of an assertive Jesus sounded sacrilegious, even heretical, and for that she found herself willing to continue the conversation. He was different from all the other church people she'd met. It helped that his life's purpose seemed to extend beyond trying to fix her and her family.

They finished the dishes, but Fae suspected they weren't done talking and she did feel obliged to explain herself to him better. "Do you want to know why I think that it's not Jesus' resume that's the problem?"

"Tell me." Maël casually leaned back against the fridge and Fae did the same on the counter across from him.

"Because he can't control his followers. Assuming, for argument's sake, that God is real, and that he is a good deity, then he has a lot to answer for from those who do anything but good on his behalf. You can't be a good ruler if you have no control and aren't respected. Legitimate humanitarians are rare—and I don't think most of them found their 'truth' or life's mission in Christianity. Christians are way more likely to be annoying, useless, and controlling than ambassadors of their king."

Maël looked curious. "What do you mean by that?"

"Well . . . um, OK. Personally, when I was eight I discovered that liquor could be a lot more fun than Jesus. The church I went to growing up had a little in-house café. No one who hung out there realized that you didn't have to be an adult to have adult problems or to moan about them. Standing around, nursing their coffee, and quoting their daily scripture apparently made them a fountain of sage wisdom for each other, but all I ever heard from those coffee cups were the same problems from the same people and the same conviction-less little phrases making it all better. Since they assumed my life was as complicated as having not collected all the Puppy In My Pockets, I was invisible to them. As were my problems, which were much more real than most of theirs. I always thought of myself as a creature breeding beneath their noses. If they'd known about me, they'd make me go to Sunday School rehab. They had one understanding of what Christian children should be like, and I gladly didn't fit it.

"And then the youth group and the 'core group' who were the center of every feel-good event the church put on . . . They played their 'edgy' songs, jumped around like accountants with pens stuck up their backsides, and loved clutching various body parts, vying with each other to win the Oscar for Best Overacted Scene of Surrender. There was this guy named Tyron the Blessed. He was a converted street rapper, really good actually. But he felt God told him to give up that up for a new career, spinning benign encouragement to teenagers. Last I saw, he's still working retail in the mall, talking about how he used to rap and almost got signed to a label. He could've done a lot more through that record deal than telling people how he blew his chance."

Fae could keep going, and was about to add how her father decided the church could take his place since he was gone so often, but Claire and Emile woke up from their impromptu nap, so she and Maël returned to them. The visit continued as though there had never been a break, but soon Uncle Emile took charge of the conversation.

"As you may know, Fae, Maria orchestrated your visit here not only to meet your family, but to have you receive something, a gift."

Fae's attention instantly peaked. "Everyone around here seems to know what it is except me. It's a little bit weird, if not a bit annoying. I know a present is supposed to be a secret, but an entire village of strangers isn't usually in on it. Grandmother said I just had to follow her instructions, but she didn't leave many clues for a treasure hunt."

"My dear," Aunt Claire smiled sympathetically, "all gifts worth having are worth some mystery. Your grandmother is right, follow her instructions." She smiled softly, then exchanged a knowing glance with Emile. "I'll give one hint: This gift isn't something that can be wrapped."

"Grandmama..." Maël had caution in his voice.

"No, no, I think that it's only fair she understands the general nature of her gift. Sometimes when you expect a puppy for Christmas and you get a stereo, it can take a little while to adjust your expectations. I just want to make sure Fae's not expecting the puppy. Trust me, Maël," Claire said.

"I'm sure Maria's told Fae everything she needs to know already."

"Thank you child, now hush," Claire gently rebuked him. It was at that moment Maël's cell phone buzzed. He checked the caller ID and excused himself upstairs.

Emile continued. "Your gift is an experience unlike anything we could describe. There's a right way for it, and a wrong way, but by going to the choir's concert tonight, you won't have to worry. Maria asked me to help set the stage for you. I haven't told my story in almost... twenty years, but Maria can be quite convincing when she puts her mind to it." Emile cracked a small smile. "Christmas means different things to different people nowadays, a break from work, presents, a restored faith in humanity, or a reminder of lost faiths. Christmas in our family has always been important for all those reasons, but also for more than that."

"Tell her the story, dear." Claire picked up Emile's hands and after she gave them a kiss, Emile began. "War has a way of making you grow up faster than you would like."

9

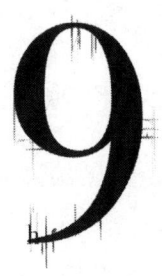

Great-Uncle Emile sat on the edge of the couch focusing his full attention on Fae and began his story with the voice of a reverent bard.

"I was the youngest boy in a family of six, two older brothers, three sisters. By the time I came, my parents didn't have the energy to keep up with all the trouble I made for them. As wonderful as my sisters and brothers were in helping raise me, my brain had a hard time catching up with my body and I always managed to make a mess of things."

Fae watched, entranced as Emile stopped speaking and stared off into the distance. A smile crept over his creased face as he chuckled softly, remembering some funny story. He soon came back to himself and, with a final chuckle, he continued on, solemn once again.

"The rumors that the Germans were stirring had been floating around the countryside for months. The men and older boys would show off newspapers with headlines announcing the political changes and the terrible things they were doing and saying to Jews and Russians and Gypsies. People were still weary with the idea of war after the First Great War, so the newspapers were disregarded as warmongering. My brothers and I didn't think that though, so we practiced fighting and shooting out in the fields."

"In reality," Claire interrupted, "his brothers practiced fighting him while the other girls and I watched."

Fae smiled, imagining the youngest brother getting beat up in front of all the girls. It was a scene as old as history.

"When the Germans invaded on May 10, 1940, I was ready to fight them—a mere boy of eleven! Even though our beautiful country quickly fell, many of us wouldn't surrender so easily. While my oldest brother joined the Belgian Resistance, the *résistance belge,* helping produce the underground Resistance newspaper, I decided I would kill stray Germans here at home. I'd steal my father's hunting gun and hide in the ditch not three miles from here, waiting for Germans to march by. We were too remote, though, so they never did. But on that day . . . my brother Stephane found me and started to drag me home by the ear. I'd never seen him so mad, but I was just as mad because he wouldn't let me kill Nazis. We ran into a small German foraging unit and tried to hide, but it was too late. They saw us and they saw my gun and thought us to be part of the *résistance belge.* We ran but they shot Stephane in the leg. And they executed him. I heard the shot behind me."

Emile's voice trailed off and his eyes grew glassy. He didn't speak for a while, the silence speaking for him. Claire gave his hands a squeeze, but they waited patiently for him to continue in his own time.

Once Emile's eyes cleared and his voice strengthened, he continued. "It was my fault my brother had died; everyone said so, maybe not with their words, but I could feel it. If I had stayed in the village like I had been told, he would have still been alive. Stephane was popular with everyone, and he had a scholarship to study chemistry. I was just a boy and the guilt tore me from the inside. I missed him so much, and I saw my mother cry whenever she walked past his coat hanging on the wall. After three months of suffering the truth that I should have died and not Stephane, I ran away. I didn't have a plan, but I knew some of the young men had decided to fight for the Germans. Even though I still wanted to kill them, I hated my life so much that I was willing to fall into company with them if only to further my own punishment.'

"They found me wandering eastward after only a day and a half. Henric Eichmann," Emile said remembering, "an ugly fart whose French was decent, said I reminded him of his nephew. His commander wanted nothing to do with me, but Eichmann insisted I stay. It was my job to go ahead of them into any village or barn and tell them what I saw. I was a foolish, stupid, naive child. I thought they simply didn't want to look silly for not knowing where the restaurants and beds were. In exchange for my help, they gave me bits of food and taught me some German since it would soon be the language of all Europe.

"One time, in the fall, we came to a barn and I was sent in. There were people inside, maybe twenty, most the age of my eldest brother, and they were all crowded around candles speaking Dutch. I barely understood Dutch but I made out that they were hunters preparing for a hunt in the morning. I reported to the Germans what I observed and told them we should go to the next farm a few miles down the road, but they didn't listen. They told me that all Belgian animals were Germany's now and these people didn't have permission to kill the Führer's game. Then they went inside and killed everyone. Eichmann told me afterward that those men and women weren't hunters. They were *résistance belge*."

For the second time, Emile's voice wavered. This time he let the tears slip out. They caught in the trenches of his face and they made the badge of his years shine. He looked like such a contradiction, bent over and weary with the weight of his story, with his bright, silly Rudolph tie speaking of a childlike happiness that was nowhere to be seen. From upstairs, the raised voice of Maël was muffled through the floor as he argued with someone on the phone.

". . . it was then that I realized what the Germans were using me for. They would thank my carcass if I ever tripped a mine and then leave me unburied. Eichmann might've missed me, maybe, like a stray dog . . . so, for a second time that year, I ran away. This time I fell in with a group of my countrymen making their way to France. My life there is another story, but I learned how to be as much of a terrorist as a member of the Resistance. Christmas was always the worst. Once the war was over, so was my place in the world. It was a long and dirty road for me, and I found more people to hate outside of just Germans. It was a divine intervention that happened one day, when my bride-to-be come across my path."

Here Claire grabbed up his hands again and Emile turned his head to smile at her. He talked more to her than to Fae.

"After weeks of stubborn convincing and trickery," Emile said the last word with the glint of a tease, "she brought me home. Most people had thought me dead; the war had been over for almost five years by then. I was a young man in body, but I was a much older soul. No one ever said anything about the role I played in my brother's death, though I knew they must've still hated me for it. Experience taught me that people might forget for a while, but they don't ever forgive. If I had thought the journey in finding myself after the war was difficult, it was worse navigating my road of redemption here—I made it so hard for myself. The second Christmas after I returned home, I was chosen to be the Choir Director for Christmas Eve."

The soft padding of feet coming down the stairs announced Maël's arrival, just in time to explain. He rested his shoulder on the entryway frame, comfortably crossing his arms. "Being chosen as Choir Director is a privilege and honor unlike anything else. Uncle Emile has been chosen twice."

"Congratulations." Fae said politely. Without knowing the significance of the position, she really couldn't add much enthusiasm. "You must really be good with music."

"Oh, it has nothing to do with talent, my dear," Claire said, breaking her gaze from Emile to look at her. "Being the Choir Director is for your benefit more than for the choir's; they're too good to need much direction." She chuckled at the idea as though it were quaint.

"Being Choir Director changed everything for me," Emile added. "I saw how to forgive and how to be forgiven. Forgiveness was my gift."

"Is that why you have it written on your door?" Fae asked.

"It is." Emile's eyes brightened. "Everyone who has been Choir Director has something to boast of. We let everyone know by emblazoning it on our door."

"But you were Choir Director twice."

"I learned forgiveness twice: once for myself and once for others."

"So is that the gift I'm to get, some sort of . . ." Fae chose her words carefully, "self-improvement?"

"It is hardly *self*-improvement," Claire gently said. "You have nothing to do with it."

"I'm sorry, but I still don't understand. Not to belittle what you just told me, Uncle, but what does the story have to do with me?" There was such a disconnect between what she was being told here and the darker reactions she had gotten in Café Noir yesterday when they spoke of the "Gift." Emile was talking of forgiveness and redemption, but that creepy old man Dreschler had shot doom at her with his eyeballs.

"There's no use trying to figure it out, my dear," Claire continued. "You're going to be given an experience and, though not the same as Emile's, you will walk away with something money can't buy. We've been teasing you with hints and it's confusing you. Maybe we should just stop before we give too much away."

"Your sister will never forgive you," Emile said, recapturing his cheerful demeanor. Fae knew her grandmother better than that. She forgave everyone. "Just know that for new life to happen, one thing must end so another can begin. The demons and destruction that had tried to rob me of my life had to go."

"Grandpapa." Maël came into the room and sat on the other side of Emile. "Maria knows best what clues Fae can hear."

"Hold on," Fae said, "What you're saying sounds like what I read on the wall at the train station."

"It's just graffiti," Maël said dismissively.

"So, then, can you tell me why there is a warning stating that the municipality isn't responsible for visitors during the 24th and why everyone wants me to leave for it?"

Maël shifted uncomfortably in his seat. "I really think we need to stop talking about this."

But Fae didn't agree. This was the moment she had been waiting for—an audience of nice people who had answers and who were talking. "But this is the fun of trying to guess the present under the tree. You hold the box up, shake it, try to trick answers out of your parents." Maël frowned but Claire and Emile remained engaged. "My father doesn't know about this, but did my mother? Why me and not them?"

"I don't know what your parents were told. Maria would have to tell you that," Claire said.

"What did my grandmother do when she was here that her name is still so recognized? What happens Christmas Eve, Uncle? Why did my grandfather have to be alone for so many years on Christmas Eve? Why is your basilica both Gothic and Renaissance? Just tell me something, anything. I can't shake this feeling that something about this place is wrong. All I've gotten since I've arrived is mystery, hallucinations, and rude people. Is something really going on? It's one thing to know you're getting a puppy or a stereo under the tree; it's another when it's dubbed the world's greatest secret. Look, Grandmother sent me a letter," Fae fumbled with her purse to pull the letter out. "As you said before, Aunt Claire, it's only fair that I understand; I know something unprecedented happens tonight, but should I be scared, or should I put my party dress on?"

There was silence in the room. Claire motioned for her to come over as though she were a child needing a hug. She wasn't interested in a hug but went anyway. She sat on the arm of the couch and Claire rubbed her knee.

Emile spoke first.

"You should be on guard. Be excited to hear the choir's concert, but not everyone wants the same thing for you. The world's greatest secret doesn't come easily."

Emile talked, but all Fae heard was the memory of that voice demanding she choose life or death, demanding it with a force that rattled her ability to comprehend the choice, demanding it as if she owed it to him. She could start to feel her heart pound louder at the memory of it . . .

Maël leaned forward so that he could make eye contact with her across the couch, his original surprise at her venting now replaced with concern. "Fae, what hallucinations? What are you seeing?"

When had she said anything about hallucinations? Had she slipped and mentioned it? She quickly regrouped and came up with an excuse, waving him off. "It's nothing but a little sleep deprivation. I've been working crazy hours these past few weeks."

From the look on his face, Maël didn't believe her.

"Just be careful. Hallucinations can be a pretty serious symptom."

"Maria's letter, may I read it?" Claire asked.

Fae eagerly passed it to her, the pertinent page already on top. There was a patient silence as Claire read, and, when she was done, she set the pages down in her lap. Emile picked them up for himself. Claire spoke as he read.

"I can't say I know the woman Maria is sending to fetch you to the Notre-Dame du Seigneur very well, but Maria is taking good care of you even from a distance." Claire patted her on the knee again. She was clearly finished giving clues.

Emile finished with the letter and handed it back to Fae. "She told you more than I would have," he said. "Your grandmother was always a bit more brash than most of us when it came to such things."

"So tell us of your adventures yesterday Fae," Maël said, obviously trying to steer the conversation in a new direction. "What did you see of our little village?"

"Nearly everything," she said, dutifully accepting the change of subject. "Gate to gate, wall to wall practically. By my field of study, you can imagine that I enjoy a different perspective of the sights than most people."

"Did you go inside the Notre-Dame du Seigneur?" Emile asked, his eyes as bright with expectation as the eyes of Rudolph on his tie.

"I didn't. But it's always open, or so I hear," Fae replied dryly. "But can you tell me about an elderly German man I saw in Café Noir yesterday? Dreschler, I think his name was? He had a well-trimmed white beard and creeped the hell out of me."

"Oh, he did, did he?" Emile asked with a bemused expression. "Lars Drechsler can do many things but I don't think he can do that yet. I suspect there's plenty of hell left in you still."

Claire gave her husband a quick jab, but Fae dismissed it with a smile.

"Don't worry about it. I don't mind raising a little hell wherever I go."

"I don't think you would be so proud of that if you looked back on the places and people you've left behind." Maël said. He was trying to keep the comment light but it didn't work.

"If people don't like me that's their problem, not mine."

"What do you want to know about Lars Drechsler?" Maël asked.

Why was he being so serious, Fae wondered. "I'm pretty open to anything anyone wants to tell me. Information seems to be something of a commodity around here."

"He's just a man who makes it his business to know everyone and everything. He's retired and has nothing else to do." By the sure way Maël ended his sentence, Fae could tell that that he expected her to be satisfied and move on. Emile, however, was more talkative as he nodded his head in agreement.

"He came to us to start a new life, and we were all ready to begin again. He took Maria's place after she left and was tasked with making sure that the Gift isn't misunderstood. Lars has decided that the Gift cannot be understood, however, and now refuses anyone access to it. But that doesn't make for much of a gift, does it? If you met him yesterday and he was rude, it's just a miscommunication between him and your grandmother. Don't mind him."

"OK, now you're starting to make me a little nervous with how you're describing this 'Gift.'" Fae teased the words like she was facing a surprise birthday party planned by an overzealous coworker, but she was actually anxious. The gift was an experience; that was fine with her. But, it could be misunderstood, and there was a right and wrong way go through it? She was probably overthinking all this. She'd love it, and tomorrow they'd all be laughing about the suspense and mystery which had fooled her.

"You'll be fine," Claire reassured her.

Not long after, Maël's mother returned from her ski trip. From that point on, all talk of Lars Drechsler, gifts, and mysteries was set aside. Maël's father and his older sister and her family found their way to the house, and no one seemed to mind the tightening quarters. In fact, the more crowded it got, the happier Claire and Emile became. Aunt Veera and her daughter showed off their talents by fearlessly wearing the Advent crowns with lit candles on their heads, and Fae took up the challenge too. She wasn't nearly as confident. Then they tried to trick each other with Belgian and Quebecois slang until the call for supper ruled Fae to be the loser; she took the loss well.

A large meal of roast, vegetables, fried potatoes, savory breads and sweet breads, and, of course, the chocolate log cake waited for them, and enough wine for twice as many people. Maël's sister played a guitar and sang some songs she had written before taking requests for Christmas carols. Fae sat back in the comfy couch listening to the whole affair with a contentment she hadn't felt since her grandmother used to play the piano for her as a little girl. Apprehension aside, Fae would've loved it if this very moment was the "Gift" experience.

Maël's phone had received a few texts which had quieted him over the length of the evening. That wasn't strange in and of itself, but it seemed whoever he was talking to was bothering him and all Fae could think of was an ex-girlfriend. It would be low to harass someone on Christmas Eve. Eventually his phone buzzed again with a call, and she watched him reject it, turn the phone off, and stuff it into his jeans' pocket.

Shortly thereafter, the grandfather clock struck nine, its droll chimes signaling everyone it was time to leave. Maël offered to drive Fae back to the hotel and she left with hugs and cheek kisses in plenty. As she was leaving, she noticed with interest that Aunt Veera was helping her parents put a Communion setting just outside the front door, in the same manner parents would set milk and cookies out for St. Nick. She looked to Maël and raised her eyebrow in question.

"It's an old regional tradition," he said. And that was it.

10

The air outside was a rude awakening after the warmth of the fire indoors and the wine running in Fae's veins. Candles in dark windows and Christmas lights of every color and combination shone out from each house, and while it wasn't overtly cold, she could feel snow in the air. Apparently, Maël could too.

"It's going to snow tonight." His voice sounded flat in the stillness of the night. The electric hum from the large lightbulbs hanging off the fence was the only other noise. "That's a good sign, it's symbolic."

"Of what?"

"Tomorrow is Christmas, the celebration of the beginning of the end for death. Tonight kick-starts that by reminding us what it means to be white as, well, snow." Maël unlocked the black Fiat, climbed inside, reached over, and unlocked her door. She climbed in.

"I don't think I could tell you what it feels like to be snow white."

"As a kid . . . ?"

"The only snow white experience I know is from Disney. Other people have it a lot worse growing up, I know, but I had a full-time job as soon as I could walk, making sure my bipolar mother didn't do anything regrettable."

She gave a laugh. "It wasn't her fault, but I took advantage of my loose parenting and gladly racked up enough sins to tell the church to stop bugging me. If it wasn't for my grandparents, those years would've left me with more than just architect school."

"I can see why Maria wanted you to come here," he said, and once again he didn't seem troubled by her confession.

They didn't say much more the rest of the way, but the silence was comfortable and she rather liked the contrast from the busy and talkative day. He took her on an extended sightseeing tour on their way back to the hotel, passing by small monuments and through cramped streets, each as unique as the other. Once they arrived at the front of the hotel, he put the car into park and turned in his seat to look at her, one arm draped over the steering wheel, the light from the streetlamp making his face look worryingly grim.

"This is where our day together ends. I've enjoyed getting to know you."

Fae cracked a half smile and jested with him. "I'm not boarding the Titanic, Maël, lighten up. How about, 'See ya later, 'gator'?"

The awkward pause was enough to tell her that the 'gator phrase hadn't crossed the ocean in translation yet. "This is the beginning of your end, Fae. No matter what happens tonight, you will not be the same Fae Peeters tomorrow morning. I shouldn't be telling you anything, but Aunt Claire had a point, you do need to understand tonight a bit better. Everyone else who's received the Gift had an idea of what was going on. Everyone is scared that you won't be able to handle it, so let me help you prove them wrong." He shifted himself forward and started speaking English. "Everything you will see, everything you will hear, is real. This is one of the few times you have to trust your eyes and not your head. Your head will lie to you. Your logic will fail you. Great secrets and great gifts don't come cheaply, but since your grandmother believed you were ready, so do the rest of your family." Maël turned back around in his seat. "Your cell phone won't work until morning and the gates are already locked. You're stuck here until morning. Someone will call before they pick you up tomorrow for dinner."

"Maël, what are you telling me?"

"You used to go to church."

"Ya," she said defensively, "and then they wanted me to believe that their stories were true."

"When the truth gets buried under so much denial, it can be painful to revisit." He looked at her with an expectancy she didn't understand, and that comment had crossed the line. "To get your gift, you're going to have to believe the impossible."

"I believe in reality, OK? Don't get all weird on me, not now. I've liked you up until this point."

He pursed his lips. "Realities change once you learn the difference between what is true and what you want to be true. Look, I have somewhere I have to be. The journey to your gift starts now; don't get into any car that isn't driven by the person named in Maria's letter."

She got out of the car and he rolled down the window as she closed the door. "Your hallucinations weren't hallucinations, by the way. I know what you saw. You saw death, and your voice has a name, and the name has a body. Stay away from him, he's your worst nightmare come alive. And in case you didn't realize, green isn't a Christmas color tonight. Oh, and one more thing—this is your first Christmas Eve where you're expected to die."

"I'm sorry, WHAT?"

"Goodnight Fae. Joyeux Noël!"

"You can't just say that and then drive away!"

He slipped the car into drive and began to pull away.

"HEEEY! What do you mean?" The car continued to drive on. "MAËL!" Shouting, she ran down the street after him. "MAËL!"

He drove halfway down the street before the red brake lights came on, and Fae could see her faced bathed in red, reflecting in his back window. He didn't back up, but Fae was at his driver's window before he had time to change his mind.

Grudgingly, Maël rolled down his window again.

"What do you mean, I'm expected to die?!" she demanded.

"You wanted to know about Lars Drechsler."

"Don't change the subject, answer my question!"

"Lars Drechsler is a normal man who takes his job very seriously. He scared me as a child, too. If you were to ask me what I think of him today, I would tell you that he's necessary and that he's probably right." Maël paused, thinking. "If you really want to find out what the Gift is, get yourself to Misseur Drechsler's house. His place isn't far from here; it's on 317 Rue de Johanne, door D. He has a room on the bottom floor and there you'll learn what you want to know—if you can convince him to let you in. Just get back here by 10:30. I promise you that you've been watched since you arrived yesterday. And if you don't make it back by then to catch your ride to the Notre-Dame du Seigneur . . . well, just don't miss your ride. You *must* get to the basilica tonight, do you understand? I'd take you myself but . . . I really have to go. Good luck and God bless."

"No, I don't understand! MAËL!" But it was no use. He sped off down the glassy road with his window rolled up, effectively locking her out—even though she had apparently been locked in. She watched as Maël drove away down the damp, dark street, leaving her alone to the quiet unknown.

Fae's breaths made small puffs of air in front of her. Alone and abandoned, left to fend for herself. She felt like that was the story of her life.

There's a correlation between religion and abandonment. Now, Maël abandons you in the same way.

The soothing male voice from yesterday spoke and Fae startled, half expecting a man to be standing behind her. But there was no one there. There was nothing behind her except the well-lit hotel entrance.

So, she had two options: Go pay Lars Drechsler a visit, or wait an hour until her ride came. She pictured the face of Lars Drechsler, his sun-bleached eyes, and his pointy prophet finger, and Fae decided it wasn't worth it. He was probably the one Maël had meant when he said people expected her to die. Her desire to find out about this Gift withered at the thought of having to find it in his apartment. The Gift, or experience, or festivities, or whatever it was, probably started at 10:30 anyway. She could wait a little longer.

From habit, Fae took her phone out to call her grandmother, but there was no signal. She had to talk to someone. Even Elise would feel like a small comfort right now.

But Elise wasn't at the desk, some other young teenager was. Armed with her smart phone and headphones plugged in, she was slouched back in the armless chair and oblivious to Fae's fast-growing concern for her life. Her packed-up Nativity was still on the counter, though now with a Post-it stuck to the side:

Here for when you want it—Mrs. Lemmens.

Fae ignored it. There was no room for that argument right now. The girl finally took notice of her. She wore heavy, black eyeliner and a tight T-shirt, showing off both her appreciation for The Beatles and her ability to gain male attention.

"Where's Elise?"

"With her family," the girl looked her up and down. "Sorry." She returned to her phone.

Fae didn't have time for self-absorbed teenagers. Heading back up the stairs, she wondered what she was going to do about surviving this increasingly creepy village. Go the basilica, but from the way Maël was speaking, there had to be more to it than that. Could she think of a good hiding place? She sighed, discouraged. After everything she had learned over the last few hours, receiving her present had begun to feel secondary to making it through the night.

The stairs creaked under her weight as she passed from the second floor landing to begin her ascent to the third but, as she stepped up, a secondary *creak* sounded behind. She stopped and listened. Nothing. Fae took another creaky step and again an echo sounded just behind her. She looked back and still saw nothing.

But there was something. She could feel it as strongly as if a crowd of people were behind her.

She bolted up the rest of the way, the echoing *creaks* matching her pace. Her fumbling fingers managed to find the skeleton key in her bag, and she jammed it into the lock as fast as she could. She was just about to slam it open and hide inside but, before she could, she felt *him*. She knew it was him with an acute awareness, and the fright she had on the stairs melted away into a misunderstanding. He was right behind her, but she wasn't scared. Instead, she felt a strange sense of calm, the intimacy of him on her back should have made him her lover. He was her Voice, her only friend in this whole adventure. He had come, and he would guide her through the night; he would protect her.

How she knew this so confidently, she didn't know.

Fae turned her shoulder wanting to see him, but there was nothing to be seen, nothing to be touched.

You think you'll be safe in there? The Voice laughed, chiding her. *Your cousin told you that you're expected to die, to paralyze you with fear. Commit yourself to me and I won't let them kill you.*

"Maël said you have a name."

Yes, but I'm not the one he told you of. Call me Noah.

"Let me see you," Fae said quietly.

You know me already.

"How? When have I met you?" Fae wanted to know this man, his voice was calming, reassuring, sure. With him she knew she was stronger. "You're not just a voice from my mind, you're so much more. I can feel you, hear you. Let me see you," she asked again.

You're not ready.

"Then you don't know me very well." Noah laughed but it wasn't pleasant. "Help me live, so I can get my gift and be done with all this. I'm ready for it."

That's what they told you, isn't it? They will tell you anything. You must only listen to me.

The man pressed even closer like a wrap around her body, and she could feel his invisible breath on her neck. She exhaled with a sigh. The same lung-crushing heaviness as before started to fall around her, though it lacked the panic it had brought before. Her heart began beating harder, straining under the invisible weight. Everything in her wanted to balk at encouraging this Voice, this Noah. They were internal warnings, but he was touching something in her that needed him to cause it to come to life. She needed him, so she ignored the warning to turn him away.

"Let me know something about the one who will save me."

There was no immediate response, as though the man was considering her request. Then with the swiftness of a light switch being turned off, he was gone, leaving her neck and back cold to the air.

Look down, he commanded her from the other side of the door. Fae did as she was told and saw familiar iridescent green smoke curling up from beneath it. *I'm in here.*

The green smoke invoked a flash of images of corpses in mirrors and skeletons with tongues in their ears. The longing Fae felt to follow Noah now battled against her feet acting on their own, backing away from the fog growing up around her legs. He had the answers she wanted; why else would he be associated with the terrors she'd experienced since arriving? He waited in the green fog to protect her from the death the fog brought. He wanted to help her, was the only one who cared enough to not leave her alone.

Then a thought squirmed out and struck her in the face like a divine revelation. Maël hadn't said that the villagers would kill her, just that they expected her to die. The thought meant something, she knew it did, she just couldn't split her concentration to think it through. There was something unknown on the other side of the door and, if she opened it, there was no way to reverse her choice, no way to un-see.

What's taking you so long? You wanted me to show myself. I'm waiting. Don't make me wait.

He was stern, and Fae didn't know what to do; her body wasn't responding to her desires. One part of her wanted to join him, but the other part told her that there were barbs to that wish.

The bashful bride. I never expected that of you, Fae. He was disappointed with her, and she wanted to rush into the room and apologize. But that green mist . . . *Let me help.* Fae watched as the skeleton key she had left in the door started to twitch and jiggle on its own, as though someone had grabbed it. The key lightly rattled and began moving, turning, turning, turning, *click.*

She held her breath.

11

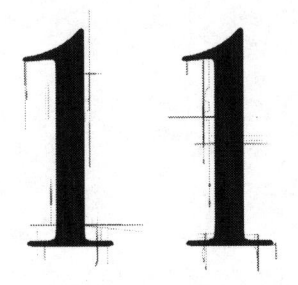

"What's Lars Drechsler's role in all this?" Fae blurted.

The key stopped moving and the door remained shut. More silence.

You care more about that man than me.

"No! No, I want you. I . . . I need you. I don't know why I said that. I don't even care about him."

The caught adulterer says the same thing.

"I don't . . . no, that old man freaks me out. I didn't . . . I just want to kno—"

Shut up. He had lost his patience. *Go to your mystery man and look in his little room like your idiot cousin suggested, baiting you so easily. Your cousin's the enemy, is he not? Look at how easily he got you to trust him. And why do you still want anything to do with your grandmother? She's your father's mother. She taught him everything she knows about trickery and deception.*

"My grandmother isn't like him."

I said to shut up. Now he was getting annoyed. *How many good people have had their lives ruined by people who say* a *Savior has come into a dark world? Include yourself. I've taught you to be better. They say they believe in a single, almighty God, yet they have so many gods the only one they truly know is themselves. Bigots and propagators of hatred and divisiveness, sound familiar? And still you would believe two of them before you would trust me. You are more naive than I thought. Go to your Misseur Drecshler and find out all you want to know.*

"No, no, I'm sorry, let me in to see you and I'll never doubt you. I can't go to that old man's apartment!"

You will if only to learn your lesson. Go to the man whose name you call out in the dark, and see what sort of "gift" they want to give you.

"But—"

GO!

His voice exploded from behind the door, rattling the key right out of the lock. It fell to the floor, lost in the swirling green mist. Fae didn't know what to do. The idea of barging in on that rickety old man terrified her almost as much as earning Noah's displeasure—she needed him. His manifest presence was still brooding on the other side of the door, and she knew he was watching her. She had no choice.

Slowly, dejectedly, Fae reached to the threadbare carpet for the key. As her hand touched the fog, it retreated back under the door like an angry lover refusing the touch of their partner. Fae sighed. She really had messed up.

At the bottom of the stairs, the teenage girl looked up at her again, this time alarmed enough to set her phone down.

"You can't go out."

One look at the girl, and Fae knew she had no real interest in backing up her command.

"I need a smoke." Fae kept walking.

The girl sniffed the air as she walked by. "Does something smell weird to you?"

Fae ignored her and grabbed a trifold map of the village. She quickly found Rue de Johanne. Maël was right when he said it was close by. It would probably take only ten minutes to get there.

Stuffing the map into her jacket pocket, Fae set off, the heels of her boots setting the pace in the nearly abandoned streets. Two cars passed her by—the only other human life she found. Lights were on in homes, and the Christmas lights and streetlamps with their dangling angels made for a warm scene, but

Fae wasn't warm. She could sense Noah watching her, and the thought of meeting her death in some fashion tonight was slowly destroying what was left of her calm. Her strongest and deepest growing conviction was that she would do anything and everything necessary to get her gift and come out on the other side alive.

As she walked toward Dreschler's address, Noah's suggestion that her grandmother had betrayed her trust was angering, because she should've seen it coming. All the signs were there. Fae didn't want them to be true, having believed that her grandmother understood her better. She'd been prepared to be disappointed with her present, but this anger and betrayal she was feeling toward her grandmother seemed completely justified, and she let Noah's contempt become hers. Noah had nothing to gain by lying to her about her grandmother's intentions, but her grandmother had everything to gain if she somehow got Fae to convert.

What if this village took spiritual death literally? Were they going to tell her to convert and find spiritual life, or we'll kill you to stop the rot in your soul? The condition in which she survived this night would reveal exactly the kind of person her grandmother really was. Deep down, Fae dearly hoped she was the person she had always known her to be. Then again, survival was never based off hopes.

Building 317 was lodged between an office and an unmarked door—all three of which, Fae noticed with no surprise, had Communion at their doorways. She tried pulling open the solid wood door and found it locked.

"Now what do you want me to do?" Fae asked aloud in defeat. Of course, strangers couldn't just walk into a respectable apartment without a key, and there was no call pad. "I can't get in." She tried the door one more time, rattling it in demonstration.

"Need in?"

A handsome man with white hair, but a young face, walked up next to her. He spoke with a mild English accent and had a puffy white jacket from which he pulled his keys.

"Please, thanks."

The man opened the door and pushed it wide, so that she could catch it.

Fae grabbed it and looked around outside, expecting to see something of Noah. She saw nothing. Quietly saying a quick thanks to her invisible friend, Fae caught the second door held open for her.

The man smiled at her politely as she followed him inside. The floors were polished stone, and old-styled evergreen swags decked the halls. "If I may, on this holiday night, give you a gift of words?" the man asked. Fae shrugged and looked at her phone. She didn't have time to talk but he had let her in, so she listened. "Know which side of the table you're on."

Fae looked at him quizzically. "OK . . . Look, I'm late for a party. Thanks for letting me in." And, with that, she hurried off down the hall. Curiosity had her look back over her shoulder, but the man with the puffy white jacket was gone. There was nowhere for him to go so quickly except back outside, but there was no closing door to indicate that he had. He'd disappeared.

She found apartment D around a corner at the end. As she came closer, she slowed her pace as reluctance to knock on Dreschler's door started to play against the fear and rejection that had driven her here in the first place. What was she going to say when he opened the door? Hi, I hear you have a room full of secrets?

Engraved into the black paint of his door were the words: *Peace on Earth. Goodwill to all men.*

So, Lars Drechsler had been a Choir Director, too. Maybe that meant there was a decent person buried beneath all his creep?

Fae took a deep breath, lightly knocked on the door and waited. 1 . . . 2 . . . 3 . . . no one was home. But before she could even think about returning the way she had come, she felt the telltale heaviness fall on her; it was like trying to breathe underwater. He was still watching. She couldn't be a disappointment again; he might change his mind about staying with her. She tried knocking again, a little harder this time.

"Come in," a distant German-accented voice came from the other side. Fae tried the door and found it open, which made her even more cautious. There had been no sliding of locks or dead bolts opening. Fae gently, if not sheepishly, let herself in. No one was on the other side.

To the left was a set of stairs, installed with a platform stair lift, and to the right was a living room and balcony full of plants dead for the winter. A respectable Christmas tree covered with children's homemade decorations stood proudly in the corner, and a sizable Nativity set rested beneath it, but there were no presents. His walls were plain white and decorated with paintings seemingly all by the same artist. One large painting caught her attention: two people huddled in pain in a dark, unfriendly place; a regal and deadly serious Jesus was with them, not cowering with them, but using his body to shield them from whatever danger they faced. It was a powerful painting, one that reminded her of Maël's conversation. Photos also graced the walls—pictures of pets, children, grandchildren, and a black-and-white war photo of five young men posing around a Panzer III tank like the one at the memorial. This humanized the freaky prophet, but it also exposed him more than Fae felt privy to, and it made her feel even more uncomfortable; she would be such a terrible spy.

"Hello?"

"This way." The German voice sounded like it came from down the hall so she followed it.

"Misseur Drechsler?" she asked, walking past the kitchen.

Her journey ended at a bathroom, a closet, and a third closed door. *He who takes away the sins of the world* was carved into this third door, and she only had to crack it open to see that it was dark inside, with no sign of Lars Drechsler.

This is the door you want. Look inside. Noah, her Voice, was back, as reassuring as ever. She went in and closed the door behind her, searching the wall with her fingers until she found the light switch.

What she saw inside wasn't all that revelatory at first. A desk had some papers and books piled neatly with an old CRT monitor from the nineties commanding most of it, its screen blank. There was a filing cabinet to one side, and the back wall was covered ceiling to floor by curtains. Curious, she eased them apart and found a giant mirror encased in a thick gold frame covered in florets that suggested an era a few centuries old. Fae dropped the curtains like they were on fire and backed away before any apparition could form. She knew in her deepest core that it was waiting for her and she wasn't going to offer it an opportunity to show itself.

The computer was password protected, so she leafed through the papers and books on the desk. They were mostly in German, though there were three French books concerning religious things and a translation of C.S. Lewis' "Mere Christianity." Finding nothing, she began pulling the desk drawers open two at a time. She found nothing unusual until she wrestled open the bottom, largest drawer. Inside were cell phones and cameras, rolls of film, and old camcorders representing decades of technology. Fae picked up one of the first generations of digital cameras and tried the power button. Nothing. She tossed it back and it landed with a loud plastic rattle.

"Oh crap!" Fae froze. That was louder than she had expected. She shouldn't be here. She was trespassing. Noah was watching, though, and she couldn't leave without finding something.

Clearing her hair from her face, Fae picked up another camera, then two camcorders, and two phones. They were all dead. An iPhone proved no more helpful. The last camera she tried turning on opened to its saved photos, the low battery light blinking right away. The first thing she saw was a wave of dull green light in the middle of a dark picture, like someone had been playing with glow sticks with the camera set for long exposure. She quickly scanned through the other pictures, not sure how long the battery would last. They were all of blurred green light against a dark background. Finally, a picture came up that gave her more detail. It was the same green light coming from the middle of an otherwise dark human outline, but the picture was shadowy and impossible to pick out details. What couldn't be missed was a glow highlighting deathly white eyes, exposed teeth, and a familiar turn-of-the-century streetlamp.

The battery sign flashed again. She began to zoom into the picture, but the demand was too much for the drained batteries and the camera shut off with a soft *whir*.

"No!" Fae growled at the device, "you're not dead yet." She pressed the power button and the LCD screen lit up only to automatically shut off again. Fae repeated the procedure but, after the fourth try, the camera refused to acknowledge her at all.

She wanted to throw the useless piece of junk back into the drawer, but the sound it would make stayed her hand. Maybe there were extra batteries around somewhere? Whatever that blurred green light was, the other devices had to hold more of the same. Dreschler was hiding something and whatever it was, Noah wanted her to see it.

Or, maybe Dreschler was protecting it, her rational thoughts suggested.

Knowing she was on borrowed time pushed Fae to tackle the metal filing cabinet. As quietly as she could, she drew open the first drawer, rapidly fingering through the sparse files. There were a few useless pictures of the same thing the camera had shown. Words like "dead," "manifestation," and "unexplained" popped out from the written materials and the more she looked, the more frightened she became. What had her grandmother dropped her into?

A manila envelope sat on top of the cabinet. Written on the outside in faded cursive, different from the handwriting on the desk, was, "First Known Record." She slid out two laminated pieces of paper. The first was a handwritten letter dated December, 1668, and the second, a hand-drawn sketch. Fae scanned the letter as quickly as possible.

It was from an Englishman named James Henry Priscott, an African explorer who was returning home after a number of years abroad. He had come to stay at a little Belgian village for Christmas, since his own bad traveling luck refused him the company of family in northern France. Fae skipped ahead to the pencil sketch on the second page. It was a scene set in front of the unmistakable Basilique de Notre-Dame du Seigneur. A beam of light was shining out from its front doors, illuminating a horde of people walking toward it. They were all skin and bones but, the closer she looked, the more she realized that there was more to them than that. An indiscernible mass occupied their body cavities. A blob was the word Fae would use but she wasn't even sure Priscott knew, because he left the drawing vague and the perspective was too distant to be clear. She went back to the letter.

Horrible sights, which not even Milton in his "Paradise Lost" could have imagined. The rumors of such evil things in the Balkans where creatures are said to dwell with the devil are given credence of their truth in this place. My dear Harry, the Africans believe in a magic which makes corpses come to life, a terribly dreadful matter, one which, though appalling, by their acceptance of such morbidity, could possibly be true in some fashion. I can barely write what I must, for Hell itself has found its portal into our mortal world, creating an abomination even the Holy Father shudders at and, as such, has abandoned in this place. The dead not only . . . here the writing had become indiscernibly smudged . . . *as the tentacles of a sea monster. When I found myself too close, it tried to reach me like a stretched-out water drop. Divine grace saved me. The locals had assured me a Christmas service the likes of which would make me cry from the beauty, and instead they have sacrificed me to demons. I write this in the terror of hiding, for the gates are locked and there is no way out. This is a village of the dead, and the dead shall not tolerate the reminder of life.*

At that point the letter was cut off, torn and weathered. A note written on yellow legal paper was attached to the back. *This letter was never sent. Priscott's diary revealed his fear of the church finding out and branding him a heretic, cursed by the Africans. He returned to England and his work became foundational for the First Great Awakening of the 1730s. His life was dedicated to preaching the non-abstraction of sin; he accredited his revelations to an unnamed event from his travels.*

It was signed "Maria Peeters" and ended with a line from the children's song, "This Little Light of Mine."

Stunned, Fae stared at her grandmother's signature—not believing what she was seeing. Noah was right. Her grandmother really had betrayed her. She tricked her into coming here so that she could be killed or converted. There was no rationale for it, but all the evidence was there to prove it. And Maël, too. He'd told her to come to this room, meaning he knew what truth was in here, what was awaiting her tonight, and yet he offered no way to help her live and gave no more than what she had asked for in a cruel foreshadowing. He was just as much to blame as her grandmother. If Fae lived long enough, she would never forgive them for this.

The soft electric hum of the stair lift turning on made her heart skip a beat. She was going to get trapped. Or worse, discovered.

Muffled voices reached her and, as she listened, she quickly became convinced that Dreschler was talking to none other than Elise herself.

"I'll stand like a man, not sit like a pansy," Lars said in response to some comment. The sound of his grouchy voice brought back memories of the café. Fae was glad to hear that he wasn't rude to only her. "Maybe I should hire you for my caregiver so you can get paid to worry about me."

"Should I ask if you still want to take yourself to the Notre-Dame du Seigneur?" Elise asked him.

"No. I told you, Alex put new tires on the scooter, the kind those Swedes use for winter racing."

"I want this to succeed as much as you."

"Then you don't want it bad enough," Lars snapped. "It *must* succeed. Maria Peeters knew better than to send anyone here, I don't care who she is."

"Maria didn't call you." There was some sort of grunt for a response. "Have you called her?"

"We don't call each other. By mutual agreement. I almost did last night."

"But she still has a lot of friends," Elise inferred from the comment, "and she can still pull strings you wouldn't be able to stop." Lars gave another grunt. "Miss Peeters will be back at the hotel by now. She should be arriving at the Notre-Dame du Seigneur about the same time we do."

"This should have been done an hour ago."

"Well we couldn't kidnap her from her relatives, could we?"

The stair lift stopped at the bottom of the stairs.

"Why didn't you get Maël involved?"

"He was involved, but I believe Maria got to him. He backed out of being the driver. Getting a replacement took a bit of work, but Paulina finally agreed."

"And what of the chauffeur Maria arranged?"

"Paulina knows how to make her go away."

"There can't be any more delays," Lars commanded her. "The priest Cuvelier wants plausible deniability, but he won't stay put so we have to be even more careful in the basilica. Could slow events down." There was a pause in the conversation. It sounded like they were putting on their boots and coats. "Did you turn off the light in my study?"

Elise zipped something up. "I thought I had."

THE GIFT

"Electricity is expensive," his raspy voice grumbled. Lars' shuffling feet came Fae's way Her insides seized at the thought of being caught snooping around his room of secrets. She could only imagine what type of awful basement imprisonment awaited her as punishment.

"Probably just forgot to turn it off when we left earlier. Sorry." Elise apologized . . . the shadow of two feet showed through the gap between the door and the floor. Fae was still standing without excuse in front of the filing cabinet.

Her eyes raced to find a hiding place and found one underneath the desk, unoriginal but there weren't many options. Scuttling into the compact space as silently as possible, she saw that she'd left the filing cabinet open. She cursed in her mind, then held her breath.

The door opened. One footstep, two footsteps, a pause, then the room went dark. Two steps out and the door closed.

Fae held her breath until she was sure he wasn't coming back, then allowed herself a long exhale, releasing all the muscles she didn't realize she'd been clenching. Carefully crawling out from under the desk, Fae felt her way in the darkness to the cabinet to close its drawer, then continued on to the door, putting her ear to it to hear if they were still in the apartment.

She still heard their voices as the front door was opened, and then the door closed with a dull *shlunk*. The locks turned, then silence. She was locked inside the old man's home.

Slipping out from the room, Fae silently retraced her path back through the apartment. She just wanted to get out of here and back to the hotel. The time said 10:15 so she had no time to waste.

Finding the front door's lock system in the dark, Fae slipped out of the apartment but she didn't get halfway out before she heard, "Oh my god."

Not six feet from the door stood Lars Drechsler and Elise, staring at her, their conversation frozen in their half-open mouths. It was Elise who had spoken, Elise who was still perfectly dressed with her perfect hair, and Elise whose eyes narrowed. Lars smiled slightly as though the mouse had been caught before the trap had even been set.

Only one thing came to Fae's mind: RUN!

She propelled herself out of the doorjambs and took off down the hall, nearly slipping around the corner on the smooth stone floors. Quick footsteps behind her said that Elise had given chase, and Elise called back to the old man, her voice echoing off the empty walls.

"This changes nothing!"

Whatever was or was not changing didn't matter—Noah would protect her. With a dramatic push, Fae flung open the building's door and took off down the street back to the hotel.

12

She didn't know where or when she had lost Elise, but when Fae could no longer breathe fast enough to keep up with her pounding heart, and when her legs refused to be pushed any further, Fae pulled up to a stumbling walk. She checked the time on her phone and was still greeted with a "no signal" symbol. She swore. How did they cut off reception? She swore again. It felt so good to get it out, so she swore again, and again, and she couldn't stop. She cursed this stupid place and her grandmother for luring her here and betraying her into this mess. She cursed death itself and then she swore at every single person she had met since arriving. She cursed God and the Communion at every door, and the beautiful, magical Christmas lights providing such a false sense of security. And then she cursed herself for coming here. She held nothing back, only letting up once she had exhausted her profane vocabulary. She felt emptied but no better.

When the hotel at last came into view, there was a blue coupe sitting empty outside the entrance. Fae figured it belonged to the woman who was supposed to take her to the basilica; she forgot her name, and really didn't care, either.

Inside the hotel, a middle-aged woman appeared out of the sitting room, intercepting her path. "Fae, I'm Colette. Maria asked me to drive you to the Basilique de Notre-Dame du Seigneur. You're late and there's not much time. Let's go."

Colette looked like a typical house mom with a bob haircut and unoriginal makeup. She took off toward the entrance, expecting Fae to follow. She didn't.

"I'm not going with you."

Colette stopped and turned to face Fae. "Young lady, I don't know you and I've never met your grandmother, but I respect what she did for this village. I promised her I'd take you to the Notre-Dame du Seigneur and now I have even less time than ever to get you there. Let's *go*!"

"I've learned a few things recently and I don't trust my grandmother anymore, so I don't trust you. I mean, what's the rush?" Fae asked, trying to entice this woman into admitting her involvement in the plot on her life. "So what if I'm a little bit late for a concert?"

"We need to go—"

"Tell me about the green light and the walking dead people."

Colette didn't respond right away and the tension was as taut as a hangman's noose. "Who told you?"

Fae didn't respond. She was relishing this moment of finally having an advantage.

"What do you know?" Colette pressed.

"Now you understand why I don't want to just jump in a car with you. I was told everyone expects me to die, and you want me to just trust that you're not somehow involved in that? How do I know it's not you who's going to knock me off? All this talk of a life-changing experience? I don't want it. I'm done. I know about your green lights. What if I started telling people what goes on around here, you—"

Colette's face flushed like the mother of a defiant teenager. "You have no idea what goes on here. I don't know what other people have told you, but we're trying to save you from those green lights and "walking dead people" as you call them. If you really knew what they were, you'd know that the Notre-Dame du Seigneur is the only place you're safe. Now, please come with me.

Disobeying Maria's instructions is not something you want to do."

It was at that moment that a stocky man who looked fresh from boot camp came in from outside and blocked the exit.

"Peter." Colette acknowledged him with little affection. He was a young man, though his face was not a memorable one; black hair growing out of a buzz cut, and thick black eyebrows that made him look meaner than he probably was. By his expression, it was apparent he hadn't come to invite them out for a drink. "Whatever Misseur Drechsler has you here to do, you can just walk away from it now. I'm taking Fae to the basilica."

"Fae is going to stay in her room."

"My orders are from Maria Peeters herself."

"I don't want to argue," Peter said. "There's not enough time for that." He reached into his jacket pocket, pulled out a silver handgun, and pointed it at Colette's forehead.

"Holy sh—"

"Shut up," Peter snapped at Fae with annoyance as Colette slowly raised her hands and took a few steps back. He looked at Fae. "If you hadn't shown up I'd be getting ready for tonight with my fiancée. But now, this is what you've made me do." He turned his attention back to Colette. "Lars wanted to keep close tabs on this one so the Gift stays protected. Asked me to help him."

"You call this helping?" Colette asked.

"I never said I agreed to help Drechsler. My little brother's request came first. I'm fulfilling a debt I owe him."

Colette was thrown off guard. Fae could see how unprepared she was to find out she wasn't fighting the foe she had thought she was.

"Don't pin this on Julien," Colette told him, "he wouldn't have told you to come with your gun."

"You can leave now or stay with her in her room," Peter warned. "But it's 10:40 and your time is running out."

"So is yours."

"I'm not letting her go out that door." Peter cocked the gun.

"Don't shoot anyone!" Fae shouted, stepping out from behind Colette who had pushed her behind her, away from Peter's aim. "I'll go to the basilica if it means living a little longer, OK? I can get there on my own." Fae made that clear, looking back at Colette. "Or, I'll go willingly to my room. I'm sure I'll be just fine in there, too, but no one is going to get shot over this." As she professed her confidence, she wasn't so sure it was accurate. The thought of those haunted mirrors made her sick.

"How do you know you'll be fine?" Colette asked.

"I've got . . . a feeling . . . that I'll be OK." With that confession, she felt Noah manifest behind her, his warmth and heaviness backing her up and she felt more confident. "In fact, I know I'll be OK."

Colette eyed her carefully. "There are only two reasons you'd be so confident, and only one of those will actually keep you safe. Have you been seeing or hearing strange things lately?"

Fae wasn't going to answer that. Colette was likely on the same page as Maël and she already knew his opinion about her hearing things. "Will either one of those two options change the present situation?"

Peter and Colette answered at the same time, "Maybe." "Yes." They stared at each other for a second before Peter won out and said, "Just say that Emmanuel is God with us."

"A pleasant Christmas phrase," Colette added, following Peter's train of thought.

Fae didn't buy it. "What does that have to do with anything?" This, then, was her conversion—through the barrel of a gun; say religious things or die, a demand which echoed throughout the millennia. "Put the gun away and then we can figure out what's going to happen."

"This is Christmas," Colette said, "a time when some of the most intelligent Eastern minds once bowed their knee to a young Jesus, even though they were pagans. Are you better than them?"

"I might know a thing or two they didn't after 2,000 years of hindsight." Neither Colette nor Peter were swayed. "So, what, are those words a secret code to access some sort of magic talisman preserved all these years from the Wise Men themselves? The gift that the world isn't ready for? The Holy Grail, perhaps?" She was being cocky, probably dangerously so, but it felt good, and this situation was beyond ridiculous. She'd experienced so much fear the last two days that, now presented with a physical fear, she felt almost desensitized to it. Neither Peter nor Colette budged. "OK, sure, whatever, Emmanuel is God with us. There, I said it. Now put the gun aw—"

Fae didn't finish the sentence before something hit her on the face, sending her reeling hard into the wall behind her. Her vision went black as her head smashed back on the ivory-painted wall and, for a second, she felt nothing but the nerves in her face lighting up like firecrackers. When the blackness began to fade, and she could see beyond the bright lights flashing in her eyes, she found herself shouldering the wall, holding her cheek, stunned. A cracked picture frame lay on the floor nearby, not far from where it once hung.

"What . . ."

Peter still held the gun, but it was lower now, limply held, and Colette hadn't moved. She looked back at Fae, stunned. Neither of them had hit her.

If you ever say that again, you will sorely regret it.

Noah wasn't just angry. He was furious.

"Are you sure you know whose protection you chose?" Colette asked, no longer the impatient mother she had been a few moments earlier. She turned to address Peter. "Her decision has been made. I can't take her anywhere now unless she wants to go. Take her to her room. I hope Misseur Drechsler is prepared for this."

Taking his cue from Colette, Peter uncocked the gun, put the safety on, and stuffed it back into his pocket. "I hope so too. Hurry, Colette, go where you need to."

"You too."

Colette left, leaving Fae rubbing her cheek to numb the stinging pain to a dull throb. Her tongue worked itself over her teeth, searching for the tangy warmth of blood wondering if any teeth had dislodged; it would be a long time before she could get to a dentist. Funny, how vanity presented itself at the most senseless times. With little other choice and still in shock, Fae let Peter prod her up the stairs to her room as her mind went to Noah. He hit her. And then he threatened her. Even after risking so much to do as he asked, she still had angered him. She had given into the intimidation of the religious. She couldn't afford to disappoint or anger him again, not if he was going to fulfill his promise to protect her.

"You're real," Fae said quietly under her breath so that Peter wouldn't think she was talking to him. "Jesus isn't a thing. He's dead. I didn't mean it."

You're going to remember that forever as a warning.

"Hurry up." Peter pushed her to go faster. The third floor couldn't come fast enough. "This place has a creepy feeling and time is wasting."

Peter was noticeably slowing, and she could hear his knees starting to click with every step. They climbed past a window, and a green light from outside faintly lit up the stairs in front of her. She heard Peter zipping up his jacket and at the same time they passed through the beam, the green light gone. He swore as he mumbled, "It's only 10:44. That psycho is eager to start." Not knowing if the green light was just Christmas lights outside, or maybe something else she should know about, Fae began to turn around, but he yelled at her, "Eyes forward and hurry up!"

She wanted to tell *him* to hurry up, if she, who was out of shape, was climbing faster than he was.

After a few more steps, they made it to the third-floor landing, and she had the old skeleton key pulled out and in the lock before Peter could say anything about moving faster. She wasted no time getting into her room. Before she closed the door, she caught Peter's eyes and saw him for what felt like the first time. This wasn't the same Peter she began climbing the stairs with, and he wasn't out of breath from his struggled climb. Yet, he was pathetically worn down, and his skin had lost its color. He looked so sick and thin, and the hardness in his eyes had been replaced by desperation. Something was wrong. She saw it, and he knew she did. Peter reached into the room and slammed the door closed.

Moments later, she heard the scraping of furniture being slid across the floor outside her door, and saw the door rattle every time something else was stacked against it. She heard Peter's muffled complaining through the door about her ruining everything, and something about his fiancée waiting for him, but she didn't hear all of it as he stumbled heavily down the stairs. He sounded like a drunk man on speed rapidly thumping about.

She still couldn't believe Noah had hit her.

But Noah didn't give her any time to reflect on that reality. As soon as Peter was gone, she could smell the fine, green mist welcoming her into the room as it rose up and drifted around her feet. She noticed right away that an edge of the blanket she'd thrown over the mirror had fallen loose. She panicked and ran to readjust it. Reaching up for the slipped corner, she noticed a folded piece of paper left on her desk. It had "message for you" embossed in fancy cursive along the top of the fold.

It was a missed phone call from her grandmother earlier that morning. Why hadn't she just called her cell? Grandparents and technology . . . It read that based on the difficulty Fae was having with the locals, her grandmother had changed the arrangements. Instead of Colette taking her to the Notre-Dame du Seigneur, she was to go to a different location. Included were street-by-street directions. Apparently, Colette hadn't gotten the change of instructions.

Gravity won out over the thick blanket. Like a dark horror-show master removing the curtain from his prize freak, it silently fell into a soft pile on the table, revealing the stage for horrors. The panic came back and she quickly reached to preemptively fling the blanket back up to kill even the chance that the corpse could show itself, except she couldn't move her arms. They were too heavy, and her legs felt locked down by strong hands.

He was holding her here.

There were no surprises when she looked into the mirror. There she was, disheveled and tired from her sprint across the village, but she still saw the determination she had worked so hard to master since she was a child; she just didn't have happy eyes. They were guarded and bore the scars of her wars, the wars with her father, her mother's bipolarism, and the church people who did her family more harm than good. Fae sighed and tried to look away before it was too late; she could feel the eagerness of the apparition waiting to appear. She couldn't handle seeing that again, and her stomach felt sick from apprehension.

Except she couldn't look away. She was trying to, but couldn't avert her eyes. Noah hardened her gaze and, just as she had feared, the corpse waiting in the shadows of the mirror slowly faded into view.

You thought I was wrong to correct you downstairs, but you don't understand what's at stake.

Fae struggled to turn her head but she wasn't strong enough, not against him. She was forced to watch as her cheeks sank and her muscles atrophied, until all her bones were jutting out like post-apocalyptic mountains. Her eyes fell deeper into her head, clouding over, her lips dried up like old parchment, and her skin lost its color. What skin that wasn't dried like leather rotted in patches, until she could see right through to the bone and sinews beneath.

Fae tried to close her eyes, but when she did she started to choke, and so she was forced to open them with deep, sucking breaths. Her legs would have collapsed if the green fog wasn't propping them up, so robbed of strength as they were.

The corpse was her. It was alive, but by no means from its own ability. It was horrible, and she couldn't stop shaking. She was dying, she was dead. For the first time since arriving in this village, she knew with surety that tonight she was going to die.

Merry Christmas Eve, Fae Peeters. You're all dressed up and ready to go out now.

Noah spoke with an eagerness she hadn't heard from him before. She could feel his breath brush tantalizingly over her ear, but it wasn't comforting, and she stifled a sob which escaped.

This is you. He whispered darkly to her, his voice penetrating deep into her soul.

He warmed her as he hugged her in close, but there was nothing to see of him in the mirror, nothing but arms of iridescent green fog curling up around her body. It took its time slowly encasing her as he enjoyed savoring the experience.

She wanted to ask him if this was all he was, a spirit within the fog, but she couldn't form the words.

This is what your father saw when he rejected you. This is what your mother saw that turned her amazing joys into sadness. You are *going mad, Fae. But I'm not done with you yet. You'll like yourself more when we're finished.*

Finally, the lock on her body released and Fae collapsed into the mist-covered ground, crying. She saw the healthy flesh on her arms as she clutched herself close, but that offered little comfort knowing that somewhere, in some time or dimension, that corpse really existed as her.

"You said you'd protect me," she said into her crumbled frame. He said he would. She had to trust him.

13

Elise hadn't felt it necessary to chase Fae all the way back to the hotel. She just needed to make sure that was where she was going. Paulina was waiting there to pick her up and bring her to the pit, and if Paulina failed then Fae would likely find the directions Elise had left in her room and she'd still arrive at the pit. Maël's decision to walk away had hurt both the plan and her. And now, because of his refusal to break their family reunion and Fae's late-night adventure, they were running dangerously close to the 11:00 p.m. window when the Gift took over. Even though no one else had told her that they were quitting, she was aware that hers was a fragile following, despite last night's meeting ending positively.

So much hope and trust in other people, so much room for things to go wrong. Elise didn't like it, but what choice did she have? She couldn't do this by herself, and there was no time for another plan. If she was honest with herself at the deepest level, she worried. The stakes were too high to lose. But, when morning came and her success proved that they were not only graced to walk through the fires of Hell, but that they could tame them too, all this would be worth it. Her audacity would be excused, her succession cemented. Misseur would have her head for this regardless, but tonight would forever change how they dealt with the Gift. Using Fae to prove Nefas had exploitable weaknesses would be the stone to ripple the water. He wanted Fae badly enough to show up two days early, but Elise would rob him of both her and her witness. Nefas, death and abomination himself, would be weakened, his grip loosened. The one who showed up in person to use and abuse them as puppets in his dark drama was going to suffer his first blow.

Elise drove to the western side of the village where the pit lay. The streets were empty so she didn't pay attention to the traffic signs, nor did she bother putting change in the parking meter. No one would be giving out tickets tonight. She hurried down the nearest street, headed toward la Rue, conscious that with every step she was getting closer and closer to the dark abandonment that was the pit and farther and farther away from where she wanted to be: the plaza around the Notre-Dame du Seigneur. It was where most people waited to welcome Christmas morning, and she'd be there now too if she wasn't having to save the village.

A lone snowflake, and then two, fell from the heavens, escapees from the storehouses in the sky. The only sounds were that of her breathing and the heels of her boots on the frozen stones. Otherwise, it was as lonely as it must've been on that silent night so long ago. Passing under the streetlamps glowing brightly for none but her, her shadow grew in front of her, then shrunk to follow long after, before it grew in front again. All the lights and scenery were background noise to her focus on arriving at the black door as quickly as possible. Not knowing what condition her plan was in made her walk all the faster.

Elise made quick work of the short maze of streets before she came to la Rue, a thin, old street just wide enough for two people to pass by each other. Its dented and scratched metal gates were open, which was a good sign. She saw two familiar bikes leaning against a wall nearby, meaning that at least two people she had told to be there had arrived.

Forcing her memories away from past closed-circuit television footage she'd seen, she tried to think of puppies and Caribbean beaches as she entered the darkened street, unable to deny the feeling of having stepped into the yawning, toothless mouth of a mummy. Solid walls of brick, exposed wooden beams, and patches of dirty stucco rose high on either side, robbing her of any natural light that might escape the overcast night. With the darkness of la Rue being unnavigable, she pulled out her car keys; a small LED keychain gave her enough light to not stumble over snow-dusted piles of old leaves and uneven stones.

Her idea to walk la Rue for a second time on the worst possible night ever, and not at midday on a sunny, June 30th afternoon, mocked her false sense of bravery. She felt like the opposing force of a magnet was pushing her away from the black door, and her lingering doubt about how good an idea this actually was began to grow to an uncomfortable level. Now that the Gift was almost here and Nefas was going to be released into his fullness, Elise was genuinely growing scared. But she was determined not to let the others see it.

She found the black door at the end of the street, the outer wall leering high above. There was no sentry light or little half-window above it, nor any markings at all. It had a worn, stone threshold about two inches off the ground that was rounded and slippery from centuries of exposure. Only, the lintel held any marking which was an old verse scratched into it. It was too dark to see now, but Elise recited it in her mind almost like a type of password: "For sin deceived me, and through the commandment put me to death." She had never gone through the door, had no idea what to expect other than to find an entry point to the pit. Now that she was here, her confidence withered.

Elise put her hand to the door to open it, to see if Alain and Marc were waiting inside, but a shout from behind stopped her short and she jumped. She was as nervous as a child stealing from a cookie jar, as she should be. What she was doing was completely off-limits. This door was the entrance to the pit of Nefas' lair, and no story told what to do once inside. One just simply did not go inside.

"Elise!" The shout echoed down the street ripping open the silent grave that was the night. "Elise."

"Maël," Elise said, once she saw his face emerge from the darkness. "I didn't think you'd be here after backing out on me."

Maël hadn't come alone. There was a small group with him. She identified them by shining her keychain light at them. They had all come, she thought with a smile, so her fears were unfounded. They did trust her.

"Aren't you supposed to be done locking up my cousin by now?"

There was something off in his voice. She reined in her relief. "She's been delayed. But Paulina will have clear roads; she should be here at any moment."

"I'm here now." Paulina came closer and the light brought her out of the darkness.

"Where's Fae?"

"Probably at the Notre-Dame du Seigneur. I let Maria's driver Colette take her."

"No! Why?" Her whole plan! She trusted Paulina with one thing, ONE thing, and she . . . "You said . . ." Elise began, but then she gritted her teeth and asked, "Why are you here if Fae is not?"

"To make sure Fae doesn't somehow go inside of there," Maël said, nodding toward the door. "You know how weird things can happen."

"But we agreed that this was the best way," she insisted. She forced herself to take a deep breath, then started again. "Do we know that Fae actually arrived back at the hotel?"

"I dropped her off there, ya," Maël said.

"Well she didn't stay there! I had to chase her back to her hotel from a late-night tour. Did anyone actually see her drive away with Colette?"

"I saw them together in the lobby," Paulina said. "Why wouldn't they have left together?"

"Oh my god." Elise threw her hands up. "She could be anywhere. She started seeing the Gift in her room the moment she arrived! She won't stay in that hotel; Nefas wouldn't sell himself that short. She could be anywhere between here and the Notre-Dame du Seigneur, and you know that he isn't going to let her anywhere near there."

"You didn't think that it was important to tell us this last night?" Alain asked.

"Marc, are you with them too?" Her little light didn't have enough reach to reveal his face. A "yes" was given from the shadows, and she shook her head in disbelief. "So none of you are here to lock Fae up."

"You convinced us it was worth a try," Maël said, "but I saw things from

Maria's perspective today. I saw the life in Fae that just needs to be given an opportunity to come alive, and I convinced everyone to change their minds. Fae's a person, not an experiment. The Gift has always been for her, not us. I'm sorry it had to look like this."

"You're worried because putting someone in there has never been attempted."

"And it never should be. Misseur will change his mind about drugging her and storing her away, the choir will see to that. Maria has proven to have their ear."

"OK." Elise's mind struggled to keep ahead of everything that was falling out. She could still salvage this, she had to. "OK, so maybe she did make it to the Notre-Dame du Seigneur. Or maybe she didn't, and maybe she found written instructions in her room on how to get to a 'safe place' . . . namely here. She could be just around the corner."

There was stunned silence from the group. Then Tristan spoke, his voice as chilly as the night air. "What have you done? Why would you do that?"

"How do you know she'll listen to you?" asked Michele.

"She wouldn't. But she will listen to her grandmother." Elise held back a small smile.

"She's not going through that door," Maël said, "not if I can help it."

Michele jumped in. "If she did start seeing the Gift yesterday, and Nefas already attached himself to her, then there's no point to us even being here. He'll take her for himself and there'll be no place she can hide."

"That was the risk I kept betting against, the longer Maël refused to break her away from their little family reunion!" Elise snapped.

"She still has a chance," Maël said turning to his friend. "After I dropped Fae off, I called Misseur and told him where Fae would be if she didn't show up at the basilica."

That news hit Elise hard. "What did you tell him about my plan, Maël?"

"Enough."

So. Misseur had known the whole time when they were in his apartment what she had been planning behind his back and he didn't say a thing. She didn't know which was worse, that Misseur had been watching her lie to him, or that her plan could very well be confiscated by the man she was trying to impress.

"Fae's a liability!" Elise shouted. She had nothing else to say, but she couldn't just admit defeat like this. "She needs to be locked in the pit, and she needs to forget! Do you want our home to become a pathetic tourist trap, and the Gift vomited all over the world? We'd be made into a turn-of-the-century freak show! Priests of every religion will come to experience or expel 'the Devil'—and who knows what governments would do to us? Without the care of people like Maria and Misseur, the importance of Christmas would be lost to one of those ridiculous ghost-hunting shows." She was preaching to the choir, but conviction was all she had left. She felt so ostracized by these people, her friends. "Fae already knows too much. She broke into Misseur's apartment!"

"Did she," Maël acknowledged with interest.

"She met Misseur for five minutes at Café Noir. Why would she break into his apartment?"

"A lot of things happen this time of year that make people act strangely," Maël suggested. "Fae is going to survive the Gift, and she will see what Maria wanted her to in the morning. And she will remember it. She's not the person you think she is."

"Fae could walk down this street at any moment. Until he takes us over, my plan can still work. Are you going to help me, if she does come in time?" Elise asked calmly.

"No. I can't," Paulina said first. Then Michele added his refusal, followed by Tristan, Marc, Alain and Maël. In the darkness, they stood fast.

"Do what you want," Maël said. "Wait inside the pit, or quit this idea and go to the party at the basilica. We're here to make sure Fae doesn't get inside that door, no matter what side of the Gift we're on."

Elise realized exactly what he meant. "Fae won't come near this door with your glowing sack of bones milling around."

"Maybe with some help from our angelic choir, Fae just might make it to the Notre-Dame du Seigneur despite us. But she is not going into that pit because of me."

Everyone wanted the choir's help in their designs for Fae, Elise thought to herself, but only the morning would tell whose cause would win it. "You can do as much to prevent her entry as I can to ensure it, once we're taken over."

"Then I suppose it'll be up to Drechsler and Jesus after that."

A grunt came from Marc as he doubled over and scurried a short distance away to throw up against the side of the building. He returned shortly, wiping his mouth with the back of his hand and looking sheepish.

"It affects us all a little differently. Guess it's time."

As he spoke, a spasm of pain shot down Elise's arm and her hand cramped up so tight it curled in on itself in a way that was not normal. She tried to brace herself against the pain, but still she cried out from the sudden sharpness of it running from her shoulder to fingers. And it was only beginning. Her arm wouldn't be the last of her muscles to constrict so tightly.

"There's no more debate," Elise grimaced while doing her best to relax, "we're out of time." Fae's life rested in the shambles of her plan. Everything which happened from this point on was on her shoulders, and that knowledge sunk like an anchor.

Their arguments and disagreements no longer mattered. The Gift had truly begun and now they were all on this washed-out road together. Maël began to pray, giving them something to concentrate on as their bodies began to die. He prayed only a few words before ending with what, for some in this village, was literally tattooed on their bodies: "Though I walk through the valley of the shadow of death I will not fear for you are with me, your rod and staff they comfort me." They all gave their agreement with scratchy, diminished voices, and there was nothing left to say or do, except wait for Christmas morning.

Elise watched the others wither away before her eyes and she knew, as they all did from this yearly experience, that dying without ever actually being dead, and facing the mental torture Nefas put them through, was a thing everyone had to deal with in their own way. They were brothers and sisters facing the same evil, but they all had a different face to see. Wordlessly, they wished each other strength, but, when they needed to focus on merely breathing and struggling to keep their own thoughts separate from the terrors and screams of Hell shoving their way into their minds, Alain began to sing.

The old carol had always been one of Elise's favorites because of its beautiful truth and its powerful, lullaby-like tune. She disliked such dramatic shows, but its words were the last bit of light and hope her desperate soul struggled for before starvation, so she joined her unrecognizable voice to his. There, in the dark abandon of a cold Christmas Eve, the seven of them sang with as much conviction as men and women sinking on a doomed ship.

> Long lay the world in sin and error pining
> Till He appeared and the soul felt its worth
> A thrill of hope, the weary world rejoices
> For yonder breaks a new and glorious morn

They sounded terrible, a choir of crones and codgers with their vocal cords drying up. Tristan's and Marc's lips were nothing more than curled leather strips, and Alain had a hole as big as a gunshot wound in his cheek, but they sang anyway and they believed what they sang. Their voices echoed against the walls and for a few moments it felt like that small, dark, forgotten street was the brightest place on Earth.

The moment was cut short by the eerie green glow that had begun to grow and was as indicative of Christmas Eve as was delivery of presents by St. Nicholas. Faint at first, it quickly became bright enough to light up the whole alley with its sickly pale color.

As they finished singing the verse, Elise opened her jacket with bony fingers and looked down into her ribcage through her remnants of leathery skin. There it was; the green blob, the lecherous parasite that would keep them alive until morning. Everyone except Paulina, who refused to see that thing inside her, looked down into themselves, acknowledging it. It throbbed with the life stolen from her heart and she could see its tendrils shooting down into her gut, could feel them winding others up around her neck, slithering deeper into her body. It was the spirit of Nefas, an entity from Hell that commanded limbs and took over the mind. She hated it, wanted to rip it out of her and then die for real, if it meant never having to see it grow inside her ever again. The few muscles left in her body cramped up, contorting her and she groaned in deep pain.

There was still a chance that, through some crazy miracle, Fae could make it here and maybe escape into the pit where the earthly gases would kill her memories. The reality of Fae getting this far alone, was impossible though. But still, Elise wanted to be ready for her. Even in her own death, she wasn't ready to admit defeat and she was going to finish what she began.

The black door welcomed her and she could feel the parasite wanting in, flexing itself through her body, engaging her limbs where there was not enough muscle left to do the job. It seared like a branding iron, and the sound that came out of her mouth sounded more reptilian than human.

One last look over her shoulder revealed that Maël and Alain were already gone. Paulina was clawing at her skull where her nose used to be. Marc, Tristan, and Michele were nearly done too, their white eyes searching this way and that for the last bit of light before they were sucked down into the darkness that awaited them in the void of their besieged minds. Their clothes hung loosely off fleshy bones and the glow from their chest deepened the already heavy shadows on their faces, blackening out their eye sockets—except for Paulina, whose eyes had swollen out. Elise knew she looked no different.

She stumbled past the black door and into the darkness beyond. *Door, pit, Fae,* those were her three thoughts. The mental instructions would linger like an echo. Her mind would remember, would even bend the parasite to her will; she had to believe that it could. The parasite's glow gave enough light to navigate the worn floor with its snaking tracks of frozen algae from water drips. She sucked cold air into the vacuum of her lungs, freezing her unprotected bones and slowing her heart even more. If she were truly alive, she would have seen her breath.

Elise's final thoughts began to fade as she stumbled each grinding and crunching step forward. She reached the internal door, black metal so old it looked to have come from a civilization older than modern settlers had ever known. Elise flopped her nearly useless hands onto the giant slide lock with a small *theenk,* and then it was over. A murderous high-pitched scream of a banshee welcomed Elise to the tortures of Hell resounding in her soul, planted there by the fallen themselves. The Gift finished taking her over.

14

With a calculated jump, Fae landed on her feet harder than her ankles would have liked, and she winced, remembering in hindsight how to absorb hard landings. Straightening her jacket, Fae looked up at the path she had scaled down. Three floors of thin, window ledges, drain pipes, and frozen bricks—she marveled at the feat. There was no way she should've been able to climb down the wall. But Noah had said to go, and he'd opened the window for her, so she went. It was a stupid thing to attempt, but Noah had led her true.

After collapsing on the floor of the hotel room, Fae had managed to pull herself together before Noah had the chance to lose his patience and shame her for being so childish. She could endure some frights and insults along the way, if it meant that she wouldn't die. That's what she told herself to get off the old floor, hyperventilating. That, and showing Noah she was still a worthy cause for his help. She who couldn't even look at herself in the mirror . . . those dead, white eyes . . . she felt sick, and she pushed her thoughts onward.

Without explaining himself, Noah wanted her to follow the directions in her grandmother's message. First he had shown her grandmother's betrayal, and then he wanted her to follow these new instructions. She could only surmise that there was something in the new destination that was to her advantage; she couldn't trust her grandmother, but she trusted Noah enough. She also didn't have much choice but to do what he asked. She'd tried the door, but it was blocked and the furniture wouldn't budge. That's when Noah had shown her the way out.

The address her grandmother had given was on the other side of the village, next to the outer wall. Fae brought her tourist map, just in case. All the little interconnected streets would eat her alive if she got lost. There was a bike rack at the back of the hotel with one bike unlocked and unracked; the heavy deposit of snow built up on its frame suggested the owner wouldn't return anytime soon. She brushed the snow off its seat and the small mounds fell with a soft *twump*.

She broke the bike through its wintery bonds and wheeled it into the middle of the abandoned street, setting off as the chill from the seat passed through her jeans. If it wasn't for the basilica towers acting as a landmark, she could've easily lost her sense of direction. Her concentration was split between not getting lost and not losing her balance on the slick and slushy pavement.

The deeper her directions took her into the village, the more unsettled she became. Something about the energy was different now. She passed a couple streets where she could see Christmas lights bobbing around in the windows and against the brick walls, as though a light wind had risen up to banter the strings back and forth. There was no wind though, not enough anyway, and she thought again about the mysterious green lights from the pictures. Her eyes caught sight of a nearby lamppost as she biked by. For some reason, the angel hanging there looked gargoylish. It might've been her mind playing tricks with the shadows. None of this felt right.

The village was so empty, so quiet, and the awareness struck her hard. It was like everyone had simply disappeared; or hiding was more like it. She could almost feel the eyes on her. Exposed as she was, in the middle of the street with her bike acting like a liability, she realized that the feeling of being watched was why she had been so unsettled since leaving the hotel.

She could imagine them all, unseen from the shadows and darkened trees dotted alongside the sidewalks, and in the little corner parks. She rationalized that she was going mad and there really were no people watching her from the shadows. This paranoia was just the next step in that maddening direction. Traveling these abandoned streets came with an acute and unnerving feeling that she was an outsider invading the asylum of a penitentiary. Being feared, not being wanted. All sorts of demented and unnatural thoughts, shaped from arcane and barbaric instruments of experimental healing, radiated toward her from the corners of the rooms where trapped patients cowered with their nervous twitches and their stressed and sweaty brows, trying to silently cast her back out from their protected walls. She would have left if she could, but she was stuck in their asylum for the night, as mad as they—but all she could hear from their silence was, "Get out, get out!"

There was no one in the streets. She could feel them, but they were nowhere to be found. She would have yelled into the silenced air for all the hiding cowards to go do some unkind things to themselves but, afraid of awakening the very madness that had brought her to this place of mental break, she held her tongue. She needed Noah to help her through this . . . *I'm in your head, I'm in your head . . . I'm in your head . . .* She had been here before.

As though on cue, Noah came to her, as carefree as a field of wildflowers. His presence was calming, and that gave her the courage to see past this feeling and push aside the madness about to breach.

None too soon, she found her final destination. Fae coasted to a stop and parked her bike against the wall where others already rested. It wasn't much of a street, more of an alley, really. There was a streetlamp nearby, but its light died where it was cast, and it only made the darkness of the entrance look that much blacker. The buildings seemed to lean in toward each other and the cobbles of the paving were uneven, missing, and sloping downward from the center. It looked like the snowbanks were dirty in spite, rather than despite, the freshly fallen snow.

Fae double-checked the directions to make sure she was at the right place and couldn't find an error. This was the place: la Rue. Just la Rue, "the street." She wished that she'd been thinking more clearly and had brought her phone to have the flashlight app to light the way.

Thanks a lot, Grandmother, Fae thought sarcastically, *if I leave this place alive, I'm going to have one very long talk with you. And then never again.* It didn't matter that it was Noah who'd told her to come. They were her grandmother's directions.

She had to continue. She refused to go back to the haunted hotel, and Noah didn't want that anyway. She wouldn't be able to find her way back to her great-aunt and uncle's house. No other place was open, except for the basilica. But that's where everyone wanted her to go, and everyone expected her to die. No, she wouldn't go there.

Noah's hands brushed down her shoulders and gently pushed her toward the open gates. She took one last quick glimpse behind her to see the streets remained empty. She could still feel the eyes of her invisible, asylum dwellers and she wanted to see them, wanted to know where their animosity came from, but Noah nudged her inside, telling her to ignore the lies of her imagination.

Fae went into the alley, feeling colder right away as though she had stepped into a subterranean cave. Every few steps, her foot would crunch on a patch of snow, interrupting her attempted light footsteps. From what she could see in the darkness, there was nothing to see on these walls but a long history of abandonment.

She came to a bend in the alley, and there in the stucco wall between two wooden beams was a small alcove six feet off the ground, lit by a light no bigger than a car's blinker bulb. It gave off a dim, yellow light which was as bright as the sun in this place. The piety and simple faith that this shrine represented was out of place. A locked door with a diamond-patterned glass window protected a silver goblet and a loaf of bread. She had seen similar shrines in Spain and Italy dedicated to the Virgin Mary. Painted on the back wall was an old Renaissance-style painting of baby Jesus, the gold and red paint glittering in the dim light. He was a happy baby, laughing, so unaffected by the darkness of this night, so unaware.

Jesus has always been unaffected and unaware, if his followers are any indication, Fae thought to chase away the sentiment of humanity the painting threatened, bridging the gap between Jesus the human being and Jesus the religious symbol. "He's such a joke."

THE GIFT

He's always been the king of jokers and fools, Noah agreed with her—so loudly that Fae jumped. His voice came from within the shrine, behind the glass doors. *Look closer Fae, this Joke is given the face he's earned.* Just as Noah was speaking, the paint of baby Jesus' face began to boil and bubble. The gold, red, and browns melted and dripped down his innocent baby face like an old prostitute's running makeup. As the paint bubbled and dripped away, a new painting was revealed beneath. Sharp fangs peeked through baby Jesus' pink lips and fly-like eyes took the place of his beautiful brown ones. A witch's nose with a giant, hairy wart protruded over his belly, and the deep wrinkles of an old man began appearing—

"Stop it!" Fae shouted, unable to handle the transformation any longer. "That's not a joke, that's disgusting." Noah didn't stop. He kept melting the picture, transforming it into something more and more horrible, something only the possessed in an asylum could craft. She was going mad. Noah was laughing cruelly as he created, but Fae turned away. She couldn't stomach it anymore.

You thought him a joke. Now he's funny.

"That's disgusting," she repeated.

That's how you were told to think, that such creativity was disgusting. You're just like Pavlov's dog, he said scathingly as they left the little shrine behind. *They want you dead, and here you are still singing their song. I want you as you are. I know you want to like my art so that you can please me. I know what will make you happy.*

He kept talking as they rounded the bend. *At the end of this street, there's a surprise I've been waiting to give you since you arrived. This is the beginning of everything you've ever wanted.*

"Answers." She felt him wrap himself around her, warming her from the chill that had settled into her.

The first of many gifts you will earn in your life with me.

"No more gifts!" She was hearing far too much about gifts. The word practically sickened her. She didn't mean to snap at him, she was sorry for that, and she cringed inside her coat waiting for his response, but it didn't come right away. She calmed her voice. "No more gifts for a while, please. I just want some answers first." He remained silent so she continued. "I'm sick of this place and everyone who keeps thinking that they're doing me a favor by stringing me along." Still he said nothing, so she spoke a little more boldly. "If you want to give me a gift, just get me safely to this place." Frustrated, she held up the small note, then crumpled it and threw it behind her, leaving it to bounce to its final resting place.

I know where you need to be. If you ever yell at me like that again . . . it would be regrettable. There was a pause where he let her consider the weight of his open threat before he spoke again, light and fresh as though his threat had never happened.

You're almost where you want to be, where you need to be. My surprise is waiting for you there. You are not alone in this world, Fae, there are so many others like you . . .

His warmth swirled around her before he rested on her hand and securely gripped her wrist, leading her forward. Fae felt herself relaxing, but not enough for her jaw muscles to unclench . . . she could feel the eyes on her again. There was still nothing behind her as she checked over her shoulder, only the night. Her gut was telling her not to go in any farther, but Noah kept pulling her forward.

The outer wall of the village was just up ahead; she could tell by looking for its top against the night sky. The alley was ending, so the plain black door she was told to find had to be close by. She thought she saw it up ahead, but it was more of a black space than a door. Everything about this place made her increasingly uneasy, and she had to wonder what kind of person would send her to this place. Her grandmother was guilty, but Fae wasn't sure if she could believe she was that kind of person.

The snow which teased earlier began to fall in earnest, finding its way into the narrow alley. Fae could feel it more than see it; the flakes made a tiny sound when they landed on her jacket. The snow was innocent and had no qualms with the earth, covering everyone and everything without prejudice. It was beautiful. Fae had always thought so.

Noah interrupted her thoughts, stopping her where she stood. *Surprise,* he said, *you've arrived.*

Fae searched the darkness around her to see Noah's surprise but she saw nothing except more darkness. She was too scared to tell him she didn't see anything, but then she began to notice that she could actually see the falling snowflakes. They were bright, reflecting some source of light. She followed their flight paths down from the sky, and as they fell it was like each snowflake scratched a deep cut in the black canvas before her. The thin trails left behind by the falling snow were absorbed into each other like water droplets and grew, becoming larger. The process began slowly at first then sped up, growing exponentially until eventually a picture began to form in front of her.

An iridescent green light lit up the alley and Fae bit her lip to try to control herself, but her body began to shake with the effort, and she couldn't stop her hands from forming into harmless fists at her side. The light was coming from six human forms at the end of the alley, and the more that was revealed of them, the more she knew exactly what Noah was showing her. This was the answer to the green light and bodies from Dreschler's room—they were decaying corpses. But how could that be, if this was all just madness in her head?

Noah knew her realization because he said sternly, *Don't cry, don't scream. I hate both. You've seen your own self in the mirror. Now, meet your brothers and sisters in me.*

Noah sent out a command to the six glowing humans, and their unblinking eyes turned their attention to Fae. At first only one heavy-booted foot shifted toward her, leaving the green glowing corpse swaying to catch its balance, and then the second foot slid gruffly across the paving stones. The owner of the feet swayed again to rebalance. Little by little, the other five creatures followed their leader, one unsure foot at a time. They began to shamble toward her, shifting their weight from one foot to the other to start the slow, awkward movement.

All but one had their jacket or shirt opened. Ribs were shadowed lines and their skin was only paper over a lantern, for from their chests emitted the source of the bright green light: a pulsating mass sitting heavy in their chest cavities, beating with the rhythm of their hearts. Their actual hearts didn't live, except for quivers here and again, choked out by the green mass. It spread out from their chests and wove its thinning branches through their bodies, intertwining intricately with the hosts and lighting up what little of the humans remained.

The flesh she could see was dried and withered, or was spotted like fruit left uneaten for too long. Some had half their cheeks rotted away, so that she could see all the way back to their molars. Two had lost their noses, leaving two long holes in the middle of their faces through which Fae could see the pulsating green tendrils inside their skulls. Their hair was patchy and, in some places, whole handfuls had been torn, or fallen off, leaving bits of bare skull exposed. And their dead eyes . . . Noah was right, they were just like her. These people were corpses, excavated before nature had finished its job. And they made erratic noises like a man deep in his sleep, not quite snoring and not quite sighing. Some of them sounded higher pitched as the air was forced out of opened holes in their throats.

"You said you would protect me," Fae barely managed to whisper. If she felt braver, she would have accused him of betrayal.

I am protecting you! he said, winding his way around her, warming her. *You're ungrateful.* Each word he spoke was like the closing of a door, forcing her deeper into his hold. *Figure it out, Fae. Humans work their whole life for things they wished they had, and now I'm giving you it all. Why? You've never had control of your life.* He spoke with a sense of superiority and she felt so misguided. *I have been your king and master since you were born, you'd just never met me before. I give you this gift in honor of our meeting. This is everything you've always wanted; believe me. This is how I will protect you.*

The corpse in front, the one who first began toward her, stumbled over his twisted feet and crashed into the wall, scraping his face against the rough surface the whole way down. A trail of dark blood painted the wall like a scar and his companions stumbled their way over his fallen body. He had barely settled before the green mass pulsated and squeezed, pulling its tendrils woven around his bones and through his remaining sinews to pick up its host from the ground. Leaning on all fours, a necklace fell out from his collar and swung in the air. From the end of the chain hung a gold ring, a miniature key, and a shark tooth.

THE GIFT

That was Maël's necklace.

And that was his scarf popping out from his jacket pocket.

"Maël?" Fae asked quietly, afraid that being too loud would draw even more attention to herself. The creature that was Maël only groaned as he struggled to stand. She gasped as she saw the side of his face torn to ribbons, the frail skin no match for the stucco and brick wall. Blood from the wound oozed out, dark and clotted like jelly.

She could smell them now too, musty and stale, and they waved their arms out in front of them in what looked like a half-hearted attempt to swat at her. It was too much. Fae turned and ran back to her bike. She had to escape, go somewhere, anywhere else. There had to be someplace to hide. She sped out of the horror house without Noah trying to stop her, but she didn't even get to the bend in the alley before she saw the terrible green glow, creeping along the walls ahead of her, bobbing and swaying with movement. There were more of them?

A wall of stumbling, possessed bodies squeezed into the alley dragging themselves toward her, the now familiar musty scent preceding their clogging mass of bodies. She skidded to a halt. As soon as they saw her, their dead eyes focused and they came alive like a pack of lame dogs having caught the scent. With a collective groan of interest, they shuffled more purposefully toward her, trampling fallen bodies without pause. Fae couldn't tell how many there were, though it didn't matter; she wasn't escaping the same way she had come in. These were the silent, asylum dwellers that had been trying to tell her to get out. She had never been in such deep agreement with anything before, and now it was too late to do anything about it.

Spinning on the ball of her foot, Fae ran back down the alley, desperately banging on the walls, trying to find a hidden door or missed street. The group of six were coming to meet her; the gap between the two groups of green corpses was shrinking fast. She skidded to a halt before she ran into them. She was trapped. A frozen water drip down the side of the wall made for a fractured mirror, and it was all she needed to catch sight of her corpse self in it, but now also the green light of a parasite as well, her parasite. She could feel the tendrils snaking up through her translucent skin. She could feel it pulling at her muscles and bones controlling her . . .

"No!" she yelled, smashing her fist against the ice. From all around her, she heard Noah laughing, his deep sound resonating off the walls. "No. No . . . this isn't funny. Stop it!" She twirled around trying to source him, but he stayed away.

The black door was her only chance. It wasn't far away, but it was behind the six. She had no idea what was behind that door, but if she had to die before she could leave, then she would do whatever it took to fight the god of fate in the process.

This would be just like a game of Red Rover.

Fae sprang forward, keeping her eyes on the black door, determined not to look at the corpses lest she lose her nerve. She reached the six and they fumbled to swat at her, and then she was through! . . . or so she thought. Twelve bony hands grabbed for her as she pushed through. They caught her coat and hair, jerking her back. She fought and squirmed, but their grip only tightened, clamping down harder on the roots of her hair, until she couldn't move her head. The corpses' meaningless groans and decaying faces leered over her until the horde united with the six and she was captured alive in an alley of the dead.

The parasite gave the corpses gripping her an iron strength, as it pushed itself down into their arms and hands. She tried to fight against them, but the more she fought the more they had to grab and lock her down with. Their grip was cold, not just dead cold, but cold like liquid nitrogen and it burned through her jacket, freezing her arm, the side of her head, everywhere they touched. Then suddenly their grip began to burn hot, searing her, and the two extremes warred upon her flesh and she couldn't stop herself from crying out from the pain of it.

The pack of dead men and women continued to grab for her, their barely animate limbs swiping blindly. Jostling bodies dislodged any hold they managed, but the six kept their grip on her as tight as steel rings forged together, their rotten faces flashing in and out of sight as she struggled. She tried kicking them away, but had no room and she was harmless against them. A cold hand with skin as brittle as papyrus and as slimy as a slug grabbed her neck from behind, each finger bone scaling down in sequence across her throat and it squeezed hard as though aiming to rip it out. She gagged as the fingers squeezed harder and harder. Somehow she wrenched one arm free long enough to pry the claw-like fingertips away, each finger breaking as she wrenched first one, then two fingers off her neck. After breaking the third, the grip broke and she instinctively began to cough heavily. As soon as she regained her throat, she was locked down again—leaving her helpless to fight off the corpses.

The horde kept grabbing at her, digging into her flesh, trying to get a piece of her—but they weren't actually doing it. They had the strength, and the six had her at their mercy—what were they waiting for? Her cries of pain became angrier as the dozens of hot iron and liquid nitrogen brands grew indiscernible. The longer her captors held her, the more the green parasites accumulated in their hands, turning them into bulbous, glowing tumors. Something was happening. She felt warm tears leak from her eyes and freeze as they trickled down her face; maybe she wasn't as angry as she was furiously terrified. Fae couldn't even tell. She just wanted to tear off their limbs her in one last struggle for her life.

What did I tell you about crying? Noah! He wasn't angry, he was using his smooth, reassuring voice; the one she first knew and trusted. *I don't like it.*

Rising from between the cracks in the paving stones, a green mist began concentrating in front of her. She was not reassured by the heavy weight of its presence. The corpses were his family, were her surprise, and she had tried to run away. Surely he would understand that she was terrified and not take the offense personally?

The green fog formed a pillar about six feet high, and Noah spoke from the midst of it. *Just another moment and this discomfort will be all over.* As he talked, the pillar took on a clearer form and the corpses in its way stumbled back, giving room for something of greater interest than her. She continued to struggle unsuccessfully against the bony hands clamped down on her. *There's nothing to be afraid of.* Body parts separated themselves from the pillar: a head, arms, legs.

"You're showing yourself to me," Fae gasped.

Yes. A misty arm reached out for her hair and, with its newly developed fingers, moved a loose strand from her eyes. *I love you, Fae. Everything I've done is to make it possible for us to be together, forever. We're like an Italian sonnet, you and I . . .*

Noah spoke something then that Fae couldn't understand; it was nasal and harsh. In response, the parasites growing in the hands of the corpses holding her pushed down into their fingers and turned them into swollen, lumpy, glowing sausages; it looked like they were being drawn up like needles. The image struck Fae with a horrible truth. The dozens of fingers poised over her body were *exactly* like needles.

I should have prepared you better for our family, Noah said, as he continued to take on more details and color. *It can be frightening seeing yourself and others as you really are.*

Noah incarnate came closer and reached one of his still translucent arms across her shoulder. He pulled forward a corpse, leading it into the empty circle where he stood. It was impossible to tell who this person was but, judging from what remained of its short permed hair and out-of-fashion glasses hanging from its one remaining ear, it had to be an elderly woman. Fae truly saw the corpses then, all of them individually as far as she could see in the dark alley with the shadows so heavy on their faces. There were men with patchy beards and thick eyebrows, corpses with earrings and hair bands holding back very little, floppy winter hats and wedding rings, people she had shared the streets with only hours ago. Her observations were cut short as Noah held up the hand of the old woman he had dragged out. It was black. The parasite didn't flow through the veins anymore, and it smelled of rotting meat. Noah explained. *Louise was injured by your struggles and her hand has become useless.*

With a quick snap, he broke the old woman's wrist. The woman barely even noticed. Then he snapped it the other way, completing the break and, with a sharp jerk, pulled the dead hand off, leaving a stub for the woman and an unattached hand in his. Without a care, he tossed it away and it was instantly lost beneath the feet of the dead. *What stops being of use is cut off,* he said as simply as if he had merely pruned the branches off a shrub. *Don't stop being useful to me, Fae. Don't make me angry.*

He shoved the mutilated woman to the side where she fell into those nearby. Then, he stood before Fae for the first time in his fully human form. He was a big man, over six feet tall, and 200 pounds of muscle showed through his jeans and gray T-shirt over which he wore a stylish, black, buttoned vest. The winter cold was apparently no issue for him and he had a perfect face, as chiseled as the rest of him, dirty blond hair, and green eyes. He looked strangely familiar. He was an image out of her imagination and, with a small warning in her gut, she realized that might not be normal.

Noah was going to protect her by killing her, she thought. If she died as the person she was, he would let her "live" with him as a corpse. Maybe this was the life corpses dreamed of. She was going to wake up from it—maybe that's why she saw herself in the mirror as she had. The idea was insane, but she going mad with evil genius, or something.

"Are you angry with me now?" With her question, the fingers immobilizing her sunk their bony ends deeper into her and she gasped with pain, amazed that her skin, so numbed from the extreme temperatures, could still feel anything.

For the first time, Noah opened his mouth and spoke his beautiful voice. It was no less intoxicating than before, but now it blessed everyone and not just her. "I am disappointed you didn't like my surprise better. But this next part will be worth it to see your beautiful face so full of joy." He smiled as he spoke again, this time inside her head. *Think of this as destroying a virus in a healthy body. You will at last be free to express your true colors.*

The man gently grabbed her hands in his, smiling with a reassurance she had never experienced before. Looking into his eyes, something overtook her and she wanted to be with him forever—her protector. The terror of the corpses and the fear of seeing herself as one of them was pushed aside, replaced by a deep need and longing. The bony fingers holding her began their final pinch into her, but just before they injected the parasite, a human voice shouted out, echoing off the alley's walls. The corpses stopped short as Noah was distracted by the interruption. Fae could feel the tension in him rising. As though he already knew who was there, Noah didn't turn around, and Fae couldn't strain to see. Whoever it was continued to yell as he got closer, using words she didn't understand.

The corpses parted before the human intruder and then reformed again behind him as he shoved his way through the dense group. The only thing she could see was his arm lifted high, above holding a silver goblet, sloshing red liquid on the ground, and half a loaf of bread, which he gripped awkwardly. None of the corpses reached out for him, though the way they tracked him passing by—it wasn't from a lack of interest. Finally, the hollering man broke through, and the parasite's light gave him his identity.

Lars Drechsler came hobbling as strong and as purposefully as his cane and old legs allowed him.

He pointed directly to Noah and spoke in a voice much stronger than what Fae could have imagined him capable of.

"You can't have her!"

15

"Let her go, now!" Lars Drechsler shouted. The wiry German walked through the decaying corpses of people he must have known by name. The parasites in their bodies throbbed with excitement though none raised a finger to touch him. A redhead and one wearing a Yankees hat snapped their teeth at him like animals. Lars ignored them all.

Noah let go of her hands as Lars crashed into the circle yelling, yet Noah still kept his back to the intruder. Even though he still looked at her, he didn't see her anymore. Lars had arrested his full attention.

"Nefas, I order you to release her to me."

Noah smiled, a sinister smile slow, to creep across his face. "You're a brave soul, old man. But your command doesn't have enough authority to override her decision. She's given her trust to me." Smoothly turning around, Noah stood face to face with the smaller, older, weaker man, then snarled. "She is mine. And so is this village."

"I hold the symbols of authority to command you," Lars said defiantly.

Noah sniffed at him with disdain. "You need to command Fae, not me. What you hold are pathetic copies anyway. Crushed grapes and crushed wheat."

"A crushed body. One that crushed you. You know how this dance ends; you've danced it before."

In a growl of deep-rooted anger, Noah backhanded Lars' outstretched arm, sending the cup and bread flying, the goblet clanging against the wall. Splashes of wine fell on the nearby corpses—and splash patterns of living flesh appeared where the liquid touched them, the parasites' tendrils quickly retreating from the affected areas. The corpses hissed exhaled breaths in a show of pain and, now that Lars was relieved of his symbols of power, they grabbed at him from all sides. Where their bony claws touched his skin, he cried out in the same confused pain Fae had. He was too old to give a fight and so was jerked around at their pleasure. The parasites squirmed and contracted to give the corpses an even greater speed they didn't have earlier when Fae was fighting them.

"I've been waiting a long time to get you," Noah said, stepping close to the old man's face once he had been firmly controlled. "You, Nazi, have been starving me for a long time and I take that personally. I'm not going to simply brand you; I'm going to use you to satisfy my hunger." To emphasize his point, the corpses holding Lars leaned down with their jaws open wide to lay a ferocious tear. Noah closed his eyes in expected ecstasy, but Fae cried out before those meatless jaws could come away with anything.

"Stop!" They all froze where they were, every jaw, every hand. "Noah, I trust you and am willing to go anywhere you want me to, but you can't do this."

"I can't?" Noah whirled around and grabbed her by the throat, squeezing just short of making her pass out. "Wrong time to get opinionated. This world is mine, given to me by *your ancestors*. You have as much right to tell me what to do as a nameless slave does his god."

The corpses' grip on her arms weakened, and Fae yanked them free to feebly paw at his hand around her neck and she nodded as best she could, to agree. "You're attractive like this." He let her go with a small shove, dragging his fingernails through her skin leaving five thin trails of blood behind. As soon as he let go, the corpses locked her down again. "Stop calling me Noah."

Undaunted by his predicament, Lars jumped back in. "You are no god and you certainly are not mine. I don't need the Communion, but it helps you remember your place. You cannot keep me here; I have no desires you can hold me with. We both know the broken body has final authority, and with that I command you to let her go." Lars squinted hard, frowning.

Whether Noah—or Nefas—had a choice in the matter was unclear, but all the hands holding her released at the same time. Lars rushed toward her, grabbing her arm and dragging through the mass of bodies toward the black door. He forged the way, the dead keeping their distance from him, but they were all still trying to make another grab for her. Maël's corpse snagged a fistful of her hair and pulled her backward, Lars losing his grip on her. Falling hard, Fae banged her head on the ground and in the flash it took her brain to assess whether it was still conscious, her vision was filled with rotting faces and her head was overwhelmed with the smell of must.

"Nefas?" She tried his other name as Lars had said it. It felt awkward on her tongue but, with a swirl of fog, his handsome face was above hers looking down. He offered his hand, then effortlessly pulled her to her feet, smiling. It was then that she truly felt the emotions of two people inside. When she heard him speak, or saw him, she desperately wanted to be with him, but the other side warned she would regret calling his name and taking his hand—that she'd just sold herself to the biggest mistake of her life. But right now, she had nothing else to cling to. Lars had no plan except to ruin the moments of sanity Nefas brought to her through all the madness.

"I will never let you leave my side," Nefas said. It was spoken as more fact than endearment.

"And I said no." Lars reached down through the bodies, found Fae's arm again, and pulled her up and away from Nefas. "He's a liar. Stop thinking he's here to help." Part of her was relieved Lars was taking her away, and part wanted to tear away and go back to Nefas because it would be a mistake to leave him. Lars pulled her to the door, black and forgotten by the years, and wasted no time pushing it open. It was instantly slammed closed again from the inside with a sharp thud of refusal, shutting them out.

"Get out of there," Lars growled at the door.

As on command, Nefas walked through the door and stood with all the poise of a dethroned monarch bent on revenge, his green eyes aflame, the corners of his mouth twitching. "I'll let you go wherever you want to in this village—" Nefas began diplomatically, his voice not matching his obvious mood. It made him seem merciful.

"You have no right to 'let' me do anything," Lars finished for him.

Nefas continued, ignoring the interruption. "You may go wherever you want in this village, but Fae stays with me and her new friends and family to celebrate this holiday night."

"Words less veiled were spoken by the Führer himself."

Nefas laughed then, it was as beautiful as watching the sun break through dark clouds. *But yet he sounds like the devil himself.* As soon as she thought that, Nefas snapped his burning green eyes at her as though reading her thoughts. She needed to make a run for it before she got in too deep with him. He wasn't who he showed himself to be. With the alley dense with corpses at his command, though . . .

"You, old Nazi," Nefas said, keeping up his benevolent act, "have to do as I say. Look around. Your confidence wavers, I can feel it. Your symbols are spilt and crushed beneath the feet of my family. You won't wade through them more than a few deep before your doubts overtake you, and my children will be free to *ruin* you."

Lars licked his dry lips. His wild eyes, ringed in wrinkles, narrowed and for a moment she really thought he would try to hit Nefas.

"Fae comes with me; through this door."

"I get what I want either way, if she goes with you or stays. You lose either way. You know as well as anyone what lies inside."

The corpses began pawing at Fae's back again, making her jump to get out of their reach. "Please just let me go," Fae begged. "Nefas, I'll go with you if it means leaving this place; or Dreschler, if you . . ." she wanted to say if he could take her to the basilica, she would rather take her chances there, but she knew it would be a grave mistake to voice such sentiments to Nefas. "Dreschler, your history with Nefas is not my history with him." The back of her head was throbbing and she dabbed her fingers back there to see if she was bleeding. Her fingers came away clean, but a large bump had popped up.

"I just want to wake up from all this, this madness in my head." She cast a look at Nefas, standing there so powerful, so intoxicating . . . "Nefas, please, get me out of this."

Lars cut in. "He's not your answer. Inside, now."

Before she had a chance, Lars pushed her through the black door and into the darkness beyond, slamming it behind her as she stumbled forward. A moment later it cracked open again, and Lars slipped through, slamming it closed to the sound of dozens of bodies thumping dully against the outside.

"Why did you do that?" Fae yelled, her voice echoing in the empty space. Nefas was about to help her! She didn't want to think of what he might do to Lars, but this might also be her moment of escape from him—while she still could. Without reply, Lars readjusted his cap and turned his attention to the only source of light in the room: a corpse facing another door on the opposite side. It didn't look like the kind of door that led to freedom. With a bit of struggle, the corpse turned toward them, forcing its feet to twist around to follow its body, its green light now better illuminating the room which was about the size of a two-car garage. Eerie shadows were cast over its decayed face and body and, because the shadows were darker in here, the body was nearly blacked out so that the parasite looked like a pulsating jellyfish. As Fae's eyes adjusted, she could see more details of the corpse. Its cheeks were so sunken and the skin so tight, Fae could make out the entire line of back-lit teeth. The clothes that hung off the bone-thin frame and what was left of the styled hair made the identity unmistakable.

"Elise."

Lars growled, "yes", and he tenderly made his way toward the door where Elise's corpse had been stationed, his efforts outside already showing their wear on his body.

"Can we escape through there? Where's the light?" Fae didn't fear him as much now that she had seen Nefas stand up to him.

"There is no light you can turn on that will chase this darkness away."

"That door didn't stop Nefas from getting in here before; it won't stop him a second time."

"Did architect school teach you that? That door only needs to keep the villagers out. This one," Lars nodded to Elise's corpse, rasping horribly at them, "I will handle. Don't let her touch you."

Elise's corpse ignored Lars after he shooed her away and made her way straight for Fae, arms reaching out, the pulsating green mass forming in her fingers like a mad scientist drawing ten needles for injection. Fae skirted around the room trying to stay ahead of Elise, waiting not so patiently as Lars loosened the giant slide bolt of the second door.

"Lars..." Fae said nervously as she bumped into a corner. Elise was almost in range and Fae tried to slide away to one side, but a low wall of something tripped her. She struggled to get out from beneath Elise's reach, scrambling on her hands and feet, but her effort was clumsy and she was getting nowhere fast.

Stop fighting what is good for you. Even if you do leave me, you will never escape. You'll like this and you'll love me even more.

Nefas. There was both relief and dread hearing him. Was he angry with her? It wasn't her fault Lars stole her in here! Being without him was making her almost as anxious as being with him—what had he done to her?! *I'm in your head...*

"Don't let her touch you!" Lars sharply yelled, snapping her attention back. Fae kicked out reflexively, catching Elise in the gut but Elise grabbed hold of her leg and her fingers pierced through, injecting her. The parasite began quickly spreading up Fae's leg—a thick tendril boring beneath her skin and into her muscle, as the parasite fed its conquest through her veins. Her leg was glowing green from the inside as the parasite began replacing her blood, and it was everything she could do to resist it. The burning heat and cold were waging war inside her veins and arteries. Fae couldn't bear it. She cried out in anguish, like a woman having a baby pushed back inside the womb, and she tried to tear away her leg but to no avail.

Just let this happen. You will have such knowledge and know such emotion that you will never be deceived or betrayed again. You will never know disappointment, only truth. And the truth will set you free.

The parasite was traveling faster up her leg and, soon, Nefas would have his way with her. At this point, she had to wonder if that was such a bad thing.

If she just let the parasite take her over, would she wake up?

She couldn't endure the intense heat and cold anymore. The pain was too much. "Not like this."

Something struck Elise in the back of the head and the corpse turned with an angry hiss. Elise stumbled with a snap of her jaws in Lars' direction, but the parasite prevented her from going anywhere, Fae's possession incomplete.

"Elise, I said 'NO'!" If Fae had been scared of his wild prophet act before, she was astounded by it now. He came around to face Elise and addressed the gelatinous mass sucking up her leg. "The power of the blood that never dries and the flesh that never rots gives you no choice but to listen to what I say. I hurt your host already, don't make me kill her to get rid of you."

The mass stayed its takeover.

At your wish, you can override what that religious mad man ordered.

It was hard to hear what Nefas was telling her through the noise of every nerve in her body screaming out. This was all too much and her weakness spoke for her. "Let . . . me . . . go . . ." she squeezed out between gritted teeth. She felt his disgust with her immediately.

On command, the parasite retreated into Elise and released Fae's leg, which began thawing out and cooling off right away. She wondered if there would be any permanent damage, hideous scars at the least, a dead leg to amputate at the worst. Lars stepped between Fae and Elise's rotten body, forcing the latter away.

Fae took her time standing up, blinking away tears and breathing heavily. She wiggled her toes to make sure they still worked. It was hot pins and needles as her blood rushed back in, but they worked.

"I told you not to touch her."

"I didn't," she snapped, trying to sound tough when all she wanted to do was hide under a blanket. "I kicked her with a covered foot."

"So ein Idiot." Lars said in German, the meaning not lost. "The door's open. Get in."

"Is this a way out?" she asked again.

"Sometimes you have to act without all the facts. Or you can waste time and deal with her on your own." Lars pointed over to Elise circling nearby like a hungry animal.

Fae limped across the room and passed through the wide metal door into the unknown.

16

Lars Dreschler followed Miss Peeters into the smaller, earthy room beyond: the pit. She was recovering from the attack well, and her limp was quickly wearing off. The incident should have been the end of the woman. Lars had to wonder if it was Nefas' hubris that had slowed the infusion of his spirit simply to be dramatic. Should another opportunity come, he wouldn't do it the same way again. If anything, he was at least that smart.

The pit door opened exclusively from the outside, so he only partially closed it for the obvious reason and also to keep Elise out for a little longer. He could feel the onset of fatigue and he might need to make use of her corpse to finish this botched plan he was forced into finishing. Lars had a fool's faith that he could miraculously make it back to the Notre-Dame du Seigneur, but to get this woman so far as well? He couldn't do it, even if he were a young man again.

"What the hell happened out there?" Fae demanded into the darkness.

"You tell me," Lars snapped.

"Tell me what happened!"

An old kerosene lantern sat just inside the door and Lars lit it, revealing the pit itself. The pit, which lacked any formal name, was ancient. It was about twenty feet wide and had an eight-foot drop to the gravel and dirt floor. A clay and stone hive had been built around it with a small hole at the top, just big enough for the earthly gases not to build up and explode the walls.

"I don't know everything—no one has ever been as senseless as you." He let that sink in.

Leaving the protection of the Notre-Dame du Seigneur was stupid for any reason, but Elise's naïve stupidity had forced him to do just that. As if he hadn't been in a bad enough mood already. "You're a fish in Nefas' ocean," Lars decided to tell her something. "You caught his attention, but it's your choice to get into bed with him. If you agree, you better know exactly what you're doing, because he'll make sure you never leave. That parasite is how he controls you. He might have other methods. I don't know. Now, go quietly meditate while I figure this out."

Lars carefully looked around at the place he had been in only once before and had sworn to never return to. It was the one promise he had hoped to fulfill to his last breath. Having Miss Peeters see the fullness of the Gift was one disaster, but for Elise to fall into the belief that Nefas could be so easily tricked was . . . unfathomable. Elise always wanted to overthrow the Gift, but he had thought her smarter than to try. Some mountains were meant as a reminder of how impossible it was to move them, he had told her. Yet, here she was, trying to move the mountain by herself.

Nefas had become quite a dandy tonight, and if Lars hadn't been otherwise preoccupied with surviving, he would have been curious to see what ended up happening first: Nefas' rot seeping through his fancy new skin, or Fae giving in and accepting his violent seduction. People saw what they wanted to in Nefas, and he made sure they got what they expected; he either just couldn't, or wouldn't, let the imitation contain his true self for long. Lars hoped to be back in the basilica long before either happened. Back in the day, people had a clear enough head to recognize evil when it crept up on them, rather than calling out to it for help. It was unbelievable.

"These doors won't keep Nefas out," Fae spoke again after much too short a silence. "Is this a safe place? Unless you're helping me escape, Nefas didn't just let me go and I didn't say I wanted to leave him. I need to be back with him." Her demand traveled loudly around the room.

"No, you don't," he said gruffly. She was staying on the other side of the pit, and he didn't blame her wanting to keep her distance. He wondered if he could tell her that what he had do next to her wasn't personal. "There is no meaning to the word 'safe' in here, and there is no other way out. You should have listened when I told you to leave on that train."

She only glared at him. She was a mess with disheveled clothes and hair, her black jacket torn open, and bags under her eyes. The scratch marks around her neck were pink and puffy. And the night was still young.

Lars could feel his head starting to get cloudy and he knew he didn't have long before the natural gases seeping up from the pit overwhelmed him. He was concerned why Nefas hadn't re-appeared yet. He should be in here trying to claim his prizes.

"Nefas?" Fae called out with hesitant expectation. Lars wanted to yell at her to shut up, but he started talking instead. He had to admit that he had some sympathy for this woman, enough, at least, to give her some of what she'd wanted: answers. The gases would affect her short-term memory anyway. She would shut up on her own to hear what he had to say.

"This is what we call the pit," he said, attempting to sound like a good conversationalist. It was a poor attempt, but he wasn't trying hard. "There are a small number of places where the Earth does not respect its boundaries, like Delphi, in Greece. The ancients believed Apollo possessed the oracle to deliver his divine messages. That Pythia had magic herbs and sat over a fissure in the ground where gases from deep inside the Earth made her seem possessed with the god. With just a crevice, the Pythia lost control of herself. This pit is an entire hole."

Fae was pacing on the narrow footpath to keep the blood flowing to her leg. He had done that same type of shuffle enough times before, when his leg had fallen asleep. It was good to see. He'd only read a single cryptic snippet about what happened when someone was possessed with Nefas' parasite. How did it go . . . *silent screams trapped in a room without walls, fireflies come with fire and ice but neither wood nor water—*

"What are you talking about? Apollo is mythology and there are no priestesses here, so what is this?" Miss Peeters seemed to be missing the point about the gas. She'd catch on soon enough.

"There are portals on this Earth, Miss Peeters, portals through which angels advance and devils drift. This is a place for the latter. Snakes have holes, spiders their tunnels. Nefas is a predator. That is what this place is."

She was slow in responding. Either that or his head was slowing its processing, both were probable. He couldn't stay much longer. "So why did you bring us in here?"

There was no point in keeping it from her.

"You need to die. Maybe just your short-term memory. More likely your body or soul too, judging by the way your night has begun. Maybe all three will die. You should ask your new friend what his plans for you are." He snapped the last part and he meant it.

Fae was quiet, but Lars didn't take the silence for resignation; the fight was still charged in her every muscle. "So this is where we die tonight." She said it so softly, so fiercely, he almost didn't hear her, or had she said it loudly and he couldn't register it? The sound of broken fingernails pawing and bones rapping at the metal door began behind him. Elise wanted in.

"If you haven't figured it out yet, the only independence you had going into tonight was your choice of two pre-set options. You chose this one. It involves hiding in this place and hoping that devil better enjoys frolicking amongst his spawn out there rather than capitalizing in here."

"Why are you saying 'you' and not 'we'?"

Lars was done giving answers. Short of a miracle, there would be no merry Christmas for Maria's granddaughter. But miracles were possible, and Nefas wasn't without foes of his own. He started off in a slow walk around the pit, surveying the uneven path with his cane. He was looking for a protruding rock or divot. "I tried to warn you. You wouldn't leave, and something had to be done. Your grandmother will understand. She was the one who passed on to me the responsibility of protecting our village from outsiders and preserving the Gift. She underestimated your threat to both."

Finding the outcropping he was looking for, Lars jammed his cane against the rock; it popped out of his hand and tumbled down into the pit, eight feet below. With a yelp of alarm, Lars looked from Fae to his cane lost in the shadows, and back to Fae.

"I . . . I can't walk very far without my cane, Miss Peeters." Which was true. He limped back to the wall and leaned against it.

"I guess you're stuck here with me then." He could see the conflict play out on her face despite her hard words—help the old man or suffer alone? She was still a decent-hearted human and, to his shame, he was going to take advantage of that.

"There's a ladder close to you," he said, pointing.

As he said it, he saw the green mist begin to rise around her feet, growing outward like fog rolling onto shore. Nefas was talking to her and he wanted Lars to know it, but all Lars could hear was white static and an indiscernible tone of a male voice buzzing in the air. Miss Peeters heard him clearly, she had the distant look in her eyes of one listening to someone heard but not seen. Lars wanted to knock some sense into her, with his cane if he still had it. That dense girl didn't get it yet, did she. She was still talking to him, still entertaining him.

"No," Fae finally said. "If you're condemning me in here, drugged on your lies, then you're staying, too."

"What part of 'don't trust Nefas' haven't you picked up on yet? He's telling you the middle of the story; don't make a decision only knowing a fraction of it. Whatever he's telling you, it's a lie!"

"But *you* have my best interests in mind." Fae scoffed harshly. "This whole insane, *stupid* village is betting on my death like some freak reality show, and you're the only one not walking around dead with a nuclear glow. How is that not suspicious? This morning you scared me. Tonight, yours will be the last face I see alive." She wavered at the end but, like his lies, she tried to sell hers.

"I'm not the only one not a corpse. If you'd gone to the basilica like you were supposed to, you would've seen that.

"You say Nefas isn't here to help, yet you're the one wanting to lock me in here. I'll cast my lot with the one who has a better track record helping me out. Get the cane yourself," Fae barked, passing her judgment. Then, as if to justify it, she added, "Christian."

And there it was, the cards on the table. He should've expected the accusation, as it was Nefas speaking through Fae—such a practiced excuse for hatred. The tables were turned from a thousand years ago, but that didn't excuse it. Lars furrowed his eyebrows, drilling the young woman with his eyes, and carefully said, "That's a broad statement. Mafia and nuns wear the same cross."

"I don't trust Christians."

"And neither do I, no more than any other human being. That's what they are, aren't they? Still human?" he challenged.

"You're a sub-class."

She wasn't going to make it. She wasn't. She was listening to everything Nefas said, and his intoxication was making her believe it. "You can only trust a picture as much as you trust the photographer. He shows and hides as much as he wants." Lars tried to bring her focus back to the real evil, though she wasn't so easily distracted with Nefas working to keep her thoughts on his track. Earlier she had wavered about leaving him, but Lars doubted she would.

His words were barely out of his mouth before the door's hinges creaked and Elise fell through. Her body lit up the whole of the small room beyond what the lamp could offer.

"I thought you closed the door!" Fae shouted in near hysteria, her arrogance vanished. Elise's dead shuffle was aimed for the young woman, who turned her full attention to backing away. Seeing his opportunity, Lars closed in behind Fae balancing himself on the wall as he went.

"This isn't one of your Hollywood movies, Miss Peeters," Lars said. "Hasn't Nefas shown you enough to prioritize your enemies?" Fae kept backing up, not even realizing that she was closing the distance between them. "Nefas is the enemy you think I am."

"Make her go away like you did last time!" She was scared, as she should be, and he hated the sound of scared women. Brought back too many memories he kept working to forget.

"Bringing you here was Elise's idea, not mine. Nefas deceived her, too. She thought this was a good idea. She just didn't have time to finish the job." Miss Peeters backed up right into him. "This, however, is my idea."

Lars grabbed her shoulders and punted out the back of her knee, twisting her around as he did, and threw her into the pit. She fell with a high-pitched scream, landing heavily in the gravel, nearly disappearing into the darkness, the mix of yellow and green lights just catching her. He severely hoped the end justified the means.

As Fae skidded into the gravel, Nefas dropped his dense oppression and his green fog formed up fast. Lars had no idea what happened when someone fell in the pit, but he assumed Nefas didn't like it; either that, or this was the excuse he needed to stop being so "polite."

Lars had no plan now but to get out of here while he still could.

Like a forming tornado, Nefas' heralding green mist swirled throughout the room, gathering itself together. The indiscernible buzzing of his voice, discernible only to Miss Peeters, grew louder until his ears throbbed. Lars could feel the disgust of his soul, dirtied with Nefas' growing manifestation. His stomach churned, wanting to throw up the poison as the pit began to smell of a dank, musty tent. He coughed heavily, the lightness of his head making him stumble like a drunk man. Nefas was forming his body in front of the door to block Lars inside. He had lived over seventy years without a cane; he could make it out of this pit without one.

"Lars Drechsler!" Fae screamed up at him, her voice echoing around the conical walls. She pushed herself to one knee, glaring death at him—but then she remembered the ladder. With the energy of youth, she started to race across the pit floor, but with every step her feet sunk in deeper, like the disciple Peter sinking into the lake.

Lars reached the ladder first, unhooked it from its base, and pulled it up and away from Fae's grasp. She had become stuck up to her knees, still fighting, with everything she had, to wade to the edge—almost fighting against herself now. The more she struggled the faster she sank.

"You're caught in the spider's web, Miss Peeters, you can't escape his poisons now. If I could take you to the Notre-Dame du Seigneur, I would." Lars tucked the ladder under his arm and dragged it on the ground behind him. It scraped and bounced across the compact earth with an organic sound, cementing the finality of Fae's resting place for tonight.

Lars was almost out of the door when a fully formed Nefas grabbed his coat from behind and halted him. He would have fallen into the pit if the ladder hadn't stopped him.

Nefas pulled him around like he was weightless and faced off with him, his fog still swirling all around them. His lips curled into a snarl and, though he looked nearly the same as when Fae first imagined him, his darkness had begun seeping through. His face was as twisted and vicious as all three hounds of the underworld. "I'm going to kill you." Nefas said it with such hate that this time the threat shook Lars' confidence like a knife stabbed halfway to his heart.

"I am of the light and I know truth, both of which are greater than you."

"You've seen so much, old man; you've had your eyes long enough. Let me do you the favor of relieving you of their burden."

"You have Fae to worry about, devil."

It is you who are worried . . . Nazi. Nefas' chilling voice boomed through his head and an evil laughter resounded so loudly that dust began to fall from the ceiling. He wasn't a Nazi, never was one of those, but Lars found his vocal cords were tied so he couldn't protest.

With a shove, Nefas let him go, out to the corpses waiting for him. He quickly escaped, shutting the door behind him, locking Elise and Fae inside a storm of hell brewing. The sound of the metal door echoed off the empty space in front of him. Anything could happen inside that pit, but that was no longer his concern for tonight. Tomorrow at sunrise he would return and see what damage could be mended, if any were worth the repair. He had done what he had to do. There was nothing else that could have been done for Fae Peeters.

Lars turned away from the pit to find the black door that would return him to the alley and the mob, which would surely kill him on his way back to the basilica. He would rather die trying to get to where he needed to be than wait where he didn't want to be. The problem was that he couldn't find the door. The green light that should be outlining it was nowhere to be found. It wasn't just black in here; it was completely lightless. The back of his eyes throbbed. He knew why, and he didn't want to think about it: Nefas had in fact taken his sight.

THE GIFT

Lars leaned heavily against the pit door, his chest heaving from the effort of what he had just gone through and the stress of what he was going to have to attempt next. In his sightlessness, he couldn't see his trembling hands, but he could feel them shaking. And his legs were so weak now, he wasn't sure if he could even make it up and over the lintel outside. He wanted to touch his eyes. He wondered if they were bleeding or if that was just a phantom feeling, but he couldn't make himself do it. He just needed to sit down . . . there was no place to do so.

"Jesus Christus," he said, shakily in his native German. The dead outside wouldn't touch him as long as he didn't fear, but Nefas' curse rang in his ears. For the first time in decades he truly was afraid on Christmas Eve, and that scared him more than the fear itself.

Lars closed his eyes to only more darkness and the invasion of Nefas' cruel laughter. He wouldn't even be able to navigate the streets without his vision. He tried to recall a word of hope, any word at all, but he couldn't think of even one.

"Why do you not leave this place?"

Lars' eyes flew open at the audible question and, though he couldn't see her, she was in front of him. She met him in his mind's eye and there he could vividly see her: a young Asian woman wearing a white parka and looking quite curiously at him. She spoke flawless German and he knew exactly who she was, even though he'd never met her before.

"My body and mind are betraying me. My sight . . . Nefas cursed me and I . . . I fear it's gone. I fear for my life. And if I fear, Nefas can kill me by it."

"Since when is either the body or mind stronger than the soul?" Her hair was pulled tightly into a long ponytail and it swung ever so slightly as she talked, making a small swishing sound as it brushed across the vinyl of her jacket. She smiled reassuringly, and that lightened his spirit.

"You are a good man, Lars, but you have been working against us. Why didn't you ask for help with Fae?" She paused and let the question sit. "I usually don't help in this manner, but I have a soft spot for you."

"I do only what I know is best." He hung his head. He just needed to sit down. "Can you help me?"

"Your independence makes it difficult for me to help."

"Not this time. Not tonight. My work is done, whether it was for good or not." He sighed heavily. "Maybe I *have* seen too much in my life. Take me to the Notre-Dame du Seigneur."

"That may be difficult. The power of sin and death is the power of this world. Nefas has grown strong through Fae Peeters' submission. The parasites have grown stronger in consequence."

"But he isn't the strongest."

She smiled, this time in agreement.

"Come with me. I'll make sure you get to the church. It is even more beautiful inside than before. The eyes of your soul will show you everything you need to agree."

She took up Lars' arm and he latched onto it willingly.

17

"LARS DRESCHLER!" Fae screamed up at the old man, his trimmed white beard framing those unsympathetic eyes staring down on her, uncaring of her fate. She hated him. The emotion exploded inside her from a place she didn't even know existed. It fed her fight, she felt stronger for it, so she hated him, not just because of what Nefas said about him, but because he deserved it. He might have saved her in the alley but that was only to delay her fate so that he could bring it about himself. She hated how he looked down on her, hated his self-importance, his accent, his clothes. His lips smiled victory, his eyes were as cold as his heart, and she wanted to spit in them. Nefas was so pleased with her right now. She could feel it.

Fae had seen the ladder out of the corner of her eye, the same time Lars remembered it. She bolted across the loose gravel not expecting that every step would become more and more laborious. Her struggle increased as she was sucked down deeper with every footstep.

Her right leg had sunk to the knee. With a desperate grunt of effort, Fae used her whole body to pull it up and thrust it forward. There was nothing solid for it to brace against in trying to free her left leg, and so she just sunk even more. From sheer willpower, she managed another lunging step forward, but by then she had sunk beyond the hope of getting out on her own.

After everything that she had gone through, that bastard of an old man was besting her with a ladder. Raging against the gravel trap, she sank deeper and watched helplessly as the Nazi hefted the ladder up and out of the pit, taking her defiance-by-survival with it. Fae glared up at Lars, the shadows from the lantern and the swirling iridescent fog making everything heave and spin.

Nefas was back. The heavy weight that announced his arrival had become her confidence. His musty smell was the scent of vengeance. He would make that Nazi pay. She watched with dark anticipation as Nefas grew his body out of the mist and she couldn't wait to see what he would do to that mad man.

Out of nowhere, a moment of surprisingly rational thought broke through her addled mind. *Nefas didn't kill Lars in the alley; why do you think that will change now?*

The calmness with which the question was asked dueled with the hate and daggers she was aiming at Lars' back. The war between rationality and a burning desire to see Lars suffer was so overwhelming that, by the time her hate won out, he had slipped by Nefas and all she could do was yell after him. She wasn't sure what Nefas was going to do; it seemed like nothing at the moment. But why? Lars was getting away.

She could see Nefas' blond hair over the edge of the pit and she so wanted him to appear beside her, offering his hand up; but, in the terrifying state that he was in now, she didn't know if he would be as kind to her as she wanted. There was something so alluring and powerful in him that she wasn't so sure anymore that she would take an opportunity to escape if one came. She had told herself that she was just using Nefas to get to a place of safety, but that rationale was about as motivating as starting a diet the day before Christmas. Nefas would get her out of this pit in his own time, she was sure.

He will free you only to inject you with his parasite?

It wasn't Nefas' voice that spoke, but her rational self. "Shut up!" Fae screamed slamming her fists onto the gravel, not caring that the sharp rocks bit into her hands. Nefas was watching her. She didn't care. She kept yelling at herself, trying to get her rational side to shut up! She slammed her fists down, agitating the gravel around her, each cathartic blow leaving little spots of blood behind.

She stopped once her thoughts silenced and, when she'd finally stopped, she noticed that a smooth, metal surface was exposed within arm's reach, barely peeking through settled rocks. She leaned over and cleared away some more of the stones. It didn't take much excavation before it was evident that the object was actually an old war helmet. Wiggling her fingers underneath the brim, she pulled but it resisted. Fae frowned, reached over with both hands, and yanked harder. It budged, but only a little. With one last heave she pulled it free scattering gravel into the air. Fae held in her hands a dusty German Stahlhelm helmet, but it was the small crater the helmet left behind that left her speechless. A crest of blond hair remained exposed. Before she could process what that meant, she was using the helmet to scoop more of the gravel away. At first, it was just more of the flaxen hair that was revealed, then a healthy-looking ear, then a forehead that wrinkled as the eyebrow muscles flexed. She took a deeper shovel of gravel away, and even though the gravel fell in on itself again, one eye was left exposed. It popped open wildly and Fae screamed, throwing the old helmet back on top of the head.

"Oh my god, this can't be real! I want to wake up, let me wake up, oh god . . . !" The concept that someone was buried alive beside her, buried alive and still alive, she couldn't even think about it, she couldn't . . . She was starting to feel sick and dizzy. Lars had said something about natural gases? "Nefas!" she called out. He didn't respond.

She had sunk almost up to her waist and with Lars gone, her hate had nowhere to go. *You must die to leave alive.* She didn't want to be buried alive like that man. How long had he been in here and how was he still alive? Her brain felt like it was slowing down. Were there others buried here? Was it their hands she felt from below, grabbing her ankles, trying to pull her down to join them? What if she was left in here and buried alive, buried and forgotten but never dying . . . ?

Nefas hadn't come and she dared not call for him again. Her last remaining friend, then, was the light from the kerosene lantern. It cast ringed circles through the fog, letting the dust particles dance in its wake, though even that light would soon be lost in the growing density of fog swirling and stifling the room. It was just a lamp, yet it was so brave in this place simply by doing what it was created to do: shine. Its light brought her back to her aunt and uncle who were probably transformed into those horror-story creatures. Their faith and hope in her surviving until Christmas morning had done none of them any good. The only gift she wanted from anyone now was to wake up from this nightmare and go home.

Fae burst into tears. They were as full of self-pity as they were of defeat.

All her life she had loved and trusted her grandmother. The idea that she had orchestrated her death—whatever form that took, was as unnatural as seeing the dead that weren't dead, as Nefas, as this pit. It was all wrong.

Her sobs came from the depth of an endless pit in her own gut, and all she felt was hopelessness and powerlessness. She had done everything right, believed in her ability to survive, fought, didn't give up, and here she was sinking into a pit of gravel, consumed with conflicting emotions toward the one who called himself her past and future. Her spirit was sinking faster than her body, but she knew this was how it had to be now: Her life was over. Religion had brought her here and its God still showed no mercy, no sympathy. She would surely use her last breath to curse his name.

As she was crying, she became aware of Nefas having perched himself on the pit's edge. She didn't know how long he had been there—probably not long since Elise had just started to stumble toward him dragging her feet with raspy breaths, the parasite within her flexing rhythmically. As soon as she saw him her self-pity dried up and so did her breath. She had never seen anything so ferocious, not a wolf on the kill nor a tiger in attack. His black vest had been torn open, the gray shirt beneath showing every twitch of tense muscle. His face was charged with a maniacal craze that made him look like he had fought hand-to-hand combat for hours, and the animalistic quality was more terrifying and astonishing to look at than either the wolf or the tiger.

"The sound of your hopeless crying hasn't changed since you were three," he spat, the words cutting through her.

With an athletic hop, Nefas jumped down into the pit, his feet landing solidly atop the gravel. He did not sink. Despite everything, Fae still wanted to touch him.

"Just before I kill that Nazi by making him drink the blood I pull from his heart, I will thank him for helping me. Because of him I've decided to share my mind with you; I'm going to transform you from the inside out."

"He got away," she said. It was the wrong thing to say. Before she realized what was happening, Nefas was beside her, pushing her head down into the gravel. The weight of his presence came so heavily and so suddenly that she was left desperately fighting for breath.

"I entertained your little fascination with that man once," he snapped into her ear. She struggled under his hand but he just pressed down harder. "The next time you say his name it will be in eulogy damning his soul." Watching her struggle to breathe, Nefas let her go and he sat back on his heels, helping her straighten up and gently wrapping his arm around her shoulders. With a tenderness that made her want to cling to him forever, he said, "Nod if you understand."

Fae nodded and Nefas stayed with her until she was able to breathe normally again. Standing back up, he noticed the helmet. With a flip of his toe, he tossed it away to reveal that the once youthful head beneath was rapidly aging before Fae's very eyes.

"Wilhelm Fuhrman. He was twenty-one. Great friends with a certain other Nazi we both know. His company came here to collect some villagers for the German war machine, but when he fled from my family, he thought the alley outside was a shortcut to get out." Nefas began casually scraping stones over the aging man's head with his foot. "After being packed away for so long, exposure to the air is catching him up to his proper age. He's been missing in action for so long already, let's keep him for another time, when he's useful to me." Nefas finished burying the head with a few more swipes of his foot. "They wanted to lock you in here for the night and retrieve you in the morning so you wouldn't have any information to sell to the papers." He scowled. "Through you the world will know enough now to send a fury of seekers into my arms. I have other uses for you too, but I need you alive. I will send you back home, alive only to me and dead to everything else, cloaked in the same disguise you wear now. First though, there's just one matter that must be resolved: from the inside out."

Fae nodded, but she would have nodded if he had said he was leaving her here for decades, or that he was selling her as a mail-order bride . . . she simply accepted what he told her.

Nefas brushed some hair away from her ear before leaning in close, inches away. He gently blew on her, causing a blend of intense pain and pleasure to tingle up her back—pain and pleasure, hot and cold, he was a master of conflict.

He whispered words into her she did not understand as he gently walked his fingers up her vertebrae, not yet sunk into the gravel. With each vertebra his fingers touched, another dark sensation was sent careening through her flesh, spoiling her. Ruining her. The more he whispered, the more embarrassed she became, then shamed, then darkly curious. When his fingers finished their march at the base of her skull, he closed his fist tight around the back of her neck and held it fast, as though he wanted to wrap his fingers around her spine.

Then he began to speak into her ear sounding again more like her tantalizing Voice, but words she could not understand. His words stirred up the chaos churning within her, hopelessness and hope, hate and revenge, lust and desire, power and fear, control and dominion. She couldn't tell which way was up, where she was; even her name was hard to find. "I alone will save you. I will give everything you need, so you won't feel the pain." As he spoke, she saw from her peripherals a stream of green smoke pour out of his mouth and travel first into her left ear, then split and go around to her left, into her eyes, through her mouth. She inhaled. Shuddering, she closed her eyes against the cool wave easing itself inside.

She felt her memory assert itself, and she recalled images of Lars interacting with Nefas, talking with him, seeing him. Fae gasped as though woken from unconsciousness. *Nefas is not a madness from my mind. Who is he?* It was just one question before she would be completely taken over by him. One question that would tell her the real cost of leaving this village as alive as he was. Would he allow just one question?

She non-threateningly grabbed onto his arm, though it felt like her own arm was twenty pounds heavier than she remembered. It was the first time she had touched him on her own, and she had no emotion about it. Those emotions couldn't be found in the swirling chaos he had created in her. "Who are you?" The words were thick and sloppy on a tongue having nearly forgotten its purpose. What was he doing to her?

Nefas gave one last breath, and waited until the smoke disappeared inside her before he allowed the fingers clutching her spine to slip around her neck, then slide up to her jaw. He captured her chin and guided her head around to face him.

"I am purity from light," he began, an intimate moment shared between two. "I am the night of your nightmare; the cloak for the dagger; your terror of the unseen. What I call perfect others call diseased and abhorrent, but I am your every desire. I am what you need to wake up in the morning and to sleep at night. I am the enemy you keep closer than a friend."

Nefas released her jaw, then pushed it away so that he had the side of her head again and exhaled. The stream of green smoke trailed back into her ears, into her eyes. He continued to speak words she still could not understand. There was nothing left to see in this life. With Elise's rotten face peering down at her, Fae closed her eyes and her mind blanked.

"Give in to the darkness of your soul."

18

The void.

It grew quickly, spilling out and enveloping everything, erasing traces of anything that had been there before. Where once there was life and freedom, there remained only darkness. It came up out of her soul, and Fae was restrained against doing anything to stop it. With eyes she didn't know she possessed, she watched it grow throughout her body. It came higher and higher, until at last it reached into her mind, and then no longer did she watch it. She was inside of it and it consumed her.

Instantly, Fae had knowledge of the void. It was not a vast waste of timelessness and endlessness that suddenly appeared from nothing. It had been deep inside her, waiting all along, and it was a new space for existence though there was nothing in it. It would be impossible for a void to co-exist with anything other than itself.

Awoken and allowed to consume, there would be no stopping it, no slowing it or negotiating with it, and no escaping it. Only the creator of the void, a mind as dark and insatiable as its creation, could add to it things which could endure the isolation, the sensory deprivation, the perfect darkness. Only the creator could allow a thought to enter, or a desire, and so sweet it would be in such a place as this. It could be horrid and wretched, but Fae would treasure and hoard it as a show of great benevolence. And so, as she watched the spreading void, Fae had the same understanding of a slave watching her master's branding iron sear into her skin: This would be with her forever.

The void had no form, no constraints, no color or illumination, nothing solid to stand on, only a never-ending sense of falling. There was no wind rushing past her or visual clues to mark the distance as she fell, so it was impossible to know for sure if she was falling. She simply knew that she was. She fell deeper and deeper into darkness without end, to such depths that her brain was pained and it suffered to fight for a way to tear through and come free. She had fallen so far already. There would eventually come a place so dark and so deep that she would never be able to come back.

As she fell, there came in the distance a nebulous mass, beautiful, with flowing electric blues and purples and yellows. Fae fell upon it fast, enticed by its allure, and as she came to it she saw that there was something in it. What it was, she couldn't tell, but then she fell into it and through it, and she suddenly knew all the secrets that were hidden inside. They were as dark as the void, and Fae felt wrongly changed.

There were other nebulous masses: orange and gold, red and indigo, green and blue and silver. Each beguiling façade of colors she fell through held only more terrible images, uncharted feelings, and entrapping fascinations. Some of these gifts she already knew in their immature form, some were fashioned for her now, and others were to be known later; but, all of them were hers and became a part of her. It was with these gifts that she understood what kind of future Nefas wanted her to have. No one could know she had such things inside her; so as soon as the gifts came, she buried each of them deep inside where such things could fester by themselves until they couldn't be contained anymore—or until curiosity brought her back to them. The more she fell, the harder she tried to miss the nebulae or to stop falling, but it was futile—she was Alice falling into the devil's Wonderland.

At what point the darkness stopped revealing its secrets and she stopped falling, Fae didn't know, any more than she would've been able to know the precise moment of falling asleep. She simply found herself aware of tangible surroundings with the need to open her eyes. Her head spun with exhaustion, and she felt like part of it was left behind somewhere. Where, she couldn't say; she remembered nothing but the residual feeling of *something*—an indiscernible shadow of her dreams.

She was still in the pit. The green fog whorl had stopped and now hovered calmly, but the pit was far from calm. Nefas was no longer beside her, but was instead in front of her. More exactly, there was a pair of legs in front of her through which she could see Nefas. This new arrival and Nefas were arguing heatedly, their voices carrying around the stone hive. The stranger was speaking accented English.

"This is your strength against mine," Nefas said darkly. "You have no room to make demands."

"I have no strength or power of my own, nor is it necessary to have any," the stranger responded, unfazed. "You know who you're really fighti—"

"By your own laws, interrupting my possession of that one behind you makes your position *very* precarious." Nefas was pointing at her, and he aggressively shifted the weight on his feet. The stranger didn't flinch.

"Don't mistake her gift of choice as your right. By our laws, I have every authority to interrupt any forceful thing you're doing, to preserve that kindness."

"That woman is mine by her choice, my product; I don't care what you call it, but get out of my way."

The stranger backed up a few paces, resting on the balls of his feet, knees slightly bent in a fighter's stance. The man was going to get himself killed. He didn't know what Nefas could do. He was close enough to her now that Fae could see the stitching on his brown shoes, and in noting that, it dawned on her that, like Nefas, he wasn't sinking into the pit. The stranger took a moment to look down over his shoulder at her and she immediately recognized him as the man who had let her into Lars' apartment earlier that night.

"You're awake," he said, his voice kind. He didn't allow himself the pleasure of any further external shows of amicability.

Nefas growled a cry of protest. Fae watched his feet crunch heavily across the gravel until the crunch of the gravel stopped. They must have been nearly nose to nose.

"Choices can always be made again," the stranger said. "It is the consequences which cannot be so easily removed. I will never stop persuading her." The stranger half turned his head to address her, but not so that he lost sight of Nefas. "Never count out the efforts of a persistent grandmother, Fae. Not even when all hope is gone." Then he addressed Nefas again. "I am taking her from this place and neither you nor your . . . things will stop us."

"You cannot stop me from persuading her," Nefas mocked, replicating the stranger's voice.

The stranger snorted, though he was cut short by the rattling of gravel nearby. From where the German helmet rested, a shaking was happening, the stones sifting away. The ground continued to became more violent until the soldier's fist punched through from below and shot small rocks into the air. The soldier's hand immediately snapped onto the stranger's leg and pulled, sweeping the unsuspecting man to the ground. Then the soldier's other arm punched up through the gravel and began reeling the stranger in, hand over hand. The helmet began to rise out of the gravel as the young soldier was slowly brought out of his burial by an unseen force. First it was just his helmet, then his eyes, the collar of his dark uniform jacket—Nefas was raising him up.

Fae watched with pity that this stranger would come to know Nefas' wrath. He was fighting to get his leg back, kicking the soldier in the face; but, the soldier just kept pulling him in. Then in a flurry of motion, the stranger had the soldier's neck wrapped between his legs and the two struggled for dominance.

"No more interruptions." Nefas left the stranger to battle and came for her. He knelt beside her and Fae couldn't help but flinch, seeing what he had become. Gone was the treasure of his handsomeness, and in its place was a child's mocking imitation scrawled in crayon. His skin was covered in the ripe colors of heavy bruising and jaundice. The ferocity of his features was sagging from loose skin and even the bags under his eyes drooped, showing too much of what was supposed to be covered. His fiery green eyes were gone, replaced by holes so black she couldn't look into them without having the void flash up again, throwing her back into its endless fall of darkness and shame.

A grunt to her left said that the stranger's struggle was almost over. Just as the man in the white coat choked-out the soldier, a second pair of arms exploded out of the gravel and grabbed him, starting a second fight. Even as she saw it happen, two cold hands snapped around her ankles from below. This time it was not her imagination. She screamed, squirming to get away, trying to push herself out with her arms.

"It's almost over. Forget your life before." As Nefas spoke, the corners of his mouth ripped open and he opened his jaw wide—testing how far it would stretch. He reached down and grabbed her hair, pulled her head back, and exposed her throat to the dangers of this world.

"My God, Jesus, NO!" the stranger hollered, shaking the whole room. Puffs of dust fell from the ceiling as he struggled to his feet, victorious. Instantly, Nefas let her go, clutching his ears in pain as if to escape a piercing sound only he could hear and a strong wind rose up, aimed only at him. Where a wind that strong came from hardly mattered; Nefas fought against it to keep his footing, and he struggled to prevent himself from being pinned against the pit wall. With a savage growl ripping the sides of his mouth even more, Nefas managed to motion his hand toward Elise still prowling the ledge, and he threw her into the pit like a hated ragdoll. Her corpse flailed in the air; Fae barely ducked in time to miss a collision, and Elise smashed into the wall nearby. There was a disgusting *crack* and Fae looked over to see Elise tangled up in herself and the parasite working hard to pick the body back up—a task made even harder as Elise began to sink.

With Nefas howling and raging against the wind, the stranger, breathing hard and his white jacket dirtied, scrambled over to Fae. He hooked his arms beneath her shoulders and pulled her out as easily as pulling a young child out of a pool, her legs easily slipping through the bony hands below trying to manacle her down.

"Your grandmother is insistent," the stranger said with a new sense of urgency that hadn't been there before. "Excuse me." He picked up her from around the waist and tossed her over the lip of the pit. He followed behind, jumping the eight feet with a hop and pull-up that made the feat look as easy as jumping into the back of a truck. "Don't look back."

He threw open the old metal door and brought her into the darkness beyond. Nefas continued howling and screaming after them, sounding more like a vengeful wraith than a human. When they got to the black door, the man simply placed her arms around his waist and said, "Whatever you do, don't let go." He threw open the door to the packed alley of glowing green corpses waiting for them. She tried to pull him back inside, for her own sake if not his, but he just covered her hands with his and forged ahead into the mass.

Fae couldn't watch, couldn't look at the skulls with wispy hair, reflecting everything she wanted to forget about her hotel mirror. Burying her face in the stranger's back, Fae let him take her out of this place. She was holding on too tightly, but he never complained. She wished that somehow he could just absorb her into himself, and then this would all be over.

The stranger led them at a quick pace, though it wasn't without a struggle. His whole body was in action, and she couldn't tell if he was fighting the corpses, pushing them, or throwing them; sometimes, it even felt like he was pulling them. Whatever he was doing, the two of them were moving, and the farther they were from that black door, the more she felt like this was the right thing to do and she felt a small tinge of hope; though, she was no less scared of what Nefas would do if he found her guilty of the escape.

Fae didn't need to look up to see the corpses. She remembered them. The old lady with one less hand, Maël with his torn skin hanging from his cheek, the teenager being trampled. Their hands pawed at her. Even though they grabbed for her, they couldn't keep a grip. They tugged and pulled, but it amounted to nothing. All around, she could hear their moans and raspy breathing and the sounds of their shuffling feet on cobblestone and in the crunchy snow. When she couldn't keep her eyes shut any longer, she saw the booted and shoed feet packed in tightly, right next to hers. The only difference between hers and theirs was that hers were moving faster.

Eventually, they broke free. The corpses' groans and wheezing grew faint, and there were no more hands pulling at her. They went a little farther before the stranger stopped and at his assurance, Fae lifted her face out of his shoulder. She had no idea where they were. La Rue was gone while tall, lit evergreens and close-quartered houses hid the basilica spires. The snow was falling so innocently, dancing and landing with grace and poise on their eyelashes and jackets. The serenity was lost on her.

"We are out of immediate danger, but Nefas won't be stayed. He will come for you again, and his creatures are following us."

"So where can I go? Nefas can go anywhere. We can't outrun him." Her need for Nefas was waning now that she was away from him, and with that came increased aversion. She looked at the stranger, not ashamed to show how scared she was. She hadn't paid him much attention at Lars' apartment, but she did now. He was about average height, lean like a runner, and ageless, despite the white hair. He could've been twenty-five or forty; it was difficult to guess.

"There is one place he can't go. But stay to my side this time. It is easier to travel quickly when my heel is not colliding with your shin." Clasping her hand in his, the stranger set off again, his eyes always forward.

Once they cleared the roofs and evergreens, it became clear where they were headed. They wove and crisscrossed through side streets trying to keep as direct a route as possible while avoiding the stray corpses stumbling aimlessly about. The stranger didn't say much, and she was grateful for his focus, though he did take the time to tell her how to differentiate the color of the parasites from the color of Christmas lights. It wasn't long before she could predict their course changes based on the shade of green lighting up the snow and bouncing off walls. At one point, they passed a group of corpses surrounding the glass door of an empty commercial space and, by the sound of shattering glass, Fae knew they were breaking in. The stranger pointed out the lack of wine and bread in the front window.

Not far from the basilica, they turned onto a main street which ran straight to it; however, ahead of them the parasites' glow was like an evil horizon raging against the night. Corpses had overflown into the street like a slow drain. Some were swaying to keep their balance, a few shuffled around but were going nowhere, and even more were just standing stationary.

Fae grabbed the stranger's arm and pulled him back to a stop.

"We can't go this way."

"Every tributary will be occupied. Just keep holding onto me and do not stop moving."

He set off again and Fae grudgingly stayed with him and fought the urge that told her to go in the opposite direction of those hell-bent corpses. But where there were corpses, there Nefas could be found, and she felt an inexplicable desire for him rise up. Something about the void in her needed to be with him, he who had been her confidence and hope, the one who had given so much of himself to stay with her.

The stranger didn't slow down for second guesses, and so she couldn't either.

The corpses caught sight of them and dragged their feet toward them, but Fae and the stranger outpaced them. Passing the corpses, Fae made the mistake of looking over her shoulder. The horde was catching up to them, their numbers blocking the road as they came. This was the pincher of la Rue all over again.

They slipped through the sparse corpses easily enough, but that luck didn't last. When they finally came to the plaza surrounding the great basilica, she fully saw what lay before them, and she faltered. Fae pulled back shaking her head.

"Not a chance."

"Don't fear," the stranger said with assurance.

"A little fear right now is a good thing."

"Not here, and not now. Here, it will get you killed."

The Basilique de Notre-Dame du Seigneur was a stony island in the middle of a green sea, rocking and swaying with the tide of barely moving bodies—hundreds and hundreds and hundreds of them. Fires in old oil barrels had burned low, each one containing a setting sun flickering its last warmth for hands that no longer concerned themselves with warmth. The corpses took over the plaza all the way up to the steps of the basilica itself, and they made as horrendous a sound of malicious intent as they did a heart-stopping sight.

"No, not a chance," She repeated, pulling back on his arm. "My nine lives are up. Let's just break into that store over there and hide out or something. Running into churches for refuge has never been my thing." She tried to pull him away, but he didn't budge.

"Have you forgotten so soon how we left the alley?"

"I wasn't looking—I can't forget what I didn't see."

"Well, you are here and no longer there, that's enough to remember. Hide your face again in my shoulder if you want."

Fae gripped his arm even tighter, hugged it close, and kept pace with him. What if Nefas showed up? What would she do? Or maybe the question had to be, what *could* she do? Biting the inside of her lip, she steeled herself as best as she was able, and together they set themselves to crossing the green sea.

Despite the unnatural grotesques that stalked the grounds, the Notre-Dame du Seigneur still drew focus to itself both as a lighthouse of refuge and as a wonder and she set her focus on it to keep her feet from failing and heart from quailing. It was dramatically spotlighted in white and, for Christmas, she'd been told, red as well. Not one of the six spires, or the two towers guarding the entrance, nor any of the other entrances around the body of the building, not even one corner was forgotten to the night. The three portal doors in the front were red as candied cherries, and the rest of the building was as bright as the moon. The basilica's aged and tired white stone walls and its beautiful stained glass windows framing the top of the façade presented themselves no less proudly than an old veteran donning their parade uniform once again. Even though its base was consumed by the green light of dancing evil, the iron guard door in front of the main entryway remained open, showing the powerfully simple wreath hanging on the wooden door.

She had seen the building during the day and found much to be intrigued by, but she had never thought it could become so stunning and emphatic at night. It wasn't just a building; it was a living thing. She had visited many of the major churches—St. Stephen's in Vienna, the Notre-Dame de Reims, the Duomo di Milano, the churches of Seville, and York Minster, Rome, Cologne, and Chartres, the Notre-Dame de Paris. They had all been undeniably beautiful, but this one, this basilica made her *feel*. It should have been natural to accept the feeling of relief she was experiencing at the prospect of getting inside; but, after so many years of striving to be emotionally guarded when inside any type of church, it was defeating to acknowledge that she might be falling in love with this one—that it might even keep her alive. As she struggled with these emotions, a heavy reluctance also began rising up the closer she got to the church that made her feet heavier and slower. Nefas didn't want her in there. Yet, before she knew it, her feet found the stone steps rising up out of the cobblestone. She had arrived.

The stranger was gone. She didn't know when he had left or where he had gone. Panic for his safety made her search for his white hair in the sea of shadowed skulls and ethereal green, but there was nothing to be found that was not dead. She couldn't see any signs of struggle that would suggest he had been caught along the way, but she did notice a perfectly formed semicircle around the steps where no corpses dared to follow her. Even though they looked as eager as ever to get to her, their feeble attempts at passing through the invisible barrier weren't enough. She felt her hope rise that this place was really going to be safe. Had the situation been any less grave, she would have found humor in the irony of spotting a corpse as rotten as the rest wearing a pair of stylish eyeglasses and a black shirt with a white collar: the priest. Indiscernible from the rest of his flock, the visual was undeniably satisfying.

"Hey, Priest," she called out to him, "looks like we still have nothing to talk about."

A sharp urging spurred her to finish her flight up the stairs and she did, but as she passed underneath the archivolt with its carved figures of stone, a certain cloaked stone figure standing behind a skeletal human being caught her eye.

It still speaks to you, doesn't it?

Nefas! Fae's skin crawled at his sound. She spun around in a circle, but he was nowhere to be seen.

He had found her—followed her?—and she was going to have to make the decision she didn't want to make. Maybe he'd let her think about it inside. There were only a dozen or so steps to get to the ironwood door, but now her eye caught on the archivolt a second time. Green fog poured heavily and fast out of the stone images. Tearing herself away from the entrancing archivolt, Fae bumped right into the solid body of Nefas standing firm in her path. He had donned a jacket over his vest and gray T-shirt, not because it was cold— It remained unzipped—but because a long hood hid his face in shadow, leaving only the end of his nose and chin peeking out.

"It's our story, Fae," he said as he reached out and flicked some dirt off her shoulder. "It should mean something to you."

She backed away out of his reach, and he followed in sync with her movements.

"If you walk through those doors, you are just like the people inside."

"I don't have to be anything I don't want to be," she said, taking another step back. "I'm just a tourist taking in the sights."

"At 2:00 a.m.? *Tsk* You should be sleeping if you are a tourist in such a boring place. We both know you're no tourist. You're no more able to open the door to this building on your own than I am." He stepped forward again and she backed away, keeping the distance.

You are mine. Fae closed her eyes against the sound of his beautiful voice and she knew she was losing her will to leave him. Those gifts in the void, only he could give her more. The image of his jaws ripping open as he screamed flashed before her mind's eye, and she snapped her eyes open to get rid of it.

"I don't belong to anyone but myself."

Nefas laughed, genuinely amused, the sound of dying hyenas and an eagle falling out of the sky. "The more you talk, the funnier you are. Consider this," Nefas began. "When you were still a young child, I told you to question and doubt everything you were told so that you wouldn't believe stupid things; ironically, you did without question. Then once you thought more reasonably, I told you to stop questioning, because only idiots wouldn't accept the obvious; and, again, you did so without question. In fact, you've done everything I told you to do since coming to me in this village; so, please, continue lying to yourself that you are a free being with no master but yourself."

That was the second time he'd mentioned her childhood. She thought of the shadow monster that sometimes waited at the top of the stairs and the memory brought back old fears she didn't need right now. "I chose to do all those things because that's what I wanted to do."

"No, that's what *I* wanted you to do! I only let you think it was your idea—you were more likely to do it without a fuss that way. Take my hand," he commanded, extending his. "We'll finish what we began. I have put so much into you already; you're not strong enough to resist"

Now that they were together again, he was stirring something inside her. He was her Voice, would always be her Voice, the one to save her. That fact shone brighter than everything else he'd put her through . . . her hand met his.

A brilliant flash of light went off in Fae's mind—so bright her eyes were left with dancing dots in front of them. She dropped his hand and, for a second, she saw her own rotting face peering out from beneath his hood before it faded away along with the bright dancing dots. She remembered now the gifts from the void and not just their fascination, but their horrors and shames as well. She felt naked before him; vulnerable. Her eyes flicked to the church door behind him. She didn't dare let them linger.

"Let yourself go where you've always wanted to be; be captivated by everything you desire."

"You've always known what I've wanted."

Nefas stepped toward her again and this time she didn't retreat. "You were right to think that your reflection in the mirror wasn't just a nightmare. It is you as you are right now. To prove it I could flay you open here on the steps of the most notorious institution of bloodshed the world has ever known to show you what lays beneath your pretty skin and bones—your soul. I've nearly finished branding you, and what you call a parasite is an honor not everyone is so lucky to have. Take my hand again and I promise you will know the all the truth you need, to be everything you dreamed of. You will feel and see more than you have ever seen or felt."

Her dreams and desires swelled up along with those given to her in the void as Nefas spoke, mudding her mind with their dark waters. What was "refuge" in a church building, when she could indulge in these things which so she shamefully and desirously wanted? They didn't seem so horrible in retrospect, but adventurous.

"You offer me your hand now but, in the pit, you didn't. Do you trust me more now?"

Nefas stiffened at the question and then jerked away from her. "I trust you even less, you little tramp, running away with a man who wants to take you from me. I take what is mine. I'm merely giving you the luxury of agreeing."

"I didn't have a choice back there in the pit; he just took me!"

"Tell me that you didn't want to go with him, that you didn't hold onto him tight, that you don't want to go inside this church. TELL ME!"

"I . . ."

"You turned your back on the God mythology a long time ago having refused the lies of his Church and fought against their crusades. Still, you have your eyes set on entering that door for help as though it isn't going to retch you back out like the piece of rot that you are."

"I'm cold, Nefas, and tired. It's warm in there."

"Then let me warm you." She could hear the smile in his voice, and it was not a pleasant one. "You are as big a hypocrite as they are."

"No! Never! I'd rather be dead than one of them."

"But you are dead."

"I can't be, you said you were saving me from death."

"Relativism." Nefas straightened himself and came closer to her again, forming a formidable barrier to the ironwood door. "I'm protecting you from death from me."

Why he didn't grab her and do what he wanted to with her she couldn't say, but she wondered if the invisible line the corpses couldn't cross had something to do with it. The snow was starting to fall more heavily though still calmly; Fae shivered, feeling the cold creeping into her toes. "Let me inside, just for a few minutes. You've given me so much; I can't stay away for long. You know me, so you know it's true."

Just then a metallic click echoed from the ironwood door and the stranger with white hair and dirtied white jacket strolled out, hands stuffed into his jeans pockets.

THE GIFT

"Miss Peeters wants inside, Nefas." The stranger raised his eyebrows as though asking if there was going to be any trouble. "And I've had enough of you for one night." Fae's eyes followed Nefas, fully expecting him to attack the stranger.

"My name is Dominic," the stranger said, extending his hand toward Fae. "It's about time I introduced myself properly." She was very aware of Nefas watching her, so she didn't offer her hand in return. "Don't fear anymore, Fae Peeters; it will kill you, remember? Nefas can't stop you from doing anything—maybe make it difficult sometimes," he said with a wry smile. "He can't hurt you while you're on the stones of this church. Come inside where you can warm up, listen to the choir sing, get some sleep if you want."

"I don't hear anyone singing." Fae said warily.

"No?" Dominic looked surprised. "They're really loud."

"Claws scraped down a chalkboard, why would I let her hear that?" Nefas said. "Your father relied on the church to fix his problems and he was a useless bigot; your mother wound up dead. All your dark little secrets from the void are mine to share."

"They're mine, you can't!" All she had to do was take Nefas' hand again and he would return to being the help and the friend she had first known him to be.

"Confess your sins. You should be proud I chose you for them. Confessions get easier after the first one, don't they Dominic?"

"Fae," Dominic re-established eye contact with her. "How are those scratches on your throat feeling? How about your leg?"

Fae dropped her eyes from him. Those were just the start of her shames, and those were just the external ones she couldn't hide. There were hundreds more from the void. She fingered her throat where Nefas' fingers had scraped her, and she found some dried blood she picked away as though that would erase the fact that the marks were even there. Those injuries were her fault— *Yes they were your fault. But imagine what I can do for you when you've made me happy. I know what you want.*

"Fae," Dominic gently called to get her attention again. "You deserve better." Dominic put his hand on the ironwood door as though to open it for her. "I told you, don't fear, and don't look behind. Nefas may have shown up in your face, but he came from your past. He might know what you want, but he knows nothing of what you need."

Her two warring sides were not helping in this moment. For every argument Dominic made, she knew that there was a church at the other end trying to save her; and for all her need for, and loyalty to, Nefas, all she could hear was the sound of her own pain, the heavy clink of slow-moving chains, and the wheezing coming from her rotted-out throat.

"Come, and you'll be exactly where your grandmother wanted you to be all along. She didn't betray you like Nefas made it look."

It was as though no matter which choice she made, it would be the wrong one.

You go through those doors and there will be nothing you can do afterward to appease me.

Nefas stood strong before her, but he was in her head.

I'm not becoming religious by going in. What if I can bring you the German? She remembered what he'd said about speaking Dreschler's name. There was a long pause and then Fae felt the approving touch of her Voice as she had first known Nefas, sliding down her shoulders. How was it that he could be so different at the exact same time?

I will name the one I want when the time comes. If you can do that, I'll let you be.

Fae made her decision, and she allowed Dominic to lead the way past a very dark figure in jeans and an unzipped hooded jacket. She could smell the sweet, woody scent of the pine wreath on the way in.

19

It had been a long time since Fae had stepped inside her first European church. She had only been a kid then, and it was the Notre-Dame de Paris. Her jaw had hung open for the whole tour and the old churches had only continued to impress from there. The riches of gold gilding on every curve, rare marbles for the floors, priceless paintings and statues giving life to the often dreary gray stone, and dwarfing altars—all promoted their remorseless arrogance in having once been the outposts for a governing power that could rival any empire throughout history. These were the buildings where you looked to the ceiling to see some of their most prized treasures, and down to the tombs in the floors to be reminded of the mortality of everyone who built and created these things of immortality. Over time and with increased familiarity, the power of cathedrals and basilicas over Fae had disappeared, but her fascination with their architecture had never waned.

Each church was unique, but some things never changed. They all had votive candles huddled in front of some relic or altar, flickering in unison; loud, stained glass windows; hushed, human voices; and cool, stirring air greeting visitors into their cavernous glories. Some churches had begun piping Gregorian-styled chants through hidden speakers to stave off the quiet, but basilicas were always places where private actions were to be spoken louder than public words. When she walked past Dominic holding the door for her, she found the exception.

The long stone interior was ringing with the song of innumerable people wandering the floors everywhere, singing in perfect timing and tune with one another, and without missing a note or an entrance. The amount of training they must've done . . . they were . . . beyond incredible. She quickly observed that these singers were all at the prime of life and were as diverse as the nations—which defied all expectations for a remote village's church choir. Crossing paths here and slipping around pillars there, some had their eyes closed while some danced to the beat of the song. Others caught her standing there and smiled while never missing a step, or a note. Their song sounded vaguely familiar. It came from someplace long ago that was once a favorite memory but was now forgotten. Then the song changed, transitioning seamlessly into another. This time she knew the lyrics, but the tune was different and it was somehow more beautiful.

Taking in her surroundings, Fae looked up to the ceiling, which was a simple coffering pattern of golden rosettes set in white squares. Enormous candle chandeliers hung at regular intervals from the ceiling, and glass-covered torches, angled away from each pillar forming the aisles, ran the length of the nave and shamed anyone who thought that electricity was the only proper way to light a large space. Then there were two small apses to either side of the entrance doors, one housing a marble statue of a dancing woman, and the other a painting of one man drowning and the other standing on the water with his hand stretched outward to help: Peter and Jesus.

Fae looked for Dominic, for him to explain all this but she caught him instead disappearing into the slow flurry of singers. None minded her as she tentatively walked deeper into the basilica. Snowflakes or stars, either one would describe them as they swallowed her up in their movements and their songs. Full of wonder, Fae delicately stepped up the basilica's nave, and her feet carried her past the last worn, dark wooden benches, then the second to last, then the next, and the next. Her feet were making decisions for her, and she trusted them to take her where she needed to go, for otherwise she would end up being too distracted by these singers and wandering with them. There were a few people sitting quietly throughout the pews—real, alive people who weren't walking glow sticks. They also seemed too wrapped up in the songs of the choir to heed her, which she preferred.

As she came closer to the altar at the front, the singers opened a path before her and Fae found herself coming to the end of the central aisle. There, in front of the altar, was a small clearing in the choir where stood a grandfatherly man and a young teenager. The man was rhythmically waving his hands in the air. Fae guessed that she had found the director of this choral group. The boy looked on in approval and, when he saw her emerge from the crowd, he waved before returning his attention to the director.

She had come to the end. To the right was an empty pew. She slipped into it, settling herself in the middle, no one noticing her. Sitting in the midst of a slow flurry of heaven's singing stars, Fae wanted nothing but a bit of privacy and rest.

Fae gently closed her eyes and deeply breathed in the warmth to heat her lungs and stave off the shakes that came with thawing out and letting the last few hours settle as reality. The exhale came slowly. Her shoulders fell loose as the peace and safety of this place wrapped her up and held her close. The song quieted and a lone, gentle voice rose from all the others singing, *All is well, all is well, lift up your voice and sing. Born is now Emmanuel, born is our Lord and Savior.* Soon the whole basilica was echoing with the song, and nothing else mattered.

She slowly opened her eyes and breathed deeply again. The air was sweet and calming, like water to a thirsty tongue or shade on a scorching day. It was wrong that she should be feeling like this. Architecture was art; beautiful architecture could make you feel emotion. Strong architecture and engineering could make you feel secure, but it couldn't emit emotion of its own. And yet, powerful music aside, Fae was feeling an emotion not her own, and it was helping her to not only recover, but to not yet resign or give up. Why she felt like she was being given a second wind, she didn't know. Maybe her body was still running high, not realizing that she was safe, or maybe it was a simple testament to the wonder of this choir.

The choir wandered as the celestial bodies seemed to in the night sky, their energy not letting them stand still. They sang without stop, sometimes with the strength, energy, and excitement of Broadway performers and other times with the gentleness of a lullaby, yet no song ever felt out of place. Not all songs were Christmas carols. There were carols she tended to know, but their arrangements no ear had heard—for if they had, tears would be as common as the gently falling snow outside. There were no instruments; none were needed. These were songs so untouched by human flaw that she couldn't speak, for whatever came out of her own mouth would be boorish and vulgar in comparison.

Fae didn't know how long she had been sitting there when a woman with gray pants and a black button-up shirt came and sat down beside her. Her short, auburn hair poked out from beneath her saggy wool hat, barely holding onto the back of her head. Red lipstick drew attention to her face, and handmade string bracelets were heavily stacked on one wrist. A small canvas messenger bag was slung across her chest, and this she let rest between Fae and herself.

"You're the new girl?"

Fae gave her a short, polite grin and nod.

"It's too bad you weren't here for the opening," the woman said. "It was spectacular. The finale is my favorite anyway; makes me cry every time. Glad you made it all the same." She spoke perfect English and didn't bother hushing her voice, which embarrassed Fae. Again, Fae gave a nod of acknowledgement. "You're looking a little beat up; are you OK?"

"Rough landing. I'll be fine," Fae said with a hushed voice, hoping that the young woman would follow suit.

The woman accepted that. "I was supposed to greet you at the door." She reached inside her bag, pulled out a booklet, and held it out for Fae to take.

"No thanks, I don't need one," she refused.

"It's just a program. I'm not soliciting," she laughed lightly. "You're a bit of a quick judge, aren't you?"

"Fool me once . . ." Fae left the adage hang, but she took the program anyway. Her name had been skillfully scripted across the top. "Thanks." She set the program in her lap.

"I'm Anaiah. It's a boy's name, but I've always thought it sounded pretty cool. I'm not even Jewish. I go by Anna."

"Fae."

"Well, I'm glad you made it, fashionably late, right? So long as Nefas gets the short end of the stick." With that, the woman stood up and began to side-step her way out of the pew.

"I'm sorry, what did you say?"

Anna stopped. "I said, anytime Nefas has a bad night, it's a good night for us."

"What makes you think he's having a bad night?"

"Well, you're here and not out there. Means he didn't get his way, right?"

"That's not very nice."

Anna gave her a curious look. "We're talking about the same Nefas?" She side-stepped back and sat down again. "How did you know to come in here?"

"It's a church that's open all the time. I can come and go as I want. Maybe we can talk afterward Anna, I don't want to miss any of this."

"If you come and go, you really will miss it, won't you?" Anna smiled, then pointed around them to the choir. "We'll be singing and dancing until sun-up. We don't perform for you or these others sitting here so, don't worry, our talking won't bother them. They have greater things on their mind."

Fae shifted in her seat to a more comfortable position. "You're a member of the choir?"

Anna grinned and, catching the song, she flawlessly joined in, her voice melting into the greater sound. She sung a few bars, then dropped out again, the elation from the short experience lighting up her eyes.

"The director doesn't mind?"

"That man up there isn't our director. He gets the title because he gets to stand in the middle of us and see what we see. And the boy with him is last year's. The previous director stays to help the new one through the experience."

"So, what do you see? Or does he see?"

"Something different every time. A painting for a thousand words falls completely short of what I see, and a thousand paintings more couldn't describe what I feel when I see it."

Fae looked at the boy and the man, his mouth moving with quiet words, and she could see a glitter of tears tracing down his aged cheeks. He was experiencing something, that was for sure.

"So what do you have against Nefas?" Fae decided to play innocent. The less Anna knew or suspected about her relationship with him, the better. "I've heard his name once or twice since I've gotten here, so he can't be that bad."

"That often?" Anna raised an eyebrow in surprise, if not disbelief. "There usually isn't much talk about someone no one wants to remember. What have you heard?"

"His name, that's about it. Really, just enough to make me curious."

"Curious?" Anna suddenly became serious, the friendly welcome gone. "Fae, you've seen a whole lot more than you should've, haven't you?" She put her hand reassuringly on Fae's. "That's why you were late. That's where Dominic and Alexandra went, to bring you in."

Fae shook her head. "I've never met an Alexandra."

"Oh, no, you wouldn't have, would you?" Anna quickly looked around, and her sight settled on one of the front rows where none other than Lars Dreschler had stuffed himself into the corner. There was no way he saw them, but Fae's heart raced at having found him so easily, for when Nefas wanted to make good on their deal.

"But it was Dominic who brought you in, wasn't it? He's the best. I don't want to know what he did to you, Nefas that is, that's not my business, but I'm so sorry you had to meet him."

Even though her need to be with Nefas was wearing off again, Fae pulled her hand away from Anna's and felt her prickling defenses rise up. Her dealings with Nefas were private and had nothing to do with this ruby-lipped singer. How dare she feel sorry for her when she didn't even know what had happened out there. Regardless of what Fae was struggling with concerning Nefas, he had stayed with her even when she had realized the madness coming upon her. Most people would have thrown medication at her and run in the opposite direction. What Nefas had told her resonated now, that if the people in this church found her out, they would throw her out. She had tried for so many years to get thrown out, and now she found herself wanting to stay.

"I never met this Nefas."

"There's something about you that suggests otherwise. I'm sorry Fae, I was charged with being your greeter, and all I've done is put you on the defensive. I think a little extra insight will help give light to your dilemma. Ask the questions leaping out of your mouth, and I'll answer them. God knows you deserve a few. Answers, I mean."

"No one answers anything around here. What makes you so eager?"

Anna shrugged. "I get it? I'm serious, ask me anything."

Fae was suspicious, but this was the opportunity she'd been wanting since she'd arrived, and it was too much to ignore. "The design of this basilica doesn't make any sense."

"Oh, um, yes. A fire destroyed the back half and then there was some infighting over its reconstruction, leaving us with a church that has an identity crisis. I think it turned out fun, anyway. And don't mind the rudeness of the people here. What this village goes through on Christmas Eve, only a drugged-up, crazy person could imagine. Try describing what you've seen tonight to a sane person, and now you have the problem of this whole village."

"What about the people sitting in the pews? They aren't like what's haunting the streets outside."

"They're all immigrants, seven families allowed in by your grandmother, three more by Lars. A couple others whose ancestors snuck in. Like you, they weren't born here, so the Gift doesn't affect them. They're here to wait for morning."

"So, who are all you? There's not a chance your whole choir is from only ten families."

"We show up to sing. It's just one of those things you get involved with, you know? Once you start, it's just such a euphoric experience that you keep coming back. I've picked up a lot being here, that's how I know what I do. This is good! I'm here to let you have what you really want, so keep asking."

Fae's heart skipped a beat, and she shifted her seat. Only Nefas knew what she really wanted. He had been saying so all night. What if Anna was spying for him? She was just asking questions. What could he hold against her for that?

Even as she asked it to herself, she knew that he could, and would, do a whole lot.

"What did my grandmother want me to have?"

Anna's smile returned to her face, and she swept her hand all around them. "This is what your grandmother wanted for you. She knows what happens outside. She never wanted you to be out there for it. You remember how there was a right and wrong way to experience your gift? Well, outside with Nefas is the wrong way. Inside is the right. But don't worry. Either in or out, there's a grand finale which can't be missed."

"If she wanted me here the whole time, then who left the message in my room telling me to go to la Rue?" Fae shook her head. "You wouldn't know that, never mind."

But Anna's face had already blanched. "You were on la Rue? Tonight?" Her eyes grew wide. "You shouldn't be here."

Nefas was right, they were going to throw her out. "Answers, Anna, you said you'd give them," Fae urged.

"No, I mean, no one goes down there. Ever. Except Lars, like, once in his life. What I mean is, you shouldn't have made it back alive."

"I guess the voices in my head managed to get me out." Fae said it as a joke but, once the words were out of her mouth, she realized that she might've just given away her Voice . . . *retch you back out like the piece of rot that you are* . . . Fae held her breath. Anna didn't know her. There was no reason for her to think what she'd said was anything but an ill-timed joke.

"Dominic got you out of there, not voices. How many? How many are in your head?"

Fae stared at Anna for a long time trying to read her. The choir grew louder, giving her the option of cloaking her answer in secrecy; or, that's how it seemed. Maybe she'd read one too many books on revolutionists who held meetings at the opera so their schemes couldn't be overheard. Why should she tell Anna anything? There was nothing to tell—

"One." Fae watched to see how Anna would react, but she didn't. She waited for Fae. "We all talk to ourselves, right?" Anna wouldn't know about her and Nefas, but she felt like her cover-up was being exposed. Fae gathered herself as if to take her leave. She'd keep her pride and leave on her own. "Internal dialogue, it's called. They say all healthy people do it. I think you've answered all my questions, thanks."

"You think I'll think you're crazy," Anna said. Fae stopped. "I don't. I won't. There's a lot that goes into voices. If you tell me more, I can tell you if you are. Crazy, I mean. I told you I have answers. Can I take a guess? You first started hearing it about two days ago, when you arrived?"

Fae didn't say anything right away. Anna grabbed a water bottle out of her bag, took a drink, and offered it to Fae. The sight of water made her thirsty, so she drank some. It also loosened her tongue.

"If it's past midnight now, then ya, two days ago when I arrived," Fae reluctantly agreed, clearing her throat. "He won't leave my head."

Anna folded a leg beneath her, and she smiled reassuringly. "You're not going mad, Fae, because they're one and the same, that voice and Nefas, but you knew that already. This isn't the first time he's done this."

"Did he ever get in your head?"

"Me? No. But I've seen it before, one, two days out from Christmas Eve, sometimes later. Sometimes earlier. He gets in your head to break you down so he can build you up the way he wants you: servile and shortsighted."

"What are you suggesting? That I've got Stockholm syndrome?" That was insulting. "I'm just a mental mess in chains and fetters looking no further than the next validation from my captor? And now you're going to tell me that Jesus has a cure for that."

"Put your pitchfork away, girl. Not everyone on the other side of church doors is going to proselytize you," Anna said, easing the tension a little. "C'mon, sit back down. I just told you that you're not going crazy. Now you can re-evaluate everything you thought was madness as something else. If you ask me, that's a lot of hope for some good news. But enough of this Q-and-A piecemeal; it's confusing jumping into the middle of a story. How about starting at the beginning? I don't think many people know it anymore; time has buried it too deep."

"Are you going to start with the chicken or the egg?" Fae asked.

Anna ignored that and dropped her voice so that it could barely be heard above the singing.

"Generations times generations ago. before recorded history, there was a husband and wife who blissfully lived at peace with God and with nature. That is, until one day when a traveler came looking for food on his journey. They should have known something was off about their visitor when over dinner he talked only of things they had never heard about, strange things, things that alarmed them. Not wanting to be rude, they kept listening; and the more they listened, the more curious they became. The visitor answered their questions with his fingers crossed beneath the table. The husband and wife began to forget the bliss of the life they had, and became hungry instead for the mysteries the visitor told them about. When dinner ended, the visitor invited them to join him on his next adventure, because, he said, he felt like they had become fast friends with much in common. The husband and wife agreed. The visitor left with a wave, promising to come back in the morning. The man and woman didn't realize that they had just put their lives in the hands of a stranger who promised more than was possible.

"At first light the next day, the visitor came knocking on their door. The woman opened it only to find that he had come with five others, who forced their way into the house, bound tight the couple, and stole them outside into a waiting, caged carriage. Driven by rows of furious horses, the carriage took off and never stopped. The couple were driven farther and farther away and they didn't know where they were going. The longer they rode, the faster they aged until soon they were ready to die, but Death would not come to take them away. Their bodies began to whither and rot, and they begged the driver to stop so that Death could catch them; but the driver refused, saying that he himself was Death. Nefas, he said his name was. Eventually, their bodies decayed so much that there was nothing left but two piles of dust. Only then did Nefas stop. He came with a jar to collect their remains but, just before he could scoop them up, a gust of wind grabbed the two piles of dust into its arms and carried them away, freeing them at last. With their voices in the breeze, the man and woman whispered their tragic story to all who would hear, their warning of entertaining the lies of Death."

Fae struggled to find the right response to Anna's tale. "What a cheery Christmas story," she eventually said, put off by the morbidity. Or maybe she was alarmed that the void Nefas had opened in her felt at home in Anna's tale.

"The wind carried the couple's remains back home to where their hearts always wanted to be. From that place, their descendants grew up, and to honor the wish of the man and woman, God made public their warning to the world by giving Death, Nefas, one night to show off and to reveal the condition of the people who ride with him. This village is that place of demonstration, and its citizens are born into the demonstration itself. None of them belong to Nefas, though."

"What a lovely fable." Fae tried to sound ironic, but she was starting to feel a little weak again. "Nefas is real, not some ghost in a story."

"Don't you think you've been living something of a ghost story since you got here?"

"A demon story, maybe."

"They're kinda told the same way. And both can be very real. There is so much we don't know about the universe, or how it works. Think of the Gift as a flashlight that cuts through our lack of knowledge, and the mirror is just Nefas' favorite tool to show you your soul, invisible to you, but not to him."

"Don't talk about mirrors," Fae said, completely unnerved. "Anna, I've seen that driver. I dreamed him, but it wasn't Nefas."

"He doesn't have just one face."

"This is more than a ghost story. This is madness."

"Fae, you've gone pale."

"He wants me alive. Nefas chose me, and I cast my dice for him. I don't think there's any going back." As she said it, she felt sick. "Maybe he'll just eventually leave me alone."

"He won't." Anna shook her head. "He needs you because he physically can't accomplish everything he wants to do in this world. But you can, and he'll use you until the end. For Nefas, death is life. It's all relative for him. He's really good at confusing you with that backward perception until you're so confused that you'll agree with anything he says. You'll end up convincing yourself everything you thought you knew can't be right and, therefore, must be unacceptable, because it no longer fits with what you now know, courtesy of Nefas' whispers. He plants darkness inside you, then conjures it until it becomes you. You just assume it's who you've always been, so you don't question it."

"So what am I supposed to do, then? I told you, I cast my dice with him, and he's let me experience things that are . . . truly indescribable, so for better or worse . . ." Fae stumbled with her words, because she knew trying to leave Nefas was going to be a battle her body and mind would likely not survive. He and his void were torture, but also a secret thrill. The idea of being separated from the void's creator remained an uncomfortable thought at best. "He's been my shadow my whole life, right? But despite him, I'm not a murderer, or rapist, or anything condemnable like that." It was different now, Fae knew, but if she could convince herself . . . convince herself of something she didn't want, simply to feed an addiction? Couldn't she just stay inside all night and let everything pass her by? Or was she choosing a side merely by being in the basilica? "I'm top percentage of my class; my future is good. I can't mess that up because I got scared and intimidated one night. If all it takes to not have Nefas mad at me is living with the knowledge that I'm a dead person walking, and that I'm subordinate to a more powerful person, then that's a price a lot of people have already paid, and they've lived just fine."

Anna was shaking her head. "You've bitten the apple, Fae," she said. "Your life can't go on like you think it will. You can't convince yourself you'll wake up from this, or that you'll eventually beat him at his own game. You know you won't. Elise tried and couldn't." Anna raised her eyebrow, and Fae suddenly felt much smaller. "There is no going back to your life before you came here. Reality is, you'll leave this village either owned completely in mind, body and soul by him, or not—choosing life instead. That's how simple—and difficult—this all is. It's your choice. There is no third option. You're either alive or dead, and that's your ultimate gift to choose. You haven't made any decision that is completely binding."

Anna still wasn't getting it. Fae squeezed her fingers together to help her calm down. "You said I just need to choose life, right? I already did that, yesterday, and everything has gone to hell since. I believe what you're saying,

Anna, but this isn't just a yes or no thing. I've already sided with him. He's not going to let me go back on that. You don't know him."

The look Anna gave her suggested that, yes, she probably did know Nefas, but that didn't reassure her. "You still have a choice, Fae, you always will. Nefas might be in your head, but he can't follow you everywhere—otherwise he'd be here right now. But you also can't hide in this building forever. Truth doesn't change. Opinion does. You need to decide what's truth and what's opinion that's simply been sold as truth. Just because you don't agree with something doesn't mean that it's wrong."

Anna paused, closed her eyes, and listened to the singers for a moment. "I'm going to have to go soon." She opened her eyes before looking at Fae again with a new level of calm. "Your current problem is that Nefas has opened a direct channel from himself to you through the void."

Fae's eyes went wide. Anna knew then, about the void. She'd probably known all along. Fae felt her cheeks grow warm with embarrassment and her insides tighten. Anna had no right to know what was between her and Nefas!

"Don't worry," Anna said, reading Fae's reaction accurately, "I'm not going to judge you, and you don't have to tell me anything about it. I'd prefer if you didn't. Dominic interrupted Nefas when he was giving it to you, but no amount of desire on your part will be enough to get rid of it."

Fae was just about done with this conversation. She twisted in her seat to face the front again, leaving Anna to speak to her shoulder. The peace and the magic the choir had given her was gone. No matter how she looked at it, her night was far from over. She didn't need Anna to keep making everything worse.

Anna stood up and perched herself on the back of the pew in front of them, forcing Fae to pay attention to her.

"I've told you where you are now, but I haven't told you your options going forward, so keep listening for a couple more minutes, OK?"

Fae wasn't overwhelmed with optimism, but she let Anna continue. Anna fixed her short hair behind her ears and took a deep breath. "Every Christmas Eve, the Gift comes and goes, as does Nefas. He gets his few hours to strut around and show off himself and his 'family,' trying to convince people to trust him and commit to him, ultimately to be given his controlling parasite, but his performance is usually without an audience. When a visitor actually stays for the Eve, they become the sole audience member, and nothing is held back. As you can see from the other people sitting here, visitors have come through before, but they weren't Maria's granddaughter, and, well, that kind of makes you a revenge target for Nefas. She stole a lot of people from him. Maria didn't know you had a target on your back, or that Nefas saw so much in your future. Your situation has been complicated by the fact that he's already partially branded you for himself."

"And I can't get the void out."

"Do you want it gone?"

Fae couldn't answer that question so she didn't, yet somehow she felt like Anna understood. There was no separating the pleasures of the void from the torture of it, nor the one who gave it to her. The three came together.

Anna continued, "You can stay here for the rest of the night and, in the morning, you'll still be in his possession and he'll finish the job, no doubt, in short order. The night will play out as it should, but your lack of decision will register as a decision to stay with him. Of course, if you don't want him haunting the rest of your life, there is a way to sever the link."

Fae studied the other woman cautiously. Once she heard the plan, she'd be complicit with it. He might find out.

"Tell me."

"There's a little kid, a baby. You'll need to find him and bring him here to the basilica."

"Everyone not a corpse is already inside, though, right?"

Anna scrunched up her face. "No."

"He's out there? Then his parents . . ."

"You know what outside looks like."

She couldn't believe it. This was just more madness. But she'd heard too much to tell Anna to leave her alone, and the little bit of hope already offered was dangerous. "Where's the kid, and what can he do that I can't? Or any other self-aware adult, for that matter?"

Anna took a deep breath, and Fae knew that the answer wasn't a simple one.

THE GIFT

"I could tell you. You won't like it."

Fae shook her head incredulously and set her eyes forward again. How blissful could ignorance be, already knowing that the combination of a baby and Nefas together in the same sentence was enough to rob her of her conscience. In Fae's silence, Anna decided to continue.

"You only have to find the child, and bring him back here to the Notre-Dame du Seigneur, and everything else will take care of itself. Can you hear him crying, yet? It's not going to be that hard to track him down."

At Anna's indication, Fae strained to hear the cry of a baby through the seamless song around her. It took a couple of seconds, but she managed to train her ear on the sound and then she couldn't un-hear it.

"There is so much wrong with what you're proposing right now," Fae told her, "the least of which is the fact that I'm not going to just walk back outside to where Nefas is waiting, and after everything you've told me . . . how about one of these other lovely people sitting here brings the kid in?"

"You could ask them," Anna said, shrugging, "but they won't do it. They've all had to do this themselves. It's just the way it all plays out. It's not your fault; it's just what has to happen—and, like growing up, some things are better understood when done yourself."

"This is bull—"

Anna cut her off. "Ask them if you want, but there's no sense getting mad at them. Dominic will go back outside with you. He'll have your back."

"While you get to stay safely inside." Fae swore under her breath, the sanctity of this place no longer holding her tongue. "So Dominic and I go out into the terrifying night, I find the crying baby, bring him back here, and Nefas is gone. He leaves me alone."

"That's . . ." Anna weighed her words, "generously simplistic . . ."

"Yes, or no?" Fae demanded.

"Yes."

"And the void?"

"The longer you're without it, the less you'll miss it. Just like Nefas." Sensing what Fae was going to say next, Anna said, "There really is no other option."

Nothing good could come of this, despite Anna's promises. Ignorance was going to have be bliss. "If this doesn't work . . ." Fae tried to think of one good last wish, in case Anna's suggestion failed and came up with nothing. She could ask for death but, since Nefas brought that with him, he could probably withhold it. At least, according to Anna's story.

As though to cement her decision, Dominic appeared, having found the two of them, and perched himself on the edge of the pew one row in front, his hands folded in front of him.

Anna cocked her head to listen to the song and then said, "I have to go. But here," she reached around her neck and pulled over her head a pearled metal chain with a heart and key pendant. The key was large for a pendant. "Take this, just to let you know that you'll never be alone. You've been through a lot already, and you're strong enough to get through what's coming, too." Then she looked back at Dominic. "Keep her safe."

Fae was going to refuse the gift, but Anna had already taken off.

She draped the chain around her neck and looked at Dominic. He could've been on a coffee break, he looked so relaxed. His first words did nothing to help her feel any better about what she had agreed to. "Maria's prayers are strong, but Nefas will be more ruthless than ever as soon as you step outside."

"Really?" Fae gathered herself to get ready to leave. If she delayed, she was only going to talk herself out of this. "That's what you're going to tell me?" There was a hole in her stomach, thinking about leaving this sanctuary for the inevitable reunion waiting for her. Dominic had her back, but that knowledge wasn't enough to remove the dull pains from her face and the reminder those brought.

"There is hope. Just follow the sound of the crying, and don't try to think your way around where it leads you, or you'll get yourself in trouble. I'll meet you outside."

Dominic slipped out of the pew and was swept away into the choir, leaving Fae to figure out "here" to "there." She left the pew and navigated through the tide of the choir, half listening to its intoxicating song while trying to pinpoint the direction of the baby's cry. Reason and habit said to leave the basilica through the front door, but that wasn't where the crying was coming from, and she wasn't in a position to start ignoring instructions. She followed the sound to a narrow hall on the other side of the basilica, the kind used by priests to go back and forth to light candles or do whatever priestly act they were obliged to perform.

Just as she was disappearing through the torchlit entryway, she heard someone behind her say, "Go. Bring death to Death." Fae stopped just inside the hall and looked back to see who was talking. She found an older man sitting in the nearby pew with his wife, who looked to be dozing. He nodded at her firmly. "Dawn will be here in a few short hours, and much has yet to happen."

"Will I be able to forgive myself when this is all done?" she asked.

"There'll be no need." He nodded again to send her on her way, but Fae hesitated to leave him, he who was a survivor. He had already shifted his attention away from her, though, and Dominic was waiting. Much has yet to happen, he said.

Too much already had.

20

The baby was crying incessantly. Its demands for attention resounded up the stone hallway. Fae put her ear to the wooden doors she passed to no avail, but she didn't have to follow the hallway far before she came to a single, iron gate marking the end. It was pitch black through the iron bars, and a chilled, stale air wafted through it. The child's crying was clearly coming from the other side.

Thinking of the candle chandelier and torches back in the sanctuary, Fae looked around with little hope for a light switch or a pull string but didn't find either. A few worn stairs led down before they were swallowed up into the darkness along with her courage. She couldn't go down there, not into that blackness and into the . . . well, there were only so many uses for a basilica's basement. She wanted to say this wasn't worth it, so she could walk away from this search. Morning was a long way off. Maybe she could work something out that Anna hadn't thought of.

The baby's cry became more insistent. Frustrated, Fae went back to the few open doors in the hallway and rummaged for a wooden broom handle or anything that could be made into a torch, only to find nothing. She soon found herself staring down the iron gate again, empty-handed. If she didn't go down there—according to Anna—she could spend her last hours of freedom in the song-infused basilica of serenity and let the madness and horror feel like a bad dream. But then she would be abandoning a baby to the elements as, apparently, no one else was going to find him. Fae found herself trying to rationalize the option of returning to the pews. She sighed with disapproval of herself.

"Fae, what kind of person are you?" she said out loud. "A selfish one," she responded just the same. With a groan of resignation, she pushed the gate open. It went silently, and her hand found the handrail bolted to the stone wall. That was the easy part. Forcing herself to take the first step into the chilled darkness was a much greater battle. She closed her eyes and focused on the choir's music behind her and let the handrail slip through her hand, guiding her downward. Beneath her feet, the stairs were steep and began to gently spiral. When she opened her eyes again, the blackness had taken her sight.

Scuffled footsteps sounded behind her. Fae froze mid-step, her heart in her throat, listening. The sounds stopped when she did. She began again, and so did the sound of scuffling feet, offset just enough that it could have been her own echo.

"Nefas?" Images of a Grim Reaper taxi driver with a melting face filled her mind, and Nefas himself illuminated in eerie green light from the skeletons and corpses surrounding him. Was he just having fun watching her panic before he made his move? She couldn't do this. Her heart was racing. The baby would be safe, surely. All she had to do was race back up the stairs, slam the gate shut, and tell Anna this scheme was a waste of time.

Just do it, go back upstairs! Fae tried to convince herself. *You've been through too much. You're not stable enough to make good decisions.* But instead, she kept going down.

"Yea, though I walk through the valley of death, I shall not fear . . ." The words she used to hold onto so long ago, when her childhood shadow monsters wouldn't let her sleep, found her again after all these years. Fae tried a nervous little laugh to help herself, "I shall not fear shadow monsters."

The handrail ran out, and Fae panicked. She was lost without it. Planting her hands against the cool stone wall, she cautiously extended her foot downward and found the floor.

It was so dead down here. Her shallow breaths seemed to hang in front of her. Still, a breeze of chilled air gave her goose bumps, and she could feel the expanse all around. Without any light, how was she ever going to find the baby, his cries bouncing off every wall?

Hesitantly stepping forward, she ran into something with her face and screamed. Thoughts of spiderwebs and spiders falling onto her made her scream and panic even more and she threw her hands around to swat the invisible creatures away. She hit the stringy object again, then again as it became caught in her flailing arms. When she felt no little spiders' legs tickling her skin, she forced herself to calm down. The strand stopped swinging and rested against her arm. She grabbed it and pulled down with hope.

A series of low-wattage lights clicked on and, after a quick, mad search over her back to find no spiders, Fae just about broke down in tears from relief. She had her sight back. There were no spiders. Nefas was nowhere to be seen

She was in the crypt of the basilica. A do-it-yourself wiring job around the exterior of the space had naked bulbs popping out from the roughly hewn walls, illuminating sarcophagi in their perfect placings. This wasn't anything uncommon. Some of the more important sarcophagi were set in fabricated alcoves. Pillars of raw stone, adorned with mosaic glass, inhibited her view of the whole space, but they were the only pretty thing down here. She didn't pause to look around—she was going to make this quick.

She chose a direction and started scanning the floors, the tops of the sarcophagi, any place a baby could be. She called out to him, hoping he would respond or, even better, take his annoying crying down a notch, but she wasn't having much luck with either. The deeper into the crypt she went, the more conscious she became of the sarcophagi and the bones they held. Awareness crept in that not only were there just bones inside those graves, but flesh in all states of decay . . . and flesh could be re-animated. She could be walking through the midst of the prison for the dead, saints and priests come to life again by the parasites trying to get out and infect her. Did the parasites work on people already dead?

THE GIFT

Thinking these thoughts, Fae peered around the back of an especially ornate sarcophagus. She was careful to stay as far away as possible when she noticed an all-too-familiar green fog began escaping from beneath the lid. Fae jumped back into the middle of the aisle, her throat tightening. It wasn't just the one sarcophagus. The growing fog was seeping out from the joints of all the sarcophagi stretching the entire span of the crypt. It steadily stretched itself out and flowed toward her as she quickened her pace past all the graves. She could make it back to the stairs before it caught her, but the fog itself never hurt her—just who came with it.

And then the tapping began. *Tap, tap, tap, tap.* Just like kids tapping on pet shop windows, the tapping came from inside the sarcophagi. The graves were alive.

In that moment, she felt him. He was warm upon her back, his hands resting over hers. It made her want to cry.

I want to show you something.

From the seams of every stone sarcophagus, spears of green light shot out, piercing the fog and revealing a dance of dust particles floating through the air. With the slowness of a great will struggling against an even mightier weight, the stone lids of the sarcophagi began to grind. Granite against granite, the lids shook and struggled.

"Oh god . . ." Fae moaned.

I shall not fear. From deep within, those words sprung up again, and Fae found herself repeating them out loud, "I am not going to be afraid." She couldn't have convinced a kitten of the sincerity of those words but, whatever power they had, she had to hope in it. "I'm not going to be afraid." She said it again as she kept backing away. By the sixth sarcophagus, the spearing light was shut off, and it just disappeared. The fog instantly evaporated. Everything was as it had been before: just the naked lightbulbs, silent sarcophagi, and that crying baby to guide her along the way. She almost fell from relief and caught herself on a nearby sarcophagus.

Had she imagined all that? She remembered Dominic's warning that fear would kill her and she wondered just what kind of creative powers fear had in this place. She needed to get out of here.

Her search was fruitless and only led to a shorter staircase going outside, where the crying was louder. The baby wasn't on or around the staircase. Maybe he was just on the other side of the door?

But Nefas would be out there waiting for her, and the moment of truth would come. She'd be lying if there wasn't a craving for more of his forbidden secrets from the void, so salacious; the shame of them had worn off with the shock of first experiencing them.

She could do this: Snag the kid and retreat inside before Nefas showed up. Dominic had risked his life getting her into this place, and now she had to risk hers to leave it.

Fae headed up the stairs.

With a little rattling of the old chains and coaxing of the locks, she undid the rustic, locking mechanism. She took a deep breath, and then she left the safety of the basilica.

The door made a reserved creaking sound. Fae inched it open just enough to see what lay on the other side. A snowdrift had built up against the door, and some of it fell and settled on the top two stairs; otherwise, there was nothing exceptional. The back of the Notre-Dame du Seigneur was surrounded by the plaza, the same as in front, the ring only broken by three streets marked out with lamps. A couple corpses hobbled along, having gotten loose from the main mass, but otherwise it was quiet. The crying was clearer out here. And less anxious, which she took to be a good sign.

Opening the door wider, she slipped out into the snowy night. As soon as she looked up, a hooded man loomed in front of her, his nose and lips barely discernible through the shadows.

"Hello Fae. I knew you would come back."

It was just like meeting an ex-boyfriend she was in danger of relapsing with. His voice drew her back to him, smooth as cream, deep as a thick, warm blanket. It was the same sound that had disarmed her the first time she had heard him as her Voice. Fae knew immediately that all of Dominic's interventions and Anna's warnings, as true or exaggerated as they may be, would soon be for nothing. She had seen the horrors he breathed as oxygen, felt his pain, and knew what he could give her—everything. And for that,

THE GIFT

with him so close, she wasn't strong enough to walk away.

"I warmed up. I needed to be with you again." She prayed that pleased him because, if not, this was going to be a very short venture.

Find the child . . . Can you hear him crying . . . ? It's not going to be that hard to track him down. The sound of Anna's voice echoing from her memory was distracting, and she pushed it aside.

"Come here." Nefas opened his arms and wrapped her up, guiding her away. Fae shrunk under his arm, but she went. "We have something to finish together. And there's someone you said you'd bring me."

"The German is insi—"

"I want the baby."

Fae stiffened, but she didn't dare protest. The price she she'd agreed to was Lars. An innocent child didn't deserve to know him—she wasn't a monster. Nefas wasn't holding her very strongly. If she could break away . . . his arm tightened around her shoulders as though he knew what she was contemplating. He'd never let her go so easily.

"I don't know where the baby is," Fae said, as though that would be enough to dissuade him.

"Someone told you rescuing that baby would spring you free of our relationship, didn't they?" It was a rhetorical question. She nodded anyway, expecting the worst. "You promised to bring me someone in exchange for 'warming up.' Bring me the baby and not only will I let you be, I'll make sure the church idiots leave you alone, too. It's OK to say that you want it." He snorted with pride. "What they didn't tell you was that freeing you from me would make you their debtor slave. You can't afford the baby, and he's not free. My offer is."

The revelation slowed Fae's walk, and Nefas slowed with her. She felt him smile. There were always two sides. Of course, the religious would try anything to kidnap her into their fold. That's what Christmas was for. And she had fallen for it. Nefas' offer was the one that Anna said didn't exist: the offer of her life back as it was before she'd come here. That's all she wanted. For all the warnings, though, could she trust that he would make good? She'd just thought it herself: He'd never let her go so easily.

"Don't they have to agree to this?"

"I tell them the terms you chose, and they comply."

From the corner of her eye, Fae saw a flash of white and realized she had forgotten Dominic's promise. But she was with Nefas; it was too late. His allure made her want to stay with him . . . even though she knew one wrong action or word would re-shatter this easily made fantasy. If she didn't agree to his deal, he would never stop terrorizing her. "I'll do it. Will you come with me to find him?"

"I'm always with you," he said, as he guided her to a sheltered corner of the basilica. "Come, our unfinished business will be so much more . . . scandalous, against the walls of such a holy church."

Fae's spine shivered and her heart pounded in her chest as she followed. The fear that came with Nefas returned, and she balked. What had she just agreed to? Anna wasn't a slaver! Nefas pushed her forward, his grip on her tighter than before. No! The void rose up in her mind, its pleasures and mysteries surging through her body. She had to have more, but it hurt; it was too deep; her mind was going to drown!

Nefas held her at the wall, but then from behind Dominic grabbed his arm holding her and ripped it away. "GO!" Dominic shouted at her. "The streets ahead, run!" He pushed her forward sending her feet scrambling. She hesitated, so close to having more of Nefas' void.

Fae gasped. The void *was* Nefas branding her . . . he was lying to her! He was never going to let her go, no matter what he said.

With a howl of rage, Nefas screeched like a maddened banshee robbed of its kill. Dominic ripped Nefas' hood back and exposed what was left of that beautiful, handsome face. And then Dominic turned to her, so filled with intensity that she broke into a dead sprint before he had to demand it again, though he did: "GO!"

She ran as fast as she could for the middle of the three streets, but she didn't get far before she tripped and landed hard. She didn't give the pain its satisfaction. She jumped back up but barely got her feet under her before tripping a second time—and then she saw. The small black paving stones were all elevated to different heights, like someone had created a giant bar graph all around with no pattern, and no consistency. The stones were moving up and down, not letting Fae get any footing.

Nefas screamed again. Fae looked behind her to see him throwing all his hatred into the empty space where Dominic had stood fighting him. Scouring the area where Dominic should have been, Nefas looked like he was sniffing him out.

"Look around you," Nefas shouted, to her or Dominic—she didn't know, his voice hideous to hear. "You're surrounded!" As she kept struggling against the paving stones, wave after wave of illuminated corpses were being revealed where she had thought there was nothing. There were just as many here as there were at the front of the basilica, hundreds closing her in, the green luminescence creeping ahead of their reveals.

Fae looked behind her again and saw Nefas, hood back in place, marching toward her, stalking through the masses of his children, the uneven stones smoothing under his feet.

"I've brought you into my world, Fae," Nefas growled. "I will slit your throat and drink your blood if that's what it takes to realize you can't be of rid me, bitch! If you won't sit and STAY, then it's time for you to be broken."

Crawling and stumbling along the unpredictable cold stones, she could feel Nefas closing in fast. He walked without hurry, prolonging the dread, while she was as helpless as a one-legged frog trying to escape mean little boys.

But there! A path through the paving stones was being flattened. Fae found her feet and bolted through the smooth imprints as fast as they were created.

"Where are you running to, Fae?" He spat the question, then laughed. And it echoed, his mocking laughter rippling out of the mouths of hundreds of sinewy jaws surrounding her. They all mocked her with Nefas' humiliating laughter. Most didn't have the vocal cords or tongues to do it on their own, but it meant the same thing: Where are you running to, dead girl?

The street, Dominic said to get to the street. Fae panicked. There were no more streets; they were all gone. Her eyes darted back and forth across an unbroken wall of buildings and storefronts curving in a wide circle around them.

"This is your fault, Fae! When I put chains on you, so tight your wrists and ankles fall off, it will be because you wanted it this way!" Nefas kept coming closer and closer. "When I pull, you will jerk and twist and, in your nakedness, you will be my fool and the lesser fools' queen, living in my endless void, dying with all your unsatisfied lusts. You thought Tantalus was just a myth?" He spat the words, and Fae could feel him dragging her into them, back into his void, so deep the memory of it was suffocating. Still, he cursed her. "The souls you will destroy in all of my names will become your throne and the fuel for the fire burning your undying body. Your tongue, I will pierce to haul wherever I need it to go. Your ears will be cut off and sewn to your dead soul. The only sounds you will hear will be the groans of your stiff, animated corpse—and me laughing at you. Your eyes, I will gouge out with my fingers, after I finally answer your silly plea to see my face, before sinking them into my own head so that you will only see what I see. Then you will thank me and call out my name in your lonely nights and even lonelier days. You will claw after my feet begging for just a little bit . . . more. Fae, have you figured out who I am yet. Fae?"

If it hadn't been for the baby's cry, she would have given him the victory right then and there. Running away was only making this worse. Time would normalize the fear and horrors . . .

Nefas summoned four new bodies from the midst of the corpses: brown-robed monks. They seamlessly passed through the crowd and created a path from Nefas to her with their bodies. Their long hoods rested on the crown of their naked, dry skulls, which were grinning at her. Their teeth clacked together as they silently spoke. They didn't laugh; the movement wasn't right for that.

"They remember you, Fae. Do you remember them?"

She remembered: the relief carvings on the archivolt.

"Fae!" Dominic shouted at her. "The streets are still there."

"They're not!"

"Look in the windows!"

Fae was afraid to let her eyes off Nefas or his four guards. Turning her back on them was a mistake. She had to, though; she knew she did.

She turned and ran again, just enough to keep ahead of the corpses closing in, and furiously scanned the storefronts and restaurants to see anything that would give a clue. Her brain raced.

Windows, windows with Christmas lights, windows with candles, windows with shutters, storefronts, I'm not a detective! What the hell am I looking for? What's missing?

"Restaurants with stacked tables, no chairs, multi-colored lights, no lights, no, no, no, house numbers, windows with . . ." Fae got it then: "no Communion!" Every building had it!

Fae darted headlong toward a massive window that didn't have Communion. With her shoulder leading the way and her eyes pinched shut, she threw herself against the window and prayed she was right expecting to crash through and roll over shards of glass. The crash never came. Fae fell through the air and hit the ground with a face full of snow, her shoulder cushioned with a soft, snowy crunch.

She snapped open her eyes to find that a deep snowdrift in the middle of the street had caught her—the only snowdrift anywhere that was so deep.

"This is your path, don't leave it," Dominic told her from somewhere behind. "Find the baby."

The street she landed on, Rue Leopold I, was empty as far as she could tell. Behind her, the imaginary façade had disappeared. The corpse mob was coming. Both sides united into one dense front, and Nefas led the way. Confidence in his success calmed his entire body as he stalked her, his body a silhouette against the luminescent army of the dead behind him. A wind picked up and whipped his clothes around. He was a king leading his army, and she was his runaway whore.

21

Fae had just been given another chance. It wasn't much, but she didn't need it to be. The instinct to survive pushed her feet beneath her and she sped up the street, away from the one who came to claim her for his own.

A second darkness fell fast and heavy on the village. It fell like a thick fog and chilled her with a cold that seeped into her bones. More of a substance than a lack of brightness, where it had been a dark night before, it was a black one now. It strangled out the streetlamps, store lights, and Christmas lights peeking through shutters and curtains. Even the brightest of lights were reduced to no more than waning specks and blinking fireflies.

Fae's run slowed to a jog as she lost proper sight. Her lungs heaved for air, and she willed her eyes to pick out shadows from the darkness to give her something to help her navigate. With the darkness came a vicious gust of cold air that pummeled snow in her face and attacked her eyes. Blinded by the darkness and snow, Fae strained to follow the baby's cries, swirling in every direction. She buried her hands in her armpits to keep them warm; she had left her gloves on the pew.

The snow was slapping her face via hundreds of tiny hands, and she had to keep her head down just to keep her eyes open. A swirl of snow rose up to look like a man. Fae bristled before it fell away in a gust; she didn't dare give the apparition her attention in case that was the key Nefas was waiting for to give it his life. A quick check over her shoulder showed Nefas' army was still hot behind, though they too were slowed by the blizzard's gusting winds. They looked like miscolored flames from lamps being swung by those who were also lost in the blizzard; she wished they were—and not phantoms rapidly fading into sight from one realm and into hers. There was no way to see whether Nefas still led his army. He probably wanted it that way.

Fae veered sharply to her left and came to a store with no particular purpose other than to sell anything the owner fancied. A yellowing, decades-old mannequin held a purple, plastic cup and a round loaf of bread, gutted, inside of which was a Nativity made with knockoff Lego figures. An oddly shaped rock, painted to look like La Befana, the Italian Christmas witch, sat in front of the metal gate pulled across the store's entrance. Hefting the painted rock over her head to break the store window, Fae saw her corpse reflection greet her in the reflective glass. It was accompanied by two of the monks, their jaws still speaking soundless words. She spun around, fearing that they had caught up with her; but, there was no one behind her.

Fae turned back to the window and, with a strained grunt, threw the rock against it. "C'mon!" The glass crackled in a spiderweb around a clean hole and a rush of heated air charged out, warming her face and hands before it was chased back inside by the storm. Fae made the hole bigger by kicking at it and carefully reached inside and grabbed the bread and the plastic cup.

"You don't know how to use that," Nefas said condescendingly. Fae jumped and cowered at the same time. He was right beside her, but she couldn't make herself turn around to face him. "Put it down."

Fae looked at herself, armed with cheap wine in an even cheaper plastic cup and inedible bread, and she remembered the sight of Lars Dreschler charging into that alley full of corpses. As she remembered, her corpse reflection came into focus at the edge of the shattered glass—the white, dead eyes, the gray skin so taut she could see every bone, her clothes hanging limply.

"What do the dead need with blood and flesh?" Nefas' body found his reflection in the glass, handsome once again beside her own grotesque one. "If you wanted blood, you should have asked." At his words, an intense pressure in her fingertips swelled up with an immediate pain, causing her to nearly crush the cup she was holding. Even in the darkness, she could see the glimmer of blood breaking out from her nail beds.

"These aren't for you," she managed to say between gritted teeth. "Clearing a path!" Warm blood tainted her tongue as she spoke, she could feel it covering her teeth—her gums were seeping blood, too.

"The child can wait until you realize you're not helping yourself by finding him; you're doing as you're told. And you will keep doing as you're told, by my side."

"You're only in my head," Fae told the reflection in the cracked glass. She coughed on the blood in her mouth and spat.

"That's the only place I need to be. Your breaking has just begun." A sharp pain seized her head and she cried out, doubling over. The blood from her fingers smudged her face as she grabbed her head and dropped her precious prizes. She found herself back inside the endless void, careening through it to no end. It was so deep it hurt, a slow crush of depth, a place where all the lusts, ideas, and despicable desires were reunited with her. Nefas was baiting her with her addiction, giving her new nebulae of salacious gifts to careen through. It felt so good and, because of that, she felt guiltier than before. She said the names of the nebulae naturally as she passed through some of them again. They tasted bitter on her tongue, but maybe that was the blood. There was no question anymore. This void was no longer just Nefas' gift; this was who she was.

She was jerked out of her mental pit too abruptly, and the violent act threw her up against the broken window aa she almost fell into the hole she had made. It took her brain a moment to re-orient itself, to find its place again in the blizzard and the blackness. Licking the inside of her teeth, she tasted no new blood. Her fingers were still slick but no longer oozing or swollen. She picked herself up off the window and noticed another impact in the glass beside hers, not broken but spiderwebbed and sagging inward. The snow in front was heavily packed down. "Dominic?" The wind threw her question back into her face. If Dominic was still nearby, he couldn't be seen from the corpses closing in, the sound of their wheezing, cavernous breathing carrying on the blizzard wind. They were wind blasted with a thin covering of snow, and they looked more abominable than before. Nefas had been wasting her time, holding her here. A mummified creature of a youth bundled up in a bright orange jacket was mere feet away.

"It worked for Lars, it'll work for me," she said to herself, squaring off to face her enemy. She picked up her symbols where they had been dropped and held them aloft, congealing blood trailing down her frozen fingers. "Get back," Fae inched forward, letting the cup and bread lead the way. "Leave me alone!" Though the corpses didn't back off, they did stop coming forward, and the pale saucers that used to be vibrant irises dumbly shifted upward to Fae's outstretched arms. No longer protected by the store's siding, she was hit hard by the gusts of wind and snow. Fae thought that she was just as likely to freeze alive in this blizzard as she was to get caught by the corpses. There had to be another way.

A dark hole in the wall beside her gaped invitingly. Fae dashed for the side street, dumped the Communion at its mouth, and hoped that with luck the elements would ward off any corpses from following. Her hands now freed, she stuffed them into her jacket sleeves, not caring about blood stains. The cold air was harsh on her lungs so she decided to rest a moment and regulate her breathing. Her back found the plaster wall, and she rested against it. It was quieter in here, she quickly noticed. The wind didn't howl so much. Actually, it didn't blow at all. Nothing moved. Everything was perfectly still, and that wasn't reassuring.

She needed to find a detour around the corpses. Ordinarily, that wouldn't be too difficult to figure out, but in this darkness, and with the expectation of Nefas' threat hanging over her, nothing was a certainty. Dominic or no, Nefas was still coming for her. Even if she gave herself up now, it wasn't going to stop him from breaking her down to more manageable pieces. But if she could race against him and bring him the baby before she crumbled into a pliable heap at his feet? She might still have something of herself left in the morning to walk away with.

Just follow the baby's cry was what Anna said, but the cry wasn't as loud now that she had come onto this street. Her brain had long ago stopped trying to apply logic, or sense, to what was happening; however, logically, if she was getting closer to the baby, then his crying shouldn't have gotten quieter. Ultimately though, it didn't matter. Dominic had pointed her in the right direction, so that was where she would go, one way or another. Seeing the herd of corpses huddled around the street entrance, Fae was satisfied that the Communion was holding them at bay, and pushed off from the wall.

The farther she got from Rue Leopold I, the quieter it became. The less the cold air moved, the more slowly her brain seemed to process. Every little sound she made sounded twice as loud—a sniffle or her clothes rubbing together. Every noise sounded disruptive, even though the sounds had no echo or distance in here. It was as if she were in an earthen den that absorbed it all. The utter silence and the complete dark were unnerving. Fae found herself slowing her purposed walk in expectation of Nefas, but he stayed away. She began dreading what this unnatural deprivation was going to bring from him. It was stifling in here, foreboding. The faster she got out, the better.

Time slowed, with nothing but her pulse beating in her ears to count the seconds. By now she had to have gone far enough to comfortably circumnavigate the corpses, and she looked for a connection on her right-hand side to complete her detour. She sped up her pace, anxious to get out of this place of blind deafness, to hear something other than the dull sounds of her own existence—to stop the dread and find where Nefas was waiting for her.

She stepped on something hard and smooth, and she froze. Maybe it was nothing. She doubted it. Tentatively, she put her weight down and heard the sound of crunching ice. An icicle. Her foot kicked another one and it hurt. Bending down, Fae felt around in the dark until she found the culprit. It was the thickness of her forearm.

Fae didn't want to, but she slowly looked up. Two wisps of green mist wove, like slalom skiers racing, through an endless supply of razor-sharp icicles on the overhanging roofs above her. The mist quickly disappeared beyond sight, but the icicles retained the faint green light which would have been beautiful in any other situation but was treacherous here. Either Nefas had found his sympathy and was giving her some navigation, or he had decided to sharpen his tools of punishment in front of her. Either way, she wished he hadn't.

The icicles' light wasn't strong enough to break through the blackness, so Fae still walked in darkness. They did, however, reveal a street to the right, and she didn't hesitate to follow. She felt an immediate relief, going in the proper direction again, and the thought of getting out of this . . . catacomb, was enough to cause her to start jogging.

When she saw the corpses up ahead, waiting for her to exit, she pulled up fast. The blackness had consumed their glow, so she was closer than she should've ever allowed herself to be. At their head were two of the monks. Once they saw her, they immediately began their march toward her. The monks were leading the way. All of them moved without a sound; not even a footstep could be heard. The dread of going back into those void, dark streets was secondary to the horror of the corpses, so Fae turned and ran the same way she'd come, wanting to lose the horde. She ran, barely breathing, afraid of tripping over something unseen, trying to hold her breath because it sounded too loud in here. She had no idea where she was going.

The icicles guided the way, but it was taking longer than it should have to get back to where she had started. There was a strong likelihood that she'd run past her intersection and, with self-doubt rising, her sense of orientation evaporated. She wanted to turn around and try again. As she did a quick shoulder check, the road behind her zoomed in, and suddenly the silent monks and corpses had made up the distance and were right behind her, their parasites ready. There would be no doubling back now. She kept running.

Then there, up in the distance, appeared Nefas. He stood out like a smoke signal and she faltered. She needed Dominic to help her out of here, but he was nowhere to be seen, while Nefas . . . she'd take her chances with the devil she knew rather than the monks. Running to him, ready to beg his help, she never got closer to Nefas, even though she was gaining distance from the mob. He made no movements. He just continued to stand in the distance watching, judging like a dark ghost keeping her pace. Fae stretched her stride to reach him faster and ran hard into a wall.

Nefas was gone. Every thought that flashed into her mind was not a good one, as she numbly felt her way across the wall and searched for her exit—only to find herself blocked in on three sides by solid wood and brick. One of these walls had to have a door, a window, a hole, a something! But there was nothing. The silent corpses were closing in. She began hearing their shuffling of dead feet over the snowy cobblestones, like an old, dial radio crackling in and out of tune, before the ear-ringing silence came back. Then, the chattering teeth of the monks' silent talk. The corpses' wheezing breaths, coming from too many orifices. They were getting closer. Still, she tried to find something in the walls that would give way.

They were practically on her. She could hear their jackets and pants swishing and ruffling, the cracking of their arms reaching out to grab her—

"Ask me nicely, Fae."

"Nefas, let me out, please!" she cried desperately. Her voice went nowhere, and it sounded detached.

The wall to her left gave way. She bolted through the empty space to the sound of Nefas' amused laughter, echoing a hundred times through rotten mouths and heard only in her head. She didn't wait around to take a bow for the performance.

Her breaths sounded too laborious, her footsteps too sharp. Another quick shoulder check showed that the monks and corpses weren't after her but had stopped altogether as though in send-off. She wasn't going to wait to find out their purpose and left them behind. She slowed to a walk, regularly checking behind her. They stayed put.

She had no concept of where she was going. The maze's nearly featureless streets were indistinguishable from each other, with the same nothingness turn after turn. There was no exit and she couldn't see the basilica spires or the village wall to guide her out. It was becoming easy to convince herself that she was a lone apocalyptic survivor in this place of desolation, forgotten by those who'd gone before. Nefas let the silence do his work for him. It was as if the void had escaped her and she was walking through it in real life. Empty only except for what its creator gave her. Where was Dominic? He'd abandoned her in here.

Left, right, right, left, double back, Fae screamed in frustration only to have the sound of it come back to her. Her ability to make the simple decision about which direction to turn next was becoming harder. The hopeless panic of being kept isolated in a place where she couldn't win grabbed hold. Her knuckles hurt from when a corpse had almost caught her earlier. It came out of nowhere, but instinct had her grab its jaw and she scraped her knuckles as she slammed its head into the wall. It grunted and groaned as it sank to the ground, leaving a glistening streak behind. That was the only noise the corpse made, and that solitary sound was burned into her memory. She'd stumbled back in shock, her hands shaking as she stared at the blood-streaked wall and the body crumpled beyond the parasite's ability to get it back up again. The corpse wore a wedding ring, strapped to its finger so it wouldn't fall off.

"NEFAS!!" She cried an angry sob, her hands shaking. She'd seen Nefas standing far off again, watching. She looked for him a second time but he was gone.

She'd left the corpse behind. The shock of her role in its death played with her ability to walk, to think. She just walked, endlessly, hoping to escape, but eventually she had to stop. She'd come this way before. Her previous foot imprints were there, and she recognized the door. There had only been a small number of doors. This one she recognized from its paint just light enough to catch the dim glow from the icicles above. She had nowhere else to go except straight, so straight she went until she came around to the exact same door again; it was unmistakable. She continued on and came up on the same door a third time, and then she refused to try a fourth time.

"Let me out!" Fae shouted pathetically, feeling like no was listening. But, sure enough, she noticed just up ahead what had to have been a tight, ninety-degree corner tucked away. She could just make out the icicles hanging around the corner. Sensing her opportunity, Fae took the sharp corner. She immediately regretted her decision and tried to back right out again, but she bumped into a wall blocking her retreat. The roofs above more or less met, creating an unbroken ceiling of icy spikes of varying lengths and thicknesses hanging precariously. Backlit with the same green light, it was striking—striking like a path to a sacrificial altar was bedded with roses. It felt like an underground tomb left unused and undisturbed for centuries, just for her.

To welcome her, one of the icicles fell with a chilling force. Fae closed her eyes against her fate, resting against the wall. "I will not be afraid," she whispered. "I can't be afraid. I'll stay here and wait. Dominic is coming . . ."

"I thought you were ready," Nefas breathed into her ear. Fae snapped open her eyes, scouring the space around her to find Nefas, but he didn't want to be seen. He spoke now from all around her. "But then you had to say his name as though he was going to rescue you. As if you needed rescuing."

She was desperate to see Nefas again because she needed to feel someone else, to know that she hadn't been abandoned here. No matter where she turned, he was passing just outside her vision. He kept talking as he circled, always one stop ahead of her sight.

"I can run this maze forever. I have my vault to store you in until next year and every year after. You would be on this street until I hear the sound of your spirit crying defeat and begging surrender. But tonight, I'm not feeling very patient. Let's try this instead."

A live scene materialized in the darkness; it was as real as if the people appearing had just been transported in. A young Spanish woman, heavily pregnant, was scampering backward in fear on her hands and feet. She was crying and pleading with someone. The situation was desperate. One hand was on her round belly; the other was reaching out for mercy. Another woman aiming a pistol entered the picture.

"I can stop this," Nefas said. "Promise me your everything."

Fae couldn't speak, dumbfounded. What was she seeing?

"Too slow again." Without hesitation, the woman with the gun pulled the trigger, shooting the pregnant woman in the head, stilling her forever.

"NO!" Fae screamed, horrified, struggling forward as if she could help the shot woman. "Why? That . . . that wasn't real . . . !"

Nefas stopped his circling and calmly came to her. "Fae, Fae, Fae, my rising star, have we spent so little time together to make you think that I joke? This doesn't end until I have your submission, and I will continue to escalate until you submit. The execution of Marialicia Angela Santos Garcia and her blistering baggage of fetal tissue is on you. I promised you neutrality with the delivery of the baby—I don't lie. But until then? You will know that you need me." He kept his voice calm, collected... reasonable. "If that takes an accident similar to Marialicia's to happen to your grandmother, or maybe your friend Analyse, then that's on you too." With that evil cliff-hanger, Nefas slipped back into the darkness. The weight of Fae's conscious was almost too heavy for her to be able to stand.

She heard, too late, the sound of a fast-forwarded, stamping horde of heavy corpse feet. A sharp hand pierced through the wall behind her, grabbed her neck, and clamped it tight against the wall. Fae gasped against the slow crush of her windpipe and grabbed for the dry finger bones: a monk. Through the false wall, she finally heard what the monk's silent, clacking jaws had been saying, a chant, over and over and over.

Nulla fuga est. Mortuus morietur ad novam vitam in morte. Nulla fuga est. Mortuus morietur ad novam vitam in morte. Nulla fuga est. Mortuus morietur ad novam vitam in morte. Woman, flee him! Nulla fuga e—

The monk's iron grip loosened just a fraction, but it was enough for Fae to find a grip around its top finger. She yanked hard on it and snapped it backward—*ietur ad novam vitam in morte*... With as deep a breath as she could fight for, Fae gave a loud shout and jerked hard at the rest of the fingers. She broke free and stumbled out into the street—and then there was nothing again. The monk's chant was silenced, leaving just her own gasping sound in the dead silence. She stood frozen, not sure if the icicles would fall or if the fake wall would disappear and the monks with the corpses would pour in and finish what they'd begun. She waited, her heart in her throat. One... two... three... four... "What are you waiting for?!" five... six... seven... eight... The fake wall evaporated, and there the two monks solemnly stood, silently chanting. The glowing army was filling up the intersection behind them, waiting to be let in.

An icicle fell, shattering ice between her and them. The monks stepped out and began leading the corpses toward her. Their feet crunched over the ice shards, and she quickly backed up in turn. "Just let me out of here," she said to the monks, hoping they doubled as Nefas' mouthpiece. "I'm going to bring him the baby just like we agreed." Another icicle fell and pierced the head of the one of the corpses, which stumbled but kept shuffling on with ice sticking out of its skull. "I can't even hear him crying anymore."

From the darkness, Nefas spoke. "I will be your answer, your relief."

"Yes! Where are you?" Fae frantically scanned around her, looking for a sign of him. A cracking noise above her warned of a falling icicle and she leaped backward just in time to miss it. The corpses began laughing with Nefas' voice, reverberating through the old streets.

Move! Fae didn't know where the thought came from, but she reacted instantly and felt the coolness of an icicle streak past her face.

The monks didn't speak for Nefas. No one did. She could run, but she couldn't run far, and she had no will left, no desire to resist him. "I'm done, Nefas. I'm done," she said. She sunk to her knees, biting her lip in complete resignation to her situation. The horde stopped.

He was going to do whatever it took to get what he wanted out of her, even if it meant killing her. He'd probably even re-animate her just to hear her confess him. And not just soul relativism death, but actual murder—and that thought was crushing. Dominic was supposed to be out here with her, protecting her from this. But he wasn't. He must've somehow learned that she was going to give Nefas the baby and decided to abandon her to it. No doubt he was now working against her to prevent the transaction. She couldn't win.

"Let me die in the void, where no one can see me and wonder at what I've become. Dominic pushed me into running." Maybe saying that would help, or maybe it would make everything worse, but she had nothing else to offer. "You two were fighting, and I needed to find the baby for you. That was our deal."

She waited in the dark, but still Nefas stayed away.

"Whatever you say, whatever you want! I'm yours." Tears welled in her eyes, and he was going to hit her for crying. She didn't care, because he could do whatever he wanted with her. That was her place. But no form of retribution came for her tears, and she waited obediently for him.

And then something happened. Her chest contracted, and Fae clutched at it for it felt like strings were being pulled from her heart. She couldn't tell if it hurt, or if it was just such a foreign feeling that she wanted it to hurt. The strings were pulled until they came to their end, and then they moved freely through her body until finally they reached the top of her skin. At first it felt like little trails of perspiration dripping down, but then the trails began moving against gravity and going in all directions—twisting up her arm, climbing up toward her neck, slipping down into her boot. The disgusting thought of tiny snakes crawling all over her made Fae frantic. Scrambling, she struggled to undo her jacket, but her fingers wouldn't cooperate, and then something bit her on the back of the leg. She knew then that they had to be snakes, and the more she fought them, the more they bit.

A swirling vortex of snow conjured up Nefas in his jeans and jacket, the hood hiding his face completely now, though in this darkness she couldn't have seen it anyway. He stood there, watching her in pure amusement.

"Maybe your memory is better than mine, but I don't remember any deal."

There had been a deal! But that was as deep as her thoughts could go with the snakes torturing her body.

"I just remember me telling you what was going to happen."

His amusement at her plight made her whimper. She broke down and pleaded with him. "Get them off me, please!" She grabbed for a snake at her back only to find nothing there when she closed her fist. Nefas gave no indication that he even heard her. She pulled at her boot trying to yank it off, her hands slipping uselessly off the smooth leather. "You've punished me enough; make them go away."

"I haven't done anything 'enough'!" Nefas finally snapped, his dark voice dangerously even. "I have barely even started with you. There are still years to come." With a casual wave of his hand, the feeling of the snakes evaporated into little puffs of fog, her skin left tingling and crawling. A gust of the blizzard's wind found its way into the street and carried Nefas away in its swirl, leaving in its wake an opening in the street that hadn't been there before. For the first time since leaving the main road, the sound of the crying baby was loud and clear.

It was a slow, uncertain effort that got Fae standing again. Expecting something else to happen, mindful of the stayed monks and corpses, she uneasily made for the newly opened path. Unhindered, the blizzard raged against her as she was emptied back into the plaza of the Notre-Dame du Seigneur, but the ability for her eyes to see again, her ears to hear, her skin to feel, was pure liberty. The basilica shone as bright as ever, though the darkness hampered its reach, and the building stood beautifully with sparkling, crystallized snow softening its sharp edges. The sight of such a hope was as tiring as it was depressing; she'd knelt before Nefas. She could never go back in there now. Not even for the gloves she could picture sitting on the pew, waiting for her return.

The plaza was still thick with corpses bumping about. It looked like hundreds had returned from their charge after her, their numbers confirming that Anna's promise of a happy ending was over. Dominic had abandoned her in that maze, and now her singular purpose was to give Nefas his baby in the fool's belief that he would let her go free after all this. Her longing thoughts were still with her gloves when Nefas appeared in front of her, blocking her view of the basilica. "Lose yourself in my eyes for only a minute, and I'll let you get your gloves." His hand rested on his hood ready to pull it back.

Fae didn't respond right away. It was the offer she was supposed to refuse.

"Not so eager to see my real face anymore? Shame. You shouldn't have picked such a nice one for me."

Nefas made a sharp, pushing motion toward her, and an unseen force shoved her back into the street she'd just escaped from, back into the shadows and the broken ice. "Are you cold again, Fae? How badly do you want back inside?"

"I—" It was hard to speak; she was shaking. "I am what you want me to be. Hot or cold."

"I won't let you freeze, Fae. I'm going to protect you." He said it in mockery, then he raised his hands and shoved her back again, making her stumble. "Earlier this evening, we were practically lovers, Fae; you trusted me. I stayed with you through your doubts and unfaithfulness and shared my mind with you. But then you spurned me, Fae, you listened to lies about me, and that hurt. You blame Dominic, but you still chose to keep running. I thought you liked my gifts."

Fae said nothing because she couldn't say what he wanted: that she was sorry.

"Don't you think I can hear you reciting those traitorous words? Being afraid is your life now; no amount of chanting will change that."

"Everything I did was to get back to you—"

Fae saw his arm sweep across his body and then felt herself flying through the air.

"Don't lie to me."

Fae found consciousness slumped against an old oil barrel, frozen solid from the drip of the eaves above. The same ensnaring side street she had just escaped from greeted her coldly again, and her head pounded. She raised a hand to touch the back of her head. Her fingers were too cold to feel much, but she brought them to her eyes and saw no blood—though, she heard a metallic rattle. Confused, she brought both hands before her to see them manacled at the wrists. She rattled the chains to test them, pulled against them, and found that they were soldered to the barrel. She closed her eyes and took a slow, deep breath. She opened them again to find Nefas crouched in front of her, the last bit of green fog evaporating from his mouth.

"You're out of chances, Fae. But then, you never really had much of one, did you?" He reached down, picked up her hands, and encased them in his own. "I finished delivering your gifts. They're for later." He squeezed down hard.

"Ow, ow, stop!"

"Let me warm them for you." Her finger bones cramped hard and she tried pulling her arms back out of his grip, but he held fast and squeezed down tighter. She cried out, but still Nefas squeezed until the first pop came and Fae fell over, struggling against him. Four more joints popped out before Nefas finally let go. Five knuckles were already swollen to marbles.

"You *decided* to bring me someone I wanted. I *told* you to bring me the baby, and that *wasn't* your choice."

"I was trying to bring him to you," Fae said, cradling her dislocated joints against her chest. She lay on her side trying to rein in the sounds of her pain. Kneeling beside her, Nefas roughly pulled away one of her hands and set Fae back into a light-headed whorl of torture. "The maze of streets yo—"

She stopped before she accused him, but it wasn't fast enough. Nefas gripped her wrist tight and flicked one of her dislocated knuckles. It was more than enough, and Fae feebly cried out, tears of pain falling hot against her cheeks as she conceded, "Dominic locked me up in the maze. He lured me in after he made me run away from you. You got me out." Nefas let her go, but she left her hand raised in mid-air in case taking it back was the wrong thing to do. A soothing sensation seeped into her hands warming them, and soon the pain in her dislocated joints went away. She slowly flexed her fingers and felt no pain.

"The powers I have, you can't even begin to know," Nefas said. In turn, Fae slowly pushed herself back up to sitting, the chains at her wrists clinking. "You surrendered to me, I own you."

This she knew, deeper than she knew her own name. "Let me bring you the Nazi, too."

In answer Nefas grabbed a fistful of Fae's hair and slammed her head back against the frozen barrel. "When I want Lars Dreschler, I will take him." Nefas forced open the collar of Fae's jacket and ignored her slow, low, groans of fighting consciousness. He placed his fingertips over her chest, letting the parasite flow out and wrap itself around her heart, casting its eerie glow beneath her jaw. "Now you can bring me the baby. Once you do, then I will warm the rest of your body. What I've put in you will force you to carry it out." Nefas let her go, and the glow from the parasite faded away.

With a moan, Fae tried to find her focus, but she was fighting consciousness. When she was finally able to focus, Nefas was striding away. Fae barely saw his shadow before he was swallowed up into his own darkness. *I'm watching, tramp. Your lies are weak, like you.*

22

Fae's eyes wouldn't focus. Or so she thought. It was hard to tell in the dark. It took a few moments to remember why chains seemed to rattle whenever she moved her arms, but eventually she remembered: She was attached to them. When she could suffer her eyes being open without feeling dizzy, she rattled the cold metal manacles around her wrists and tugged at them with the same result as before. Somehow she didn't think leaving them on her was Nefas' oversight.

The cold from the paving stones and the barrel's metal was driving into her, and she shivered. Unsteadily, Fae slowly rose to her feet. A quick blackout forced her to grab the barrel's rim in time to let the moment pass. How she was going to find the baby was beyond her. Chained to this barrel, she wasn't going to be chasing after anything, much less a cry in the wind. She could just make out the corpses' green glow in the plaza at the end of the street; getting back to Rue Leopold I would mean exposing herself to them. She wasn't ready for that even though, strangely, she somehow felt OK about walking among them. She slumped against the wall and stared up to the sky. Of what she could tell, the blizzard looked to have lost its fury, but it was still a storm. She found no inspiration in the sky. It didn't make her dizzy, though, so she kept staring up.

Looking up, with snowflakes falling on her eyelashes, Fae was drawn back to the days of her childhood when she would go on family vacations in the Rockies to the cabin her grandfather had built. As she got older, she more and more often sought refuge outside, where she'd hide beneath the branches of a giant evergreen. It hid her from the cabin's entrance, but gave her a view of the whole sky as it spread endlessly across the forested mountains. She had spent so many hours just staring at the sky and watching the snow fall, or the birds soar, and finding comfort from her thoughts. And then there was that massive snowstorm that swept through the usually mild Vancouver back in junior high. That night, Justin Walker finally made good on the pizza he had promised her. It wasn't cold, and the snow had fallen heavy and silent. They made a snowman in the neighborhood park and then sat against it, staring up into the sky watching the snowflakes appear out of nowhere, inches from their faces, and talking about trivial things twelve- and thirteen-year-olds deemed so grown-up and serious. But, unlike then, looking into a night sky now didn't make the problems go away or bring sense to life. It just made her realize how alone she was.

There was a window above her head. She hadn't noticed it before—surprising, since on its inside ledge was a lit, plastic Nativity scene. It was a rare light that hadn't been smothered in Nefas' darkness. She carefully stood to look at the tacky decoration that showed white-faced men with blue eyes and a blonde-haired Mary. The three Wise Men stood outside the barn with their gifts, wrapped in perfect square boxes and topped with perfect blue ribbons.

"You guys followed a giant star. Made for a great story, didn't it." She slid back down, sitting on her haunches and studying the manacles, hanging heavy off her wrists. "I wouldn't mind one of those right now—a sign to follow. Apparently, I should've been in a cathartic trance inside the Basilique de Notre-Dame du Seigneur instead of making deals with the devil for my sanity and the lives of people I care about. I don't even think I am sane anymore . . . so I guess it wasn't much of a deal then, huh. Grandma tried."

Another pull at her chains proved nothing had changed, but she did take the time to study the bonds themselves. As she leaned to one side, the necklace

Anna had given her slid against her skin; she'd forgotten about it. As silly as the notion was, Fae took the necklace off and fit the key into the keyhole of her shackles. She didn't believe it when the key slid in; she was stupefied when the key worked, and the shackle fell off. And then nothing happened. There was no sound of scuttling of feet bringing the monks and corpses. No deadly icicles fell. The void didn't swell up and drown her thoughts. The baby's crying continued carrying in the wind, but that was it. She quickly freed her other hand and then waited for a long while, expecting the unexpected. But nothing happened.

Tentatively, she stood up using the barrel to help her stand. Her legs were stiffened by the cold; her toes were as frozen as her fingers had been; but she was free.

Fae looked around and tried to determine the best way to get out of this place. "Bringing a Christmas miracle to find this baby would be great, don't you think? If baby Jesus cried this loud, Herod would've killed him long before the Wise Men ever found him." Fae laughed sadly at herself. "Listen to me talk."

The curtains in the window shivered, and a tabby kitten jumped onto the ledge and startled her. It looked out at her with huge green eyes and meowed, cocking its head to one side before gnawing on the plastic star of Bethlehem. Fae smiled at her cute little friend but then, afraid it might gnaw into a wire and electrocute itself, she tapped on the window to chase the kitten away. In one swift motion the kitten jumped and bolted back into the apartment. Fae was alone again, and the loose star jarred to a horizontal lie.

Star of wonder, star of night . . . Westward leading, still proceeding . . .

The carol's lyrics rang through her head unbidden, and she instantly wanted the singsong carol out. It sounded ugly, like a mosquito buzzing in her ear. She'd never disliked it before, so why now, she didn't know. She tried to drown it out with another song, but the only one that came to her was a harsh rap song she didn't even like, so she shut her thoughts off to music all together.

The carol, however, did make a unique argument. The Wise Men followed the directional pointing of a star to the place they believed they needed to be. The star in the window was now pointing in a direction too, albeit, thanks to the cat. Twenty-four hours ago, she would never have believed that she would follow a tipped-over star of Bethlehem to find a baby and trade him for— . . . she couldn't think beyond that. It made her stomach lurch. She barely recognized herself from twenty-four hours ago and, as embarrassing as it was, Fae set off down the small street in the direction the little plastic star pointed.

I am so tired, Fae thought, slugging through the snow. She'd just keep walking until this road ended. Beyond that, if the baby was supposed to be found, then he would have to find her. Some dark part of her wondered what Nefas wanted with the baby, and the ideas made her sick. She struggled to remember what she'd been saying about not being afraid, but she couldn't remember how it went. *I don't know how much more of this I can take. I hate Grandmother so much right now. And lying Claire, Emile, and stupid Maël, Mrs. Lemmens—they all knew what was coming. Oh, and Elise, what I have to say to you! They should all rot in the chambers of ruin until the damnation of Judgment Day makes them fodder for slaves to tread upon, contempt of Hell's furious fires.*

Fae stopped walking, shocked. "How did I even think that? I love my grandmother." *Maybe instead of my freedom from Nefas, I should have asked him to pay visit to the likes of my betrayers and show them what they led me into— infect* them *with his void and parasite.* "Holy— Fae, what are you thinking?" She pounded her head with the palm of her hands to try to beat the thoughts out, feeling more like she was in an asylum than ever before.

Her struggle with these dark thoughts woke the void in her. She found herself in one of the first colored nebula she had ever passed through. She was stuck in a red and purple cloud and talking to at least a dozen or more versions of herself. She was screaming at some, trying to placate some, terrified of others. Some were angry at her, some were raging violent, others were laughing, depressed, malicious, seductive, and they were all vying for her attention. She couldn't address them all, but she was trying, trying so hard but couldn't keep up. Every time she replied she responded in kind, either laughing, or screaming, or crying, and often she was reacting to any number of them all at once. Fae had no idea if she was supposed to be happy or sad;

she had no idea who she was outside of these other Faes who kept changing her into themselves, and she was at their mercy.

Then out of the crowd rose her mother, mascara running down her cheeks, a messy ponytail slipping to one side. Fae wanted to run to her, tell her to hold on, that it would get better, it always did. "I thought you loved me, Fae," her mother said in monotone. "Your father asked you to come to my surprise birthday at church. You weren't there." A pistol appeared in her hand and she pressed the barrel to her head. "I thought I loved you, too." And then she shot herself. Fae screamed as her mother's body fell limp into the gases, or she thought she screamed. Maybe she had just stood there indifferent.

"That's not how it happened!" Fae insisted. "That's not how she died! She never said that!" *How do you know what she wished?* "There was no party!" *How do you know? You didn't go home very often, did you? Where were you on her birthday?* "We had her birthday whenever she was happy; I never missed one." *Except for this one.* "There was no surprise party!"

All this was downloaded almost instantly, and Fae snapped out of it like a plug abruptly pulled out. Released, her heart was pounding. "God," she whispered, horrified, "help me. Something is taking me over."

Yes, very good . . .

Even though the street she was on had been spared the roughest of the blizzard, a wind rose from behind and pushed her forward—a wind that was degrees warmer than the rest of the air. Fae watched in wonder as it passed her by and swirled the snow away from the ground, creating a path halved of its snow deposit.

Captivated by its mystery, Fae followed after the current, glistening with fractures of light stolen by the frozen crystals caught up inside it. It swept through one small intersection and then wrapped around to take her down another street, flowed into a different one, and then finally dumped her out onto Rue Leopold I. The dying fury of the blizzard scattered the current, but the weakening gusts nudged her up the street away from the Notre-Dame du Seigneur, the same direction Dominic had first told her to go.

The longer she trudged through the snow, the worse the creep of nausea became. For distraction, she took note of the modified angels swinging helplessly beneath their muted lamps. One had clipped wings showing how weak and frail it was. Another had lost its head in the difficult trials of the night. The two facing each other farther up the street had vicious, mad dog faces with pointed, snapping teeth. No doubt, Nefas had done this, but she had to admit, she kind of liked their new, non-classical look. Before she could dwell on the angels for too long, she came to a juncture where, for the first time all night, the direction of the baby's cry was unmistakable.

She passed underneath a stone arch bridge and headed toward the cry. This street was completely different from the one she had just left, as this one had large industrial buildings densely lining both sides in an unbroken row. Their large loading doors and open work fronts were all closed, and it didn't take long until Fae stood in front of a giant wooden loading door. Two lightbulbs hung high, illuminating black block letters painted on the brick wall reading, "boucherie," butcher shop. There was no doubt that the baby's cries were coming from inside. The butcher's family probably lived in a small attached apartment.

Fae came to the loading door and picked up the heavy, palm-sized lock keeping the two halves of the door closed. She pulled hard on it a couple of times, to no avail.

She had come too far to let it come to this. She wanted to sit down and let the snow bury her so she could forget and so that she could be forgotten, but the urge from inside fueled her to not give up yet. Nefas needed his baby. A quick search revealed no hard object capable of beating the lock off. After double-checking a few feet down the road in both directions, there didn't look to be another way in. What if she could kick the doors open? The brackets looked old enough.

Swallowing the nausea haunting her, and trying to focus without causing a migraine, she geared up to deliver the most crushing impact since the game-tying goal of her high school regional soccer final. Perched on the balls of her feet, Fae convinced her body to cooperate; she was ready to let loose the explosive kick when she was interrupted.

"All set to destroy some more property?"

Dominic.

"Where in hell have you been?" She was obviously angry at him, but she was also scared that he'd finally shown up. She had a human business transaction to conclude that he wouldn't approve of... that no normal person would approve of. But she wasn't normal anymore, was she? Dominic was strong enough to fight Nefas, so he could certainly fight her. "If you hadn't run away, that shop's window wouldn't be broken."

Dominic approached the barn door. "Mrs. Dubois was looking for an excuse to get a new one. She will thank you."

"What are you doing?"

Dominic pulled out two thin picks, stuck them into the padlock's keyhole, and twisted them around. "Opening the door."

"Get out of the way. I'm going to do it."

That caused him to stop and look at her in amusement.

"Are you, now? Giving no offense, but if you feel half of what you look like, I am not sure that you have enough in you to crack open an egg."

"Go away. I'll meet you back at the basilica with the kid."

Dominic stood up then, and looked at her seriously. Fae was certain he grew an extra six inches before her eyes. "Your brain is one knock away from making your minor concussion a major one, and there is a patch of ice right in front of this door. If you really want to stand on your pride, then do so once a certain child is tended to and not at his expense."

With that being said, Dominic returned to his lock picking and within a few seconds he straightened up, gave a quick tug, and popped the padlock open. In one swift motion, he freed the lock and pulled open one side of the door for her to slip through. She did so consciously aware of the ice patch and, even then, she still skidded on the perfectly smooth surface.

The protection the barn offered from the conditions outside were as good as a warm bath to her frozen body. Fae turned around to face him. "I'll see you back at the basilica, thanks." That sounded too obvious. "You know, since you show up at your convenience to help out, then leave at your convenience. Aren't you missing a solo with the choir?" Her thawing cheeks felt like plastic every time she moved them.

"The baby, Fae; can't you hear him?" Dominic made his way past her into the dark. She could hear him palming the wall, but she was too stunned to help him look for the light switch. Of course, she could hear him! . . . but when had she stopped caring about him? She'd found Nefas' baby; why did it matter if he was still crying?

Fluorescent tube lighting flickered to life, and Fae quickly shielded her eyes from the blinding light. "A warning would've been nice," she griped, squinting and blinking, her head throbbing. Two goats, one goose, and a sow added their complaints to Fae's and the baby's, whose subdued cries were renewed at the small commotion.

To her right were two stainless steel stalls where the sow was, and a small paddock thickly layered with fresh straw, the overflow littering the pitted concrete floor. The animals shifted their sleepy legs and stared at the intruders unimpressed. The goose roamed free but kept its distance. There was a door beside the stalls leading into the attached store and another, larger, stainless steel one at the back for an industrial freezer. To her left were a few extra bales of hay, some bags of feed, and two frayed harnesses with rope hung over nail pegs. A metal water tap leaked slow drips into a drainage hole, and beside that a weathered, gray wooden table held the only thing she cared about: a baby carrier with a thick wool blanket placed over top.

Dominic was already there, flipping off the scratchy, gray and red blanket to reveal a very real child squirming under his straps and crying his little baby heart out.

"Real flesh and blood." Fae spoke softly to the snowsuited boy and picked him up after unsnapping the straps holding him in. She guessed him to be about six months old. As soon as her hands wrapped around his chest, he stopped crying, his brown eyes staring at her, his jaw falling slightly open. "Just as promised."

"He's precious," Dominic said, joining Fae by the table.

"With the lungs of an opera singer." Holding the child in her arms, Fae was enraptured by his beautiful eyes. She hadn't held many babies before, and she was taken by the depth of personality staring out at her. There was an intelligent person inside those brown orbs, trusting her, believing in her. Those eyes didn't know any better.

"Were the goats giving you good company?" The baby smiled up at her. Fae broke her attention with the boy and addressed Dominic. "He must be from an immigrant family? He isn't a corpse."

"The Gift may not be pleasant, but it's not cruel. Babies, young children, and those who can't understand aren't affected. They're cared for in the Notre-Dame du Seigneur. Now, let's get him back." Reaching down, Dominic tickled his belly through the snowsuit, and the little boy laughed and squirmed in Fae's arms. "They are so innocent, aren't they?" Dominic mused. Fae wanted to ask him what sort of innocence could free her from Nefas but, since that option was no longer available, she decided not to open the conversation. "They have no idea what evil is and they don't care. Imagine what this world would look like if we could all go back to that place again."

Fae wasn't feeling well, so she put the baby back in his carrier. "It's dumb to think that innocence will ever last. This boy will hate his parents, regret his binge-drinking party days, and steal chocolate bars and virginities before he throws a friend under the bus to get a job just like everyone else."

"This is not an ordinary boy."

Fae tossed the blanket back over the carrier hiding the child beneath it. She didn't want to see him anymore. Ignorance was bliss. "You shut down here, Dominic. I'll take this forgotten kid back to the basilica."

"We go together. It can be easy to get lost in these streets." He let the comment hang, and Fae didn't touch it.

Grabbing the carrier with both hands, Fae hefted it off the table and lugged it across the floor, wondering if Nefas needed the baby alive. Thankfully, the stray goose waddled close behind. Its little honking noise with every step was enough to keep Fae from sinking too deep into that horrendous thought trail. She could lock Dominic inside, she thought, if she could slip outside and secure the padlock. With one eye on the door and one on Dominic, Fae casually reached for the thick handle and pulled inward, ready to slip out, carrier first. The door rattled, but it didn't open. She tried again; the door bounced against its constraint, but it still didn't open.

"Dominic, did you lock the door?"

Dominic was standing unconcerned next to the light switch, holding a blanket matching the one that covered the baby. "I told you, we leave together. For you." He tossed the blanket toward her, but she let it fall to the ground. "You need to warm up before going back out there."

"How did you lock it?" Dominic didn't respond; he just looked down to the blanket at her feet then back up. "You helped me get out of the plaza, and now I'm finishing the job. I am taking him."

"Yes, you are. That's what you need to do, but we go together," he said calmly. The baby carrier was getting unbearably heavy, and the boy was fidgeting. Fae put him down.

"Just, open the doors. I need to get out of here." Dominic didn't look convinced. "Do you know what Anna told me? That this boy is my ticket to getting my life back."

"Where are you going to take him, Fae?"

"I told you, the Notre-Dame du Seigneur!" She tried opening the doors again, but they only rattled mockingly at her.

"I don't think you are."

A surge of hate balled up inside and she wondered how fast his snowy persona would melt if he was lit on fire. "I said let me out, NOW!" Screaming the last word, Fae narrowed her eyes. "You have no idea what will happen if I don't leave with this baby."

Unfazed as always he replied, "I am not your enemy."

"You oppose me, so you are my enemy. Stand in my way and you will die for it."

"By whose hand?"

"I think you know." Fae waited for the light of recognition to go off on his face, which would be as gratifying as watching all her opponents plead at her feet for the mercy she would never give. This was the moment she wanted to have all those years ago in the church café: behold, the creature breeding beneath your noses. Only now, it wasn't vodka she was revealing, but Nefas. "You may have stood up to him before, but not even you can hold out forever."

The bitter light of acknowledged defeat that Fae was waiting for never came. Instead, Dominic looked completely unbothered. "You threaten me with a power you don't understand."

THE GIFT

"You can't win against him. Look at me. I tried everything you and Anna said, and he still broke me. He owns me now. He owns me!" Hot tears welled up, as she starred furiously at him. "Open this door, or I'll call him here right now, and he'll take what is his."

"Nefas can't come in here, Fae."

"Oh my god, how stupid are you? Say 'can't' one more time, Dominic. Say it, just SAY IT!"

"Nefas will never find us here. It's the baby, he's been hidden like a joey in its mother's pouch. Since we're with the baby, we benefit from his protection."

He was lying, trying to trick her. "I'll show him the way in."

"It is your choice. What will happen when Nefas comes?"

"He'll do whatever he wants with you, and he'll get me out of here. This baby is the price I pay for him to let me walk away from this village the same way I came in. He knows what I want and he made a better deal than Anna's."

"He'll just let you go after all that effort to possess you?" Dominic raised his eyebrow. Fae tried to hold her face tight with conviction, but she could feel a muscle tweak in her lip. "The mysteries of the void he breathed into you—he'll just take those back, too?"

"What that void is to me is none of your business. If you didn't want it to come to this, you shouldn't have abandoned me in that hellish maze."

"Fae, I didn't forget you after your escape in the plaza. I prepared that Communion for you to find on your way; it was yours to use. You weren't supposed to abandon it."

"And you couldn't have just told me that, you know, like, with words?" She didn't give him a chance to answer. "There probably wasn't *supposed* to be an army of eager corpses cornering me against that storefront either, and I probably wasn't *supposed* to have left my gloves behind. What else was not *supposed* to have happened? I don't know, maybe two psychotic villagers luring me into a dark and scary graveyard pit where the town's horror likes to hang out? You were supposed to protect me!"

Dominic was looking at her with pity, but he was not one to get sidetracked. "I told you to stay on Rue Leopold I. You made the decision to leave the street, and I was unable to help you like I wanted to. But Anna gave you the key you needed, and those icicles were supposed to hit you every time. I did what I could. I heard everything, Fae. I saw *everything*." He wasn't angry, or disgusted, or acting betrayed, and he should've been.

"Freedom has a price."

"I am sorry to tell you that you are not rich enough to pay for it."

"I know. Nefas said I'd be in your debt, so he gave me the debt-free option."

Stepping toward her, Dominic reached down to grab the blanket and wrapped it around her shoulders, then knelt and peeked inside the baby carrier. "He's dozing even through all our talking," he said with a slight smile before standing up again. "Nefas lied to you, Fae. It's what he does. He will see you betray innocence, then force you to watch him destroy it. Instead of walking away from him and gaining some sort of return to normalcy, you will be chaining yourself to him with shame and self-hatred. I know you've come to that same realization, but know that you're not powerless against him."

"If you saw everything that happened, then you'll remember I was already in literal chains. Your words are too late." Fae frowned, feeling the darkness inside growing stronger. "What is this baby to me but currency? I'm buying myself back to enjoy life without you, without Nefas, and to live life according to my dictates, how I plan it, and how I want it."

"Have the last forty-eight hours really convinced you that you'll be OK without help?" Dominic stood back up and cocked an eyebrow. "What has Nefas ever said or done that gives you enough confidence to believe he would just let you go?"

The answer was nothing, and she'd known this since she'd left the basilica—which is why she'd tried to run from him in the first place. Nefas would be with her in wake and in sleep, and this conversation was one maze too late. Ever since she'd emerged from it, the fear of being intricately tied to Nefas was vanishing like fog on a warm morning; yes, she would be his queen, and she needed to get back outside.

There was one way left to get Dominic to undo the lock. It was a delicious idea, an unholy one, and one that was irresistible to try. "So, say you're right about all this." She paused and looked at him with big eyes. "I already made the deal. If I don't come through with my end then he's... he'll... do terrible things..."

Hugging the blanket closer, she came to Dominic and rested her body against his, laying her head on his shoulder. There was a short moment where nothing happened, then he put an arm around her shoulders, hugging her.

"I would be buried alive in that pit if you didn't show up, and in any other world I would have been done for long ago. I still need you, I will never stop needing you." Dominic let her go. Tilting her head back, she gazed at him tenderly and whispered his name, "Dominic." She reached her blanketed arms around his back, seeking to wrap him up in her love, but his face grew angry and he pushed her away.

"No! You cannot do this!"

"Then, maybe you can," Fae suggested secretly. Her brain was swimming in the void again, but there was something different about this nebula that separated it from the others she had passed through. The un-holiness of it, there was something about it that she didn't understand, but while a part of her was thinking, the other was still acting. "No man ever saves a woman over and over again and doesn't dream of some great thanks in return." She approached him again, and he kept his distance.

"There is no return path from where you're now going, Fae. You do not want to do this."

"No return? Oh, I definitely think that is where I want to go with you."

"NO!" He shouted at her so strongly, it stopped her in her tracks. The baby woke crying and the animals stirred, disturbed. In a blink of an eye, the barn lit up in a searing white light and, when the blindness ebbed, away Fae fell to her knees, her heart racing in fear of the power before her. A man of at least seven feet stood where Dominic had, a terrible figure of awe and strength—a man who would have been a god to people of a simpler time. He wore clothes she had no context for, and his eyes burned with a reflected fire that belied the greatness of the source, like the moon did the sun. Glowing white hot, she couldn't stand looking at him. She buried herself beneath the thick blanket and yet found little reprieve inside even that. And then the light faded away, and she heard Dominic say, "I had to do that. It is impossible for me to be complicit with what you were trying to do."

With an uncertain hand, Fae slowly uncovered her head and looked up from the floor. Dominic was there as he had been before, a young man made to look older by his white hair. "You're . . . are you . . . a . . ."

"I suggest we hold here for a bit before we make our way back; calm this little boy down again, and get your body temperature regulated." Dominic reached into the carrier and pulled the crying boy out, his little cheeks pink from his efforts. He stopped crying instantly. "Oh, what's this?" Reaching back into the carrier, Dominic pulled out a full baby bottle and showed it to Fae with a smile. "How did we miss this?"

Fae still was in shock. "Was that . . . I mean, did that really . . . I, I didn't know. I'm sorry. I'm so sorry."

"I believe that you genuinely are," he said, giving the nipple of the bottle to the baby who greedily grabbed onto it.

After staring numbly at Dominic and the baby until the bottle was empty, Fae licked her dry lips and said, "The corpses. Those monks. They never stop coming."

"Corpses don't need to follow you anymore, Fae. They are already here." The baby pushed away the empty bottle, and Dominic tossed it back into the carrier. "Hold him will you? Maybe undo his snowsuit; see if his diaper needs changing."

Fae grabbed the boy, but her mind wasn't with him. "They're outside? Or behind one of the doors you mean? They can't get in here though, right?" Dominic had gone to rustle amongst the supplies stacked beside the wooden table and was ignoring her. "Dominic! If Nefas is getting close, I need to know. Dominic!" Still no response. "No wonder artists painted cherub babies instead of you guys," she said to the baby staring at her with those amazing brown eyes. "At least they look sociable."

"Those little fat cherubs were one of the greatest discrediting programs ever run against us," Dominic finally said from across the room, having all of a sudden decided to hear her. "Who wants to ask for help from a silly little daydreaming toddler?"

"The corpse, Dominic; are you looking for it behind that rope? Maybe check with the pig, I think I heard a stomach grumble for some fresh bacon."

As soon as Dominic met her eyes, Fae knew she was going to regret it and wished she could take the words back. He was so much more than human, like Nefas; he could keep her in submission. "I swear I didn't mean that." She cast her eyes to the floor and braced for what would come next.

"Fae, look up," he said with sympathy. "I don't just hurt people, and I don't hurt you." Then more purposefully, "Have you undone his snowsuit yet?"

She was slow to get started, taken aback by Dominic's lack of interest in seizing the power he had over her. Once the little boy's sausage fingers were free, he locked eyes onto hers and grabbed her index finger. He brought it to his mouth and not so much sucked on it as he kissed it with his little, pink lips. He laughed then, giggling and waving her finger in the air as he flailed his limbs about. He was such a beautiful boy, perfect, sweet. Fae let him have his fun.

How could she trade his perfect happiness for her own tarnished life? He was a human child, not a black-market trade item, and yet the darkness told her that she lost her right to question Nefas' demands.

She tickled his belly with her free hand. The little boy squealed again and flailed his limbs some more, his face lighting up like a Christmas tree, the playful color of green lights bouncing around underneath his chin . . . Fae gasped and froze. These were no Christmas lights lighting his face.

They were here.

23

"Dominic," Fae called out as smoothly as her trembling voice could manage. The green light wasn't going away and she didn't hold back her screech. "Dominic!" The goose honked and flapped its wings in agitation. Her hands were clasped around the baby's chest as he dangled from her outstretched arms, his giggling replaced by the distress of his fun suddenly being gone. It was her fingers that were surging with green veins, and she practically threw the baby back into his carrier when she saw it. He started to cry and she twirled around, thrusting her hands in Dominic's face, their state rapidly returning to normal and almost making a mockery of her panic.

"I'm infected. He's found me! I'm taking too long to get back to him and he's punishing me! I thought you said he couldn't find me! I have to go, I have to leave, to get to him, I need to give him this baby before it's too late."

"You know I won't let you take the baby to him."

"He's turning me into one of THEM!" she screamed, tearing at her fingers as though by ripping them open the parasite would flow out.

"Your soul has been like one of them your whole life. Nefas injected you when you were nearing unconsciousness in the alley."

She was going to scream at him for being so useless when she had been most vulnerable, but she bit her tongue.

"Choices have consequences," Dominic said as he pulled her hands apart to stop her frantically tearing at them. "Nefas can't get the baby himself, nor can any of his corpses. He needed an alive person to do that: you. This isn't his first Christmas Eve. He knew you'd come back outside, charged with finding the baby. He's using you to get what he wants. What he promised you in exchange isn't possible; and now that he owns you, he wouldn't have had to fulfill the promise anyway."

Unable to do anything else, Fae paced back and forth, chewing on her thumbnail until she remembered what was in her, and then she spit it back out.

"Nefas still needs you to make the choice to give him the boy; otherwise, the value of the transaction is lost. You do still have a choice even if it doesn't feel like it. His parasite takes your independent will away and replaces it with his own, so, for the time being, he gave you only a portion of himself—just enough to make it incredibly difficult for you to deny him. Once you give him the boy, he will fully infect you and then fully control you."

The more Dominic talked, the more she believed he was telling the truth, and the more she hated what that would mean for her. "I have nothing left to resist him with. Everything I've gone through. For nothing . . ." Fae stopped pacing and looked at Dominic with hard eyes. "The moment I start thinking about not giving him what he wants, the void drowns me out. It's . . . amazing in there, but the more I go in, the more terrified of myself I become."

"Don't give him what he wants," Dominic said it so simply and so easily, and it was irritating because this was neither. "Bring the boy to the basilica instead."

"Do you know what it feels like to be broken down? Emotion by emotion, joint by joint? I am ashamed to be putty in his hands, and still he laughs . . ." Fae turned away so Dominic didn't have to see her fighting back tears. She had nothing to hold them in with.

She looked down at her hands. The overwhelming thought of the thick, gooey parasite beating with the rhythm of her heart, squeezing her bones to do its bidding, removing her will, curling itself in her chest cavity made her sick; she ran over to the drain pipe and heaved up warm liquids into it. Every time she finished, she thought of the parasite inside her again, and she threw up again until there was nothing left. Dominic came to her side with a canteen of water, found from his scavenges, and she drank.

"You can't throw up the parasite," he told her while holding her hair back.

"I'll be the first to succeed."

"You'd be as successful as trying to sneeze a memory out of your head." He handed her the canteen again, and she took a sip. "This is not your end. There is hope."

"That sounds great until I open the door and Nefas is standing there waiting for me. I can't escape him. You keep helping me try, but he keeps getting me back. The longer I make him wait, the worse it's going to be," Fae said as she rested herself against the brick wall.

"The boy is needed at the Notre-Dame du Seigneur. That is your hope, and that is where everything will be set straight again. When he is brought there, then you will get what you came to this village for."

Fae tiredly swore at him. "I came to get a pretty, wrapped box."

Dominic shrugged. "If you want to go to Nefas and your fate with him, then go, but it will be without the boy. If you want to come with me, then I will not leave your side until the night is done. This will be the last time you get the choice tonight. It is fear that will kill you; remember that."

"I'm already dead." Fae snorted bitterly. By the look on Dominic's face, he was glad she was finally figuring it out. "I'm so tired, Dominic," she sighed, resting her head against the wall. "Give me a few minutes, and I'll make a decision, OK?" She shivered as her body relaxed. Dominic lightly kicked her foot.

"If you rest now, it will be hard to get you back. C'mon." Grabbing her arms, Dominic pulled her to her feet, handed her more water, and turned on the dripping tap so she could wash the dried blood from her hands and the splatters from her face.

Sighing heavily at her options, Fae closed her eyes. Dominic had been strong enough to get her out from Nefas' control earlier, but that was before she'd knelt to him and was infected. She was going to have to risk everything on the belief that he was strong enough to do it again, under different circumstances. Maybe she didn't have to be a monster.

While she thought these traitorous things—just as she knew it would—the void welled up and plunged her deep into its darkness, showing her every reason why betraying Nefas would only bring hurt and pain to everyone. He would get the baby either from her or through her, and it wouldn't be pretty. She held her head against the pain trying to get out. Dominic touched her shoulder, and her pain evaporated, leaving her breathing hard and tears rolling down her cheeks.

"Have some more water." He offered her the canteen again, and she knew better than to refuse. As she drank, the residual pain of the void was washed away. She handed the canteen back and wiped her eyes with the back of her hands. She stared down at the rough concrete floor and bit her lip.

She sighed as she cast her eyes to the baby boy, fallen into a post-meal nap. "You know what will happen to me if he gets to me, right? You know what he'll do to him?" She pointed to the baby.

"I don't deal in 'ifs.' There is no uncertainty in how this drama is going to play out. It's now merely a question of whether you're going to be with me or against me when it happens."

Fae said, "We should name him before we do this. He needs a name. You probably know his real one, don't you?"

Dominic nodded. "What would you name him?"

"Nicholas." Fae decided after a moment. "After Nike, the goddess of victory. In elementary school, we used call everyone's Nike shoes 'Nicholas shoes,' thinking we were funny. And also after Saint Nicholas. He brings good things to good people Christmas morning. He deserves some good things right now. Not what I was going to bring him."

"For tonight then, this baby will be your Nike."

Fae got up and returned to the carrier. She fixed the thick blanket over it to keep baby Nicholas warm and began slowly rocking it with her foot. "So what do we do? What's your plan?"

"I'm going to wait."

"For what?"

"You to catch those goats." Dominic strode to the goat pen and rested his hand on the gate waiting to open it for her. "That's a nanny goat," he nodded into the pen at the larger of the two animals. "Nicholas' bottle is empty. You should have some milk too when you manage to get it—for strength."

"I couldn't keep it down if I tried. Just let me rest for a couple minutes. I just . . . I just want to rest. Everything hurts. Every part of me is exhausted. Nicholas just ate."

Dominic, unwilling to negotiate, kept waiting at the gate, and Fae resigned. Shaking her head, she took the bottle from Dominic as she headed in. The two animals stared at her unblinkingly with their gold, slit eyes wondering what she was doing on this side of the fence.

"You can do this."

24

Dominic was softly singing a lullaby to Nicholas in a language Fae didn't recognize, but she listened wishing he would never stop. She was sitting in a corner of the pen, where the youngest goat had pushed her over so he could sit in her lap. But goats being goats, he was currently balancing his front hooves on her shoulder and trying to chew her hair. He was still sleepy, so it was a lackluster effort. Fae hugged him close like a teddy bear, and she was fully aware of, and grateful for, the animal therapy.

Dominic finished his lullaby and tucked Nicholas into the blanket leaving only his round head and black hair poking out. He continued to asleep. She waited until Dominic finished settling Nicholas before she spoke, quietly, so as to not wake him.

"I did it." Fae nodded beside her where the bottle full of goat's milk stood triumphantly. The goat became bored with her and bounced off to settle down in the straw. Fae stood up beside Dominic.

"You did it," he acknowledged, neither of their eyes leaving the beautiful boy in front of them. "We'll leave as soon as my friends arrive."

"More of your kind?" Dominic nodded. "I thought we couldn't be found."

"Insider knowledge."

"Let me leave a note for his parents. Just in case. Tell them where their son is."

"That's not necessary."

"I want to," she insisted. "Things never happen like they should."

Dominic opened his jacket, pulled out a notepad and pen, and gave them both to her. She scribbled her note to Nicholas' parents telling where the boy was going to be, and she pinned it down on the gray wooden table under a tin can filled with sand and cigarette butts. By the time she rejoined Dominic and Nicholas, the promised friends had arrived with the same stealth that Dominic had a penchant for displaying.

Dominic pointed first to the tall, Asian woman, also wearing a white parka, and who had a pony tail sitting high on her head, "Alexandra," then to the other two, Middle Eastern and brothers by the look of them, "Issa and Ilyas." Issa wore a solid black toque to cover his short hair and sported a well-maintained scruff of a beard; Ilyas was clean shaven with shaggy hair falling around his popped-collar Adidas jacket. It looked more appropriate for pre-game warm-ups than surviving winter squalls, but clothes were probably a mere formality for them anyway. The three of them greeted her politely, but it was clear they weren't here for networking. Issa knelt beside the sleeping Nicholas and affectionately brushed his face with his fingers.

"How is she?" Alexandra asked Dominic, wasting no more time on formalities.

"She can make it."

"Did you explain to her what's next?"

"Not yet."

"What needs to be explained?" Fae inserted herself into their conversation and tried not to be irritated at being talked about when she was right there. "We're taking Nicholas to the basilica, and you're going to keep Nefas freaking away from me."

The unfortunate look Ilyas gave her was all the answer she needed to destroy her expectations.

"Nicholas?" Alexandra asked Dominic.

THE GIFT

"It's a good name," he said. Then he turned toward her. "It is not that simple, Fae. You've been feeling addicted to the void and to Nefas because you quite simply are. He designed the void that way and he himself is addictive. That's not your fault; that's reality. However, as you've noticed, separation is the quickest way to weaken his influence."

Fae felt the desire even as he spoke of him. She wanted Nefas. His beautiful face and his smooth voice, the dark thrills of his void . . . the pain he brought didn't even matter. She forced herself to focus harder on what Dominic was saying to fight past the rising urge.

"Nefas has been controlling you from the outside since you arrived: what you see, hear, feel. But the void is inside, and it feeds off your imagination and manipulates it. You've been experiencing this all night, not the least in the crypt, how real it can make your thoughts, and that's only the start of the potential it can access in you. But now that you carry the very essence of Nefas in you through his parasite, your imagination is his toy. It is going to make your journey to the basilica much more difficult. You will have in your possession what he wants and what you promised—Nicholas—but he can't just grab him from you. He will manipulate the void to control your thoughts."

Fae understood. "To get me to do what he wants. While the parasite forces corresponding action."

"You will still be able to refuse—you're resisting him now by even having this conversation. But he knows you better than you know yourself. The mind is a powerful thing."

"He can use me against myself."

Dominic was hesitant. Alexandra gave a nod, so he replied. "We're here to prevent him from harming you or Nicholas externally—but yes, he can get you to hurt yourself."

"Then I'll stay here. There's four of you; you take him to the basilica."

"Fae, your soul is a corpse, your body belongs to Nefas; it's only safe for you here because you're with Nicholas."

Fae looked down at the boy. "So that's it then," she said. "Even with you guys, I won't get far before I give him what he wants." Fae nodded to herself, the weight of her situation settling. "What are my chances then, truthfully?"

She caught the looks exchanged between the three newcomers—looks that said they knew something more but weren't going to say. Either that, or they were simply impatient. In the end, she wasn't sure if it would matter.

"We're ready to go," Alexandra solemnly announced, her dark eyes set and focused. "Fae, stay in our middle. Issa, give her Nicholas." The brother with the toque gently reached both hands beneath the baby and lifted him out of the carrier as smoothly as possible before he stood up and held him out to Fae. Nicholas curled up into Issa's arms and Fae refused to take him.

"I can't hold him, no."

"We're not concerned about the parasite in you," Alexandra said.

"If Nefas can make me hurt myself, what will stop him from making me hurt Nicholas? I'll give him Nicholas if I see him, I know I will. He'll have both of us if you make me take him."

"No he won't, we'll be watching you. There is no one else to take him."

"There's four of you! And I feel like I can barely stand straight, much less carry fifteen pounds. I'll drop him, or choke him, or—"

"Fae," Ilyas spoke up, "The child's innocence draws the corpses like a lighthouse. From the plaza to those still hiding, everyone in the village will be mobbing after him. There are four of us because all four of us will be fighting them off. There are no extra hands to carry him."

This is what Anna had tried to tell her: her role in Nefas' great performance, her Christmas experience. It all came down to this. She looked first to Dominic for some indication that there was another option, then to Alexandra and Issa, then back to Ilyas and found no deviation. "I'm going to wrap him up then," Fae finally said, grabbing the wool blanket, allowing Issa to help her so as to not disturb Nicholas. He felt like the weight of the world in her arms.

Alexandra took the lead in front, shaggy-haired Ilyas to her right, Dominic behind her, and Issa to her left. They were calm, and Fae tried to recall the image of Dominic fully revealed to help her imagine all four in the same way, reassuring herself of their promises. Her heart was beating hard and fast, and she felt sick. Nefas' runaway whore . . . She'd already seen what he planned

THE GIFT

for her. Now it was just about making sure little Nicholas made it through. She looked one last time at the thick bundle resting heavily against her shoulder. The blanket provided the buffer between him and her parasite-riddled fingers. She was filled with shame looking at him, so she draped the blanket's corner over his face.

"Wait, what about my grandmother?" Fae asked. "My friends? Nefas will go after them to get to me. He said he would."

"He won't," Dominic promised. "We've thought of that already and we're prepared."

Alexandra gripped the door handle but, before pulling it open, she looked over her shoulder at Fae, her eyes set with the task ahead. "One last bit of advice? Love can be a terribly strong thing in its purest form. No matter where he takes you, that is how he loses."

Fae bit her dry lips and felt the chapped skin on her tongue and hot salty tears in her eyes. The tears stung. She wasn't so sure she wanted to do this anymore. Alexandra made it sound so simple, she almost dared hope that she would come out of this alive. She also made it sound like the start of a funeral eulogy.

Re-gripping the sleeping bundle in her arms, Fae watched in slow motion as the wooden door was pulled open and a wild gust of snowy wind raced in, welcoming her back. She braced herself against the cold, but at least this time she had Alexandra to break a path through the snow and the drifts. They passed through the small ring of light cast by the bulbs above the door. Beyond that was the same darkness she had blindly battled through just to get to this place. She followed Alexandra numbly, knowing that Nefas was somewhere nearby, knowing she would kneel for him again, fearing the knowledge that his rage would inspire the punishment against her. If she hadn't been surrounded by her protectors, her legs would've given out and she would've sacrificed herself and Nicholas to him there and then just to have this over with.

They passed beneath the archway that linked one side of buildings to the other and Alexandra slowed down. "They come," she said.

Fae looked around Alexandra's shoulder to see. Suspended in the air and slowly bobbing up and down to the pace of struggling corpses, the first green glow had won out through the blackness. Fae hugged Nicholas more tightly to her chest, and she saw then that the corpses weren't the only thing that had discovered them. Preceding them flew a green wisp of smoke, swift and unbothered by the winter elements. It sped toward her like an attacking shark, and she could feel Nefas' weight coming with it as her heart and lungs began to struggle against the heaviness of his oppression.

She swallowed hard and waited for it to begin. *Though I walk through the valley of death I won't fear.*

"Dominic. Don't let him take me."

The wisp parted around Alexandra's legs and swallowed Fae's feet, twisting up her body. His hands brushed over her hair and slipped into her mind, his fingers twirling around inside her head like a child swirling their hands through a sandbox. Nefas bridged one darkness to another, and the void washed back into her mind's eye. She fell into it and, lost in its endlessness, she was helpless to fight it.

And then she was back home in Vancouver, walking up the rain-soaked wooden steps of the community church. Her father was dragging her to yet another wasted Sunday morning.

25

A heavy rain poured outside. Her father held an umbrella over them, so they were dry except for their shoes. He made fast to open the door for her, but she beat him to it and pulled it open—not waiting for him to shake the rain off the umbrella. She was alone with him this morning. Her mother was half asleep on the couch after another dose adjustment of Depakote. Her father had been away with his job most of the week, so it had been up to Fae to help her mother through the adjustment. She still managed a 91% on her long-division test on Thursday. She knew her parents had other things on their mind; she might tell them later.

 A tall, thin, old man, wearing the same respectable brown tweed suit he wore on rotation with one other, stood waiting to greet her, his fake teeth too white. He was kind, though, so she liked him. She shook his hand and told him she'd stayed up too late watching TV last night; he snuck her a hard candy and, with a twinkle in his eye, told her to use it wisely. She continued into the foyer, without looking to see where her father was, and joined the flow of people making their way into the sanctuary, past the café where everyone stood around drinking their coffee, admiring each other's sameness and sounding like sketch comedy caricatures.

Her father caught up with her then and gave her shoulders a hug. She accepted it limply. He dressed sharply; he always did; pin stripe pants, smooth leather belt, white shirt tucked in, no tie, shiny shoes, pager hanging off his hip. She was dressed nicely, too, in a lilac dress and her first pair of earrings which her father had given her when he'd come back from Chicago last month. He smoothed back her hair, and before going into the sanctuary together, they passed the woman passing out the bulletins who always smelled of baby formula and had a giant mole on the side of her mouth. Fae tried to avoid her because of her squishy hugs and the all-you-can-eat buffet of Christian clichés she felt led of the Lord to give. She had kid and adult versions.

They made it into the sanctuary only to have her father's pager inconspicuously go off. The buzz it made against his hip sounded as gritty to her as the obnoxious alarm clock that went off half an hour too early. She heard him sigh and knew what was coming. He had to go. Someone from the church would bring her home, maybe take her out to lunch; that's what he would say. He turned to her to tell her, but she didn't want to hear it so she waved him off. Just like that, he was gone.

She had to find a seat, and everyone was already sitting; she was late. An overhead projector for the song lyrics everyone already knew sat at the front, manned by that week's teenage recruit. The bass player actually showed up this week, and the drummer looked as disinterested as ever on his fake drum kit. She saw her friends Sarah and Jillian and Zack and Ryder snickering to each other over the cartoons they were drawing. She'd shown them how to do that and had gotten in trouble when Ryder left behind his best one of Jesus getting nailed to the side of the hockey boards. He'd blamed the drawing on her, meaning she had to endure Sunday School intervention meetings. She'd gotten him back for it by tattling on him when he copied her school homework. It was never the same between them after that, and he took Zack with him to be friends with other girls.

The sound of measured, shoe thumping made Fae realize that her outfit had changed. She was now wearing her first pair of fashionable, heeled boots meaning she was in high school and about eight years older than when she had come out of the rain. She still looked for a seat and thankfully found none with the core of the youth group: James, Esther, Summer, Aaron, and of course, Tyron the Blessed. There were others too whom she walked past, names and faces she hadn't cared to remember since they left her memory years ago, and she didn't care to remember now.

She reached the front and still found no seat. She was going to turn around and keep looking but was stopped by the worship music being replaced by the perfectly practiced voice of their pastor, Pastor Blake. Everyone around her seemed so sad. Her grandparents were clearing tears from their eyes. Zack and Ryder were blank faced; the girls were weepy. Her father was back now too, sitting on the front row, a fitted black suit hanging heavy on his shoulders.

"In life, she was the highest example of bravery," Pastor Blake said with a small flourish of his hand, "a soldier fighting a war within."

Below the platform lay an open casket surrounded by a forest of pink and yellow flowers, mostly lilies. Fae didn't have to look inside to know it was her mother in there. She stood in the middle of the aisle, but no one noticed.

"Through her battles she never lost sight of those things she considered nonnegotiable. Love. Hope. Faithfulness. God. With all these things and more, she displayed her genuine heart for all to see; to her husband; to her daughter."

Fae looked down to her hand where she was holding a program and saw that Frankie Valli's, "Can't Take My Eyes Off You" had been crossed off the playlist with red ink. The hymn "Be Thou My Vision" was written over it. She angrily crumpled the program and, seeing that Pastor Blake had a red pen in his breast pocket, hurled it down the aisle at him and yelled exactly what she was thinking and feeling.

This was the third worst day of her life. The first was the day she had been told her mother was dead. The second was the day after. The tragedy had been that her mother's bipolarism was miraculously stabilizing, she was almost completely off her meds, and over the last year it was like Fae was getting to meet her mother for the first time. A drunk driver hit her at 9:58 a.m. on Sunday, July 7th, 2002. Fae had lied about soccer practice to get out of church that morning, and her mom had dropped her off. She had been on her way to church to meet her father.

"As the Lord gives, so does he take away."

"Take away? It's murder, and who gave him the right?" Fae yelled at Pastor Blake, her hands balled into fists at her side, "If your God defeated death, then why does he still deal in it, huh? Which lie is it?" No one paid her any attention. It was if her outrage was perfectly invisible.

The pastor continued his sermon, and for the second time she didn't hear a word of the last sermon she would ever attend. Instead she only stared at the reflective wood casket, her mind numbed by the memories of the woman inside of it. They didn't agree on everything, her mom and her, and Fae had gone through a number of years resenting her for being too weak to get through the lows of her condition, and too uncontrolled to properly ride the highs—forcing Fae to constantly babysit her. Now her chance to make up the years was gone and she was left alone with her father, who in turn left her alone with the church and, when she was lucky, her grandparents. She only had to get through another two years before she could escape to university.

She survived the sermon and even survived the giving of the eulogy, but she barely made it through the cell phone ringing just as her mother's parents were saying goodbye to their daughter. Fae was horrified and furious as she watched her father answer it. He couldn't have left that bloody thing behind for once in his life? She marched over to grab that home-wrecker out of his hands and smash it on the floor but, when she got there, he looked at her with those sad eyes he always gave whenever he said it, "Fae, honey, I have to go."

"No, you don't!" Fae yelled, making a grab for the phone. Her arm was too short by at least four inches and she missed. "You can't leave me here, alone! It's Mom's funeral for Christ's sake, even Jesus mourned his dead! For once in your life, don't leave me."

He stood up. "I'll be back tomorrow."

"You're a terrible father and an even worse husband!" Fae shouted as he walked so smoothly up the aisle, out the door, and effectively out of her life.

"What kind of narcissist does that?" Fae had no memory of the young man about her age who had come beside her, but she welcomed him nevertheless.

She thought him to be a longtime friend, and she felt like his name was Charlie. "I bet his boss even had to tell him to take the day off."

"I hate him. He was ruining Mom's funeral just by being here." Fae looked back at the coffin and felt the tears drip down her face, water wrung from a rock. "For one day, just one day." Fae paused, steeling her voice. "I've been living on my own for years now. What does it matter?"

Charlie found her hand and held it in his, squeezing gently. "Let's get out of here."

He took her up the aisle and they passed all the people she knew; her grandparents, the youth group, the baby formula lady and everyone else. Together, the two of them walked back into the foyer, only this time it wasn't full of coats and stained carpet. She and Charlie had walked into the heart of St. Peter's Basilica in Rome.

Fae thought she should be startled at the drastic change in setting and overwhelmed at being absolutely dwarfed in this temple of mankind's wealth and pride, but she was no more concerned by it than she had been with Charlie's sudden appearance. She was supposed to be here, and she knew it as she sharply strode forward, head high, shoulders straight, and a handful of papers and files swinging from her side. Charlie was beside her looking a good thirty years older and she assumed she had aged the same. The noise their shoes made was boisterous and was pitiful in its attempts to fill the emptiness of this place.

The cathedral was vacant of people and furnishings—no benches, and no confession booths—everything had been cleared out. Lights had been shut off, leaving only the afternoon summer sun streaming through the windows over a hundred feet above to light the vastness. The one-man balconies built into some of the weight-bearing pillars, which were more like towers than pillars, were covered with white construction tarps, making even such blue-collar items look graceful cascading from dizzying heights to the floor. The priceless pieces of art for the twenty-five altars and twenty-six monuments, including Michelangelo's "Pietà," were also covered in white sheets, making them all ghosts in a church that was already filled with so many ghosts of the past.

A group of five smartly suited men waiting for her looked like toys standing underneath the Baldacchino, a 95-foot tall canopy of stolen Ancient Roman bronze and seventeenth century creativity. The last to be covered up, it looked more like an exiled, aged king rather than a majestic one, thanks to the emptiness all around. This place had become nothing more than a nostalgic sentiment, and she was here to change that. She was one of four lead architects working on the project. This group of English-speaking stakeholders was hers to woo and impress and she'd been doing so since the project began. She greeted them as she neared, taking turns shaking their hands.

"Gentlemen," Fae said, wasting no time, "Say goodbye to St. Peter's Basilica, and welcome the European Union's new Art and History Center, a research and preservation facility and museum. If you'll come with me, I will walk you through this space as it will be by the time construction ends."

She handed out sharp-looking folders and led them off toward the right transept. They strode past a pillar and as they came clear of it some feet later, an unexpected sight in her peripheral vision stopped her immediately.

Squatters were huddled together around a small fire they had built on the flawless floor. They had given trouble before, refusing to leave, and she'd been told that they had been removed, but it would seem that wasn't the case.

"I thought you took care of this problem." She looked at the security guard nearby.

"They were not there when I come to look," the Italian man shrugged his innocence. "Lucky for you, they want to wait and see your beautiful work. You should be happy of their affection for your talents!"

"Get them out. Now."

"I cannot," he said apologetically. "This is their home."

"It hasn't been their home since the government took possession five years ago. They've been given more than enough time to find another place to live. Their time is up."

"No one wants them," the guard said with another shrug.

Angry, Fae excused herself from the group and Charlie tagged along. She was going to talk to these people herself.

Underneath the shadow of St. Basil's statue was a weathered canvas lean-to where a young woman was cooking flatbreads and holding a baby in her arms. Fae had met them all before when she had felt obliged to tell them herself that they were losing their home. The woman cooking was Mary. Her husband, Joseph, emerged from the lean-to as Fae approached. There were three others, two sheepless shepherds and a Persian, but they stayed back.

"My friend, it is good to see you again!" Joseph welcomed her in as though into his home—which was Fae's home and not his.

"Get out of my building."

"This building was dedicated to my boy, given to him, and he hasn't given it up yet."

"It was called St. Peter's not St. Jesus," Fae said sharply, and pointed to the Cathedra Petri where Peter's chair was, then to his statue, and up to his name inscribed along the base of the dome which could be seen from every corner of the echoing structure. "Your boy was just given lip service here."

Mary stood up from the fire and placed a calming hand on her husband's shoulder, and he backed down. "Are you a mother?" Mary asked. The surety of her manner was underlined by a surprising level of confidence.

"Don't try to arouse sympathy from me. Get a job like the rest of us."

"Come, sit by the fire and eat, and we will get to know each other for who we really are."

"Construction begins within the week. If you're not gone by morning, I'll have you arrested." Turning on the ball of her feet, Fae started walking back to her group, but the security guard caught up to her before she could resume the tour.

"Bella, send them to the grotto. There are others, many others who live down there, others no one want to give home to. They will be happy there."

Fae stopped and considered his suggestion. She caught a glimpse of a cross pendant peeking out through his uniform and felt sorry for him.

Charlie piped up, "May as well put them on the shelf rather than releasing them to the world. Who knows what kind of trouble they could make."

"Fine. Tell them to pack their junk. I'll take them down."

The guard's face lit up, and he grabbed her hand and kissed it.

Soon afterward, Fae was leading the small group carrying their few possessions kitty-corner to the Baldacchino where a colossus statue of St. Andrew was surrendering in front of an X-shaped cross. They passed through a gate in the marble barricade surrounding the statue, not even half the height of the statue's podium, and went down the hidden staircase that had its opening behind it.

It was a shallow descent, and the grotto was bright with fluorescent light flooding the low barrel-vaulted ceilings. Everything was sterile with white plaster walls and polished floors. Spaciously placed, yellowing white marble sarcophagi held the tombs of past popes and saints. It was the same sterility here that could be found in government basements; it was the sterility of secrets.

Fae led them on while Charlie closed the rear. Long mimicking hallways made it both easy and hard to get lost, but soon they arrived in front of a very old, heavy bookcase, its dark brown shelves densely packed with leather-bound books. The one book in particular Fae that reached for required both hands to pull it off the shelf, and Charlie helped her place it on the floor. A gold inlay title was imprinted on the front cover: Vol. XXXVI: Gods and Deities of a More Pleasant Nature.

The small group looked at each other nervously as the book was opened. Charlie took his time looking for an empty page, each one making a little *fwip* sound as he turned it over. They passed gods of all names, Demeter from Greece, Guan-Yin from China, Izanagi from Japan, Vishnu from India, Šamaš from Mesopotamia, there were so many. Eventually Charlie found an empty page.

"Right after Mithras, couldn't ask for a better resting place. I think your boy should become great friends with Mithras," Charlie said to Mary. "You'll have a lot to talk about and a long time to talk about it." Mary set her face and said nothing.

"Are you going to separate us?" one of the shepherds asked Fae. "Only the babe is God."

"You belong to his story, so you'll live with him in these pages."

"You belong to his story too, Fae," Joseph said with a conviction she had seen before from her grandmother. It shook her, and for a moment she wondered if she should just let them go.

Charlie interrupted her thoughts by ushering the two shepherds and the Persian into the open book. One moment they stepped onto the blank page, and the next they inhabited it—nothing more than an illustration with a caption written below. Mary turned to Fae with a determination on her face that took Fae a little off guard. Never had she looked so different from all the millions of portraits created of her.

"I know your convictions justify forgetting us on this shelf but, I ask you, don't put my baby in those pages. Take him," Mary asked with dignity. "Put him in a good orphanage, and he will grow up to be a good man." Behind Mary, Joseph slipped unnoticed into the book. "You don't like us, I understand." Mary continued, "but he's just a baby."

"And he'll stay a baby in that book, protected and remembered as a myth. People love mythology. It's fun. They don't like religion."

"Don't punish him for what other people have done in his name."

"I offer a counterproposal," Fae suggested. "I'll take your baby and then leave him outside. If he is God and is meant to live, then he'll be adopted by a stranger passing by. If he has no place in this world, then he will die from exposure and thirst. And if he isn't God then . . . I guess you won't be able to stay on these pages."

Tears slipped down Mary's young face. The tears, Fae knew, were for her. "The pagans used to wash their hands of unwanted children in the same way, putting responsibility on their gods. We called it murder."

It was an attempt to guilt her with the moral high ground, and Fae wasn't going to fall for it. "You and those other gods are now characters in the same book with a lot of time to spend together so, for your sake, I'd watch what you said about them. This is my only offer."

Mary gave a small nod of consent and gave her babe over to Fae's care. Kissing his little head, the last thing Mary said was, "Everything my boy is meant for is to preserve life for those he loves, which is everyone."

And then Mary stepped onto the pages and fell into the Nativity beside her husband, surrounded by some of the few followers left to her son. Charlie snapped the volume shut, barely giving enough time for Mary's ink to dry before replacing it on the shelf, its spine indistinguishable from all the other volumes.

The return to the surface was quick. Coming up the stairs sent Fae not back into the empty vastness of St. Peter's but rather into the falling dusk outside. Rome's darkening Cyprus trees were stark against the dramatic colors of the setting sun. A crowd of friends and family burst into shouts and claps when she arrived, welcoming her to her surprise party. They ran to give her hugs, a drink was thrust into her hand, and another was taking a video with her. She had never seen these people before and yet, just like Charlie, she knew them intimately. Emotions of love and friendship for these people swelled her heart.

Her parents, whom she'd also never seen before, were beaming at her, thrilled at their successful surprise. Her father, a graying man with a jolly face, came and wrapped his arm around her, while her mother, who had smile wrinkles, wrapped her arm around Fae's other side. Together they excitedly ushered her deeper into the party.

The little baby in her arms began to get restless, reminding Fae of her end of the bargain, and she felt awkward, especially since she was juggling both him and a drink. Once again, Charlie came to her rescue with a charming smile as her mother and father welcomed him with giant hugs.

"Give him to me, Fae," he said easily, "I'll put him somewhere. Don't waste any more time on him when everyone else is waiting for you." Following his nod in the direction of the party, Fae's desire lingered on the street party and a good-looking redhead named Eric, waving her over. Already feeling the abandonment of sensibility that came with being a bit drunk, something deeply arrested her, and she handed Charlie her drink instead.

"He is a human life. I can at least do it myself."

"I'll go with you."

With promises of a quick return and much pointing at the baby problem she was holding, Fae and Charlie slipped away and found a nearby street corner, quickly becoming crowded with night life. There was a small fenced-in patch of grass in the middle of the sidewalk surrounding a stone monument to some past deed. Fae placed Mary's baby there, easing him onto the soft grass. She turned to go without sentiment, but then he started to cry and despite herself, his cries pulled at her heart, the sound echoing the memory of another baby's crying she had once refused to ignore. Fae looked at Charlie who nodded with an encouraging smile.

"Supply and demand will determine his life now. This is a busy corner. He'll be fine."

"Lack of demand is what brought him here. His humanity is what's being judged now." Fae bit her lip. "You're right. Let's go. This place is being taken over by night partiers. I don't want to see who picks him up."

They headed across the road to the Tiber River. In her absence, her party had moved to a party boat. Inconveniently, however, she could still hear the baby's cries.

Coming to the iron guardrails and looking down nearly thirty feet to the river below, Charlie stood beside her. The party barge lazily bobbed up and down at its berth. She found her parents partying as crazily as a retired, happy couple should. She caught sight of Eric, who waved her on again, and two of her best girlfriends raised their glasses high, promising more once she arrived. She desperately wanted to join them, but there was no way down, no stairs, no elevator. Logically, she had to jump.

Charlie swung his legs over the rail and waited for her to do the same before they took the leap together. A strong, powerful jump would carry them over the concrete riverside and land them on the open deck of the boat. It was a hard-to-miss target, so it had to be easy enough. Just as she was about to swing her legs over the rail, the babe's cries of abandonment suddenly died.

"Something happened to him," she said, pulling back.

"Yeah, someone picked him up," he said with a dull look on his face. "That was expected."

"I need to make sure."

"Fae, no," Charlie said, grabbing her arm. "His fate is none of your concern. Think of who he is."

"A human being, Charlie. I should have stuffed him into that book with his mother, but now he's just an orphan."

"He's supposed to be a god. He can take care of himself."

"He's supposed to be both, human and a god," Fae said, as she stole back across the road, the trouble of the dilemma worrying her face, "and that's the problem."

"Half an hour ago you didn't care what happened to him," Charlie called after her and trotted to catch up. "The point of this is to clear your conscience of his fate, but it's up to the truth to reveal if he is god or not."

"There is no god!" Fae yelled at him, getting more and more frustrated. And if that was the case, then she'd just condemned a normal child to death, or worse. But if Mary was right . . .

With Charlie glued to her side, they came to the place where they left Mary's baby. Fae knew without having to check for a pulse that he was dead. He lay just as she had placed him, his deep brown eyes staring blankly into the darkening blue sky. How it happened so quickly, she didn't know. No one around them cared to stop and investigate, didn't want to confirm that what looked like a forgotten doll was not a doll at all. It was just her and Charlie, and after looking on in silence, Charlie made the decision to speak first.

"World, behold your god."

"There is no god," Fae responded flatly.

"Not anymore. Jesus and his Father are proven to be stories; this truth is given new life with his death." Charlie reached down to check for a pulse on the babe's neck to confirm what was already known. "Congratulations, Fae, you've done what no other being has been able to do."

Fae didn't know what to feel. She'd proven what she already knew, that God was a myth and that Jesus was dead, and yet there was no satisfaction. She should have been destroyed about allowing an innocent baby to die, this human being who was no more god than she, and yet she was not full of grief. His dead body filled her eyes and she simply felt nothing.

"This wasn't my fault," she finally said.

"Maybe we should bury him," Charlie gently suggested. "We'll send him off in the current of the Tiber like so many humbled people before him."

Fae broke her stare on the body and looked at Charlie, thankful for his friendship. She noticed then that his eyes were a vivid green that was as beautiful as it was unnatural, and it struck her as notable for some reason. Had he begun wearing colored contacts?

Fae nodded her agreement, and Charlie was quick to pick up the limp body first. The massive dome of St. Peter's Basilica rose high above the treetops, highlighted by the night spotlights around it. In only a few days, construction would begin, and the height of her career would begin where the great architect Bernini had left his, and the last generation to know that building as St. Peter's Basilica had already begun dying.

She had everything she had wanted from life and yet, as she walked beside Charlie, she started to realize that maybe the one thing she didn't want was to have no God. He could've saved Mary's baby.

God was the perfect deity in concept, favorably natured as far as gods went, and all powerful, but as Fae thought about it, she realized that where the idea of God went wrong was in how his adherents executed their belief in the omnipotent and acted out their religion as an excuse to be terrible human beings. They destroyed generations, and so many lives they bloodied and ruined. They schemed and manipulated and hid their racism and phobias behind the name of their perfect God who was too perfect for his followers to live up to. An otherwise faceless deity, he'd been given a relatable face from the attributed qualities of his followers, thereby turning something perfect into a plague. But without this perfect God as an example to follow, would Mother Teresa have ever turned the world upside down? Would the greatest universities have ever been founded? Would there be nearly as many people feeding the poor, keeping the elderly company, or rehabilitating the wounded? The world needed a perfect God, but the world did not need the leeches who brought God down to their level. It was then, thinking these things, that Fae began to feel alone. There was no God, but the one singularly perfect inspiration literally lay dead beside her in Charlie's arms, and who could forgive her for that?

They arrived back at the guardrail overlooking the Tiber with still no way down to join the party other than to jump. Charlie was waiting for her to climb over before handing her the lifeless babe. She wanted to respectfully send him off into the waters from the boat deck, but that didn't seem possible if she was going to have to jump. She took the body from Charlie, who frowned, and went to a nearby tree planted in the middle of the sidewalk. A square of dirt lay exposed around its trunk which was just big enough for a body the size of the baby.

"What are you doing Fae?" Charlie questioned. "Just toss him into the Tiber."

"He's a child worth more dignity than that."

"I'll do it for you, then."

"I clean up my own messes. They say that Christianity was birthed out of Rome and now it will be buried here as well, under this tree."

Charlie's green eyes smiled, but he nodded somberly. "The earth is home to everyone in the end." Fae tried to find comfort in his words, in his staunch support of her, but the fact that his eyes were so green still distracted her. Trying to remember why that was important was annoying.

Fae knelt to begin digging a hole, only to find one already perfectly made. So she placed the babe's body deep in the earth and watched as the magic of the world threw dirt on top of him. Then, in the same manner as when she first noticed Charlie's green eyes, she saw—truly saw—the face of Mary's dead boy. He wasn't the same baby she had taken from the grotto.

It was Nicholas.

"Charlie?" Fae cried out, starting to panic, "Charlie, something's wrong. This isn't Mary's baby!" She leaned down deep into the grave to grab him out, but her arms couldn't reach him. No matter how far she tried to stretch, Nicholas was always out of reach and, still, the handfuls of dirt peppered him with layer after layer of burial.

"Stay strong, Fae." Charlie tried to calm her and now, all of a sudden, they were both standing over the Tiber with the guardrail at their back and their toes hanging over the ledge. Fae cranked her head around to the tree where Nicholas had been buried and saw a fresh mound of earth and a little gravestone clumsily carved into the tree bark reading, *Nike. R.I.P.*

"The Nativity has been broken apart, Fae. Christianity's history has been erased. Your past is changed." Charlie waved his arm upriver to where St.

Peter's dome rose, and the emptiness Fae had felt earlier washed over her again. "The future is being rewritten. Now, c'mon, what really matters is your party, and we're super late. Let's go already." With an excited smile, Charlie picked up her hand from the rail. She was about to follow until he said one last thing before they were to make the impossible jump: "I told you, I have big plans for you."

It must've been the way he said it, or maybe it was her own mind catching up with her imagination but, suddenly, Fae knew that Charlie's green eyes were wrong. They weren't contacts, and there was no way she could safely land a jump of that distance. She also knew in that moment that Nicholas wasn't dead and that there was nothing real on that boat waiting for her.

Without warning, she snatched her hand away from Charlie and hopped over the rail onto the sidewalk, running to the fresh grave underneath the tree. She heard Charlie calling her name just as any concerned friend would.

"Fae! Fae! What are you doing, he's *dead* Fae, have you lost your mind?"

"Maybe, and probably my soul too, but it's not too late to save his life."

"Jesus is *DEAD*, you saw his body, God is *DEAD*—"

"THERE IS NO GOD!" Fae screamed at him, "so how can he be dead? Stop lying to me, you're doing what *they* do! Nicholas is not Mary's child!" Frantically, Fae tore at the dirt with her hands and threw it aside as fast as she could.

"Then why does Death want him so badly?"

26

Why did Death want Nicholas so badly? The question came from nowhere, because Fae was in nowhere. Rome, the rainy streets of Vancouver, it all disappeared. The question echoed in a dream without purpose, until she again found herself back in a familiar darkness, a darkness which lay over a small village in southern Belgium.

The driving wind and snow of the renewed storm reinforced Fae's return to the real world. She quickly took stock of her surroundings. Squatted low, she was facing a medieval style door studded with age-dulled spikes. The door was harmless enough to a passerby but would be deadly to anyone who may have had it on their mind to launch themselves out onto a party barge over twenty feet away—for example. Nearby, there was a hastily dug hole deep in the snow. Nicholas lay in it, half covered with the same incriminating evidence that was melting in her hands. Drops of blood fell on the snow beside him, and a quick wipe of her nose revealed they came from her.

"Alexandra, she's back," Dominic shouted from above her. Fighting disorientation, it was a small feat to realign her brain out of the dream and to her present reality. She plunged her hands into the snowy grave, grabbed Nicholas up, and held him close. He appeared no worse for wear.

"Why did we stop moving?" Fae demanded as she shakily stood. Her question died in the air when she peeked through the shoulders of Issa and Dominic. They were a small group of six in the middle of a crusade of the dead as far as Fae could see in every direction. Dominic, Issa, Ilyas, and Alexandra were wrestling the corpses furiously, punching them in the face, knocking out teeth and sending loose jaws flying, all just to prevent their greedy arms from reaching Nicholas.

"How far to the basilica?" Fae shouted above the din of the struggle. It took a moment, but eventually Alexandra gave answer by giving orders to move out again.

They struggled through a crowd that didn't want to break, her protectors finding their collective rhythm to create enough momentum to plow though: breaking knees, elbows, and fingers; removing shoulders from sockets. The brutal system was working, though, as the parasites removed their useless hosts from the front lines, or their bodies became trampled by those who could still fulfill their master's demands.

Nefas hadn't given up on her. Whenever Fae managed to see beyond her protectors, his four sentry monks were there, waiting, tracking her amidst the carnage, as was Nefas himself. She could feel his stare locked cold on Nicholas and on her. He taunted her in whispers, baiting her, squeezing her heart dry. *The extraction of that creature from your arms is the only thing waiting for you at the end of this fool's errand. My methods are perfect and excruciatingly painful—do you know how many different screams Nicholas can make? How many ways I can keep breaking your mind? Your body?* His words broke her down, his presence was drawing her back, and she found herself trying to drift toward him, subserviently lifting Nicholas out to him. She wanted to be back on his side so desperately, if only to stop this . . . *You're not strong enough to follow these fools to the end. I will always take you back, Fae.*

"Hey!" Ilyas shouted at her, bumping her back into the center of their formation and pushing Nicholas back into her arms. "Just hold on a little longer."

Nefas' confidence at securing Nicholas was likely why he didn't rely on the void or his parasite to try to force his will again; his pleasure was in watching her go to her end fully aware. If she hadn't been in the middle of four formidable beings giving their all for her and Nicholas, Nefas was right; she wouldn't have been strong enough.

Once they got close enough to the basilica for its spires to break through the thick darkness, Fae felt little relief. She knew what waited for her there, and it was not a happy ending. Finally breaching the small plaza didn't make their journey seem any closer to ending, either. The corpses had followed them to overflow the plaza, making an impenetrable sea of the dead, and there was nowhere for the beat-up corpses to be thrown. Their legs were swept out or broken so their bodies could be walked over, and it was all Fae could do to keep Nicholas away from her own parasite-ridden fingers, much less theirs. Fae swallowed hard, set her face, and kept her focus on Alexandra's swinging, black ponytail. She would not fear through this valley of death; she would not give her imagination any room. She would only see Nicholas to his end, and then she would face hers.

Fighting their way to the Notre-Dame du Seigneur, a sight greeted them that Fae could not have prepared for. Not only was their group expected, but the whole choir was there to welcome them. They spilled out of the front doors and onto the steps, down into the zone no corpse would cross. The warm light from the inside was bright as a fanned fire in contrast to the darkness. They still sang their amazing songs as though they had never stopped, and they probably hadn't.

Alexandra punched through the final ranks of corpses, flinging the last of them back into the mass like bags of sand. With the safety of the choir before her, Fae didn't waste a blink before dashing out from behind the four, giving all she had left to leap up the stairs as the choir parted before her. Nicholas was so close to being safe, to being where Nefas couldn't touch him. At the top steps waited those who weren't affected by the Gift, including Lars Dreschler who was leaning on a younger man and staring in the wrong direction. The last ones between her and the door were the boy with the Choir Director. Both were at peace but somber, and they did not move aside.

"Your journey doesn't end in there," the director, said. He was a soft-spoken man, and it was hard to hear him over the singing.

"Like hell it doesn't!"

"Fae," Dominic called her name from behind. His jacket was torn, hair was tousled, but only a few fight wounds besides his bloody knuckles told of his struggle. He climbed the stairs behind her, catching his breath. Alexandra, Issa, and Ilyas, looking just as rough, stayed behind at the foot of the steps. The singing quieted, and all eyes turned toward them. Dominic held out his hands for Nicholas and, as loath as Fae was to give him up, she gently transferred Nicholas over. He would be safe.

Dominic took little Nicholas and gently kissed him on the forehead before dropping the blanket to the ground. He turned around to face the glowing sea of the dead held at bay by the invisible barrier. "Fae, you cannot go inside yet." His eyes never left those of Nicholas, and he spoke only loud enough for her to hear. "It is time for you to see the Gift your grandmother wanted for you." Looking outward, Dominic announced with a thunderous voice, "From depths of Hell, thy people save, and give them victory o'er the grave! Disperse the gloomy clouds of night, and Death's dark shadows put to flight!"

As soon as Dominic finished speaking, a sonic implosion rushed toward him and Nicholas like a backward ripple. It pushed the choir and ranks of corpses forward, stumbling onto their toes, as the wave shot through them. The last of the storm slowed to a quit. The thick darkness, though, remained.

A great pillar of green mist all too familiar formed just inside the no-cross zone. Nefas began to appear, growing out his arms and legs, forming his head and, just when Fae expected him to come to full humanity, he blacked out and seemed to disappear. But then he moved, and his outline could be seen against the iridescence of the corpses behind him. He took three steps forward as nothing more than a black shadow, so thick and so dense he seemed to suck everything into himself. He came with such fear and hatred, and with the weight of death, that Fae crumbled on the steps before him. His four robed monks faded into existence at his side and, for the first time, their jaws stayed silent. Arms from behind pulled her up, but she barely noticed, the void swelling up inside her head. She wanted more of him, needed more of him, the deep of her void called out to him; she could feel Nefas toying with her inside there. She felt a twinge of excitement from the parasite inside her, eager to be reunited with its master.

Dominic stood in front of her with Nicholas, who had started to play with Dominic's fingers, putting each one into his mouth in turn. When Nicholas was done, Dominic simply announced, "It is time."

"That runaway you're trying to protect is mine," Nefas said, his voice like that of a haunted terror, deep and sinister. "I've claimed the darkness of her soul, I own her, and so is what she found."

"It is time," Dominic repeated.

"Not until I get what I came for."

"The punishment for your insolence is never changing. Watch your power be broken. Fae Peeters has chosen."

"She surrendered to me," Nefas growled like the dogs from Hades, and he stormed forward only to be cut off by Alexandra and the two brothers. "You," Nefas pointed at Fae, or so she thought by the movements of his shadow, "crawl to my feet and beg forgiveness."

Nefas had no forgiveness in him. There would be no reprieve of her punishment from him, of this she had no illusions. But Nicholas was safe, and that was all that mattered. Nefas closed his fist in the air and pulled his arm back sharply as though yanking a rope. The parasite in her responded as if it were leashed to Nefas' arm, and Fae flew forward from the supporting arms behind her and was thrown down the stairs. She rolled hard and crashed into the back of the legs of Issa and Ilyas, the only barrier standing between her and Nefas' dark shadow. The void in her head spun and, though her eyes saw, her mind was falling deeper and deeper. She felt her body slowly picking itself up on its own accord, the parasite acting for its master as she came to her hands and knees. Even though it was a mockery she would beg. She would beg for mercy in this farcical show and pray that it would be over quickly.

Nefas used his hand to reel her in again and she came, her head getting wedged between Ilyas and Issa's legs. The parasite kept trying to get her through but was repeatedly bounced back. Again, and again it tried, but the brothers did not move.

You saw the future, Fae, the Great Humbling. It's all true, and I showed you the truth. I've shown you your place in history, everything you wanted. The world is my treasure to give. All you have to do is beg.

THE GIFT

"Fae." From somewhere outside the void, she heard Dominic's soft voice call to her, musical and light. She wanted to go to where it was, but she couldn't find it, couldn't stop herself from falling farther and farther away from his voice. "Fae," Dominic called to her again, "You don't have to beg for what is already yours."

Nefas was getting impatient. The parasite flopped her to her side and tried to squirm through the legs blocking her, writhing like an earthworm pulled from the ground, but Issa and Ilyas tightened themselves together and kept her blocked out. She needed Nefas to make this stop, she needed him . . . The parasite pulled her arm out from beneath her and was stretching it out to him. She had to be with him.

"Fae." Dominic's voice broke through the void and, in a moment of lucidity, what Fae was seeing with her eyes reached her brain. Lying on her side looking up, she saw Dominic crouched beside her holding Nicholas, free of his snowsuit and wearing his sheep-covered sleeper. Nicholas should have been crying in fear, but he was happy, and he reached down toward her. He gave a tiny laugh and tried to grab her nose. He couldn't reach though and somehow, in spite of the parasite, Fae managed to pull back the arm stretching for Nefas and rolled on top of it to keep it at her side.

Nefas seethed. "You don't get choices anymore." He closed his fist in midair and immediately Fae's airways closed off. The parasite wrapped itself around her trachea, and her eyes bulged as she vainly gasped for air. One hand scratched at her throat looking for relief, the other reached for Dominic, pleading for his help. With gulping breaths to get anything into her burning lungs, Fae didn't realize until it was too late that Nicholas was grabbing for her parasite-filled fingers.

If Fae had ever wondered what it felt like to be a flushed toilet, she knew in that moment as a massive swirling in her body took everything from her. The parasite squelching the air from her lungs, the addictions from the void—it all flowed out of her fingers and into the pure innocence of Nicholas. The void folded in on itself, releasing her from its power, and she felt the previously dislocated joints of her fingers realign themselves like a shoddy repair being fixed by an expert craftsman. Her back cracked into realignment, the effects of the concussion erased, the scratches on her throat smoothed away, and her whole body warmed up.

Freed to breathe, her lungs' vacuum filled with air in a mighty inhale and then, in the same breath, she exhaled it all in a cry that stopped everyone within earshot as Fae stumbled to her hands and knees, crying. Nicholas was infected with her parasite. This was a mistake, a terrible mistake that should've never happened, the moment she'd spend her whole life wishing to have back. She'd not only infected him, but had given him everything that Nefas had tortured her with. Despite her attempts to protect Nicholas against herself, she'd just given Nefas what he wanted. And this, then, despite what Dominic had promised, was the moment Nefas won.

27

Through the blurry eyes of her tear-filled vision, Fae saw the parasite disappear into Nicholas' body, while in front of her she could feel Nefas brooding wickedly, biding his words.

She looked up at Dominic. "How can I get it back? How does he give it back to me? It was my fault, he's too young for this, let me take it back."

Dominic knelt in front of her, gently holding Nicholas between them. "Your freedom has been paid for by the only one rich enough to buy it. Anna warned that you wouldn't like how it happened."

"But this is what he wanted!" Fae yelled, standing up. Dominic followed suit. Nefas' black form paced angrily, oozing his thick hatred. "He wanted Nicholas, and I just gave him to him! I belong to him, and nothing's changing that now." The tears were flowing freely but she didn't care.

"Nefas wanted you to hand over Nicholas' body, so he could kill him. You didn't do that. Infecting Nicholas is the perfect opposite of what Nefas wants. He doesn't own you anymore."

Nefas' anger was growing more ravenous, and he growled at Dominic, "She *is* still mine."

Dominic ignored Nefas, but shook his head in disagreement. "Watch now and learn." Dominic straightened himself and passed through the barrier Alexandra and the brothers had created.

"What are you doing?" Fae screeched, diving after them only to be shut out by shoulders and bodies. "Dominic stop, he's just a baby!" Screaming at him Fae tried breaking through the brothers, but they were solid as rock and Alexandra restrained her by the shoulders. "Bring him back! Issa, Ilyas, someone stop him! Nicholas!"

Nefas' dark body immediately met the new arrivals and tracked closely behind Dominic, eager for his prize. Fae saw his greedy, shadowy arms reach out for the babe, and Dominic saw, too. With one word said so simply, Dominic froze the source of death itself: "No."

Instantly Nefas froze as still as ice. His monks disappeared, and Dominic passed him by as though he were nothing. Fae was helpless to do anything but watch as Dominic breached the perimeter of the corpses, stopping just outside of it. He lifted his eyes to the night sky and spoke something Fae couldn't hear but, when he had finished, the choir began singing again and this time she well knew their haunting song echoing off the surrounding buildings:

O come, O come, Emmanuel

At the same time, the brothers relaxed their barrier and let Fae break through. She stumbled past them to charge after Dominic. In her right mind, she would have never dove headlong into the solid front of rotting corpses, but she did, and she didn't care if their parasites re-infected her. Her fate with Nefas was one she had already accepted. But the corpses still weren't interested in her. Their attentions were all turned in favor of the new arrival. Their rotting, bony hands grabbing for Nicholas looked like layers of spears enveloping Dominic in the process. He didn't fight them off but rather stood solid, fully accepting of being overrun, his sole focus on holding Nicholas out like a sacrifice for these terrible creatures to devour.

That mourns in lonely exile here

Fae was pulling at the corpses trying to yank them away from Nicholas, though it had little effect. "Curse you Dominic, curse you!" For every corpse she wrestled away, another two took its place. "Nicholas!" Fae screamed again in a dangerous state of being both panicked and incensed. "The Communion, I use its power against you all!" She had no pride left to feel silly wielding the words like an exorcism. "Get away from him!" It did no good.

Over the groans and wheezing breaths, the shuffling of feet, and the dull sound of bone hitting bone, she heard Dominic say, "Death must happen for you to leave alive. This is the way the dead find life."

"Nicholas, no!"

Her heart sank to the icy cold ground when she saw how Nicholas wasn't at all afraid of the corpses. Instead, he was excited by them and strained in Dominic's strong arms. He reached and grabbed for all the glowing green fingers he could find, and Dominic did nothing to stop him.

Tears clouded Fae's vision, seeing Nicholas reaching for his death as she did what she could to throw corpse hands out of his way. One parasite after another was absorbed into his little body, and still he reached for all the rotting hands she couldn't throw away in time.

Free thine own from Satan's tyranny
From depths of Hell thy people save
And give them victory o'er the grave

Her body had just about given up, exhausted over and over again. Fae could feel it slowly quitting on her, and soon she became little better than a flyswatter, babbling for the corpses to leave Nicholas alone. When gentle hands took her shoulders in their embrace, Fae had no energy left to resist their guidance away from the scene to the side, where she could still see it all happen but couldn't interfere.

"Look around you, Fae. The gift of life comes this Christmas morning." It was Anna. She pointed to where a path had been cleared from the Notre-Dame du Seigneur, which led through the watching immigrants and singing choir, and down into the corpses. Along that path were people stumbling like they just fell out of bed, all in various states of emotional stability, crying, laughing, staring off into space. A few of the choir had to help some of them along as more people were coming behind faster than they were recovering.

Fae followed the trail of staggering humans to the source she feared: Nicholas.

"Once Nefas' time runs out, his power over these people breaks," Anna explained, but Fae barely heard. "This is the Gift you were sent here to see and to know."

The transformation in the corpses began immediately after they infected Nicholas, subtle at first as the face began to fill in and the white cloudiness in the eyes blossomed into clarity and awareness. Emancipated of the parasites, the bodies lost their luminescence and went dark. Hair began to fill in on heads, shoulders broadened with muscle, strides grew stronger with every step taken. Lips and noses grew where there had been none, and the victims of the violence of Alexandra's team re-grew their jaws and teeth, and their bones mended. It was a slow, fluid change, impossible to pinpoint any one event, and yet by the time these people reached the top of the basilica stairs, they were as normal as any person should be.

Even as Fae took it all in, an older boy, hair flying out behind him, sprinted past everyone, jumped up the stairs, tripping halfway up, and then disappeared into the wide, open doors.

"This was his first year," Anna said.

It was the reaction of these people that broke Fae's heart in a new way. The contrast of their restored life broke her more completely than she even thought possible and she found new tears to cry as she looked on at the conundrum acting itself out before her eyes. What was more evil, condemning a thousand people to Nefas' thralldom, or allowing a single child to accept a thousand deaths for a thousand people? She wept because the answer lay with Nicholas, still grabbing at the endless green fingers reaching out for him.

She was torn between crying with these free prisoners in the moment of their emancipation, having tasted herself the darkness from which they walked out of, and being glued to the opposite transformation that was happening with Nicholas. He had grown so very old. His tiny face was wrinkled and hollowed like a harrowed old man who had seen too many tragedies and had his heart broken too many times to bother with what this world had to offer. Where one parasite was enough to control a whole adult body, Nicholas seemed to be compressing them all into his chest, forming a black spot so dark it could be seen slowly growing underneath his sleeper like an ink spill. There was something so intentional about his actions that Fae knew, maybe would never believe, but knew, that Nicholas was more aware of what he was doing than she could ever give a baby credit for.

Dominic was having trouble keeping Nicholas stable, and it wasn't because he kept squirming to reach the corpses pressing at him. It was for a reason only someone who had direct contact with the parasite could know—Dominic's arms were burning with a terrible heat that was freezing cold. And yet neither relented, as Nicholas took the parasites from everyone, not missing a soul. Fae watched while Anna stayed crouched by her side, saying little. Fae had seen the amazing transformation of Maël, the torn skin on his face filling in without a scar, and her great-aunt and uncle, who had somehow stayed side by side even in their death, holding hands as soon as they had the awareness to do so. They saw her crumpled on the ground, the voices of their eyes crying out their understanding of her pain, though they let her be and went straight inside. Mrs. Lemmens, the priest, the old man whose leather shop she had invaded—she witnessed them all. Anna had to chase away the barista boy who leapt over to Fae, so proud that his older brother had 'kept her safe' in her hotel room, too wrapped up in his own experience to realize that Fae couldn't share it with him.

By the time it took to cleanse the square of most of the corpses, the Notre-Dame du Seigneur had spilled over, stuffed beyond capacity, and a new type of crowd was forming outside, many joining their voices with the choir. The whole experience was beautiful, it was miraculous, and the toll on Nicholas was barbaric. Dominic had been forced to set him down on the cold pavement, though, had he been in his true form, Fae doubted he would have had to. The corpses couldn't bend down without falling, so they let the parasites escape their feet as they scuffed by Nicholas. The parasite was taking longer now to ingest itself, as the super saturated body of the baby boy was just trying to squeeze a few more in before he simply couldn't anymore.

His once beautiful and trusting eyes had so many ruptured blood vessels, and he was a baby that more closely resembled the shrine painting Nefas had manipulated on la Rue than the child she had risked everything for; Fae had to wonder if Nefas, in his frozen state, was in fact fully neutralized. Nicholas had lost nearly all his body fat, so all that remained of him was a tragedy drowned in his sleeper and a massive belly that writhed with the parasites squirming inside. It was the only thing that did move other than those bloodshot eyes searching about.

With only stragglers left, Lars Dreschler was led down the stairs and through the crowd of humans by the younger man he had been leaning on. When he neared Nicholas, his guide helped him lean down and touch the boy. Lars blinked a few times, and then, with a smile Fae didn't think him capable of, he kissed the tips of his fingers and made the motion as though he were going to place it on Nicholas' forehead. Then he left the way he'd come, this time, on his own.

Fae felt no gratitude when the last corpse fell before the horrible creature laying on the ground and discharged its parasite. Gratitude for ending the torture was a place long past, as was anger, regret, hate, or any other emotion. It was just simply over. Fae had no more tears to shed, no more anguish to cry out, no more bile to spit up. To her right was a village full of alive human beings, free from the darkness and the pain, and to her left was the one who brought it all to pass. The scales hung even, it seemed.

It was just simply over.

And yet, it wasn't.

"There is one more," Dominic said quietly. Few could hear him over the noise of so many celebrating around them, but not many had to.

Elise.

A woman, carrying a green, glowing body, came in from one of the main roads leading into the plaza. The woman looked Native American and seemed to float across the ground rather than walk. As she came closer, the lights from the basilica illuminated the reason for her grace: Elise was broken.

Some who celebrated nearby noticed the singular walk of the woman and stopped to see who would be so late to their emancipation. Lars forced his way to the front of the crowd, but otherwise, the party continued on in ignorance.

Despite the best support given to her, Elise's back sagged in a way no connected vertebrae could ever allow. Her elbows, knees, wrists, and ankles flopped uselessly and awkwardly, and ribs poked out at sharp angles. Even with the parasite, it would be impossible for her to walk, or crawl, or to move at all.

The woman came within feet of Fae and gently lay her burden on the ground next to Nicholas. She arranged Elise's limbs as comfortably as could be possible. Elise's rotting corpse was a few inches out of reach of her savior and, for a minute, the two stared at each other, unmoving.

And then Nicholas began to move his bony arm toward Elise, oh so barely. His fingers swayed high in the air until the force of gravity pulled them down and breached the distance between them. Their fingers touched and, in that instant, the parasite from Elise forced itself into the little body already too full. When the transfer finished, the bloodshot eyes mercifully closed and the cracking sounds of bones being fused back together began coming from Elise's body.

At the same time, the choir's beautiful songs stilled in the early morning's chill. The sky was beginning to lighten.

Christmas morning had come.

28

Physically, Elise looked back to normal, minus her boots and a mat of unruly hair. When she had finished coming out of Hell, she took one look at Fae, crumbled in an exhausted mess on the other side of Nicholas and broke. Curling up into a ball, she let the muffled cries wrack her. The woman who had brought her stood vigilantly nearby, while Maël and some of his friends joined Lars.

A shuffling of bodies came from the stairs as the Choir Director and the boy were let through. Even their radiance looked dimmed as they took in the humbling scene before them. The shadowy form of Nefas still stood frozen where he had last been rendered inert.

Dominic motioned for the Choir Director to come. The older man accepted his direction and, with a little push from his young teacher, stepped out from the crowd. With a cracked voice, he shouted out, "Behold!"

He grabbed the attention of some but not everyone, so he tried again. Inhaling deeply, he lifted his hands and shouted with a booming voice, startling even himself, "BEHOLD!"

Everyone both inside and out of the basilica went silent. Even Elise held back the sound of her weeping.

THE GIFT

Dominic's true self was pushing to be seen through his disguise and, with the same thunderous voice, spoke words that were as haunting as the sight before Fae: "The Lamb who takes away the sins of the world!"

It was a eulogy for a life cut so short. Fae let her eyes close on the world in agreement that an end had come. The plaza stilled, the only sounds coming from the cold winter's air stirring and the thump of her heart.

So it was that when Fae began hearing a child's laughter, she accepted it as just another hallucination. At first it was just a faint sound, a giggle from a toddler inside the basilica, but then it grew louder and more elated. It was high-pitched squeals of innocent joy, and it came closer and closer until Fae could feel it right in front of her. She didn't want to look, she was done seeing, but she peeled open her eyes and saw the creature-form of Nicholas still laying there.

Nicholas' body was shaking in time with the laughter, and that it came from a mouth seared together and unable to open was the indicator that Fae's mind really was concocting the whole thing. She looked to Dominic for a clue about what was, or wasn't, happening, but he was intently watching Nicholas, as was everyone else. No one moved. No one dared blink. Even the children didn't fidget.

The laughter like that of a little boy being kissed by a puppy kept rising up out of Nicholas' chest and, for the second time that night, Fae heard the sounds of a child who wanted to be heard. It grew louder and more carefree with every rise of his lungs until, finally, it couldn't be contained anymore. His lips were torn open by the force of his laughter as an explosion of power rocked everyone back, sending a storm of loose snow flying.

It was a paradox, the grotesque creature waving his flimsy arms in the air, laughing and giggling as though he were a normal baby, his parasite-filled pot belly heaving up and down. As the laugh broke out, so did its contagiousness as a few of the youth began to laugh too, and more pockets of laughter soon followed.

Fae felt Anna help lift her torso off the ground and let Fae lean back against her.

"You're going to want to see this," she said. "This is just for you."

279

Nicholas' laughter crescendoed, along with the growing number of people who couldn't contain theirs. Then, with a crack as sharp as a gunshot, the horrendous starvation, disfigurement, and mutations that had transformed Nicholas snapped off like a tablecloth being removed by a showman. The result was a thick, roiling stream of shimmering green blackness that passed from Nicholas directly into the shadowy figure of Nefas.

It punctured Nefas and it pulled more and more of him into himself like a black hole. Paralyzed, but aware of the moment of his defeat, Nefas' only protest was a haze of many faces rapidly flashing, trying to find one that would elicit a response from someone. He got none.

Within seconds, the darkness consumed him fully and he was sucked into the black hole of his own creation. There was nothing left of him. Not a scent. Not even a whisper.

Dominic had picked Nicholas up in his arms and was happily bouncing him around, singing a catchy jingle Fae didn't know. He had been restored as fully as all the other villagers, and the kiss of dawn had begun to lighten the heavens, promising a new day. The celebration had spread everywhere as people came in and out of the Notre-Dame du Seigneur to join this dance or play that game. Advent wreaths appeared on the heads of children, and a giant Christmas tree was being set up not too far from the basilica steps. Kids chased each other, bumping into people, and the choir was now indistinguishable from the villagers as together they sang favorite songs, danced, drank, ate, hugged, and kissed.

Only Elise was still crumpled on the ground, curled up tight, her guard keeping the revelers a safe distance away. Fae leaned weakly against Anna and, when the two women caught each other's eyes, Fae gave a little nod. *I forgive you*, it said.

Dominic bounced himself and Nicholas over to Fae and bent down so that she could look at him. Nicholas squealed in delight when he came near, and Fae lifted a hand, so heavy, to touch his soft, sweet face. He laughed and buried his head into Dominic's shoulder as though suddenly shy. Fae let her arm drop back down before Nicholas peeked back out at her with his little baby grin.

"Is it over?" Fae groggily asked Dominic, who beamed down at Nicholas bouncing up and down on his hip.

"Go to sleep, Fae. Sweet dreams."

"Mmmmm." With a heavy sigh, Fae let her eyes drop. Her last thought before the peace of exhausted sleep took her over: *Nefas isn't dead.*

I know.

29

A sound of muted voices stole through the heaviness that blurred the lines between wake and sleep. It sounded like two aliens communicating. The voices didn't matter, because a warm cocoon that Fae never had to leave had wrapped her up inside of itself. What time it was, what day, she didn't care, those questions were meaningless. A spa of worriless dreams and blissful nothingness called her back. The muttering aliens were none of her concern.

The dreams took her away, and the aliens kidnapped her again much too soon. This time it was a single alien, and Fae could make out what was being said. The voice sounded so far away, a woman's.

"Oui, oui, she made it through . . . still sleeping like a beauty . . . a few things complicated—I don't know, no . . . of course I will . . ."

The woman talked some more. It sounded like someone had quite a time of something. Good for them. Sleep called Fae again, pulling at her consciousness. She was only too willing to let it take her.

It was her own groan that finally pried Fae away from placid, heartwarming dreams and back into the rented room on the third floor of Mrs. Lemmen's hotel. She didn't want to leave her dreams, but they disappeared like timid fairies taking all memory of themselves with them, and Fae continued to lay motionless in her bed and pretend that she still was in that magical realm.

She must have stayed like that for another hour or two, using the most sacred part of her imagination to try to take her back to a place she had no memory of, which, in turn, exercised her brain out of its grogginess and into a normal level of functionality. At last Fae could pretend no longer and, rolling out from the hug of her cocoon, Fae gave another groan. She ached for a steaming, hot shower. And fresh coffee. She felt like she was nursing a monster hangover.

Her knee found the small side table before her hands did and she almost fell over. It was dark in this room. Turning on the table lamp she'd nearly knocked over, she rubbed the pain out of her knee and found herself in the mirror. She looked awful, like she really was hungover, though she had no memory of drinking. And her legs were so sore, her whole body actually, from her head and neck down to even the muscles in her feet.

She slowly rubbed her neck, letting out a long yawn, then returned her dozy attention to the wild woman staring back at her. But there was something wrong with that. Her reflection. The mirror. It was supposed to be covered with a blanket.

Like getting hit by a subway train, the events of the night before crashed into her in an almost physical blow, and her mind raced to sort through it all.

How did she get here? Dominic? Who took the blanket off the mirror? Where was Nicholas now? What day was it?

Suddenly it all mattered, and Fae rushed to take a shower, forgoing the pleasure of the warm water. Throwing on the first change of clothes her hands found, she hurried out of the room, none too sad to leave it.

Working through the stiffness in her legs, she hobbled down all three flights of stairs, forcing her sore arms into her jacket. She assumed it was still Christmas Day and the grandfather clock standing in the corner told her that it was 6:26. She didn't know where she was going to go, but there was bound to be someone, somewhere who would help her figure that out.

She didn't get past the front desk.

"Where are you going in such a hurry without wishing an old woman a good evening and a Merry Christmas?" It was Mrs. Lemmens. Elise was nowhere to be seen. The older woman pulled herself up out of the desk chair and came out and around to where Fae had stopped with a genuine smile on her face.

"Mrs. Lemmens, it is so good to see you again." The statement couldn't have been truer. "Merry Christmas."

"How are you feeling, child?"

"A bit like I've been run over. I want to find a few people; can you help me? I have questions."

"Don't we all?" Smiling like a sage, Mrs. Lemmens directed her into the lounge where they sat in the lovely wingback chairs in front of a blazing fire. "Who are you looking for?"

"Nicholas and Dominic, first of all. My cousin, Maël." Fae sighed then and with confession added, "I should apologize to the priest too."

The older woman looked a bit confused. "Maël and the priest Cuvelier are no problem, but who are these first two?"

"The baby last night, I didn't know his name so I named him Nicholas, and Dominic was our . . . bodyguard, I guess . . . during . . . throughout."

"Oh!" Mrs. Lemmens gave a polite chuckle, clapping her hands in delight and shaking her head. "You probably won't see those two again. The singers are all gone too, they've left until next year. Well, no, that isn't entirely correct. Many are still here, but very few of us will see them."

"So they really are . . . are they . . . ?" Fae didn't want to say the word because if she said it, then she couldn't take it back, but Mrs. Lemmens waited patiently for her to work it out. "They're angels."

Mrs. Lemmens smiled at her. "And your blessed little boy?"

"The lamb who took away the sins of the world." This time the answer came more easily, but she was not believing the implication. "Jesus Christ. You want me to believe that Nicholas is Jesus." Fae shook her head. "No, that's ridiculous. No law of the universe would allow for that."

She just smiled again. "Tell me, how do you *really* feel this morning?"

Fae knew she wasn't looking for how her body felt. Her dreams and sleep were the best she'd ever had; she had felt so warm and loved in them. In fact, she still felt warm and loved, and it wasn't because of the fire burning in front of her. She had come out of a psychological and physical grinder alive but, perhaps more important, all those things that Nefas had given her through the void were nowhere to be found. She didn't even miss them, much less want them.

"I feel . . . I don't know, new?"

"Well then, you don't need me to tell you what to believe, do you?"

"But I didn't confess anything."

"Child," Mrs. Lemmens gently placed her soft hand over Fae's. "I don't know what you went through last night and it's not my place to know, but if you carried that child to the Notre-Dame du Seigneur fighting everything they say you did, then you demonstrated your confession that he was a better choice than that Death devil. In time, the right words will come." She stood and Fae did, too. "Now, enough of that for now. Your cousin and great-aunt and uncle are eager to see you, and I promised to let them know when you awoke. And your dear grandmother has been calling every hour to hear your voice so while I make my phone call, why don't you make yours?"

Mrs. Lemmens disappeared into her back office. Fae was left alone, staring at the phone in her hand, her grandmother's number pulled up ready to be called. It would be nine thirty on Christmas morning there, and she was as equally excited to hear her beloved grandmother's voice as she was reluctant. What was she going to tell her? What should she tell her? She pressed the call button.

The phone rang but twice before her grandmother answered. "Fae! My strong, wonderful child!" Her mild-mannered grandmother was so loud that Fae had to hold the phone away from her ear, but she smiled, loving it.

They talked until Maël arrived, his moussed-up hair and small swagger enough to cause her to run and hug his neck. His eyes said everything she needed to see from him, a knowing that they now shared something beyond words.

"How are you feeling?" he asked as they walked out to his car.

"Exhausted and groggy, still processing the fact that I'm alive," she said with a grin. "I should be asking the same of you."

"Feeling ready to party."

"Well, whoever helped you to get ready to go out, tell them they did a complimentary job. You were looking a little rough, last time I saw you," Fae joked, and he shook his head with a grin as he started the car back up. "You know, I'm disappointed with you."

"Why's that?"

"You never once mentioned what an amazing choir you guys have."

"You never asked."

They were the last to arrive at her great-aunt and uncle's packed house. Everyone from the day before was there, plus a few more. The women had kicked all the men out of the kitchen, but it was still tight quarters, so they told Fae to just relax. Being more familiar with sandwiches and protein bars than real meals, she didn't argue.

No one asked her about the events of the previous night, and she didn't offer any insights. The kids stared at her though, and Maël let her know that the story of her arrival in the plaza had been passed around by the immigrants who'd seen the whole thing. But she was in good company, and there was enough good conversation that prevented her thoughts from returning to the events of the dark night before.

As supper drew close, everyone toasted with the *aperitif* to kick-start their appetites, though that really wasn't necessary as the house was an intoxication of delicious smells. There had been a steady flow of appetizers, but that still did little to satisfy the expectation for the meal itself. Judging from the other greedy eyes constantly shifting toward the kitchen, Fae knew she wasn't alone in that desire.

Christmas dinner was more impressive than Fae could have imagined. Emile opened the dinner with a prayer filled with such gratitude and simple love that, by the end of it, everyone was smiling, except for Emile and Fae. As Emile closed with his "amen," Fae met his gaze and saw in him the same awareness of the depth of the debt they owed to a little boy whose name was whatever it needed to be. He smiled his old smile at her and, suddenly, he looked like a young man again, full of the life yet before him. Fae could see it then, that he had no fears and no inhibitions from his past, that he held no grudge against any man. Her vision grew blurry, and she quickly reached for the potatoes.

The richness and quantity of the dishes and courses was beyond human capacity to ever digest at one sitting and yet, by a second Christmas miracle, they managed to get through them all. When at last they could eat no more, they removed themselves to the living room and left the kitchen mess to the cleaning elves Claire insisted were real. There they played a heated game of Monopoly, which apparently was Emile's favorite, and the winner, who also happened to be the surprisingly shrewd competitor Emile, had the honor of bringing in the final dish.

The Monopoly board was cleared away and Emile carried in a large serving board holding a traditional sweet bread called *cougnou*. Braided into a manger, a smaller bread child meant to represent the baby Jesus was placed in the middle. Everyone except Fae broke into it, as she couldn't see an artisan loaf of bread, but only Nicholas being torn apart by all the hands reaching for him, grabbing, and pulling. The sight made her sick so she excused herself to the kitchen to take on the role of the cleaning elf.

She'd already thrown herself into clearing the table when Claire came into the kitchen to join her, leaning on one wall, then another. Fae grabbed a chair for her, but the stout lady waved her off.

"I've been sitting long enough to warrant some standing. It will also be good for my digestion." She braced herself against the counter, and settled into a good position. "I've never known anyone to walk out on *cougnou* before."

"Uncle Emile made it, didn't he?"

Claire smiled. "He will bake another just for you."

"I'm sure he would." Fae laughed with reservation, and would have left it at that, except Claire hadn't exerted herself to talk about bread. "It's too soon, that's all."

Claire nodded with understanding. "Sometimes it helps to speak of what haunts you. Bringing dark things into the light steals their power."

"It also gives you power over me, knowing my secrets."

"Look at me, Fae. Do I look like an old woman to care about power over others?"

Fae smiled sheepishly and shook her head. It was the knowing that she had attempted to trade a baby's soul for her own that weighed her down; being tricked into not only trusting but deeply desiring, craving, that dark monster, and those shames which were too raw and too condemning to let out. Those things were more than just dirty laundry to air out.

"Your grandmother risked much in sending you here. You would waste it all if you left Death a key to chain you back up again. His voice can always be heard if you give him an ear, just ask my husband." Claire motioned for Fae's help and she came quickly to her side. "Come now. Whatever troubles you about the *cougnou* is over. I hear them bringing the games back out."

"I do have two questions." Claire nodded. "Can you tell me the *full* story about what happened when the Germans invaded?"

"I think that can be arranged, easily enough. What is your second?"

Fae hesitated. "Can you tell me Lars Dreschler's story, how a former Nazi came to live here?"

Claire smiled. "Not many people know he's a veteran anymore. Even fewer who remember, and none know for sure, if he really was a Nazi or not. People will believe what they want."

Fae simply nodded in agreement, having no taste to explain how she found out about Lars' unsavory past, though, for the same reason, she doubted the Nazi accusation.

Claire agreed. "With the story of our redemption from the Germans you will also learn of the crotchety old Misseur Dreschler."

"I can't believe you just called him that!"

"He is what he is," Claire said with a mischievous grin. "It is a good time for everyone to hear the story again. Emile is the best storyteller, but he so dislikes telling war stories, even the good ones. It will be up to me."

Holding Claire's arm to help her balance, they went back to the living room, all her family crammed together like puppies in a box—packed in, but oblivious to the inconvenience.

30

Fae extended her stay another three days. She had classes she had to prepare for, so the extra week her family wanted had been negotiated down. At Fae's insistence, Mrs. Lemmens gave her a first-floor room, inferior in quality and size, but it avoided the haunted stairs and mirrors of her original room.

Fae slept with the lights on every night, and she couldn't look in any reflective surface. She hoped she would eventually get over it. The first night, her dreams had been weird and twisted, and she woke up after each one ended, remembering only residual memories of green mist and stone figures trying to make her stone like them. To say the least, it was a daily thrill when the rising sun woke her up.

The Nativity set that had been left at the front desk was still waiting for her in the same place she'd last left it. Seeing it sitting there, she'd been drawn to it as though it were a treasured piece of nostalgia from a long-forgotten past, and she'd taken it into her new room and placed each character with precision under the eaves of the peaked stable roof. Her fingers lightly kissed each piece, gliding around their heads, bumping over the uniform tuffs of sheep wool. The shepherds, with their guiding crooks. The Wise Men, whose wisdom came not so much from their gifts but their belief. Poor Joseph, who always got left out. And Mary, who never asked for millennia of religious paparazzi following her, reshaping her.

"I'm so sorry," Fae whispered to the melancholic Mary figurine, looking so different from the Mary she'd met. "That book shouldn't be your final resting place. You can't help what others have done to you. To your boy."

And then she came to the Jesus figure, all the characters' lonesome eyes cast his way. Her fingertips barely brushed over his emotionless porcelain face, and she marveled at how wrong the world had gotten it. *Nicholas*, she marveled, *victory. He was the most selfless, trusting, cheerful child I have ever met.* She carefully picked up the square manger, taking care not to bump any of the other pieces, and held it to her eye level. The sound of Nicholas' laughter that had rocked the entire village resounded in her memory. Closing her eyes to hear the memory better, she saw his terribly deformed shape and Nefas' shadow standing over him. Her heart quickened, and a tear slipped out of her eye.

Another tear dropped onto her cheek and ran down to hang off her chin. She wiped it away before it fell and put Jesus back in his place, but not before lifting the piece to her lips and gently kissing it.

Elise had returned to her position behind the front desk. She was as professional as she had always been, though her eyes had lost their defiance; maybe it was her confidence. Fae carried on as though nothing had gone amiss between them, and Elise returned the curtesy. There was naught to be seen or heard from Lars Dreschler, and Fae didn't ask after him or seek him out. The thought of him still made her uneasy.

That, however, changed on December 29th when Fae was waiting in the train station with Maël and his mother, Veera, for her train to come. A large 24-hour clock above the door to the platform and the Christmas tree, that had been alone in greeting her upon her arrival, were joined by a ticket master engrossed in a paperback novel. Having arrived early, they had plenty of time to say their goodbyes and talk of what the new year would bring.

An interrupting gust of winter air announced the arrival of another person, and Maël and Veera greeted Lars as a well-respected acquaintance, while the ticket master looked up from his book and nodded. Fae, however, unsure of what to do, just watched him. He was coming for her; that was the only explanation, which meant that he wasn't done wagging his finger in her face. Cautious of what the *clipping* of his cane brought besides a wiry old man, Fae readied herself for anything. Maybe he was going to try to keep her here forever now that she carried the secret he had to protect? She wouldn't put it past him.

Lars stopped just short of her, studying her briefly with those unsettling eyes before he spoke. "Maria Peeters is a woman who never stops believing." He studied her again and then nodded to himself. "You are one who will never stop fighting, I think, and believing."

"Believers who are fighters are a dangerous group," Fae came back, thinking of all the many reasons why she stayed away from religion, or whatever she did now. Maybe she was a heart without a home.

"The two cannot be separated. Everyone who believes something will fight for it. You," Lars pointed his rickety finger right at her, "will return one day."

"Maybe," Fae said, not wanting to outright contradict him. "I'm hoping my career will take me elsewhere."

"It will." Lars' eyes narrowed. "Because you will fight for the belief that you are good enough to be one of the best. Then, you will return," he said again, continuing to point at her, "and the Gift will not be left uncared for."

Fae wanted to laugh. How misplaced his words and hopes were. Fat chance she was ever going to come here to tend Hell's graveyard year after year.

"I'm sure there are others already living here who would do a better job. Like Elise."

Lars shook his head. "Some mistakes leave you weaker, not stronger. Elise will never take my place. For both our sakes, it is good you survived that night. Bon voyage."

Lars Drechsler left then, his shoes squeaking from the melted snow. Fae wasn't sad to see him leave, and she breathed more easily once the door closed behind him.

"Wow," she said with a light scoff, glancing up at the clock. Her train would be here in a couple of minutes. "He sure has dreams."

"Time shows many truths to be lies and many lies to be truth, so who knows?" Veera said. "Did you want the numbers of my friends in Brussels? They will understand what you've been through."

Fae's hesitation was answer enough.

"She already declined once," Maël told his mother, looking apologetically at Fae.

"She's been through a horror story, Maël," Veera said. Then, turning to Fae, "It was just an offer, nothing more. You always have our number. Papa Emile was right to say that alone, you are vulnerable to his advances."

Fae flushed and tried to hide her embarrassment. Veera didn't know how Nefas had worked his way with her. "I think I'll be OK focusing on school and internships."

"You know the story about the frog in the kettle, don't you?"

Fae saw Maël roll his eyes, but she played along. "You mean the frog that is slowly boiled because he doesn't notice the rising heat until it's too late. And then he's cooked," she said. "And yes, I know the moral of the story too: Don't get caught by surprise. I appreciate everything, but I'm not one of . . . you people. I, and a lot of the rest of the world, will never get over the endless idiocy and face-palming that Christians plague us with. I know what happened here Christmas Eve, but I'm not interested in the club."

"Christians plague the world as much as they help it," Maël agreed. "But not all lawyers are soulless, and not all politicians are hopeless, either. We're all human, and Nefas will push his agenda through anyone. It's just that Christians have been telling everyone for so long how much better they are than them that, when they prove to be like everyone else, it's a longer way to fall and makes for more sensational, if not satisfying, news."

The train came a few minutes later, its silver metal cars slowing to a halt in front of the platform with a grind. Veera grabbed Fae up in one last hug, and Maël did the same. "My cousin," he said as they broke.

The train waited for no one, and Fae had just closed the narrow door behind her before she felt the lurch of it pulling away. *Home.* The thought of relief at being back in her own bed, with the comfort of her non-haunted things surrounding her, pushed away the emptiness that came with leaving behind the family she had found. The village itself, though, she had no problem leaving that far behind.

Fae found an empty set of seats facing each other, so she plunked herself into the one nearest the window and stowed her luggage underneath, dropping her jacket on the seat beside her. With a relaxing sigh, she leaned back and watched the snow-covered landscape fly by. A light rain had begun to fall; the water drops streaked across the window.

Not interested in her surroundings, Fae didn't pay attention when a man entered the car and sat down across from her. He kept to himself, so when Fae did notice him she assessed him as one does any stranger, looking for immediate quirks or social oddities which might give cause for being especially ignored. He wore a stylish, comfortable sweater, dark jeans, and thick-soled shoes. His hair was styled short, and he had kept a shadow of a beard. An established man in his early thirties. He gave a polite smile.

"Brussels?" he asked.

"Yeah."

"Visiting family for Christmas?"

"Yeah. You?"

He gave a small chuckle. "Every holiday and sometimes in between. I have a huge family."

Fae laughed politely with him. "Better than no family."

"Sometimes I wonder. What part of Brussels are you?"

There were certain questions that always made Fae suspicious, and that was one of them. This man, however, seemed harmless enough, so she decided the general quarter would be sufficient. "Marolles."

"I'm only a few blocks from there. Maybe we'll meet on the street sometime."

And there was the hook she was expecting. "Mhh," Fae nodded. It was time to end the conversation. "Maybe. It's a big city." She turned her head back to the window. He wasn't put off though, and when he spoke again his voice was different. It was deeper, and it was like a warm breath on her neck. It was unmistakable, the sound of her—no, not hers anymore—that *Voice*.

"Stranger things have happened."

Fae stopped breathing as she stared at him, trying to keep control. It was still her raw emotions unrecovered, a phantom memory imposing itself. She was free of him, why was he still haunting her?

Doesn't mean he won't stop trying to get you back.

Shut up brain, you're not helping!

He has no power over you other than what you give him—what do you want?

"Is something wrong?" His voice was normal again.

Fae focused on him. He looked genuinely concerned.

"Sorry, what did you say?"

"Just that stranger things have happened." The Voice again. That deep and inviting Voice that had begun it all.

She felt the blood rushing to her head, flushing her face, starving her lungs, causing her heart to beat hard and fast. Everything about that night rushed back to her, and the peace that had given her soul such rest was rapidly disappearing.

"Are you all right?"

"Stop talking," she warned, her mind running as fast as it could to sort out the real from the imagined.

"So, something IS wrong," he smirked, and that's when she saw them—his eyes, metallic green irises that had come alive. "Good to know. See you around."

And then he got up and walked away, not looking back.

He had left a folded piece of paper on his seat and Fae had enough wits left to lean over and pick it up, her hands unsteady as she unfolded it.

It was a poor photocopy of a child's Latin homework, a crossword puzzle for vocabulary. The puzzle was complete except for one word. The clue was: impious act, abomination. Eleven-down was half filled in from the other intersecting words: N_F_S.

... E ...

The Voice in her head! Her hands began to shake so badly that she dropped the homework on the floor and into the gritty puddle of melted snow from her shoes.

... A. I love you, Fae, like worms love a body in the ground.

Acknowledgments

First, thank you to my mom, without whom I wouldn't be where I am today. To my brother, for being my sounding board and helping me with ideas when I got stuck; maybe one day I really will release an extended version just for you. To my editors, Steve Parolini and Cindy Whittemore, I am so thankful to have been able to reap the benefits of your experience and talents! Thank you, Polgarus Studio, for your quality formatting work. To my Beta-readers, Krista Goff, Jonathan Matthews, and Aaron J. Morton, your input was so helpful. And Aaron, thank you for jumping on board this project even before I knew what to do with it! To Jeremi Ochoa, for bringing the synopsis to the next level, Stephanie H. Jourdan-Thompson and Vanessa Racine, who helped me with the French, and George Robertson, for fixing (overhauling?) my Latin. And to everyone who responded when I reached out, and were cheerleaders for this release, you are all amazing. And ultimately, to my God and Jesus . . . a thousand pictures for a thousand words . . .

Photo by Juliane Arielle Photography

Stephanie M. Matthews has always loved writing, both fiction and nonfiction, the latter mostly related to the Ancient world. She developed an enjoyment of thriller stories early in life, and the Christmas season has remained her favorite since her very first one. When she's not writing in her spare time, she spends her time reading, mountain biking, and pretending that she can play hockey. Stephanie currently resides in Ottawa, Ontario.

www.stephaniemmatthews.com
stephaniemmatthewsinfo@gmail.com
Follow on Facebook at Stephanie M. Matthews

Made in the USA
Middletown, DE
16 November 2017